The
Rock Rats

Ben Bova

NEW ENGLISH LIBRARY
Hodder & Stoughton

Copyright © 2002 by Ben Bova

First published in Great Britain in 2002
by Hodder and Stoughton
First published in paperback in 2002
by Hodder and Stoughton
A division of Hodder Headline
A New English Library paperback

The right of Ben Bova to be identified as the
Author of the Work has been asserted by him in accordance
with the Copyright, Designs and Patents Act 1988.

ISBN 0 340 76959 9

Printed and bound in Great Britain by
Mackays of Chatham plc, Chatham, Kent

Hodder and Stoughton
A division of Hodder Headline
338 Euston Road
London NW1 3BH

To Charles N. Brown and the *Locus* team

Yet each man kills the thing he loves,
    By each let this be heard,
Some do it with a bitter look,
    Some with a flattering word,
The coward does it with a kiss,
    The brave man with a sword!

Some kill their love when they are young,
    And some when they are old;
Some strangle with the hands of Lust,
    Some with the hands of Gold:
The kindest use a knife, because
    The dead so soon grow cold.

Oscar Wilde
The Ballad of Reading Gaol

Prologue: Selene

Amanda clutched at her husband's arm when Martin Humphries strode into the wedding reception, unannounced and uninvited.

The Pelican Bar went totally silent. The crowd that had been noisily congratulating Amanda and Lars Fuchs with lewd jokes and lunar 'rocket juice' froze as if somebody had doused the place with liquid nitrogen. Fuchs patted his wife's hand gently, protectively, as he scowled up at Humphries. Even Pancho Lane, never at a loss for a quip, simply stood by the bar, one hand holding her drink, the other balling into a fist.

The Pelican wasn't Humphries' kind of place. It was the workers' bar, the one 'joint' in Selene's underground warren of tunnels and cubicles where the people who lived and worked on the Moon could come for relaxation and the company of their fellow Lunatics. Suits like Humphries did their drinking in the fancy lounge up in the Grand Plaza, with the rest of the executives and the tourists.

Humphries seemed oblivious to their enmity, totally at ease in this sea of hostile stares, even though he looked terribly out of place, a smallish manicured man wearing an impeccably tailored imperial blue business suit in the midst of the young, boisterous miners and tractor operators in their shabby, faded coveralls and their earrings of asteroidal stones. Even the women looked stronger, more muscular than Humphries.

But if Humphries' round, pink-cheeked face seemed soft

I

and bland, his eyes were something else altogether. Grey and pitiless, like chips of flint, the same colour as the rock walls and low ceiling of the underground bar itself.

He walked straight through the silent, sullen crowd to the table where Amanda and Fuchs sat.

'I know I wasn't invited to your party,' he said in a calm, strong voice. 'I hope you'll forgive me for crashing. I won't stay but a minute.'

'What do you want?' Fuchs asked, scowling, not moving from his chair beside his bride. He was a broad, dark-haired bear of a man, thick in the torso, with short arms and legs, heavily muscled. The tiny stud in his left ear was a diamond that he had bought during his student days in Switzerland.

With a rueful smile, Humphries said, 'I want your wife, but she's chosen you instead.'

Fuchs slowly got up from his chair, big thick-fingered hands clenching into fists. Every eye in the bar was on him, every breath held.

Amanda glanced from Fuchs to Humphries and back again. She looked close to panic. She was a strikingly beautiful woman, with the wide-eyed innocent face and lusciously curved figure that made men fantasize and women stare with unalloyed envy. Even in a plain white jumpsuit she looked utterly stunning.

'Lars,' Amanda whispered. 'Please.'

Humphries raised both hands, palms out. 'Perhaps I phrased myself poorly. I didn't come here for a fight.'

'Then why did you come?' Fuchs asked, in a low growl.

'To give you a wedding present,' Humphries replied, smiling again. 'To show that there's no hard feelings . . . so to speak.'

'A present?' Amanda asked.

'If you'll accept it from me,' said Humphries.

2

'What is it?' Fuchs asked.

'*Starpower 1*.'

Amanda's china blue eyes went so wide that white showed all around them. 'The ship?'

'It's yours, if you'll have it. I'll even pay for the refurbishment necessary to make it spaceworthy again.'

The crowd stirred, sighed, began muttering. Fuchs looked down at Amanda, saw that she was awed by Humphries' offer.

Humphries said, 'You can use it to return to the Belt and start mining asteroids. There's plenty of rocks out there for you to claim and develop.'

Despite himself, Fuchs was impressed. 'That's . . . very generous of you, sir.'

Humphries put on his smile again. With a careless wave of his hand, 'You newly-weds need some source of income. Go out and claim a couple of rocks, bring back their ores, and you'll be fixed for life.'

'Very generous,' Fuchs muttered.

Humphries put out his hand. Fuchs hesitated a moment, then gripped it in his heavy paw; engulfing it, actually. 'Thank you, Mr Humphries,' he said, pumping Humphries' arm vigorously. 'Thank you so much.'

Amanda said nothing.

Humphries disengaged himself and, without another word, walked out of the bar. The crowd stirred at last and broke into dozens of conversations. Several people crowded around Fuchs and Amanda, congratulating them, offering to work on their craft. The Pelican's proprietor declared drinks on the house and there was a general rush toward the bar.

Pancho Lane, though, sidled through the crowd and out the door into the tunnel, where Humphries was walking alone toward the power stairs that led down to his mansion at Selene's lowest level. In a few long-legged lunar strides she caught up to him.

'I thought they threw you out of Selene,' she said.

Humphries had to look up at her. Pancho was lean and lanky, her skin a light mocha, not much darker than a white woman would get in the burning sunshine of her native west Texas. She kept her hair cropped close, a tight dark skullcap of ringlets.

He made a sour face. 'My lawyers are working on an appeal. They can't exile me without due process.'

'And that could take years, huh?'

'At the very least.'

Pancho would have gladly have stuffed him into a rocket and fired him off to Pluto. Humphries had sabotaged *Starpower 1* on its first – and, so far, only – mission to the Belt. Dan Randolph had died because of him. It took an effort of will for her to control her temper.

As calmly as she could manage, Pancho said, 'You were pretty damn generous back there.'

'A gesture to true love,' he replied, without slowing his pace.

'Yeah. Sure.' Pancho easily matched his stride.

'What else?'

'For one thing, that spacecraft ain't yours to give away. It belongs to—'

'Belonged,' Humphries snapped. 'Past tense. We wrote it off the books.'

'Wrote it off? When? How in hell can you *do* that?'

Humphries actually laughed. 'You see, Ms Director? There are a few tricks to being on the board that a grease-monkey like you doesn't know about.'

'I guess,' Pancho admitted. 'But I'll learn 'em.'

'Of course you will.'

Pancho was newly elected to the board of directors of

Astro Manufacturing, over Humphries' stern opposition. It had been Dan Randolph's dying wish.

'So we've written off *Starpower 1* after just one flight?'

'It's already obsolescent,' said Humphries. 'The ship proved the fusion drive technology. Now we can build better spacecraft, specifically designed for asteroid mining.'

'And you get to play Santy Claus for Amanda and Lars.'

Humphries shrugged.

The two of them walked along the nearly-empty tunnel until they came to the power stairs leading downward.

Pancho grabbed Humphries by the shoulder, stopping him at the top of the moving stairs. 'I know what you're up to,' she said.

'Do you?'

'You figger Lars'll go battin' out to the Belt and leave Mandy here in Selene.'

'I suppose that's a possibility,' Humphries said, shaking free of her grip.

'Then you can move in on her.'

Humphries started to reply, then hesitated. His face grew serious. At last he said, 'Pancho, has it ever occurred to you that I really love Amanda? I do, you know.'

Pancho knew Humphries' reputation as a womanizer. She had seen plenty of evidence of it.

'You might tell yourself that you love her, Humpy, but that's just because she's the only woman between here and Lubbock that won't flop inta bed with you.'

He smiled coldly. 'Does that mean that you would?'

'In your dreams!'

Humphries laughed and started down the stairs. For a few moments Pancho watched him dwindling away, then she turned and headed back toward the Pelican Bar.

As Humphries rode down to Selene's bottommost level, he thought, Fuchs is an academic, the kind who's never had two pennies in his hands at the same time. Let him go out to the Belt. Let him see how much money he can make, and all the things that money can buy. And while he's doing it, I'll be here at Amanda's side.

By the time he reached his palatial home, Humphries was almost happy.

Data Bank: The Asteroid Belt

Millions of chunks of rock and metal float silently, end-lessly, through the deep emptiness of interplanetary space. The largest of them, Ceres, is barely a thousand kilometres wide. Most of them are much smaller, ranging from irregular chunks a few kilometres long to objects the size of pebbles. They contain more metals and minerals, more natural resources, than the entire Earth can provide.

They are the bonanza, the El Dorado, the Comstock Lode, the gold and silver and iron and everything-else mines of the twenty-first century. There are hundreds of millions of *billions* of tons of high grade ores in the asteroids. They hold enough real wealth to make each man, woman, and child of the entire human race into a millionaire. And then some.

The first asteroid was discovered shortly after midnight on January 1, 1801, by a Sicilian monk who happened to be an astronomer. While others were celebrating the new century, Giuseppe Piazzi was naming the tiny point of light he saw in his telescope *Ceres*, after the pagan goddess of Sicily. Perhaps an unusual attitude for a pious monk, but Piazzi was a Sicilian, after all.

By the advent of the twenty-first century, more than twenty-six thousand asteroids had been discovered by Earthbound astronomers. As the human race began to expand its habitat to the Moon and to explore Mars, millions more were found.

Technically, they are *planetoids*, little planets, chunks of rock and metal floating in the dark void of space, leftovers from the creation of the Sun and planets some four and a half billion years ago. Piazzi correctly referred to them as planetoids, but in 1802 William Herschel (who had earlier discovered the giant planet Uranus) called them *asteroids*, because in the telescope their pinpoints of light looked like stars rather than the disks of planets. Piazzi was correct, but Herschel was far more famous and influential. We call them asteroids to this day.

Several hundred of the asteroids are in orbits that come near to the Earth, but by far most of them circle around the Sun in a broad swath in deep space between the orbits of Mars and giant Jupiter. This *Asteroid Belt* orbits the Sun more than six hundred million kilometres from Earth, four times farther from the Sun than our homeworld.

Although this region is called the Asteroid *Belt*, the asteroids are not strewn so thickly that they represent a hazard to space navigation. Far from it. The so-called Belt is a region of vast emptiness, dark and lonely and very far from human civilization.

Until the invention of the Duncan fusion drive the Asteroid Belt was too far from the Earth/Moon system to be of economic value. Once fusion propulsion became practical, however, the Belt became the region where prospectors and miners could make fortunes for themselves, or die in the effort.

Many of them died. More than a few were killed.

Three Years Later

1

'I said it would be simple,' Lars Fuchs repeated. 'I did *not* say it would be easy.'

George Ambrose – Big George to everyone who knew him – scratched absently at his thick red beard as he gazed thoughtfully out through the window of *Starpower 1*'s bridge toward the immense, looming dark bulk of the asteroid Ceres.

'I di'n't come out here to get involved in daft schemes, Lars,' he said. His voice was surprisingly high and sweet for such a shaggy mastodon of a man.

For a long moment the only sound in the compartment was the eternal hum of electrical equipment. Then Fuchs pushed between the two pilots' seats to drift toward Big George. Stopping himself with a touch of his hand against the metal overhead, he said in an urgent whisper, 'We can do it. Given time and resources.'

'It's fookin' insane,' George muttered. But he kept staring out at the asteroid's rock-strewn, pockmarked surface.

They made an odd pair: the big, bulky Aussie with his shaggy brick-red mane and beard hovering weightlessly beside the dark, intense, thickset Fuchs. Three years in the Belt had changed Fuchs somewhat: he was still burly, barrel-chested, but he had let his chestnut brown hair grow almost to his collar, and the earring he wore was now a polished chip of asteroidal copper. A slim bracelet of copper circled his left wrist. In their individual ways, both men looked powerful, determined, even dangerous.

'Living inside Ceres is bad for our health,' Fuchs said.

George countered, 'Plenty of radiation protection from the rock.'

'It's the microgravity,' Fuchs said earnestly. 'It's not good for us, physically.'

'I like it.'

'But the bones become so brittle. Dr Cardenas says the rate of fractures is rising steeply. You've seen that yourself, haven't you?'

'Maybe,' George half-admitted. Then he grinned. 'But th' sex is fookin' fantastic!'

Fuchs scowled at the bigger man. 'Be serious, George.'

Without taking his eyes off Ceres' battered face, George said, 'Okay, you're right. I know it. But buildin' a bloody O'Neill habitat?'

'It doesn't have to be that big, not like the L-5 habitats around Earth. Just big enough to house the few hundred people here in Ceres. At first.'

George shook his shaggy head. 'You know how big a job you're talkin' about? Just the life-support equipment alone would cost a mint. And then some.'

'No, no. That's the beauty of my scheme,' Fuchs said, with a nervous laugh. 'We simply purchase spacecraft and put them together. They become the habitat. And they already have all the life-support equipment and radiation shielding built into them. We won't need their propulsion units at all, so the price will be much lower than you think.'

'Then you want to spin the whole fookin' kludge to an Earth-normal g?'

'Lunar normal,' Fuchs answered. 'One-sixth g is good enough. Dr Cardenas agrees.'

George scratched at his unkempt beard. 'I dunno, Lars. We've been livin' inside the rock okay. Why go to all this trouble and expense?'

'Because we have to!' Fuchs insisted. 'Living in micro-gravity is dangerous to our health. We *must* build a better habitat for ourselves.'

George looked unconvinced, but he muttered, 'Lunar g, you say?'

'One-sixth normal Earth gravity. No more than that.'

'How much will it cost?'

Fuchs blinked once. 'We can buy the stripped-down spacecraft from Astro Corporation. Pancho is offering a very good price.'

'How much?'

'The preliminary figures work out . . .' Fuchs hesitated, took a breath, then said, 'We can do it if all the prospectors and miners put in ten per cent of their income.'

George grunted. 'A tithe, huh?'

'Ten per cent isn't much.'

'A lot of us rock rats don't make any income at all, some years.'

'I know,' said Fuchs. 'I factored that into the cost estimate. Of course, we'll have to pay off the spacecraft over twenty or thirty-year leases. Like a mortgage on a house, Earthside.'

'So you want everybody here in Ceres to take on a twenty-year debt?'

'We can pay it off sooner, perhaps. A few really big strikes could pay for the entire project all by themselves.'

'Yeah. Sure.'

With burning intensity, Fuchs asked, 'Will you do it? If you agree, most of the other prospectors will, too.'

'Whyn't you get one of the corporations t' do it?' George asked. 'Astro or Humphries . . .' He stopped when he saw the look on Fuchs' face.

'Not Humphries,' Fuchs growled. 'Never him or his company. Never.'

'Okay. Astro, then.'

Fuchs' scowl shifted into a troubled frown. 'I've spoken to Pancho about it. The Astro board would not vote for it. They will sell stripped-down spacecraft to us, but they won't commit to building the habitat. They don't see a profit from it.'

George grunted. 'Lot they care if we snap our bones.'

'But you care,' Fuchs said eagerly. 'It's *our* problem, George; we have to solve it. And we can, if you'll help.'

Running a beefy hand through his thick mop of hair, Big George said, 'You're gonna need a techie team to do the integration job. There's more to puttin' this habitat of yours together than just connectin' tinkertoys, y'know. You'll need a flock of geek boys.'

'That's already in the cost estimate,' Fuchs replied.

George huffed a mighty sigh, then said, 'All right, Lars, I'm in. I guess it would be pretty good to have a base with some decent gravity to it out here in the Belt.'

Fuchs smiled. 'You can always have sex aboard your own ship.'

George grinned back at him. 'Believe it, mate. Believe it.'

Fuchs went with George to the ship's main airlock and helped the bigger man get back into his hard-shell spacesuit.

'They're testin' lightweight suits back at Selene, y'know,' he said as he slid into the rigid torso and worked his arms through the stiff sleeves. 'Flexible. Easy to put on.'

'And the radiation protection?' Fuchs asked.

'Magnetic field surrounds the suit. They claim it's better'n this stuff.' He rapped his knuckles against the torso's cermet carapace.

Fuchs gave a little snort of disdain. 'They'll need years of testing before I'd buy one.'

As he wormed his hands into the gloves, George said, 'Me too.'

Handing the bigger man his fishbowl helmet, Fuchs said, 'Thanks for agreeing, George,' he said. 'It means a lot to me.'

George nodded solemnly. 'I know. You two want to have kids.'

Fuchs' cheeks reddened. 'It's not that!'

'Isn't it?'

'Well, not alone, no.' Fuchs looked away from George for a moment, then slowly admitted, 'I worry about Amanda, yes. I never thought she would want to stay out here with me. I never thought I would be out here this long.'

'There's a lot of money to be made here in the Belt. A *lot* of money.'

'Yes, yes indeed. But I worry about her. I want her to be in a safer place, with enough gravity to keep her from deconditioning.'

'And enough radiation shielding to start a family,' George said, grinning. Then he pulled on his helmet before Fuchs could think of a reply.

2

Once George had cycled through *Starpower 1*'s airlock and jetted back to his own *Waltzing Matilda*, Fuchs went down the ship's narrow central passageway to the compartment where his wife was working.

She looked up from the wallscreen as Fuchs slid the compartment door open. He saw that she was watching a fashion show beamed from somewhere on Earth: slim, slinky models in brightly coloured gowns of outrageous designs. Fuchs frowned slightly: half the people of Earth displaced by floods and earthquakes, starvation rampant almost everywhere, and still the rich played their games.

Amanda blanked the wallscreen as she asked, 'Has George left already?'

'Yes. And he agreed to it!'

Her smile was minimal. 'He did? It didn't take you terribly long to convince him, did it?'

She still spoke with a trace of the Oxford accent she had learned years earlier in London. She was wearing an oversized faded sweatshirt and cut-off work pants. Her golden blonde hair was pinned up off her neck and slightly disheveled. She wore not a trace of make-up. Still, she was much more beautiful than any of the emaciated mannequins in the fashion show. Fuchs pulled her to him and kissed her warmly.

'In two years, maybe less, we'll have a decent base in orbit around Ceres, with lunar-level gravity.'

Amanda gazed into her husband's eyes, seeking something. 'Kris Cardenas will be happy to hear it,' she said.

'Yes, Dr Cardenas will be very pleased,' Fuchs agreed. 'We should tell her as soon as we arrive.'

'Of course.'

'But you're not even dressed yet!'

'It won't take me a minute,' Amanda said. 'It's not like we're going to a royal reception.' Then she added, 'Or even to a party in Selene.'

Fuchs realized that Amanda wasn't as happy as he'd thought she would be. 'What's the matter? Is something wrong?'

'No,' she said, too quickly. 'Not really.'

'Amanda, my darling, I know that when you say "not really" you really mean "really." '

She broke into a genuine smile. 'You know me too well.'

'No, not too well. Just well enough.' He kissed her again, lightly this time. 'Now, what's wrong? Tell me, please.'

Leaning her cheek on his shoulder, Amanda said very softly, 'I thought we'd be home by now, Lars.'

'Home?'

'Earth. Or even Selene. I never dreamt we'd stay in the Belt for three years.'

Suddenly Fuchs saw the worn, scuffed metal walls of this tiny coop of a cubicle; the narrow confines of the ship's passageway and the other cramped compartments; smelled the stale air with its acrid tinge of ozone; felt the background vibrations that rattled through the ship every moment; consciously noticed the clatter of pumps and wheezing of the air fans. And he heard his own voice ask inanely:

'You're not happy here?'

'Lars, I'm happy being with you. Wherever you are. You know that. But—'

'But you would rather be back on Earth. Or at Selene.'

'It's better than living on a ship all the time.'

'*He's* still at Selene.'

She pulled slightly away, looked straight into his deep-set eyes. 'You mean Martin?'

'Humphries,' said Fuchs. 'Who else?'

'He's got nothing to do with it.'

'Doesn't he?'

Now she looked truly alarmed. 'Lars, you don't think that Martin Humphries means anything to me?'

He felt his blood turning to ice. One look at Amanda's innocent blue eyes and full-bosomed figure and any man would be wild to have her.

Coldly, calmly, he said, 'I know that Martin Humphries wants you. I think that you married me to escape from him. I think—'

'Lars, that's not true!'

'Isn't it?'

'I love you! For god's sake, don't you know that? Don't you understand it?'

The ice thawed. He realized that he held in his arms the most gorgeous woman he had ever seen. That she had come to this desolate emptiness on the frontier of human habitation to be with him, to help him, to love him.

'I'm sorry,' he muttered, feeling ashamed. 'It's just that . . . I love you so much . . .'

'And I love you, Lars. I truly do.'

'I know.'

'Do you?'

He shook his head ruefully. 'Sometimes I wonder why you put up with me.'

She smiled and traced a fingertip across his stubborn, stubbled jaw. 'Why not? You put up with me, don't you?'

With a sigh, he admitted, 'I thought we'd be back on Earth by now. I thought we'd be rich.'

'We are. Aren't we?'

'On paper, perhaps. We're better off than most of the other prospectors. At least we own this ship . . .'

His voice faltered. They both knew why. They owned *Starpower* because Martin Humphries had given it to them as a gift.

'But the bills do mount up,' Amanda said swiftly, trying to change the subject. 'I was going over the accounts earlier. We can't seem to stay ahead of the expenses.'

Fuchs made a sound somewhere between a grunt and a snort. 'If you count how much we owe, we certainly are multi-millionaires.'

It was a classic problem, they both knew. A prospector might find an asteroid worth hundreds of billions on paper, but the costs of mining the ores, transporting them back to the Earth/Moon region, refining them – the costs of food and fuel and air to breathe – were so high that the prospectors were almost always on the ragged edge of bankruptcy. Still they pushed on, always seeking that lode of wealth that would allow them to retire at last and live in luxury. Yet no matter how much wealth they actually found, hardly any of it stayed in their hands for long.

And I want to take ten per cent of that from them, Fuchs said to himself. But it will be worth it! They'll thank me for it, once it's done.

'It's not like we're spendthrifts,' Amanda murmured. 'We don't throw the money away on frivolities.'

'I should never have brought you out here,' Fuchs said. 'It was a mistake.'

'No!' she contradicted. 'I want to be with you, Lars. Wherever you are.'

'This is no place for a woman such as you. You should be living comfortably, happily—'

She silenced him with a single slim finger across his thin lips. 'I'm perfectly comfortable and happy here.'

'But you'd be happier on Earth. Or Selene.'

She hesitated a fraction of a second before replying, 'Wouldn't you?'

'Yes,' he admitted. 'Of course. But I'm not going back until I can give you all the things you deserve.'

'Oh, Lars, you're all that I really want.'

He gazed at her for a long moment, then said, 'Yes, perhaps. But I want more. Much more.'

Amanda said nothing.

Brightening, Fuchs said, 'But as long as we're out here, at least I can make a decent home for you in Ceres orbit!'

She smiled for her husband.

3

'Build a habitat big enough to house everyone living at Ceres?' asked Martin Humphries, incredulous.

'That's what the rumble is,' said his aide, a winsome brunette with long-lashed almond eyes, full pouty lips, and a razor-sharp mind. Even though her image on his bedroom wallscreen showed only her head and shoulders and some background of her office, the sight of her set Humphries' mind wandering.

Humphries leaned back in his wide, luxurious bed and tried to concentrate on business. He had started the morning with a vigorous tussle with a big-breasted computer analyst who nominally worked in Humphries Space System's transportation department. She had spent the night in Humphries' bed, yet even in the midst of their most passionate exertions he found himself closing his eyes and fantasizing about Amanda.

His bedmate was in the shower now, and all thoughts about her or Amanda were pushed aside as Humphries talked business with his aide, whose office was several levels up in Selene's underground network of corridors.

'It sounds ridiculous,' Humphries said. 'How reliable is this information?'

The aide let a wintry smile cross her tempting lips. 'Quite reliable, sir. The prospectors are all talking about it, back and forth, from one ship to another. They're chattering about it all across the Belt.'

'It still sounds ridiculous,' Humphries grumbled.

'Beg to differ, sir,' said the aide. Her words were deferential, but the expression on her face looked almost smug. 'It makes a certain amount of sense.'

'Does it?'

'If they could build a habitat and spin it to produce an artificial gravity that approaches the grav field here on the Moon, it would be much healthier for the people living out there for months or years on end. Better for their bones and organs than sustained microgravity.'

'Hmmph.'

'In addition, sir, the habitat would have the same level of radiation shielding that the latest spacecraft have. Or even better, perhaps.'

'But the prospectors still have to go out into the Belt and claim the asteroids.'

'They are required by law to be present at an asteroid in order for their claim to be legal,' the aide agreed. 'But from then on they can work the rock remotely.'

'Remotely? The distances are too big for remote operations. It takes hours for signals to cross the Belt.'

'From Ceres, sir,' the aide said stiffly, 'roughly five thousand ore-bearing rocks are within one light-minute. That's close enough for remote operations, don't you think?'

Humphries didn't want to give her the satisfaction of admitting she was right. Instead, he replied, 'Well, we'd better be getting our own people out there claiming those asteroids before the rock rats snap them all up.'

'I'll get on that right away,' said the aide, with enough of a smile curving her tempting lips to show that she had already thought of it. 'And mining teams, too.'

'Mining operations aren't as urgent as claiming the stupid rocks.'

'Understood,' she said. Then she added, 'The board

meeting is this morning at ten. You asked me to remind you.'

He nodded. 'Yes, I know.' Without another word he tapped the keypad on the nightstand and her wallscreen image winked off.

Slumping deeper into the pillows, he heard the woman who'd spent the night in his bed singing in the shower. Off-key. Well, he said to himself, music isn't her best talent.

Fuchs. The thought of Lars Fuchs pushed all other notions out of his mind. He's out there with Amanda. I never realized she'd stay out in that wilderness with him. She doesn't belong there, living in a crummy ship like some gypsy, some penniless drifter wandering out there in the empty wastes. She should be *here*, with me. This is where she belongs.

I made a mistake with him. I underestimated him. He's no fool. He's not just prospecting and mining. He's building an empire out there. With Pancho Lane's help.

The young woman appeared at the bathroom door, naked, her skin dewy and flawless. She posed enticingly and smiled for Humphries.

'Do we have time for one more? Are you up to it?' Her smile turned just a tad impudent.

Despite himself, Humphries felt stirred. But he said gruffly, 'Not now. I've got work to do.'

And he thought, This twat could get possessive. I'd better transfer her to some job back on Earth.

Martin Humphries drummed his fingers impatiently on his desk, waiting for the lame-brained techs to make all the connections so the board meeting could get underway.

After all these years, he fumed to himself, you'd think

that setting up a simple virtual reality meeting with half a dozen idiots who refuse to leave Earth would be an easy matter. He hated waiting. He loathed being dependent on anyone or anything.

Humphries refused to leave Selene. His home was on the Moon, he told himself, not Earth. Everything he wanted was here in the underground city, and what wasn't here could be shipped to Selene upon his order. He had fought Selene's legal system to a standstill to prevent them from exiling him back to Earth.

Earth was crippled, dying. The greenhouse flooding had wiped out most coastal cities and turned hundreds of millions of people into homeless, starving wanderers. Farmlands withered in droughts while tropical diseases found fresh territories in what used to be temperate climates. Electrical power grids everywhere faltered and sputtered lamely. A new wave of terrorism unleashed man-made plagues while crumbling nations armed their missiles and threatened nuclear war.

It's only a matter of time, Humphries knew. Despite all the efforts by the so-called world government, despite the New Morality's fundamentalism and relentless grip on the political reins of power, despite the suspension of individual freedoms all across the globe, it's only a matter of time until they start nuking each other into extinction.

Safer here on the Moon. Better to be away from all that death and destruction. What was it Dan Randolph used to say? When the going gets tough, the tough get going – to where the going is easier.

Humphries nodded to himself as he sat in his high-backed chair. He was alone in his sumptuous office, a mere twenty metres from his bedroom. Most of Humphries Space Systems' board members also lived in Selene now, yet hardly any of them were allowed into the house. They stayed in their own homes, or came to the HSS offices up in the Grand Plaza tower.

Damned waste of time, Humphries grumbled to himself. The board's just a rubber stamp, anyway. The only member who ever gave me any trouble was Dad and he's gone now. Probably trying to tell St Peter how to run heaven. Or more likely arguing with Satan in hell.

'We're ready now, sir,' said his aide's silky voice in the stereo earplugs Humphries wore.

'Then do it.'

'Are your goggles in place, sir?'

'I've been wearing my *contacts* for damned near fifteen minutes!'

'Of course.'

The young woman said nothing else. An instant later, the long conference table that existed only in Humphries' computer chips sprang into existence before his eyes, each seat filled by a board member. Most of them looked slightly startled, but after a few seconds of turning in their chairs to see if everyone was there, they began chatting easily enough with one another. The half dozen who were still on Earth were at a disadvantage, because it took nearly three seconds for signals to make the round-trip from Moon to Earth and back again. Humphries had no intention of holding up the proceedings for them; the six old farts had little power on the board, no need to worry about them. Of course, they each had a lot to say. Humphries wished he could silence them. Permanently.

He was in a foul mood by the time the meeting ended, cranky and tired. The meeting had accomplished nothing except very routine decisions that could have been made by a troop of baboons. Humphries called for his aide over the intercom phone. By the time he had gone to the lavatory, slipped his VR contacts out of his eyes, washed his face and combed his hair, she was standing in his office doorway, wearing a cool powder-blue pantsuit accented with asteroidal sapphires.

Her name was Diane Verwoerd, born of a Dutch father and Indonesian mother, a teenaged fashion model in Amsterdam when her dark, sultry looks first attracted Humphries' notice. She was a little on the skinny side, he thought, but he paid her way through law school anyway and watched her climb his corporate ladder without ever once succumbing to his attempted seductions. He liked her all the more for her independence; he could trust her, rely on her judgment, which was more than he could say about the women who did flop into his bed.

Besides, he thought, sooner or later she'll give in. Even though she knows that'll be the end of her job in my office, she'll crawl into bed with me one of these nights. I just haven't found the right motivation for her yet. It's not money or status, I know that much about her. Maybe power. If it's power she's after, she could be dangerous. He grinned inwardly. Playing with nitroglycerine can be fun, sometimes.

Keeping those thoughts to himself, Humphries said without preamble as he stepped back to his desk, 'We need to get rid of the rock rats.'

If the statement surprised her, Verwoerd showed no hint of it. 'Why should we?' she countered.

'Simple economics. There's so many of them out there claiming asteroids that they're keeping the price of metals and minerals too low. Supply and demand. They're overdoing the supply.'

'Commodities prices *are* low, except for food products,' Verwoerd agreed.

'And sinking,' Humphries pointed out. 'But if we controlled the supply of raw materials—'

'Which means controlling the rock rats.'

28

'Right.'

'We could stop selling them supplies,' Verwoerd suggested.

Humphries waved a hand in the air. 'They'd just buy their goods from Astro. I don't want that.'

She nodded.

'No, I think our first step should be to establish a base of operations on Ceres.'

'On Ceres?'

'Ostensibly, it will be a depot for the supplies we sell to the rock rats,' Humphries said, sliding into his commodious high-backed chair. If he desired, the chair would massage his body or send waves of soothing warmth through him. At this moment, Humphries wanted neither.

Verwoerd gave the appearance of thinking over his statement for several moments. 'And actually?'

'It'll be a cover for putting our own people out there; a base for knocking the rock rats out of the Belt.'

Verwoerd smiled coldly. 'Once we open the base, we cut our prices for the supplies we sell the prospectors and miners.'

'Cut our prices? Why?'

'To get them buying from HSS and not Astro. Tie them to us.'

Nodding, Humphries said, 'We could give them more favourable terms for leasing spacecraft, too.'

Now she took one of the upholstered chairs in front of his desk. Crossing her long legs absently, she said, 'Better yet, lower the interest rates on purchase loans.'

'No, no. I don't want them to own the vessels. I want them to lease the spacecraft from us. I want them tied to Humphries Space Systems.'

'Under contract to HSS?'

Humphries leaned back in his chair and clasped his

hands behind his head. 'Right. I want those rock rats working for me.'

'At prices that you set,' she said.

'We allow the prices for raw ores keep going down,' Humphries mused. 'We *encourage* the independents to bring in so much ore that the prices are forced constantly downward. That will drive them out of the field, sooner or later.'

'Leaving only the people who are under contract to HSS,' Verwoerd agreed.

'That way, we gain control of the costs of exploration and mining,' he said, 'and at the other end we also control the prices for the refined metals and other resources that we sell to Selene and Earth.'

'But individual rock rats could sell to companies on Earth on their own, independently,' she pointed out.

'So what?' Humphries snapped. 'They'll just be under-cutting each other until they drive themselves out of business. They'll be cutting their own throats.'

'Supply and demand,' Verwoerd murmured.

'Yes. But when we get the rock rats working exclusively for us, we'll control the supply. No matter what the demand we'll be able to control prices. And profits.'

'A little on the devious side.' She smiled, though.

'It worked for Rockefeller.'

'Until the anti-trust laws were passed.'

'There aren't any anti-trust laws in the Belt,' Humphries said. 'No laws at all, come to think of it.'

Verwoerd hesitated, thinking, then said, 'It will take some time to drive out all the independents. And there's still Astro to consider.'

'I'll handle Astro when the time comes.'

'Then you'll have complete control of the Belt.'

'Which means that in the long run it won't cost us

anything to set up a base on Ceres.' It was a statement, not a question.

'That's not exactly how the accounting department will see it.'

He laughed. 'Then why don't we do it? Establish a base on Ceres and bring those rock rats under our control.'

She gave him a long, careful look, a look that said *I know there's more to this than you're telling me. You've got a hidden agenda, and I'm pretty sure I know what it is.*

But aloud, all she said was, 'We can use this base on Ceres to centralize all the maintenance work, as well.'

He nodded an acknowledgement to her. 'Good idea.'

'Offer the lowest possible terms on the maintenance contracts.'

'Get the rock rats to come to HSS for maintenance,' he agreed.

'Make them dependent on you.'

He laughed again. 'Gillette's dictum.'

She looked puzzled.

'Give 'em the razor,' he explained. 'Sell 'em the blades.'

Dossier: Oscar Jiminez

The illegitimate son of an illegitimate son, Oscar Jiminez was picked up by the police during one of their periodic sweeps through the barrios of Manila when he was seven years old. He was small for his age, but already an expert at begging, picking pockets, and worming his way past electronic security systems that would have stopped someone bigger or less agile.

The usual police tactic was to beat everyone mercilessly with their batons, rape the girls and the better-looking boys, then drive their prisoners far out into the countryside and leave them to fend for themselves. Until they got caught again. Oscar was lucky. Too small and scrawny to attract even the most perverse of the policemen, he was tossed from a moving police van into a roadside ditch, bleeding and covered with welts.

The lucky part was that they had thrown him out near the entrance to the regional headquarters of the New Morality. The Philippines were still heavily Catholic, but Mother Church had grudgingly allowed the mostly Protestant reformers to operate in the island nation with only a minimum of interference. After all, the conservative bishops who ran the Philippine Church and the conservatives who ran the New Morality saw eye to eye on many issues, including birth control and strict obedience to moral authority. Moreover, the New Morality brought money from America into the Philippines. Some of it even trickled down enough to help the poor.

So Oscar Jiminez became a ward of the New Morality. Under their stern tutelage his life of crime ended. He was sent to a New Morality school, where he learned that unrelenting psychological conditioning methods could be far worse than a police beating. Especially the conditioning sessions that used electric shock.

Oscar swiftly became a model student.

4

Kris Cardenas still looked little more than thirty. Even in a gritty, shabby one-room habitat carved out of one of Ceres' countless natural crevices, she radiated the blonde, sapphire-blue-eyed, athletic-shouldered look of a Californian surfer.

That was because her body was filled with therapeutic nanomachines, virus-sized contrivances that pulled apart molecules of fats and cholesterol in her bloodstream, repaired damaged cells, kept her skin smooth and her muscles taut, acted as a purposeful immune system to protect her body from invading microbes. Nanotechnology was forbidden on Earth: Dr Kristine Cardenas, Nobel laureate and former director of Selene's nanotechnology laboratory, was an exile on Ceres.

For an exile who had chosen to live on the ragged frontier of human settlement, she looked happy and cheerful as she greeted Amanda and Lars Fuchs.

'How are you two doing?' she asked as she ushered them into her quarters. The twisting tunnel outside her door was a natural lava tube, barely smoothed by human tools. The air out there was slightly hazy with fine dust; every time someone moved in Ceres, they disturbed the rock dust and the asteroid's gravity was so slight that it hung in the air constantly.

Amanda and Fuchs shuffled their feet across Cardenas' bare rock floor and made their way to the room's sofa – actually a pair of reclining seats scavenged from a spacecraft that had limped to Ceres and never made it out again. The seats still had safety harnesses dangling limply from them. Fuchs coughed slightly as he sat down.

'I'll turn up the air fans,' Cardenas said, gliding to the control panel set into the room's far wall. 'Settle the dust, make it easier to breathe.'

Amanda heard a fan whine from somewhere behind the walls. Despite being dressed in a long-sleeved, high-buttoned jumpsuit, she felt chilled. The bare rock always felt cold to her touch. At least it was dry. And Cardenas had tried to brighten up the underground chamber with holowindows that showed views of wooded hillsides and flower gardens on Earth. She had even scented the air slightly with something that reminded Amanda of her childhood baths in real tubs with scads of hot water and fragrant soap.

Cardenas pulled an old laboratory stool from her desk and perched on it before her visitors, locking her legs around its high rungs. 'So, how are you?' she asked again.

Fuchs cocked an eye at her. 'That's what we come to you to find out.'

'Oh, your physical.' Cardenas laughed. 'That's tomorrow, at the clinic. How are you getting along? What's the news?'

With a glance at Amanda, Fuchs answered, 'I think we'll be able to go ahead with the habitat project.'

'Really? Has Pancho agreed—'

'Not with Astro's help,' he said. 'We're going to do it ourselves.'

Cardenas' eyes narrowed slightly. Then she said, 'Is that the wisest course of action, Lars?'

'We really don't have that much of a choice. Pancho would help us if she could, but Humphries will hamstring her as soon as she brings it up to the Astro board of directors. He doesn't want us to improve our living conditions here.'

'He's going to establish a depot here,' Amanda said. 'Humphries Space Systems will, that is.'

'So you and the other rock rats are going to pursue this habitat programme on your own?'

'Yes,' said Fuchs, quite firmly.

Cardenas said nothing. She clasped her knees and rocked back slightly on the stool, looking thoughtful.

'We can do it,' Fuchs insisted.

'You'll need a team of specialists,' Cardenas said. 'This isn't something that you and your fellow prospectors can cobble together.'

'Yes. I understand that.'

Amanda said slowly, 'Lars, I've been thinking. While you're working on this habitat project you'll have to stay here at Ceres, won't you?'

He nodded. 'I've already given some thought to leasing *Starpower* to someone else and living here in the rock for the duration of the project.'

'And how will you earn an income?' Cardenas interjected.

He spread his hands. Before he could reply, though, Amanda said, 'I think I know.'

Fuchs looked at his wife, clearly puzzled.

'We can become suppliers for the other prospectors,' Amanda said. 'We can open our own warehouse.'

Cardenas nodded.

'We can deal through Astro,' Amanda went on, brightening with each word. 'We'll obtain our supplies from Pancho and sell them to the prospectors. We can sell supplies to the miners, too.'

'Most of the mining teams work for Humphries,' Fuchs replied darkly. 'Or Astro.'

'But they still need supplies,' Amanda insisted. 'Even if they get their equipment from the corporations, they'll still need personal items: soap, entertainment videos, clothing . . .'

Fuchs' face was set in a grimace. 'I don't think you would want to handle the kinds of entertainment videos these prospectors buy.'

Undaunted, Amanda said, 'Lars, we could compete against Humphries Space Systems while you're directing the habitat construction.'

'Compete against Humphries.' Fuchs rolled the idea on his tongue, testing it. Then he broke into a rare grin. It made his broad, normally dour face light up. 'Compete against Humphries,' he repeated. 'Yes. Yes, we can do that.'

Amanda saw the irony in it, although the others didn't. The daughter of a small shopkeeper in Birmingham, she had grown up hating her middle-class background and the lower-class workers her father sold to. The boys were rowdy and lewd, at best, and they could just as easily become dangerously violent. The girls were viciously catty. Amanda discovered early that being stunningly beautiful was both an asset and a liability. She was noticed wherever she went; all she had to do was smile and breathe. The trick was, once noticed, to make people see beyond her physical presence, to recognize the highly intelligent person inside that tempting flesh.

While still a teenager she learned how to use her good looks to get boys to do what she wanted, while using her sharp intellect to keep one jump ahead of them. She escaped her father's home and fled to London, took lessons to learn to speak with a polished accent, and – to her complete astonishment – found that she had the brains and skill to be a first-rate astronaut. She was hired by Astro Manufacturing Corporation to fly missions between Earth and the

Moon. With her breathless looks and seeming *naïveté*, almost everyone assumed she had slept her way to the top of her profession. Yet the truth was just the opposite; Amanda had to work hard to fend off the men – and women – who wanted to bed her.

It was at Selene that she had met Martin Humphries. He had been her gravest danger: he wanted Amanda and he had the power to take what he wanted. Amanda had married Lars Fuchs in part to get away from Humphries, and Lars knew it.

Now, here out on the fringe of humankind's expansion through the solar system, she was about to become a shopkeeper herself. How father would howl at that, she thought. The father's revenge: the child becomes just like the parent in the end.

'Humphries won't like competition,' Cardenas pointed out.

'Good!' exclaimed Fuchs.

Shaken out of her reverie, Amanda said, 'Competition will be good for the prospectors, though. And the miners, too. It will lower the prices they have to pay for everything.'

'I agree,' said Cardenas. 'But Humphries won't like it. Not one little bit.'

Fuchs laughed aloud. 'Good,' he repeated.

Two Years Later

5

As soon as he stepped out onto the surface of Ceres, Fuchs realized that this was the first time he'd been in a spacesuit in months. The suit still smelled new; he'd only used it once or twice. *Mein gott,* he said to himself, I've become a *bourgeois.* The suit didn't fit all that well, either; the arms and legs were a trifle too long to be comfortable.

His first venture into space had been *Starpower 1*'s ill-fated maiden voyage, five years earlier. He'd been a graduate student then, heading for a doctorate in planetary geochemistry. He never returned to school. Instead, he married Amanda and became a rock rat, a prospector seeking his fortune among the asteroids of the Belt. For nearly two years now, he had abandoned even that to run a supply depot on Ceres and supervise the habitat project.

Helvetia Ltd was the name Fuchs had given his fledgling business, incorporating it under the regulations of the International Astronautical Authority. He was Helvetia's president, Amanda its treasurer, and Pancho Lane a vice-president who never interfered in the company's operations; she seldom even bothered to visit its headquarters on Ceres. Helvetia bought most of its supplies from Astro Corporation and sold them to the rock rats at the lowest mark-up Amanda would allow. Humphries Space Systems ran a competing operation, and Fuchs gleefully kept his prices as low as possible, forcing Humphries to cut his own prices or be driven off Ceres altogether. The competition

43

was getting to the cut-throat level; it was a race to see who would drive who out of business.

The rock rats obviously preferred dealing with Fuchs to dealing with HSS. To his pleasant surprise, Helvetia Ltd prospered, even though Fuchs considered himself a mediocre businessman. He was too quick to extend credit on nothing more than a rock rat's earnest promise to repay once he'd struck it rich. He preferred a handshake to the small print of a contract. Amanda constantly questioned his judgment, but enough of those vague promises came through to make Helvetia profitable. We're getting rich, Fuchs realized happily as his bank account at Selene fattened. Despite all of Humphries' tricks, we are getting rather wealthy.

Now, gazing around the bleak, battered surface of Ceres, he realized all over again how lonely and desolate this place was. How far from civilization. The sky was filled with stars, such a teeming profusion of them that the old familiar constellations were lost in their abundance. There was no friendly old Moon or blue glowing Earth hanging nearby; even the sun looked small and weak, dwarfed by distance. A strange, alien sky: stark and pitiless. Ceres' surface was broodingly dark, cold, pitted by thousands of craterlets, rough and uneven, boulders and smaller rocks scattered around everywhere. The horizon was so close it looked as if he were standing on a tiny platform rather than on a solid body. For a giddy instant Fuchs felt that if he didn't hang on, he'd fall *up*, off this worldlet, into the wild wilderness of stars.

Almost distraught, he caught sight of the unfinished habitat rising above the naked horizon, glittering even in the weak sunlight. It steadied him. It might be a ramshackle collection of old, used and stripped-down spacecraft, but it was the handiwork of human beings out here in this vast, dark emptiness.

A gleam of light flashed briefly. He knew it was the little shuttlecraft bringing Pancho and Ripley back to the asteroid's surface. Fuchs waited by the squat structure of the airlock that led down into the living sections below ground.

The shuttle disappeared past the horizon, but in a few minutes it came up over the other side, close enough for him to see its insect-thin legs and the bulbous canopy of its crew module. Pancho had insisted on flying the bird herself, flexing her old astronaut muscles. Now she brought it in to a smooth landing on the scoured ground about a hundred metres from the airlock.

As the two spacesuited figures climbed down from the shuttle, Fuchs easily recognized Pancho Lane's long, stringy figure, even in her helmet and suit. This was the first time in nearly a year that Pancho had come to Ceres, doubling up on her roles of Astro board member and Helvetia vice-president.

Tapping on the communications keyboard on his left wrist, Fuchs heard her talking with Ripley, the engineer in charge of the construction project.

'. . . what you really need is a new set of welding lasers,' she was saying, 'instead of those clunkers you're workin' with.'

Rather than trying to walk in the low-gravity shuffle that was necessary on Ceres, Fuchs took the jetpack control box into his gloved hand and barely squeezed it, feather-light. As usual, he overdid the thrust and sailed over the heads of Pancho and the engineer, nearly ramming into the shuttlecraft. His boots kicked up a cloud of dark dust as he touched down on the surface.

'Lord, Lars, when're you gonna learn how to fly one of those rigs?' Pancho teased.

Inside his helmet Fuchs grinned with embarrassment. 'I'm out of practice,' he admitted, sliding his feet across the surface toward them, raising still more dust. The ground felt gritty, pebbly, even through his thick-soled boots.

'You were never *in* practice, buddy.'

He changed the subject by asking the engineer, 'So, Mr Ripley, will your crew be able to assemble the latest additions on schedule?'

'Believe it or not,' Ripley replied archly, 'they will.'

Niles Ripley was an American of Nigerian heritage, an engineer with degrees from Lehigh and Penn, an amateur jazz trumpet player who had acquired the nickname 'Ripper' from his headlong improvisations. The sobriquet sometimes caused problems for the mild-mannered engineer, especially in bars with belligerent drunks. The Ripper generally smiled and talked his way out of confrontations. He had no intention of letting some musclebound oaf damage his horn-playing lip.

'Your schedule will be met,' Ripley went on. Then he added, 'Despite its lack of flexibility.'

Fuchs jabbed back, 'Then your crew will earn its bonus, despite their complaints about the schedule.'

Pancho interrupted their banter. 'I've been tellin' ol' Ripper here that you'd get this job done a lot faster with a better set of welding lasers.'

'We can't afford them,' Fuchs said. 'We are on very tight budget restraints.'

'Astro could lease you the lasers. Real easy terms.'

Fuchs sighed audibly. 'I wish you had thought of that two years ago, when we started this operation.'

'Two years ago the best lasers we had were big and inefficient. Our lab boys just came up with these new babies: small enough to haul around on a minitractor. Very fuel efficient. They've even got a handheld version. Lower power, of course, but good enough for some jobs.'

'We're doing well enough with what we have, Pancho.'

'Well, okay. Don't say I didn't make you the offer.' He heard the resigned, slightly disappointed tone in her voice.

Pointing a gloved hand toward the habitat, which was nearly at the far horizon, Fuchs said, 'We've done quite well so far, don't you think?'

For a long moment she said nothing as the three of them watched the habitat glide down the sky. It looked like an unfinished pinwheel, several spacecraft joined end to end and connected by long buckyball tethers to a similar collection of united spacecraft, the entire assembly slowly rotating as it moved toward the horizon.

'Tell you the truth, Lars old buddy,' said Pancho, 'it kinda reminds me of a used car lot back in Lubbock.'

'Used car lot?' Fuchs sputtered.

'Or maybe a flyin' junkyard.'

'Junkyard?'

Then he heard Ripley laughing. 'Don't let her kid you, Lars. She was pretty impressed, going through the units we've assembled.'

Pancho said, 'Well, yeah, the insides are pretty good. But it surely ain't a thing of beauty from the outside.'

'It will be,' Fuchs muttered. 'You wait and see.'

Ripley changed the subject. 'Tell me more about these handheld lasers. How powerful are they?'

'It'll cut through a sheet of steel three centimetres thick,' Pancho said.

'How long does it take?' asked Ripley.

'Couple nanoseconds. It's pulsed. Doesn't melt the steel, it shock-blasts it.'

They chatted on while the habitat sank out of sight and the distant, pale Sun climbed higher in the dark, star-choked sky. Fuchs noticed the zodiacal light, like two long arms outstretched from the Sun's middle. Reflections from dust motes, he knew: microscopic asteroids floating out there, leftovers from the creation of the planets.

As they started toward the airlock, Pancho turned toward Fuchs. 'Might's well talk a little business.'

She raised her left arm and tapped the key on her cuff, switching to a secondary suit-radio frequency. Ripley was cut out of their conversation now.

Fuchs hit the same key on his control unit. 'Yes, business by all means.'

'You asked us to reduce the prices for circuitboards again,' Pancho said. 'We're already close to the bone, Lars.'

'Humphries is trying to undersell you.'

'Astro can't sell at a loss. The directors won't stand for it.'

Fuchs felt his lips curl into a sardonic smile. 'Humphries is on your board of directors still?'

'Yup. He's promised not to lower HSS's prices any further.'

'He's lying. They're offering circuit boards, chips, even repair services, at lower and lower prices. He's trying to drive me out of the market.'

'And once he does he'll run up the prices as high as he pleases,' Pancho said.

'Naturally. He'll have a monopoly then.'

They had reached the airlock hatch. It was big enough for two spacesuited people, but not three, so they sent Ripley through first.

Pancho watched the engineer close the hatch, then said, 'Lars, what Humphries really wants is to take over Astro. He's been after that since the git-go.'

'Then he'll have a monopoly on all space operations, everywhere in the Belt . . . everywhere in the whole solar system,' Fuchs said, feeling anger rising within him.

'That's what he's after.'

'We've got to prevent that! Whatever it takes, we must stop him.'

'I can't sell you goods at below cost, buddy. The board's made that clear.'

Fuchs nodded wearily. 'Then we'll have to think of something else.'

'Like what?'

He tried to shrug his shoulders, but inside the spacesuit it was impossible. 'I wish I knew,' he admitted.

6

I'm becoming dependent on this woman, Humphries thought, watching Diane Verwoerd as they rode down the moving stairs toward his mansion, in Selene's bottommost level.

She was coolly reading out the daily list of action items from her handheld palmcomp, ticking them off one by one, asking him to okay the staff assignments she had already made to handle each item.

Humphries rarely left his house. Instead, he had made it into a haven of luxury and security. Half the house was living quarters, with the other side given over to the scientists and technicians who maintained and studied the gardens that surrounded the mansion. It had been a brilliant idea, Humphries thought, to talk Selene's governing board into letting him create a three-hundred-hectare garden down in the deepest grotto in Selene. Officially, the house was the Humphries Trust Research Centre, which ran the ongoing ecological experiment: could a balanced ecology be maintained on the Moon with minimal human intervention, given adequate light and water? Humphries didn't care in the slightest what the answer was, so long as he could live in comfort in the midst of the flourishing garden, deep below the radiation and the other dangers of the Moon's surface.

He relished the knowledge that he had fooled them all, even Douglas Stavenger, Selene's founder and youthful *eminence gris*. He had even talked them into rescinding their foolish decision to exile him from Selene, after his part in Dan Randolph's death had become known. But he hadn't fooled the tall, exotic, silky Diane Verwoerd, he knew. She saw right through him.

He had invited her to lunch at the new bistro just opened in the Grand Plaza. She had turned down his earlier offers of dinner, but a 'working lunch' outside the house was something she could not easily refuse. So he had taken her to lunch. And she had worked right through the salad and soy cutlets, barely taking a sip of the wine he ordered, refusing dessert altogether.

And now, as they rode on the powered stairs back to his office/home, she held her palmcomp before her and rattled off problems facing the company and her solutions for them.

She's become almost indispensable to me, he realized. Maybe that's her game, to become so important to me businesswise that I'll stop thinking of her as a hot body. She must know that I don't keep a woman around for long once I've had her in bed.

He grinned inwardly. You're playing a tricky game, Ms Verwoerd. And, so far, you've played it just about perfectly.

So far.

Humphries refused to admit defeat, although it was obvious that this luncheon idea had been no victory. He listened to her long recitation with only half his attention, thinking, I'll get you sooner or later, Diane. I can wait.

But not much longer, another voice in his head spoke up. No woman is worth waiting for this long a time.

Wrong, he answered silently. Amanda is.

As they neared the bottom of the last flight of moving stairs, she said something that abruptly caught his full attention.

'And Pancho Lane flew all the way out to Ceres last week. She's on her way back now.'

'To Ceres?' Humphries snapped. 'What's she doing out there?'

'Talking to her business associates, Mr and Mrs Fuchs,' Verwoerd replied calmly. 'About undercutting our prices, I imagine.'

'Undercutting me?'

'What else? If they can drive HSS out of Ceres they'll have the whole Belt for themselves. You're not the only one who wants to control the rock rats.'

'Helvetia Ltd,' Humphries muttered. 'Silly name for a company.'

'It's really a front for Astro, you know.'

He looked around the smooth walls of the escalator well without replying. At this deep level beneath Selene, no one else was riding down. There was no sound except the muted hum of the electric motor powering the stairs.

'Pancho's using Fuchs and his company to make it much tougher for you to take control of Astro. The more business she does through Helvetia, the more the Astro board sees her as a real hero. They might even elect Pancho chairman when O'Banian steps down.'

'Drive me out of the Belt,' Humphries growled.

'That's what we're trying to do to them, isn't it?'

He nodded.

'We'd better do it, then, before they do it to us,' said Diane Verwoerd.

Humphries nodded again, knowing she was right.

'What we need, then,' she said slowly, 'is a plan of action. A programme aimed at crushing Helvetia once and for all.'

He looked at her, really looked at her for the first time since they'd finished lunch. She's thought this whole thing through, he realized. She's leading me around by the nose, by god. Humphries saw it in her almond eyes. She has this all figured out. She knows exactly where she wants to lead me.

'So what do you suggest?' he asked, really curious about where she was heading.

'I suggest a two-pronged strategy.'

'A two-pronged strategy?' he asked dryly.

'It's an old technique,' Verwoerd said, smiling slyly. 'The carrot and the stick.'

Despite his efforts to remain noncommittal, Humphries smiled. 'Tell me about it,' he said as they reached the bottom of the stairs and stepped off.

Once he got back to his office, Humphries cleared his calendar and leaned back in his chair, thinking, worrying, planning. All thoughts of Diane left his conscious mind; he pictured Amanda out there with Fuchs. Amanda wouldn't try to hurt me, he told himself. But *he* would. He knows I love her and he'd do *anything* to damage me. He's already taken Amanda away from me. Now he wants to drive me out of the Belt and stop me from taking Astro. The sonofabitch wants to ruin me!

Diane is right. We've got to move, and move fast. Carrot and stick.

Abruptly, he sat up straight and ordered the phone to summon his chief of security. The man rapped softly at his office door a few moments later.

'Come in, Grigor,' said Humphries.

The security chief was a new hire: a lean, silent man with dark hair and darker eyes. He wore an ordinary business suit of pale grey, the nondescript costume of a man who preferred to remain in the background, unnoticed, while he noticed everything. He remained standing despite the two comfortable chairs in front of Humphries' desk.

Tilting his own chair back slightly to look up at him, Humphries said, 'Grigor, I want the benefit of your thinking on a problem I have.'

Grigor shifted slightly on his feet. He had just been recruited from an Earth-based corporation that was floundering financially because most of its assets had been destroyed in the greenhouse flooding. He was on probation with Humphries, and he knew it.

'Those rock rats out in the Belt are getting a bigger and bigger share of their supplies from Helvetia Ltd instead of from Humphries Space Systems,' Humphries said, watching the man closely, curious about how he would respond.

Grigor said nothing. His face betrayed no emotion. He listened.

'I want Humphries Space Systems to have exclusive control of the rock rats' supplies.'

Grigor just stood there, unmoving, his eyes revealing nothing.

'Exclusive control,' Humphries repeated. 'Do you understand?'

Grigor's chin dipped in the slightest of nods.

'What do you think must be done?' Humphries asked.

'To gain exclusive control,' said Grigor, in a throaty, guttural voice that sounded strained, painful, 'you must eliminate your competitor.'

'Yes, but how?'

'There are many ways. One of them is to use violence. I presume that is why you have asked my opinion.'

Raising one hand, Humphries said sharply, 'I don't mind violence, but this needs to be done with great discretion. I don't want anyone to suspect that Humphries Space Systems has anything to do with it.'

Grigor thought in silence for a few heartbeats. 'Then the action must be taken against individual prospectors, rather than Helvetia itself. Eliminate their customers and the company will shrivel and die.'

Humphries nodded. 'Yes,' he said. 'Exactly.'

'It will take some time.'

'How much time?'

'A few months,' Grigor said. 'Perhaps a year.'

'I want it done faster than that. Sooner than a year.'

Grigor closed his eyes briefly, then said, 'Then we must be prepared to escalate the violence. First the individual prospectors, then personnel and facilities on Ceres itself.'

'Facilities?'

'Your competitor is constructing an orbital habitat there, is he not?'

Humphries fought to suppress a satisfied grin. Grigor's already been studying the situation, he realized. Good.

When his employer failed to reply, Grigor continued, 'Stopping the habitat project will help to discredit the man who started it. If nothing else, it will show that he is powerless to protect his own people.'

'It's got to look accidental,' Humphries insisted. 'No hint of responsibility laid at my doorstep.'

'Not to worry,' said Grigor.

'I never worry,' Humphries snapped. 'I get even.'

As Grigor left his office, silent as a wraith, Humphries thought, Carrot and stick. Diane will offer the carrot. Grigor's people will provide the stick.

One Month Later

The Lady of the Lake

'Ooh, Randy,' gushed Cindy, 'you're so *big*.'

'And hard,' added Mindy.

Randall McPherson lay back on the small mountain of pillows while the naked Twins stroked his bare skin. Some guys liked sex in microgravity, but Randy had spun up his ship to almost a full terrestrial g for his encounter with the Twins. His partner, Dan Fogerty, complained about the fuel cost of spinning up the ship, but Randy had ignored his bleating. Fogerty was known to all the miners as Fatso Fogerty, he had allowed himself to blubber up so shamelessly, living in microgravity most of the time. McPherson spent hours of his spare time in their ship's exercise centrifuge, or had the whole ship spun up to keep his muscles in condition. Fogerty was lucky to have a level-headed man such as McPherson to team with him, in McPherson's opinion.

The Twins were actually back at Ceres, of course, but the virtual reality system was working pretty well. Hardly a noticeable lag between a request by Randy and a smiling, slinky, caressing response from Cindy and Mindy.

So Randy was more than a little irked when Fogerty's voice broke into his three-way fantasy.

'There's a bloomin' ship approaching us!'

'What?' McPherson snapped, sitting up so abruptly that the VR images of the Twins were still wriggling sensuously on the pillows even though he was no longer lying between them.

'A ship,' Fatso repeated. 'They're askin' to dock with us.'

McPherson muttered a string of heartfelt profanities while the Twins lay motionless, staring blankly.

'Sorry, ladies,' he said, pushing himself up off the pillows, feeling half embarrassed, half infuriated. He lifted the VR goggles off and saw the real world: a dreary little compartment on a scruffy clunker of a ship that badly needed a refit and overhaul after fourteen months of batting around the Belt.

Awkwardly peeling off his VR sensor suit and pulling on his coveralls as he made his way up to the bridge, McPherson bellowed, 'Fatso, if this is one of your goddam jokes I'm gonna wring your neck till I hear chimes!'

He ducked through the hatch and into the cramped, overheated bridge. Fogerty overflowed the pilot's seat, one hand clenching half a meat pie; most of the rest of it was spattered over his chins and coveralls front. He was globulously bulbous, stretching the faded orange fabric of his coveralls so much that McPherson was reminded of an overripe pumpkin. He smelled overripe, too, and the additional spicy aroma from the meat pie made McPherson's stomach churn. Reckon I don't smell much better, McPherson told himself, trying to keep an even temper.

Fogerty half turned in the creaking chair and jabbed a thick finger excitedly toward the main display screen. McPherson saw the two-kilometre-long chunk of rock they had just claimed, dark and lumpy, and a silvery spacecraft that looked too sleek and new to be a prospector's ship.

'A mining team?' Fogerty half-suggested.

'Out here already?' McPherson snapped. 'We just sent in our claim. We haven't contacted any miners.'

'Well, there they are,' said Fogerty.

'That's not a miner's ship.'

Fogerty shrugged. 'Shall I give 'em permission to come aboard?'

McPherson had to squeeze past his partner's bulk to get into the right-hand seat. 'Who in blazes are they? And what are they doing here? With the whole Belt to poke into, why are they sticking their noses into our claim?'

Fogerty grinned at his partner. 'We could ask 'em.'

Grumbling, McPherson flicked on the communications channel. 'This is *The Lady of the Lake*. Identify yourselves, please.'

The screen swirled with colour momentarily, then a darkly bearded man's face took form. He looked vaguely oriental to McPherson: high cheekbones, hooded eyes.

'This is *Shanidar*. We have a boxful of videodisks that we've viewed so often we can lip-synch the dialogue. Do you have any to trade?'

'What've you got?' Fogerty asked eagerly. 'How recent are they?'

'Private stuff, mostly. *Muy piquante*, if you know what I mean. You can't get them through the normal channels. They were brand new when we left Selene, six months ago.'

Before McPherson could reply, Fogerty broke into a dimpled, many-chinned smile. 'We can swap you one-for-one, but our stuff is older.'

'That's okay,' said the bearded man. 'It'll be new to us.'

'What're you doing out here?' McPherson demanded. 'We claimed this rock, you know.'

'We're not prospecting any more,' came the reply. 'We've hit our jackpot and made a deal with Humphries Space Systems to process the ores. Got our money in the bank. We just thought we'd unload these videodisks before we head back home.'

'Sure,' said Fatso. 'Why not?'

McPherson felt uneasy. But he saw the eager look on his

61

partner's fleshy face. After fourteen months in the Belt they had barely cleared the payments on their ship. They needed another week, at least, to negotiate a mining contract with one of the corporations. McPherson had no intention of accepting the first offer they received. And the prices for ores just kept going down; they'd be lucky if they netted enough to live on for six months before they had to go out again.

'Okay,' he said reluctantly. 'Come on over and dock at our main airlock.'

Fogerty nodded happily, like a little kid anticipating Christmas.

7

Amanda thought again about how housekeeping on Ceres – inside Ceres, actually – was different from living on a ship. Not that their living quarters were that much more spacious: the single room that she and Lars shared was a slightly enlarged natural cave in the asteroid, its walls, floor and ceiling smoothed and squared off. It wasn't much bigger than the cubic volume they had aboard *Starpower*. And there was the dust, always the dust. In Ceres' minuscule gravity, every time you moved, every time you took a step, you stirred up the everlasting dust. It was invisibly fine inside the living quarters, thanks to the air blowers. Once they moved up to the orbiting habitat, the dust would be a thing of the past, thank god.

In the meantime, though, it was a constant aggravation. You couldn't keep anything really clean: even dishes stored in closed cupboards had to be scoured under air jets before you could eat off them. The dust made you sneeze; half the time Amanda and most of the other residents wore filter masks. She worried that her face would bear permanent crease marks from the masks.

But living in Ceres offered something that shipboard life could not duplicate. Company. Society. Other people who could visit you or you could drop in on. Strolls through the corridors where you could see neighbours and say hello and stop for a chat. The corridors were narrow and twisting, it was true; natural lava tubes through the rock that had been smoothed off enough for people to shuffle through in a low-gravity parody of walking. Their walls and ceilings were still curved and unfinished raw stone; it was more like walking through a tunnel than a real corridor. And there was the dust, of course. Always the dust. It was worse in the tunnels, so bad that everyone wore face masks when they went for a stroll.

Lately, though, people's attitudes had changed noticeably. There was an aura of expectation in the air, almost like the slowly building excitement that the year-end holiday season brought, when she'd been a child on Earth. The habitat was growing visibly, week by week. Everyone could see it swinging through the sky on their wallscreens. We're going to live up there, everyone was saying to themselves. We're going to move to a new, clean home.

When Lars had first told Amanda about the orbiting habitat, she'd been worried about the radiation. One advantage of living inside a big rock was that it shielded you from the harsh radiation sleeting in from the Sun and deep space. But Lars had shown her how the habitat would use the same magnetic radiation shielding that spacecraft used, only stronger, better. She studied the numbers herself and became convinced that the habitat would be just as safe as living underground – as long as the magnetic shielding worked.

Lars was up on the unfinished habitat again with Niles Ripley. He and the Ripper were working on a recalcitrant water recycler that refused to operate as programmed. Meanwhile, she was running the office, routing prospectors' requests for supplies and equipment to the proper inventory system and checking to make certain that the material was actually loaded aboard a ship and sent to the people who had requested it.

Then there was the billing procedure. Miners were usually no problem: most of them were on corporate payrolls, so whatever they owed could be deducted automatically from their pay-cheque. Prospectors, though, were something else. The independents had no pay-cheque to deduct from. They were still searching for an asteroid to mine, waiting to find a jackpot, yet they needed air to breathe and food to eat just as much as did miners working a claim. At Lars' insistence, Amanda ran a tab for most of them, waiting for the moment when they 'struck it rich.'

Strange, Amanda thought, how the system works. The prospectors go out dreaming of making a fortune. Once they find a likely asteroid they have to make a deal to mine its ores. That's when they realize that they'll be lucky if they can break even.

The prices for metals and minerals roller-coasted up and down – mostly down – depending on the latest strikes; the commodities markets Earthside were hotbeds of frantic speculation, despite the sternest efforts of the Global Economic Council to keep things under control. Yet there were just enough really big finds to keep the stars in the prospectors' eyes. They kept doggedly searching for the one asteroid that would allow them to retire in wealth and ease.

The real way to make a fortune, Amanda had learned, was to be a supplier to the prospectors and miners who seemed to be rushing out to the Belt in steadily increasing numbers. They did the searching and the finding, the mining and refining, but the people here on Ceres were the ones who were getting rich. Lars had already amassed a small fortune with Helvetia Ltd. Humphries' people were piling up bigger and bigger sums in their bank accounts, too. Even the Twins, with their virtual-reality bordello, were millionaires several times over.

The real profits, though, went to the corporations. Astro and Humphries Space Systems made most of the money;

only a small percentage of it stays with people like Lars and me, Amanda knew.

Amanda rubbed at the aching back of her neck. It had become stiff from staring at the wallscreen for so many hours on end. With a tired sigh, she decided to call it a day. Lars would be coming in soon. Time to scrub up and put on a clean set of coveralls for dinner and maybe take a walk to The Pub afterward. Before shutting down for the day, Amanda flicked through the list of incoming messages awaiting her attention. Routine. Nothing that needed immediate attention.

Then she noticed that one of the messages had come in not from the ships plying the Belt, but from Selene. From the headquarters of Humphries Space Systems.

Her first instinct was to ignore it. Or perhaps delete it altogether. Then she saw that it was addressed to Lars, not her. It was not marked personal, and did not bear Martin Humphries' signature. No harm in reading it, Amanda thought. It won't be a two-way conversation, face-to-face. She glanced at her mirror by the bed, across the narrow room. I'm certainly not dressed to impress anyone, she thought. But even if it is from Martin, it was recorded and sent hours ago. Whoever sent it won't see me.

She didn't bother to take-off her filter mask as she called up the message from HSS.

The wallscreen flickered momentarily, then showed an attractive dark-haired woman with the kind of sculpted high cheekbones that Amanda had always envied. The ID line beneath her image read DIANE VERWOERD, SPECIAL ASSISTANT TO THE CEO, HUMPHRIES SPACE SYSTEMS.

'Mr Fuchs,' said Verwoerd's image, 'I have been authorized by the management of Humphries Space Systems to engage in negotiations for buying out Helvetia Ltd. The buyout would include your supply depot, inventory, and all the services that Helvetia performs. I'm sure you'll find our terms very attractive. Please call me at your earliest convenience. Thank you.'

The screen blanked to the HSS logo against a neutral grey background. Amanda stared at it, seeing the woman's image, hearing her words. Buy us out! We could go back to Earth! We could live well and Lars could even go back to graduate school and get his doctorate!

She was so excited that she paid no attention to the message from the supply ship that was supposed to rendezvous with *The Lady of the Lake*.

8

'Don't you see, Lars?' Amanda said eagerly. 'We could go home! To Earth! You could go back to your studies and get your doctorate.'

Fuchs was sitting on the edge of their bed, his thin slash of a mouth turned down grimly, Amanda beside him. Together they had watched Diane Verwoerd's full message, offering him ten million international dollars for his supply service and its facilities on Ceres.

'It's a bribe,' he growled.

'It's the opportunity of a lifetime, darling. Ten million international dollars! Think of it! Ten million, free and clear, just like that!' She snapped her fingers. 'For nothing more than signing your name.'

'And getting out of Ceres.'

'And returning to Earth. We could go to London, or Geneva, if you prefer.'

'It's a bribe,' he repeated stubbornly.

Amanda took both his big, callused hands in hers. 'Lars, darling, we can go back to Earth and live comfortably wherever you choose. We can begin a new life together.'

He said nothing, simply stared at the blanked wallscreen as if he were looking down the muzzle of a gun.

'Lars, we could have children.'

That stirred him. He turned his head to look into her eyes.

'I want to have a baby, Lars. Your baby. We can't do that here, you know that.'

He nodded bleakly. 'The gravity . . .' he muttered.

'If we lived on Earth, we could lead normal lives. We could raise a family.'

'The frozen zygotes are waiting for us at Selene,' he said.

She slid her arms around his neck. 'We won't need them, Lars. Not if we live on Earth like normal people.'

He started to pull her to him, but then something crossed his face. His expression changed; he looked almost as if he were in pain.

'They want us to leave Ceres.'

'And you want to *stay*?' Amanda had meant it to be joking, light-hearted, but it sounded bitter, almost like nagging, even to her.

'The prospectors. The miners,' he said, almost whispering. 'All the others rock rats out here . . . our friends, our neighbours.'

'What of them?'

'We'd have to leave them.'

'We'll make new friends. They'll understand.'

He pulled away from her and got to his feet. 'But we'll be leaving them to *him*, to Humphries.'

'What of it?'

'Once we're out of his way, once he's bought us out, he'll be the only source for supplies in the entire Belt. No one else would dare to compete against him.'

'Astro might. Pancho—'

'He's on Astro's board of directors. Sooner or later he'll take control of Astro, too. He'll control everything! And everybody.'

Amanda had known all along that her husband would stick on this point. She had tried to keep it out of her mind, but there it was, in the open, standing between them.

'Lars,' she said slowly, picking her words with care, 'whatever feelings Martin may have once had for me are

70

long gone, I'm certain. There is no need to view this as a competition between you and him.'

He walked away from her, paced the little room in six strides and then turned back toward her, a barrel-chested bear of a man dressed in faded dark grey coveralls, his broad heavy-featured face glowering with distrust.

'But it *is* a competition, Amanda. Between Humphries Space Systems and Helvetia Ltd. Between him and Astro, actually. We're caught in the middle of it, whether we like it or not.'

'But we can get out of it,' she said. 'You can take me back to Earth and we'll be rid of Humphries and Astro and the rock rats for good.'

He strode to the bed and dropped to his knees before her. 'I want to take you back home, dearest. I know how much you want to be away from here, how brave you've been to stay here with me—'

'I love you, Lars,' she said, reaching out to tousle his dark hair. 'I want to be with you wherever you are.'

He sighed heavily. 'Then we must remain here. At least for a little while longer.'

'But why . . . ?'

'Because of them. The rock rats. Our neighbours and friends here on Ceres. We can't leave them to Humphries.'

Amanda felt her eyes misting over. 'We can't let this opportunity pass us by, Lars. Please, *please* accept their offer.'

He started to shake his head stubbornly, but then he noticed the tears in her eyes. He got to his feet again and sat heavily beside her on the edge of the bed.

'Amanda, dearest, I can't turn my back on all the people here. They trust me. They need me.'

'I need you, too, Lars,' Amanda said. 'We've been out here for five years. I haven't complained once, have I?'

'No, you haven't,' he admitted. 'You've been very wonderful.'

'I'm asking you now, Lars. I'm begging you. Please accept this offer and take me back home.'

He stared into her glistening eyes for long, silent moments. She could see that he was thinking, searching for some way to do what she wanted without feeling that he had betrayed the other rock rats in the Belt.

At last he said, 'Let me talk to Pancho.'

'Pancho? Why?'

'To see if Astro will make a similar offer.'

'And if they won't?'

With obvious, painful reluctance, Fuchs said, 'Then we'll accept Humphries' offer.'

'You will?'

He nodded, smiling sadly. 'Yes, I'll take his money and leave the Belt and bring you home to Earth.'

Dossier: Joyce Takamine

The name on her birth certificate read Yoshiko Takamine, but once she started at public school everyone called her Joyce. Her parents didn't mind; they were fourth-generation Americans, with only a vague feeling of nostalgia for the family's roots in Japan. The first time one of her schoolmates called her a 'Jap', Joyce thought she meant 'Jewish American Princess.'

Father moved them to the hills above Sausalito but when the greenhouse floods wiped out most of the electrical power generation plants in the Bay area, they were plunged into darkness along with everyone else. Those were desperate times, with half the county thrown out of their jobs. No electricity, no work. Joyce's class held their senior prom by candlelight, and there was talk of bringing in drilling companies to bore wells deep enough to tap the natural gas that lay kilometres below ground.

All the kids had to find some kind of job to help support the family. Joyce did what her great-grandmother had done more than a century earlier: migrant stoop labour in the farms down in the rich valleys of California. The floods hadn't reached that far inland, although prolonged drought was searing the orchards and vineyards mercilessly. It was hard, bitter work, picking fruit and vegetables beneath the hot sun while grim-faced men armed with shotguns kept a patrol against wandering bands of starving looters. They expected casual sex from the workers. Joyce quickly learned that it was better to please them than to go hungry.

When Joyce returned home that winter, she was shocked to see how much her parents had aged. An epidemic of dengue fever had swept the coast and even reached into the hills where they lived. Her mother sobbed softly at night; her father stared into the hot, cloudless sky, racked with bouts of coughing that left him gasping for breath. When he looked at his daughter he seemed ashamed, as if all this devastation, all this ruination of the family's plans, were his fault alone.

'I wanted you to become an engineer,' he told Joyce. 'I wanted you to rise beyond my station in life.'

'I will, Dad,' she told him, with the careless assurance of youth. And when she turned her eyes to the sky, she thought about the wild frontier out along the Asteroid Belt.

9

'He's put in a call to Pancho Lane,' said Diane Verwoerd.

She and Humphries were strolling through the courtyard outside his mansion. The big, high-ceilinged cavern was filled with flowering shrubbery, a profusions of reds and yellows and delicate lilacs blooming from one rough-hewn rock wall to the other. Taller trees rose among the mass of flowers: alders and sturdy maples and lushly flowering white and pink gardenias. No breeze swayed those trees; no birds sang in the greenery; no insects buzzed. It was a huge, elaborate hothouse, maintained by human hands. Hanging from the raw rock ceiling were strips of full-spectrum lamps to imitate sunlight.

Verwoerd could see the enormous garden beyond the ornate fountain that splashed noisily in the courtyard. The house itself was massive, only two stories high but wide, almost sprawling. Built of smoothed lunar stone, its roof slanted down to big sweeping windows.

Compared to the grey underground drabness of the rest of Selene, this garden and home were like a paradise in the midst of a cold, forbidding desert. Verwoerd's own quarters, several levels up from this grotto, were among the best in Selene, but they seemed cramped and colourless compared to this.

Humphries claimed he enjoyed walking in the open air. The only other open space in Selene was the Grand Plaza, under the big dome up on the surface, and *anyone* could take a stroll up there. Here he had his privacy, and all the heady colour that human ingenuity and hard work could provide on the Moon. Verwoerd thought he enjoyed the idea that all this was his, more than any aesthetic or health benefits he could gain from walking among the roses and peonies.

But any pleasure he might have enjoyed from this stroll was wiped away by her announcement.

'He's called Pancho?' Humphries snapped, immediately nettled. 'What for?'

'She scrambled his message and her reply, so we don't know the exact words as yet. I have a cryptologist working on it.'

'Only one message?'

With a small nod, Verwoerd answered, 'His incoming to her, and hers outgoing to him immediately after.'

'Hmm.'

'I can guess what the subject was.'

'So can I,' Humphries said sourly. 'He wants to see if she'll better our offer.'

'Yes.'

'He's playing her against me.'

'It would seem so.'

'And if she outbids me, then Astro gets full control of his Helvetia Ltd.' He pronounced the name sneeringly.

Verwoerd frowned slightly. 'He's already using Astro as his supplier. What does Pancho have to gain by buying him out?'

'She keeps us from buying him out. It's a preventive strike, that's what it is.'

'So we increase our bid?'

'No,' Humphries snapped. 'But we increase our pressure.'

Seyyed Qurrah laughed with delight as he gazed through the thick quartz observation port at his prize, his jewel, his

76

reward for more than two years of scorn and struggle and near starvation. He feasted his eyes as the irregular chunk of rock slid across his view, greyish brown where the sunlight struck it, pitted and covered here and there with boulders the size of houses.

'Allah is great,' he said aloud, thanking the one God for his mercy and kindness.

Turning to the sensor displays in his cabin's control panel, he saw that this lump of stone bore abundant hydrates, water locked chemically to the silicates of the rock. Water! In the desert that was the Moon, water fetched a higher price than gold. It was even more valuable at Ceres, although with only a few hundred people living at the big asteroid, the demand for precious water was not as high as that of Selene's many thousands.

Qurrah thought of the contempt and ridicule that they had heaped upon him back home when he'd announced that he intended to leave Earth and seek his fortune in the new bounty of the Asteroid Belt. 'Sinbad the Sailor' was the kindest thing he'd been called. 'Seyyed the Idiot' was what most of them said. Even once he had reached Ceres and leased a ship with the last bit of credit his dead father had left him, even there the other prospectors and miners called him 'Towel Head' and worse. Well, now the shoe was on the other foot. He'd show them!

Then he pictured how happy Fatima would be when he returned to Algiers, wealthy and happy at last. He would be able to shower her with diamonds and rich gowns of silk with gold threading. Perhaps even acquire a second wife. He was so pleased that he decided to take a full meal from his meagre foodstocks, instead of his usual handful of couscous.

But first he would register his claim with the International Astronautical Authority. That was important. No, before that, he must make his prayer to Allah. That was more important.

He realized he was nearly babbling out loud. Taking a deep breath to calm himself, Qurrah decided, prayer first, then register with the IAA, then celebrate with a whole meal.

He kept his ship spinning all the time, counterbalancing his habitation unit with the power generator and other equipment at the end of the kilometre-long tether. Not for him the long months in microgee, with his muscles going flabby and his bones decalcifying so that he would have to spend even longer months in lunar orbit rebuilding his body cells. No! Qurrah lived in almost full Earth gravity.

So he had no trouble unfurling his prayer rug once he had taken it from its storage cabinet. He was spreading the rug on the one uncluttered area of his compartment when his communications receiver chimed.

A message? He was startled at the thought. Who would be calling me out here, in this wilderness? Only Fatima and the IAA knows where I am – and the people back at Ceres, of course, but why would they call a lonely prospector?

Fatima! he thought. Something has happened to her. Something terrible.

His voice trembled as he answered, 'This is the *Star of the East*. Who is calling, please?'

A bearded man's face appeared on his main screen. He looked almost Asian to Qurrah, or perhaps Hispanic.

'This is *Shanidar*. You are trespassing on territory that belongs to Humphries Space Systems, Incorporated.'

'This rock?' Qurrah was instantly incensed. 'No sir! There is no registered claim for this asteroid. I was just about to send in my own claim when you hailed me.'

'You haven't registered a claim for it?'

'I am going to, right now!'

The bearded man shook his head, very slightly, just a small movement from side to side.

'No you're not,' he said.

They were the last words Qurrah ever heard. The laser blast from *Shanidar* blew a fist-sized hole through the thin hull of his ship. Qurrah's death scream quickly screeched to silence as the air rushed out and his lungs collapsed in massive haemorrhages of blood.

The Pub

George Ambrose cradled his stone mug of beer in both his big paws. They call it beer, he grumbled inwardly. Haven't seen a decent beer since I came out here. Fookin' concoction these rock rats call beer tastes more like platypus piss than anything else. The real stuff was available, but the price for anything imported was so high that George gritted his teeth and sipped the local brew.

As joints went, The Pub wasn't so bad. Reminded George of the Pelican Bar, back at Selene, except for the Twins in their spray-paint bikinis. They worked behind the bar, under the protective eye of the owner/barkeep. More'n two hundred and sixty million kilometres away, the old Pelican was. Nearly a week's flight, even in the best of the fusion ships.

The Pub was a natural cave in Ceres' porous, rocky crust. The floor had been smoothed down but nobody's ever bothered to finish the walls or ceiling. Be a shame to leave this behind when we move to the habitat, George thought. He'd grown fond of the joint. Everything in The Pub was either scavenged or made from asteroidal materials. George was sitting on an old packing crate, reinforced by nickel-iron rods and topped with a stiff plastic cushion cadged from some ship's stores. The table on which he was leaning his beefy arms was carved rock, as was his mug. Some of the crowd were drinking from frosted aluminium steins, but George preferred the stone. The pride and joy of The Pub was its bar, made of real wood, ferried in here by the daft old poppie who owned the joint. Maybe he isn't so daft, George mused. He's makin' more money than I am, that's for sure. More money than any of these rock rats.

He looked over the crowd. Men and women were jammed four deep at the bar and sitting at all the tables spotted across the place like stalagmites rising from the stone floor, four or five men to every sheila. A dozen or more stood along the back wall, drinks in their hands. A pair of women and another bloke were sitting at the same table as George, but he hardly knew them and they were chatting each other up, leaving him alone with his beer.

A strange crowd, he thought. Prospectors and miners ought to be rough, hard-handed men, outback types like in the old videos. These blokes were college boys, computer nerds, family men and women with enough education and smarts to operate spacecraft and highly automated mining machinery. Not one of 'em ever used a pick or shovel, George knew. Hell's bells, I never did myself. Lately, though, a different sort had been drifting in: snotty-looking yobs who kept pretty much to themselves. They didn't seem to have any real jobs, although they claimed they worked for HSS. They just hung around, as if they were waiting for something.

Off in the far corner of the cave a couple of blokes were unpacking musical instruments and connecting up their amplifiers. Niles Ripley walked in, loose-jointed and smiling at his friends – just about everybody – with his trumpet case in one hand. George pushed himself to his feet and shambled to the bar for a refill of his platypus brew. Several people said hello to him, and he made a bit of chat until Cindy slid the filled mug back to him. Or was it Mindy? George could never tell the Twins apart. Then he went back to his table. Nobody had swiped his seat. That's the kind of place The Pub was.

As the music began, low and sweet, George found himself thinking about his life. Never dreamed I'd be out here in the Belt, digging ores out of fookin' asteroids. Hard work, but better than prospecting, poking around the Belt for months on end, looking for a really rich asteroid that the corporations haven't already claimed, hoping to make the big strike so you can go home and live in luxury. Life takes weird turns.

The Ripper, who had been playing along with the other musicians, finally stood up and tore into a solo that rocked the cave. His trumpet echoed off the stone walls, bringing everyone to their feet, swaying and clapping in time to his soaring notes. When he finished they roared with delight and insisted on more.

The evening flew by. George forgot about the ship that he owed money on, forgot about getting up early tomorrow morning to finish the repair job on *Matilda*'s main manipulator arm so he could get the hell out of Ceres and finish the mining job he'd signed up for before the contract deadline ran out and he had to pay a penalty to Astro Corporation. He just sat there with the rest of the crowd, grooving on the music, rushing to the bar along with everyone else when the band took a break, drinking all night long yet getting high on the music, not the beer.

It was well past midnight when the band broke up, after several encores, and started to pack their instruments and equipment. People began to file out of The Pub, tired and happy. The Twins had disappeared, as usual. Nobody laid a hand on them, except in virtual reality. George ploughed through the crowd and made his way to the Ripper.

'Lemme buy you a beer, mate?'

Ripley clicked his trumpet case shut, then looked up. Smiling, he said, 'Maybe a cola, if you can afford it.'

'Sure thing, Rip. No worries.'

A few determined regulars still stood at the bar, apparently with no intention of leaving. George saw four of the new guys there, too, grouped together, bent over their drinks and talking to one another in low, serious tones. They all wore coveralls with the HSS logo over their name tags.

'Another beer for me and a cola for the Ripper, here,' George called to the barkeep.

'A cola?' sneered one of the yobbos. The others laughed.

Ripley smiled down the bar at them. 'Can't have any alcohol after midnight. I'm working on the habitat in the morning.'

'Sure,' came the reply.

George scowled at them. They were so new to Ceres they didn't realize that an imported cola cost half the Earth. He turned back toward Ripley. 'Helluva show you put on tonight.'

'They seemed to like it.'

'Ever think of playin' professionally? You're too good to be sittin' out on this rock.'

Ripley shook his head. 'Naw. I play the trumpet for fun. If I got serious about it, it'd become work.'

'You hurt my ears with that damned noise,' said another of the yobbos.

'Yeah,' said one of his mates. 'Why the hell d'you hafta play so damned loud?'

Before George could say anything, Ripley replied, 'Gee, I'm sorry about that. Maybe next time I'll use a mute.'

The complainer walked down the bar toward Ripley. 'Next time, my ass. What're you going to do about the frickin' headache you've given me?'

He was a tall, rangy sort, athletically built; short blond hair, with a funny little tail in the back, like an old-time matador. He was young, George saw, but old enough to have better manners.

The Ripper's smile started to look a little forced. Very gently, he replied, 'I guess I could treat you to a couple of aspirins.'

'Fuck you and your aspirins.' The guy threw his drink in the Ripper's face.

Ripley looked shocked, totally at a loss. He blinked in confusion as beer dripped from his nose, his ears.

George stepped between them. 'That wasn't very smart,' he said.

'I'm not talking to you, Red. It's this wise-ass noise-maker I'm talking to.'

'He's my friend,' said George. 'I think you owe him an apology.'

'And I think you ought to pull your shaggy ass out of this before you get hurt,' said the yobbo, as his three companions came up to stand with him.

George smiled pleasantly. This was getting interesting, he thought. To the beer-thrower, he said, 'Mr Ripley here isn't the sort to get involved in a barroom brawl. He might hurt his lip, y'see, and then everyone here would be upset with the people who made that happen.'

The guy looked around. The Pub was almost empty now. The few remaining regulars had backed away from the bar, drinks in their hands. A handful of others who had been leaving now stood at the doorway, watching. The barkeep had faded back to the other end of the bar, the expression on his face somewhere between nervous and curious.

'I don't give a fuck who gets upset with who. And that includes you, big ass.'

George grabbed the guy by the front of his shirt and lifted him, one hand, off the floor to deposit him with a thump on the bar. He looked very surprised. His three friends stood stock-still.

Ripley touched George's other arm. 'Come on, pal. Let's not have a fight.'

George looked from the yobbo sitting on the bar to his three standing partners, then broke into a shaggy grin.

'Yeah,' he said to the Ripper. 'No sense breakin' the furniture. Or any heads.'

He turned and started for the door. As he knew they would, all four of them leaped at him. And none of them knew a bean about fighting in low gravity.

George swung around and caught the first one with a back-hand swat that sent him sprawling. The next two tried to pin his arms but George threw them off. The original troublemaker came at him with a high-pitched yowl and a karate kick aimed at his face. George caught his foot in mid-kick and swung him around like a kid's toy, lifted him totally off his feet and then tossed him, flying in a howling slow-motion spin, over the bar. He crashed into the decorative glassware on the shelves along the back wall.

'Goddammit, George, that costs money!' the barkeep yelled.

But George was busy with the three recovered yobbos. They rushed him all at once, but it was like trying to bring down a statute. George staggered back a step, grunting, then smashed one to the floor with a single sledgehammer blow between his shoulder blades. He peeled the other two off and held them off the floor by the scruffs of their necks, shook them the way a terrier shakes a rat, then banged their heads together with a sound like a melon hitting the pavement after a long drop.

He looked around. Two men were unconscious at his feet, a third lay moaning face-down on the floor. The barkeep was bending over the one on the floor behind the bar amid the shattered glassware, shouting, 'Well, somebody's got to pay for this damage!'

'Are you all right, George?' Ripley asked.

George saw that the Ripper had a packing-crate chair in his hands. He laughed. 'What're you gonna do with that, post 'em back to Earth?'

Ripley broke into a relieved laugh and the two men left The Pub. Half a minute later the Ripper ran back in and retrieved his trumpet. The bartender was on the phone, calling Kris Cardenas, the only qualified medical help on Ceres. In his hand he held a credit chip from one of the yobbos.

10

Even after five years on Astro Corporation's board of directors, Pancho Lane still thought of herself as a neophyte. You got a lot to learn, girl, she told herself almost daily.

Yet she had formed a few working habits, a small set of rules for herself. She spent as little time in Astro's corporate offices as possible. Whether at La Guaira on Earth or in Selene, Pancho chose to be among the engineers and astronauts rather than with the suits. She had come up through the ranks, a former astronaut herself, and she had no intention of reading reports and studying graphs when she could be out among the workers, getting her hands dirty; she preferred the smell of machine oil and honest sweat to the quiet tensions and power-jockeying of the corporate offices.

One of her self-imposed rules was to make decisions as soon as she had the necessary information, and then to act on her decisions quickly. Another was to deliver bad news herself, instead of detailing some flunkey to handle the chore.

Still, she hesitated to put in the call to Lars Fuchs. It wouldn't make him happy, she knew. Instead, she called his wife. Pancho and Amanda had worked together five years earlier; they had co-piloted *Starpower 1*'s maiden mission to the Belt. They had watched helplessly as Dan Randolph died of radiation poisoning – murdered by remote control, by Martin Humphries.

And now the Humper was offering to buy out Lars and Mandy, get them off Ceres, establish his own Humphries Space Systems as the sole supplier for the rock rats out there. Pancho had tried to fight Humphries, tried to keep Astro in the competition through Fuchs' little company. But she had been thoroughly outmanoeuvred by Humphries, and she knew it.

Angry more at herself than anyone else, she marched herself to her office in La Guaira and made the call to Amanda. She paid no attention to the lovely tropical scenery outside her office window; the green, cloud-topped mountains and gently surging sea held no attraction for her. Planting her booted feet on her desktop, wishing there was some way to help Mandy and Lars, she commanded her phone to send a message to Amanda Cunningham Fuchs, on Ceres.

'Mandy,' she began unceremoniously, ' 'fraid I got bad news for you and Lars. Astro won't top Humphries' buyout offer. The board wouldn't vote to buy you out. Humphries has a nice little clique on the board and they voted the whole proposition down the toilet. Sorry, kid. Look me up when you get back to Selene, or wherever you're goin'. Maybe we can spend some time together without worryin' about business. See ya.'

Pancho was startled when she realized she'd been sitting at her desk for nearly half an hour without instructing the phone to transmit her message.

Finally she said, 'Aw shit, send it.'

The headquarters of the International Astronautical Authority were still in Zurich, officially, but its main working offices were in St Petersburg.

The global warming that had melted most of the glaciers in Switzerland and turned the snowpacks of the Alpine peaks into disastrous, murderous floods had forced the move. The administrators and lawyers who had been transferred to Russia complained, with some resentment, that they had been pushed off the greenhouse cliff.

To their surprise, St Petersburg was a beautiful, cosmopolitan city, not at all the dour, grey urban blight they had expected. The greenhouse warming had been kind to St Petersburg: winters were nowhere near as long and bitter as they had once been. Snow did not start to fall until well into December and it was usually gone by April. Russian engineers had doggedly built a series of weirs and breakwaters across the Gulf of Finland and the Neva River to hold back the rising seas.

Even though the late winter sunlight had to struggle through a slate-grey layer of clouds, Erek Zar could see from his office window that most of the snow had already melted from the rooftops. It promised to be a good day, and a good weekend. Zar leaned back in his chair, clasped his hands behind his head, looked out across the rooftops toward the shimmering harbour and thought that, with luck, he could get away by lunchtime and spend the weekend with his family in Cracow.

He was not happy, therefore, when Francesco Tomasselli stepped through his office door with a troubled expression on his swarthy face. Strange, Zar said to himself: Italians are supposed to be sunny and cheerful people. Tomasselli always looked like the crack of doom. He was as lean as a strand of spaghetti, the nervous sort. Zar felt like Shakespeare's Julius Caesar: *Let me have men about me that are fat, sleek-headed men, and such as sleep o' nights*.

'What's the matter, Franco?' Zar asked, hoping it wasn't serious enough to interfere with his travel plans.

Tomasselli plopped into the upholstered chair in front of the desk and sighed heavily. 'Another prospecting ship is missing.'

Zar sighed too. He spoke to his desktop screen and the computer swiftly showed the latest report from the Belt: a spacecraft named *Star of the East* had disappeared; its tracking beacon had winked off, all telemetry from the craft had ceased.

'That's the third one this month,' Tomasselli said, his lean face furrowed with worry.

Spreading his hands placatingly, Zar said, 'They're out on the edge of nowhere, sailing alone through the Belt. Once a ship gets into trouble there's no one near enough to help. What do you expect?'

Tomasselli shook his head. 'When a spacecraft gets into trouble, as you put it, it shows up on the telemetry. They send out distress calls. They ask for help, or advice.'

Zar shrugged.

'We've had ships fail and crews die, god knows,' Tomasselli went on, a faint ring of vowels at the end of most of his words. 'But these three are different. No calls for help, no telemetry showing failures or malfunctions. They just disappear – *poof!*'

Zar thought a moment, then asked, 'Had they claimed any asteroids?'

'One of them had: *Lady of the Lake*. Two weeks after the ship disappeared and the claim was officially invalidated, the asteroid was claimed by a vessel owned by Humphries Space Systems: the *Shanidar*.'

'Nothing irregular there.'

'Two weeks? It's as if the Humphries ship was waiting for *Lady of the Lake* to disappear so they could claim the asteroid.'

'You're getting melodramatic, Franco,' said Zar. 'You're accusing them of piracy.'

'It should be investigated.'

'Investigated? How? By whom? Do you expect us to send

92

search teams through the Asteroid Belt? There aren't enough spacecraft in the solar system for that!'

Tomasselli did not reply, but his dark eyes looked brooding, accusing.

Zar frowned at his colleague. 'Very well, Franco. I'll tell you what I'll do. I'll talk to the Humphries people and see what they have to say about it.'

'They'll deny everything, of course.'

'There's nothing to deny! There's no shred of evidence that they've done anything wrong!'

Tomasselli muttered, 'I am going to examine all the claims made by HSS ships over the past month.'

'What for?'

'To see if there are any in the regions where those two other missing ships disappeared.'

Zar wanted to scream at the man. He was nothing but a suspicious-minded young Italian, seeing nefarious plots and skullduggery wherever he looked. But he took a deep breath to calm himself and said in an even, measured tone:

'That's fine, Franco. You check the claims. I'll speak to the HSS people. Monday. I'll do it first thing Monday morning, after I come back from the weekend.'

11

There was no meeting hall in Ceres, no single place designated for public assemblies. That was mainly because there had never been a need for one; Ceres' ragtag collection of miners and prospectors, repair people and technicians, merchants and clerks had never come together in a public assembly until now. The closest thing to a government on Ceres was a pair of IAA flight controllers who monitored the take-offs and landings of the ships that were constantly arriving for supplies and maintenance, then departing into the dark emptiness of the Belt.

So when Fuchs called for a public meeting, it took some doing for him to convince the other rock rats that a gathering was necessary and beneficial. As it was, hardly forty men and women out of the several hundred in the asteroid showed up at The Pub, which Fuchs had commandeered for his meeting. A few dozen others attended electronically, from their ships in transit through the Belt. Big George was among those latter; he had left Ceres in his *Waltzing Matilda* several days before Fuchs' meeting was convened.

It was a good-natured crowd that came together in The Pub at 1700 hours that afternoon. Like most spacecraft and off-Earth facilities, Ceres kept Universal Time. The Pub's owner/barkeep had allowed his place to be used for the meeting upon Fuchs' promise that it would take no longer than an hour. The 'six o'clock swill' would proceed as usual.

'I'm no public speaker,' Fuchs said, standing atop the bar so everyone in the milling, chattering crowd could see him. Three big flatscreens had been wheeled into the back of the room; they showed nearly a score of individuals attending the meeting remotely. Many of the prospectors refused to do even that, claiming that they didn't want anyone to know where they were, outside of the usual IAA trackers, whom they tolerated only because of the IAA's tradition of confidentiality and non-interference in spacecraft operations, except for safety conditions.

'I'm no public speaker,' Fuchs repeated, louder.

'Then what're you doing up there?' came an irreverent voice from the crowd. Everyone laughed.

Grinning back at the heckler, Fuchs rejoined, 'It's a dirty job'.

'. . . but somebody's got to do it,' the whole crowd finished with him.

Fuchs laughed, a little sheepishly, and looked at Amanda, standing off by the wall toward his right. She smiled encouragement at him. The Twins stood beside her, fully clothed in glittering metallic outfits. Even in plain coveralls Amanda still looked far more beautiful than them, in Fuchs' eyes.

'Seriously,' he said, once the crowd settled down, 'it's time we talked about something that most of us find distasteful—'

'What'samatter Lars, the toilets backing up again?'

'The recycler breaking down?'

'No,' he said. 'Worse than that. It's time to start thinking about forming some kind of a government here.'

'Aw, shit!' somebody yowled.

'I don't like the idea of rules and regulations any more than you do,' Fuchs said quickly. 'But this community is growing and we don't have any laws or law enforcement.'

'We don't need 'em,' a woman shouted.

'We've been getting along okay without any.'

Fuchs shook his head. 'There have been two brawls right here in The Pub in the past month. Someone deliberately damaged Yuri Kubasov's ship last week. Deliberate sabotage.'

'That's a private matter,' came a voice from the back of the chamber. 'Yuri was chasing the wrong woman.'

A few people snickered knowingly.

'Then there was the break-in in my warehouse,' Fuchs added. 'That was no minor affair; we lost more than a hundred thousand dollars worth of inventory.'

'Come on, Lars,' a woman challenged. 'Everybody knows that you're competing against HSS. So they're playing a little rough; that's your problem, not ours.'

'Yeah, if you and Humphries are battling it out, why try to drag us into your fight?'

Glancing again toward Amanda, Fuchs answered, 'It's not my fight. It's yours.'

'The hell it is!' said one of the men, heatedly. 'This is between you and Humphries. It's personal and it's got nothing to do with us.'

'That's not true, as you'll soon find out.'

'What's that supposed to mean?'

Reluctantly, surprised at how hard it was to bring out the words, he told them, 'It means that Amanda and I will be leaving Ceres shortly. We'll be returning to Earth.'

'Leaving?'

Feeling real pain, Fuchs went on, 'Humphries has made an offer that's much too generous for us to ignore. HSS will be taking over Helvetia's warehouse and all its services.'

For several heartbeats there was absolute silence through The Pub.

97

Then, from one of the flatscreens, Big George said, 'That means HSS will be our only supplier.'

'They'll have a monopoly here!' someone else wailed.

With a grave nod, Fuchs said, 'That's why it's important for you to form some kind of government, some group that can represent you, maybe get Astro to set up another facility—'

'FIRE,' said the synthesized computer voice from the speakers by The Pub's entryway. 'FIRE IN SECTION FOUR-CEE.'

'That's my warehouse!' Fuchs blurted out.

The crowd bolted through the entryway and out into the tunnel. Fuchs jumped down from the bar, grabbed Amanda by the hand, and raced along behind the others.

Each section of the underground settlement was connected to the others by the tunnels. Airtight hatches stood in the tunnels every hundred metres or so, programmed to seal themselves shut in case of a drop in air pressure or any other deviation from normal conditions. By the time Fuchs reached the entrance to his warehouse, still grasping Amanda's hand, the hatch that sealed off the cave had long been shut tight. He pushed through the crowd from The Pub, coughing violently at the dust they had raised, and touched the hatch's metal surface. It felt hot.

'The warehouse cameras are out,' said one of the technicians. 'Must be a pretty intense fire.'

Fuchs nodded, scowling. 'Nothing to do but wait until it consumes all the air in there and kills itself off.'

'Was anyone inside?' Amanda asked.

'I don't believe so,' Fuchs said. 'Not any of our people, they were all at the meeting.'

'So we wait,' said the technicians. He fumbled in his coverall pocket, then pulled out a breathing mask and slipped it on.

Several people in the crowd murmured condolences. Most of the others drifted off, buzzing with low-voiced conversations. Here and there someone coughed or spluttered from the dust.

'He did this,' Fuchs muttered.

'Who?' asked Amanda.

'Humphries. One of his people.'

'No! What would he—'

'To convince us to leave Ceres. The money offer he made was a ruse. We haven't told him of our decision to accept it, so now he uses force.'

'Lars, I can't believe that he'd do that.'

'I can.'

Amanda looked at the few people remaining in the tunnel and said to her husband, 'There's nothing we can do here. We should go home; we can come back later, when the fire's burned itself out.'

'No,' Fuchs said. 'I'll wait here.'

'But you don't have a breathing mask and—'

'You go. I'll wait here.'

Amanda tried to smile, failed. 'I'll wait with you.'

'There's no need . . .'

'I'd rather be with you,' Amanda said, taking his big-knuckled hand in both of hers.

Standing there with nothing to do except wait, coughing in the gritty dust, Fuchs felt a seething anger rising within him, a burning hatred for the man who could order such a thing and the henchmen who actually did it.

The swine, he said to himself. The filthy, sneaking, murderous swine. A fire! In a sealed community like this. If the safety hatches hadn't worked they could have killed us all! The fire would have consumed all our air and asphyxiated every one of us!

Murderers, he told himself. I'm dealing with men who

would commit murder to get what they want. I'm taking Humphries' money and running away from this place like a lackey being paid off by the lord of the manor.

'Lars, what wrong?' Amanda asked.

'Nothing.'

She looked truly worried. 'But you were trembling. You looked – I've never seen such an expression on your face before.'

He tried to control the rage boiling inside him, tried to hide it, keep it bottled up where no one could see it, not even his wife.

'Come on,' he said gruffly. 'You were right. There's nothing we can do here until we can open the hatch and see how much damage has been done.'

When they got back to their apartment, he picked at the dinner Amanda set before him. He could not sleep. The next morning, when he and a pair of technicians went back to the warehouse, the airtight hatch was fused shut. They had to use one of Astro's mining lasers to cut it open and then wait several minutes for the big, gutted chamber to fill with breathable air.

The warehouse was a blackened shambles. The technicians, both of them young men new to Ceres, stared at the wreckage with round eyes.

'Jeez,' muttered the one on Fuchs' right as they played their hand-lights around the still-hot ruins.

Fuchs couldn't recognize the place. The shelving had collapsed, metal supports melted by the heat of the blaze. Tons of equipment were reduced to molten lumps of slag.

'What could've caused such a hot fire?' wondered the kid of Fuchs' left.

'Not what,' Fuchs muttered. 'Who.'

It's a good thing that it takes so long for communications to go back and forth, Amanda thought. Otherwise Lars would be screaming at the woman by now.

She had watched her husband, his face grimed from the ashes of the warehouse and his mood even darker, as he placed his call to their insurance carrier to inform them of the fire. Then he had called Diane Verwoerd, at Humphries Space Systems' offices in Selene.

Even though messages moved at the speed of light, it took more than an hour for Ms Verwoerd to respond. With the distance between them, there could be no real conversation between Ceres and the Moon. Communications were more like videomail than true two-way links.

'Mr Fuchs,' Verwoerd began her message, 'I appreciate your calling me to inform us about the fire in your warehouse. I certainly hope that no one was injured.'

Fuchs started to reply automatically, and only stopped himself when Verwoerd coolly went on, 'We will need to know the extent of the damage before opening our negotiations on acquiring Helvetia Ltd. As I understand it, a major part of your company's assets consisted of the inventory in your warehouse. I understand that this inventory was insured, but I'm certain that your insurance won't cover much more than half the value of the damaged property. Please inform me as soon as you can. In the meantime, I will contact your insurance carrier. Thank you.'

And her image winked out, replaced by the stylized logo of Humphries Space Systems.

Fuchs' face looked like a thundercloud, dark and ominous. He sat at the computer desk of their one-room apartment, staring silently at the wallscreen. Amanda, sitting on the bed, didn't know what she could say to make him feel better.

'We won't be getting ten million,' he muttered, turning to her. 'Not half that, I imagine.'

'It's all right, Lars. Three or four million is enough for us to—'

'To run away with our tails between our legs,' he snapped.

Amanda heard herself answer, 'What else can we do?'

Fuchs's head drooped defeatedly. 'I don't know. I don't know. We're wiped out. The warehouse is completely gutted. Whoever set the fire did a thorough job.'

Warily, she asked, 'Do you still think it was deliberately set?'

'Of course!' her husband shouted angrily. 'He never intended to pay us ten million! That was a lure, a ruse. He's kicking us off Ceres, out of the Belt entirely.'

'But why would he make the offer . . . ?' Amanda felt confused.

Almost sneering with contempt, Fuchs said, 'To put us in the proper frame of mind. To get us accustomed to the idea of leaving the Belt. Now he's waiting for us to come crawling to him and beg for as much of the ten million as he's willing to give us.'

'We won't do that,' Amanda said. 'We won't crawl and we won't beg.'

'No,' he agreed. 'But we will leave. We have no choice.'

'We still have the ship.'

His heavy brows rose. '*Starpower*? You'd be willing to go prospecting again?'

Amanda knew that she really didn't want to take up the life of a rock rat again. But she nodded solemnly, 'Yes. Why not?'

Fuchs stared at her, a tangle of emotions burning in his deepset eyes.

Niles Ripley was dead tired as he shuffled slowly across the desolate dark ground, heading for the airlock. A four-hour shift of working on the habitat was like a week of hard labour anywhere else, he felt. And riding the shuttlecraft back down to the surface of Ceres was always nerve-racking; the ground controller ran the little hopper remotely from underground, but Ripley twitched nervously without a human pilot aboard. The shuttle had touched down without mishap, though, landing a few metres from a Humphries craft being loaded for a supply run to one of the miners' ships hanging in orbit.

It'll be good to get to The Pub and sip a brew or two, Ripley said to himself. By god, I'll even spring for the imported stuff tonight.

The construction work was going well. Slower than Fuchs had expected, but Ripley was satisfied with the progress that the crew was making. Looking up through his fishbowl helmet, he could see the habitat glinting in the sunlight as it spun slowly, like a big pinwheel.

Okay, he thought, so maybe it does look like a clunky kludge. Bunch of spacecraft tacked together in a circle, no two of 'em exactly the same. But by god the kludge is pretty near finished; soon, people could go up and live in that habitat and feel just about the same gravity as on the Moon.

Got to get the radiation shielding working first, he reminded himself. Sixteen different sets of superconducting magnets and more to come. Getting them to work together is gonna be a bitch and a half.

The work was so damned tedious. Flatlanders back on Earth thought that working in microgee was fun. And easy. You just float around like a kid in a swimming pool. Yeah. Right. The reality was that you had to consciously plan every move you made; inside the spacesuit you had to exert real strength just to hold your arms out straight or take a few steps. Sure, you could hop around like a jackrabbit on steroids if you wanted to. Hell, I could jump right off Ceres and go sailing around like Superman if I had a mind to – and if I didn't worry about breaking every bone in my legs when I landed. Working in microgee is *tough*, especially in those damned suits.

Well, I'm finished for today, he said to himself, as he watched the habitat slowly disappear beyond the sharp, rugged horizon. Ceres is so small. Just a glorified hunk of rock hanging in the middle of nothing. Ripley shook his head inside his bubble helmet, amazed all over again that he was working way out here, in this noplace of a place. He started back toward the airlock again, kicking up lingering clouds of gritty dust with each careful, sliding step. Looking down awkwardly from inside the helmet, he saw that the suit was grimy with dark grey dust all the way up the leggings, as usual. The arms and gloves were crummed up, too. It'll take a good half-hour to vacuum all this crud off the suit, he told himself.

The airlock was set into a dome of local stone, its thick metal hatch the only sign of human presence on Ceres' surface, outside of the two spindly-looking shuttlecraft sitting out there. Ripley was almost at the hatch when it swung open and three spacesuited figures stepped out slowly, warily, as if testing each step they made in this insubstantial gravity. Each of their spacesuits showed a HSS logo on the left breast, just above their name tags. Ripley wondered if they might be the guys Big George had clobbered in The Pub. They had all been Humphries employees, he recalled.

They were carrying big packing crates, probably filled with equipment. In Ceres' low gravity, a man could carry loads that required a small truck elsewhere. All of them had tools of various sorts clipped to belts around their waists.

'Where you goin', guys?' Ripley asked good-naturedly over the common suit-to-suit radio frequency.

'Loading up the shuttle,' came the answer in his earphones.

'Same old thing every day,' another of them complained. 'More crap for the mining ships up in orbit.'

They got close enough to read Ripley's own name, stencilled on the hard shell of his suit. Ripley realized that they were so new to Ceres they hadn't gotten their own individual suits yet. They had apparently picked the suits they were wearing from HSS' storage; their names were lettered on adhesive strips pasted onto the torsos.

'Buchanan, Santorini and Giap,' Ripley read aloud. 'Hi. I'm Niles Ripley.'

'We know who you are,' Buchanan said sourly.

'The horn player,' said Santorini.

Ripley put on his peacemaking smile, even though he figured they couldn't see it in the dim lighting.

'Hey, I'm sorry about that brawl couple nights ago,' he said placatingly. 'My friend got carried away, I guess.'

All three of them put their crates down on the pebbled, dusty ground.

Buchanan said, 'I hear they call you the Ripper.'

'Sometimes,' Ripley said guardedly.

'Where's your trumpet?'

With a little laugh, Ripley said, 'Back in my quarters. I don't carry it with me everywhere I go.'

'Too bad. I'd really like to jam it up your ass.'

Ripley kept smiling. 'Aw, come on now. There's no reason to—'

'That big ape of yours put Carl in the infirmary with three crushed vertebrae!'

'Hey, I didn't start the fight. And I'm not looking for one now.' Ripley started to walk past them, toward the still-open airlock hatch.

They stopped him. They grabbed his arms. For a ridiculous instant Ripley almost felt like giggling. You can't fight in spacesuits, for chrissakes! It'd be like boxers wearing suits of armour.

'Hey, come on, now,' Ripley said, trying to pull his arms free.

Buchanan kicked his feet out from under him and Ripley fell over backward, slowly, softly, in the dreamy slow-motion of microgee. It seemed to take ten minutes as he toppled over; numberless hordes of stars slid past his field of view, silently, solemnly. Then at last he hit the ground, his head banging painfully inside the helmet, a thick cloud of dust enveloping him.

'Okay, Ripper,' Buchanan said. 'Rip this!'

He kicked Ripley in the side of his spacesuit. The others laughed and started kicking, too. Ripley bounced around inside the suit, unable to get up, unable to defend himself. It didn't hurt that much at first, but each kick got worse and he worried that they might tear his air line loose. He tasted blood in his mouth.

When they finally stopped kicking him, every part of Ripley's body throbbed with pain. They were still standing over him. Buchanan stared down at him for a long, silent moment. Then he unhooked a tool from the Belt at his waist.

'You know what this is?' he asked, holding it up in his gloved hand. It was a short, squat, smooth greenish rod with a helical glass flashlamp coiled around its length and a pistol grip beneath. A heavy black cord ran from the heel of the grip to a battery pack clipped to Buchanan's belt.

Before Ripley could say anything Buchanan explained.

'This is a Mark IV gigawatt-pulse neodymium laser. Puts out picosecond pulses. We use it to punch neat little holes in metal. What kind of a hole do you think it'll punch through you?'

'Hey, Trace,' said Santorini. 'Take it easy.'

Ripley tried to move, to crawl away. His legs wouldn't carry him. He could see the laser's guide beam walking up the front of his spacesuit, *feel* it come through his transparent helmet, inch over his face, past his eyes, onto his forehead.

'Trace, don't!'

But Buchanan slowly lowered himself to one knee and bent over Ripley, peering into his eyes. This close, their helmets almost touching, Ripley could see a sort of wild glee in the man's eyes, a manic joy. He moved one arm, tried to push his tormentor away; all he accomplished was to pull the name tag off Buchanan's suit.

'They didn't say to kill him,' Santorini insisted.

Buchanan laughed. 'So long, noisemaker,' he said.

Ripley died instantly. The picosecond laser pulse pulped most of his brain into jelly.

13

Lars Fuchs was sitting at his desk talking to the prospector to whom he'd leased *Starpower*. The woman flatly refused to give up the ship until the term of her lease expired, four months in the future.

'I've been snookered out of two good rocks by HSS people,' she said, her anger showing clearly in her image on Fuchs' wallscreen. 'I'm going out to the far side of the Belt and get me a good-sized metallic 'roid. Anybody comes near me, I'll zap 'em with the cutting laser!'

Fuchs stared at her face. She couldn't be much more than thirty, a former graduate student like himself, yet she looked far harder, more determined, than any graduate student he remembered. Not a trace of make-up; her hair shaved down to a dark fuzz; her cheek bones and jawline gaunt, hungry.

'I can arrange for you to transfer to another ship that's available for lease,' Fuchs said reasonably.

The prospector shook her head. 'No deal. I'm working my way around the far side. By this time tomorrow it'll take half an hour for messages to catch up with me. Sayonara, Lars.'

The screen went blank. Fuchs leaned back in his creaking desk chair, his thoughts churning slowly. There is no way I can force her to bring *Starpower* back. She's on her way out and she won't be back for at least four months. When she returns she'll either have claim to a rich metallic asteroid or she'll be so dead broke she won't even be able to pay me the final instalment on the lease.

No matter which way he looked at it, he could find no answer to his problem. If we're going back to Earth it will have to be as passengers on someone else's ship.

Amanda came through the door from the tunnel at the same moment that the phone chimed. Fuchs automatically said 'Answer,' to the phone, but then he saw the awful expression on his wife's face.

'What is it?' he asked, rising from his chair. 'What's wrong?'

'Ripley,' she said in a voice that sounded frightened. 'They found him by the airlock, outside. He's dead.'

'Dead?' Fuchs felt shocked. 'How? What happened?'

'That's what I want to talk to you about,' said Kris Cardenas, from the wallscreen.

Fuchs and Amanda both turned to her image.

Cardenas looked grim. 'They brought Ripley's body to me, here in the infirmary.'

'What happened to him?' Fuchs asked again.

Cardenas shook her head warily. 'Nothing wrong with his suit. He didn't die of asphyxiation or decompression. The suit's scuffed up a lot, but there was no system failure.'

'Then what?' Amanda asked.

She frowned with uncertainty. 'I'm going to do a multi-spectral scan and try to find out. The reason I called you was to find out if he has any next-of-kin here on Ceres.'

'No, no one closer than New Jersey, in the United States,' said Fuchs. 'I'll transfer his personnel file to you.'

'He was working on the habitat?' Cardenas asked, even though she knew the answer.

'Yes,' said Fuchs absently. 'Now the project will have to stop until we find someone to replace him.'

Amanda said, 'We're coming to the infirmary, Kris. We'll be there in five minutes.'

Cardenas said, 'Hang on. Give me an hour or so to do this scan. I'll know more about it by then.'

Amanda and Fuchs both nodded their agreement.

Instead of her usual buoyant brightness, Kris Cardenas looked grave, almost angry as she ushered Amanda and Fuchs into her tiny infirmary. It was the only medical facility on Ceres, the only medical facility between the Belt and the exploration bases on Mars. Cardenas could handle accident cases, if they weren't too severe, and the usual run of infections and strains. Anything more severe was sent to Selene, while Cardenas herself remained among the rock rats.

She was twice an exile. Because her body was teeming with nanomachines no government on Earth would allow her to land on its territory. This had cost her her husband and children; like most of Earth's inhabitants, they were terrified by the threat of runaway nanotechnology causing pandemic plagues or devouring cities like unstoppable army ants, chewing everything into a grey goo.

Her anger at Earth and its unreasoning fears had led her to cause Dan Randolph's death. It was inadvertent, true enough, but Selene had banned her from her own nanotech laboratory as a punishment for her actions and as a pre-caution against future use of nanomachines for personal vengeance. So she left Selene, exiled herself among the rock rats, used her knowledge of human physiology to establish the infirmary on Ceres.

'Have you found what killed Ripley?' Amanda asked her as she and Fuchs took the chairs in front of Cardenas' desk.

'I wouldn't have caught it, normally,' Cardenas said tightly. 'I'm not a pathologist. It damned near slipped right past me.'

The office was small, crowded with the three of them in it. Cardenas tapped a keypad on her desktop and the wall opposite the doorway turned into a false-colour display of Niles Ripley's body.

'There was nothing obviously wrong,' she began. 'No visible trauma, although there were a few small bruises on his chest and back.'

'What caused them?' Fuchs asked.

'Maybe when he fell down, inside his suit.'

Fuchs scowled at her. 'I've fallen down in a spacesuit. That doesn't cause bruising.'

Cardenas nodded. 'I know. I thought maybe he died of a cardiac infarction, a heart attack. That's when I went for the scan,' she explained. 'But the coronary arteries look clean and there's no visible damage to the heart itself.'

Fuchs squinted at the image. A human body, he thought. One instant it's alive, the next it's dead. What happened to you, Ripley?

Amanda echoed his thoughts. 'So what happened to him?'

Cardenas' expression grew even tighter. 'The next thing I looked for was a stroke. That's still the number one killer, even back on Earth.'

'And?'

'Look at his brain.'

Fuchs peered at the wallscreen, but he didn't know what was normal in these false-colour images and what was not. He could make out the white outline of the skull and, within it, the pinkish mass of the man's brain. Tangles of what he took to be blood vessels wrapped around the brain and into it, like a mass of tiny snakes writhing inside the skull.

'Do you see it?' Cardenas asked, her voice as sharp as a bayonet.

'No, I don't see . . . wait a minute!' Fuchs noticed that while most of the brain was a light pink colour, there was an area of deeper hue, almost a burnt orange, that ran straight through the brain mass, from front to back.

'That orange colour?' he said, not certain of himself.

'That orange colour,' Cardenas repeated, hard as ice.

'What is it?' Amanda asked.

'It's what killed him,' said Cardenas. 'Ruptured neurons and glial cells from the front of his skull to the back. It did as much damage as a bullet would, but it didn't break the skin.'

'A micrometeor?' Fuchs blurted out, knowing it was stupid even as his mouth said it.

Amanda objected, 'But his suit wasn't ruptured.'

'Whatever it was,' said Cardenas, 'it went through the transparent plastic of his helmet, through his skin without damaging it, through the cranial bone, and pulped his brain cells.'

'*Mein gott*,' Fuchs muttered.

'I have two more bits of evidence,' Cardenas said, sounding more and more like a police investigator.

The wallscreen image changed to show Ripley's dead face. Fuchs felt Amanda shudder beside him and reached out to hold her hand. Ripley's eyes were open, his mouth agape, his milk-chocolate skin somehow paler than Fuchs remembered it. This is the face of death, he said silently. He almost shuddered himself.

Cardenas tapped her keyboard again and the image zoomed in on the area just above the bridge of Ripley's nose.

'See that faint discolouration?' Cardenas asked.

Fuchs saw nothing unusual, but Amanda said, 'Yes, just a tiny little circle. It looks . . . almost as if it had been charred a little.'

Cardenas nodded grimly. 'One more piece of the puzzle.' She reached into her desk drawer.

Fuchs saw her pull out a thin strip of tape, not even ten centimeters long.

'This was stuck on Ripley's right glove when he was found,' Cardenas said, handing the tape to Fuchs.

He stared at it. Hand-lettered on the tape in indelible ink was BUCHANAN.

Coldly, mercilesslly, Cardenas said, 'Buchanan is a mechanic for Humphries Space Systems. He has access to tools such as hand lasers.'

'A hand laser?' Fuchs asked. 'You think a hand laser killed Ripley?'

Cardenas said, 'I got one from the HSS warehouse and tried it on my soysteak dinner. One picosecond blast ruptures the cells pretty much the way Ripley's brain cells were destroyed.'

'Do you mean that this man Buchanan deliberately murdered Ripley?' Amanda asked, her voice faint with shock.

'That's exactly what I mean,' said Cardenas, as hard and implacable as death itself.

14

By the time he and Amanda got back to their own quarters, Fuchs was blazing with rage. He went straight to the closet by the minikitchen and started rummaging furiously through it.

'Lars, what are you going to do?'

'Murderers!' Fuchs snarled, pawing through the tools and gadgets stored on the closet shelves. 'That's what he's brought here. Hired killers!'

'But what are you going to do?'

He pulled out a cordless screwdriver, hefted it in one hand. 'It's not much, but it will have to do. It's heavy enough to make a reasonable club.'

Amanda reached for him, but he brushed her away.

'Where are you going?' she asked, breathless with fear.

'To find this man Buchanan.'

'Alone? By yourself?'

'Who else is there? How much time do we have before this Buchanan takes off in one of Humphries' ships and leaves Ceres altogether?'

'You can't go after him!' Amanda pleaded. 'Let the law handle this!'

Storming to the door, he roared, 'The law? What law? We don't even have a village council. There is no law here!'

'Lars, if he's really a hired killer, he'll kill you!'

He stopped at the door, tucked the screwdriver into the waistband of his slacks. 'I'm not a complete fool, Amanda. I won't let him kill me, or anyone else.'

'But how can you . . .'

He grabbed the door, slid it open, and marched out into the tunnel, leaving her standing there. Billows of dust followed his footsteps.

The Pub was crowded when Fuchs got there. He had to push his way to the bar.

The barkeep recognized him, but barely smiled. 'Hello, Lars. Gonna call another town meeting?'

'Do you know a man named Buchanan?' Fuchs asked without preamble.

The barkeep nodded warily.

'Do you know where I can find him?'

The man's eyes shifted slightly, then came back to lock onto Fuchs'. 'What do you want him for?'

'I need to talk to him,' said Fuchs, struggling to keep his voice even, calm.

'He's a bad-ass, Lars.'

'I'm not here to start a fight,' Fuchs said. He even felt it was true.

'Well, that's Buchanan right down there at the end of the bar.'

'Thank you.'

Fuchs accepted a frosted aluminium goblet of beer, then wormed his way through the crowd until he was next to Buchanan. The man was with two friends, talking to a trio of miniskirted young women, their drinks on the bar in front of them. Buchanan was tall, with wide sloping shoulders, and young enough to have a flat midsection. His blond hair was cut short, except for a tiny imitation matador's twist at the back of his head. His face was lean, unlined, relaxed.

'You are Mr Buchanan?' Fuchs asked, putting his goblet on the bar.

Buchanan turned to him, looked Fuchs over and saw a

stocky older rock rat in a shapeless grey velour pullover and wrinkled slacks, with the build of a weasel and a sour expression on his broad, heavy-featured face. The guy had a tool of some sort tucked in his waistband.

'I'm Buchanan,' he said. 'Who the fuck are you?'

Fuchs replied, 'I am a friend of the late Niles Ripley.'

He said it quietly, flatly, but it was as if he had shouted the words through a power megaphone. Everything in The Pub stopped. Conversation, laughter, even motion seemed to freeze in place.

Buchanan leaned his right elbow on the bar as he faced Fuchs. 'Ripley won't be blowing his horn around these parts anymore,' he said, grinning. One of the men behind him snickered nervously.

Fuchs said, 'Your nametag was found in his dead hand.'

'Oh, so that's where it got to. I was wondering where I'd lost it.'

'You killed him.'

Buchanan reached slowly behind him and pulled a hand laser from the pouch strapped to his waist. He laid it down carefully on the bar, next to his drink. Its power cord trailed back to his belt; its business end pointed at Fuchs.

'If I did kill him, what're you going to do about it?'

Fuchs took a breath. The lava-hot rage he had felt only a few minutes earlier had turned to ice now. He felt cold, glacially calm, but not one nanobit less enraged than he had been before.

He replied softly, 'I thought you and I could go back to Selene and let the authorities there investigate the murder.'

Buchanan's jaw dropped open. He gawked at Fuchs, standing like a stubborn little bull in front of him. Then he lifted his head and brayed with laughter. His two friends laughed, also.

No one else did.

Fuchs slapped Buchanan's laughing face, hard. Shocked, he touched his bleeding lip, then reached for the laser on the bar. Fuchs was prepared for that. He clamped Buchanan's hand to the bar with a vice-like grip and pulled the screwdriver from his waist with his right hand.

The laser cracked once. Fuchs' aluminium goblet went spinning, leaking beer through a tiny hole, while Fuchs thumbed the screwdriver on and jammed it into Buchanan's chest. Blood geysered and Buchanan looked terribly surprised, then slumped to the floor, gurgling briefly before he went silent forever.

Splashed with Buchanan's blood, still holding the buzzing screwdriver in his right hand, Fuchs picked up the hand laser. Buchanan's fall had wrenched the power cord out of the base of its grip.

He glanced down at the dead body, then looked at Buchanan's two friends. Their eyes were wide, their mouths agape. Unconsciously, they both backed away from Fuchs.

Without another word, Fuchs turned around and strode out of the silent Pub.

Three Weeks Later

15

They held a trial of sorts. Under Fuchs' own prodding, the people of Ceres picked a judge by sorting through the computerized personnel files and coming up with a woman who worked for Humphries Space Systems as a contracts lawyer. A jury was selected by lot; no one picked was allowed to refuse the duty. For the defence, Fuchs represented himself. No less than the owner and barkeep of The Pub volunteered to prosecute the case.

The trial, held in The Pub itself, took all of forty-five minutes. Practically everyone in Ceres jammed into the rock-walled chamber. Chairs and two tables had been moved up to the bar to accommodate the accused and the counsellors. The judge sat on a high laboratory stool behind the bar. Everyone else stood.

Six different witnesses told substantially the same story: Fuchs had asked Buchanan to go to Selene with him for a formal investigation of Ripley's murder. Buchanan reached for the laser. Fuchs stabbed him with the power tool. Even Buchanan's two companions admitted that that was the way it had happened.

Fuchs' punctured beer goblet was presented as evidence that Buchanan had indeed fired his laser with intent to kill.

The only question arose when the prosecutor asked Fuchs why he had come into The Pub armed with the tool that eventually killed Buchanan.

Fuchs admitted openly, 'I knew that he was a dangerous man. I knew that he had murdered Niles Ripley—'

The judge, sitting on a high stool behind the bar, snapped, 'That's inadmissible. This trial is about you, Mr Fuchs, not about Ripley's death.'

With only the slightest of frowns, Fuchs said, 'I was afraid he would be dangerous. I had been told that he had come to The Pub before and started a fight. And that he had several friends with him.'

'So you armed yourself with a lethal weapon?' asked the prosecutor.

'I thought it might be useful as a club, if it came to a fight. I had no intention of using it to stab him.'

'Yet that's exactly what you did.'

'Yes. When he tried to shoot me I suppose I reacted without thinking of the consequences. I defended myself.'

'Very thoroughly,' the judge grumbled.

The verdict was never in doubt. Fuchs was acquitted; the killing was called justifiable self-defence. Then the prosecutor displaced the judge behind the bar and proclaimed that there would be a round of drinks for everybody on the house.

Amanda was delighted with the outcome, but Fuchs was morose for the next several days.

'This isn't the end of it,' he told her one night as they lay in bed together.

'Lars darling,' said Amanda, 'you mustn't let this get you down so. You acted in self-defence.'

'I really would have gone with him to Selene,' Fuchs said. 'But I knew he would never do that. Never.'

'It's not your fault that you had to kill him. It was self-defence. Everyone knows that. You mustn't feel bad about it.'

'But I don't!' He turned to face her. In the darkened

room, lit only by the glow of the digital clock numerals in one corner of the wallscreen, he could barely make out the puzzled expression on her lovely face.

'I don't feel bad about killing that vermin,' Fuchs said, in a low, firm voice. 'I knew I would have to. I knew he would never listen to reason.'

Amanda looked surprised, almost fearful. 'But Lars—'

'No one would do a thing about it. I knew I was the only one who would bring him to justice.'

'You knew? All along you knew?'

'I *wanted* to kill him,' Fuchs said, his voice almost trembling with fervour. 'He deserved to die. I wanted to kill the arrogant fool.'

'Lars . . . I've never seen you this way.'

'What's worrying me,' he said, 'is Humphries' reaction to all this. The negotiations for buying out Helvetia are obviously finished. Buchanan was part of his attempt to force us out of the Belt. What is he going to try next?'

Amanda was silent for a long while. Fuchs watched her adorable face, so troubled, so filled with care for him. He almost smiled. The face that launched a thousand spaceships, he thought. Well, at least several hundred.

Yet she was thinking that her husband had turned into an avenging fury. Perhaps only for an hour or so, but Lars had gone out to The Pub deliberately to kill a man. And it didn't worry him, didn't frighten him at all.

It terrified her.

What can I do? Amanda asked herself. How can I stop him from becoming a brute? He doesn't deserve this; it isn't fair to force him to become a monster. She racked her brain, but she could see only one way back to sanity.

At last she said, 'Lars, why don't you speak directly to Martin?'

He grunted with surprise. 'Directly? To him?'

'Face-to-face.'

'Over this distance that's not possible, really.'

'Then we'll go to Selene.'

His expression hardened. 'I don't want you that near to him.'

'Martin won't hurt me,' she said. Tracing a hand across his broad chest, she went on, 'And you're the man I love. You have nothing to fear from Martin or any other man in the universe on that score.'

'I don't want you at Selene,' he whispered firmly.

'We can't go to Earth unless we go through weeks and weeks of reconditioning.'

'The centrifuge,' he muttered.

Amanda said, 'I'll stay here, Lars, if that's what you want. You go to Selene and talk this out with Martin.'

'No,' he said immediately. 'I won't leave you here.'

'But . . . ?'

'You come to Selene with me. I'll talk to Humphries, assuming he'll agree to talk to me.'

Amanda smiled and kissed his cheek. 'We can put an end to this before it becomes an out-and-out war.'

Pulling her to him, Fuchs said gently, 'I hope so. I truly hope so.'

She sighed. That's more like it, she thought. That's more like the man I love.

But he was thinking, It's Amanda that Humphries wants, nothing less. And the only way he'll get Amanda is over my dead body.

'She's coming here?' Martin Humphries asked, hardly daring to believe what his aide had just told him. 'Here, to Selene?'

Diane Verwoerd allowed a tiny frown of displeasure to crease her forehead. 'With her husband,' she said.

Humphries got up from his high-backed chair and practically pranced around his desk. Despite his aide's sour look he felt like a little kid anticipating Christmas.

'But she's coming to Selene,' he insisted. 'Amanda is coming to Selene.'

'Fuchs wants to talk to you face-to-face,' Verwoerd said, folding her arms across her chest. 'I doubt that he'll let his wife get within a kilometre of you.'

'That's what *he* thinks,' Humphries countered. He turned to the electronic window on the wall behind his desk and tapped at his wristwatch several times. The stereo image on the wide screen flicked through several changes. Humphries stopped it at an Alpine scene of a quaint village with steeply pitched roofs and a slim church steeple against a background of snow-covered peaks.

That's ancient history, Verwoerd thought. There hasn't been that much snow in the Alps since the great avalanches.

Turning back to her, Humphries said, 'Fuchs is coming here to surrender. He'll try to wheedle as much of the ten million we offered him as he can get. But he's bringing Amanda because he knows – maybe in his unconscious mind, maybe not consciously – but he knows that what I really want is Amanda.'

'I think we should look at this a little more realistically,' Verwoerd said, stepping slowly toward the desk.

Humphries eyed her for a moment. 'You think I'm being unrealistic?'

'I think that Fuchs is coming here to negotiate your buy-out of his company. I very much doubt that his wife will be part of the deal.'

He laughed. 'Maybe you don't think so. Maybe he doesn't think so. But I do. That's what's important. And I bet that Amanda does, too.'

Verwoerd had to deliberately keep herself from shaking her head in disagreement. He's insane about this woman. Absolutely gonzo over her. Then she smiled inwardly. How can I use this? How can I turn his craziness to my advantage?

Dossier: Oscar Jiminez

When he finished the New Morality high school, at the age of seventeen, Oscar was sent to far-off Bangladesh for his two years of Public Service. It was compulsory; the New Morality demanded two years of service as partial repayment for the investment they had made in a youth's education and social reformation.

Oscar worked hard in what was left of Bangladesh. The rising sea levels and the terrifying storms that accompanied each summer's monsoon inundated the low-lying lands. Thousands were swept away in the floods of the Ganges. Oscar saw that many of the poor, miserable wretches actually prayed to the river itself for mercy. In vain. The swollen river drowned the heathens without pity. Oscar realized that just as many of the Faithful were drowned.

Luck touched him again, once he finished his two years of Public Service. The New Morality administrator in Dacca, an American from Kansas, urged Oscar to consider accepting a job in space, far away from Earth.

Oscar knew better than to argue with authority, but he was so surprised at the idea that he blurted, 'But I'm not an astronaut.'

The administrator smiled a kindly smile. 'There are all kinds of jobs up there that need to be filled. You are fully qualified for many of them.'

'I am?' Oscar's qualifications, as far as he knew, were mainly lifting and toting, handling simple invoices, and following orders.

With a nod, the administrator said, 'Yes. And, of course, there is God's work to be done out there among the godless humanists and frontier ruffians.'

Who could refuse to do God's work? Thus Oscar Jiminez went to Ceres and was hired by Helvetia Ltd, to work in their warehouse.

16

Selene's Hotel Luna had gone through several changes of management since it was originally built by the Yamagata Corporation.

In those early days, just after the lunar community had won its short, sharp war against the old United Nations and affirmed its independence, tourism looked like a good way to bring money into the newly-proclaimed Selene. Masterson Aerospace's lunar-built Clipperships were bringing the price of transportation from Earth down to the point where the moderately well-heeled tourist – the type who took 'adventure vacations' to Antarctica, the Amazonian rain forest, or other uncomfortable exotic locales – could afford the grandest adventure vacation of them all: a trip to the Moon.

Sadly, the opening of the hotel coincided almost exactly with the first ominous portents of the greenhouse cliff. After nearly half a century of scientific debate and political wrangling, the accumulated greenhouse gases in Earth's atmosphere and oceans started an abrupt transition in the global climate. In swift succession, disastrous floods inundated most coastal cities. Earthquakes devastated Japan and the American Midwest. Glaciers and ice packs began melting down, raising sea levels worldwide. The delicate web of electrical power transmission grids collapsed over much of the world, throwing hundreds of millions into the cold and darkness of pre-industrial society. More than a billion people lost their homes, their way of living, everything that they had worked for. Hundreds of millions died.

Tourism trickled down to nothing except for the extremely wealthy, who lived on their financial mountaintops in ease and comfort despite the woes of their brethren.

Hotel Luna became virtually a ghost facility, but it was never shut down. Grimly, hopefully, foolishly, one owner after another tried to make at least a modest success of it.

To a discerning visitor, the lavish, sprawling lobby of the hotel appeared slightly seedy, the carpeting was noticeably threadbare in spots, the oriental tables and easy chairs were scuffed here and there, the ornate artificial floral displays drooped enough to show that they needed to be replaced.

But to Lars Fuchs' staring eyes Hotel Luna's lobby seemed incredibly smart and polished. He and Amanda were riding down the powered stairway from the hotel entrance in the Grand Plaza. Glistening sheets of real, actual water slid down tilted slabs of granite quarried from the lunar highlands. The water was recycled, of course, but to have a display of water! What elegance!

'Look,' Fuchs exclaimed, pointing at the pools into which the waterfalls splashed. 'Fish! Live fish!'

Beside him, Amanda smiled and nodded. She had been brought to the hotel on dates several times, years ago. She remembered the Earthview Restaurant, with its hologram windows. Martin Humphries had taken her there. The fish in those pools were on the restaurant's menu. Amanda noticed that there were far fewer of them now than there had been back then.

As they reached the lobby level and stepped off the escalator, Fuchs recognized the music wafting softly from the ceiling speakers: a Haydn quartet. Charming. Yet he felt distinctly out of place in his plain, dark grey coveralls, like a scruffy student sneaking into a grand palace. But with Amanda on his arm it didn't matter. She wore a sleeveless white pantsuit: even zippered up to the throat it could not hide her exquisitely curved body.

Fuchs didn't pay any attention to the fact that the spacious lobby was practically empty. It was quiet, soothing, an elegant change from the constant buzz of air fans and the faint clatter of distant pumps that was part of the everyday background of Ceres.

As they reached the registration desk, Fuchs remembered all over again that Martin Humphries was footing their hotel bill. Humphries had insisted on it. Fuchs wanted to argue about it as they rode a Humphries fusion ship from Ceres to Selene, but Amanda talked him out of it.

'Let him pay for the hotel, Lars,' she had advised, with a knowing smile. 'I'm sure he'll take it out of the price he pays you for Helvetia.'

Grudgingly, Fuchs let her talk him into accepting Humphries' generosity. Now, at the hotel desk, it rankled all over again.

When it had originally opened as the Yamagata Hotel, there had been uniformed bellmen and women to tote luggage and bring room service orders. Those days were long gone. The registration clerk seemed alone behind his counter of polished black basalt, but he tapped a keyboard and a self-propelled trolley hummed out of its hidden niche and rolled up to Fuchs and Amanda. They put their two travel bags onto it and the trolley obediently followed them into the elevator that led down to the level of their suite.

Fuchs' eyes went even wider once they entered the suite.

'Luxury,' he said, a reluctant smile brightening his normally dour face. 'This is real luxury.'

Even Amanda seemed impressed. 'I've never been in one of the hotel's bedrooms before.'

Suddenly Fuchs' smile dissolved into a suspicious scowl. 'He might have the rooms bugged, you know.'

'Who? Martin?'

Fuchs nodded gravely, as if afraid to speak.

'Why would he bug the rooms?'

'To learn what we plan to say to him, what our position will be in the negotiation, what our bottom figure will be.' There was more, but he hesitated to tell her. Pancho had hinted that Humphries videotaped his own sexual encounters in the bedroom of his palatial home. Would the man have cameras hidden in *this* bedroom?

Abruptly, he strode to the phone console sitting on an end table and called for the registration desk.

'Sir?' asked the clerk's image on the wallscreen. A moment earlier it had been a Vickrey painting of nuns and butterflies.

'This suite is unacceptable,' Fuchs said, while Amanda stared at him. 'Is there another one available?'

The clerk grinned lazily. 'Why, yessir, we have several suites unoccupied at the moment. You may have your pick.'

Fuchs nodded. He can't have them all bugged, he thought.

'I'm glad you decided to meet me in person,' Martin Humphries said, smiling from behind his wide desk. 'I think we can settle our business much more comfortably this way.'

He leaned back, tilting the chair so far that Fuchs thought the man was going to plant his feet on the desktop. Humphries seemed completely at ease in his own office in the mansion he had built for himself so deep below the lunar surface. Fuchs sat tensely in the plush armchair in front of the desk, feeling uneasy, wary, stiffly uncomfortable in the grey business suit that Amanda had bought for him at an outrageous price in the hotel's posh store. He had left Amanda in the hotel; he did not want her in the same room as Humphries. She had acquiesced to his demand, and told her husband that she would go shopping in the Grand Plaza while he had his meeting.

Humphries waited for Fuchs to say something. When he just sat there in silence, Humphries said, 'I trust you had a good night's sleep.'

Suddenly Fuchs thought of hidden cameras again. He cleared his throat and said, 'Yes, thank you.'

'The hotel is comfortable? Everything all right?'

'The hotel is fine.'

The third person in the room was Diane Verwoerd, sitting in the other chair in front of the desk. She had angled it so that she faced Fuchs more than Humphries. Like her boss, she wore a business suit. But while Humphries' dark burgundy suit was threaded with intricate filigrees of silver thread, Verwoerd's pale ivory outfit was of more ordinary material. Its slit skirt, however, revealed a good deal of her long, slim legs.

Silence stretched again. Fuchs looked at the holowindow behind Humphries' desk. It showed the lush garden outside the house, bright flowers and graceful trees. Beautiful, he thought, but artificial. Contrived. An ostentatious display of wealth and the power to flaunt one man's will. How many starving, homeless people on Earth could Humphries help if he wanted to, instead of creating this make-believe Eden for himself here on the Moon?

At last Verwoerd said crisply, all business, 'We're here to negotiate the final terms of your sale of Helvetia Ltd to Humphries Space Systems.'

'No, we are not,' said Fuchs.

Humphries sat up straighter in his chair. 'We're not?'

'Not yet,' Fuchs said to him. 'First we must deal with several murders.'

Humphries glanced at Verwoerd; for just that instant he seemed furious. But he regained his composure almost immediately.

'And just what do you mean by that?' she asked calmly.

Fuchs said, 'At least three prospector's ships have disappeared over the past few weeks. Humphries Space Systems somehow acquired the claims to the asteroids that those prospectors were near to.'

'Mr Fuchs,' said Verwoerd, with a deprecating little smile, 'you're turning a coincidence into a conspiracy. Humphries Space Systems has dozens of ships scouting through the Belt.'

'Yes, and it's damned expensive, too,' Humphries added.

'Then there is the out-and-out murder of Niles Ripley on Ceres by a Humphries employee,' Fuchs went on doggedly.

Humphries snapped, 'From what I hear, you took care of that yourself. Vigilante justice, wasn't it?'

'I stood trial. It was declared justifiable self-defence.'

'Trial,' Humphries sniffed. 'By your fellow rock rats.'

'Your employee murdered Niles Ripley!'

'Not by my orders,' Humphries replied, with some heat. 'Just because some hothead on my payroll gets himself into a brawl, that's not my doing.'

'But it was to your benefit,' Fuchs snapped.

Coolly, Verwoerd asked, 'How do you come to that conclusion, Mr Fuchs?'

'Ripley was the key man in our habitat construction program. With him gone, the work is stopped.'

'So?'

'So once you acquire Helvetia, the only organization capable of finishing the project will be HSS.'

'And how does that benefit me?' Humphries demanded. 'Finishing your silly-assed habitat doesn't put one penny into my pocket.'

'Not directly, perhaps,' said Fuchs. 'But making Ceres safer and more livable will bring more people out to the Belt. With your company in control of their supplies, their food, the air they breathe, even, how can you fail to profit?'

'You're accusing me—'

Verwoerd interrupted the argument. 'Gentlemen, we're here to negotiate the sale of Helvetia, not to discuss the future of the Asteroid Belt.'

Humphries glared at her again, but took in a breath and said grudgingly, 'Right.'

Before Fuchs could say anything, Verwoerd added, 'What's done is done, and there's no way of changing the past. If an HSS employee committed murder, you made him pay the full price for it.'

Fuchs searched for something to say.

'Now we should get down to business,' said Verwoerd, 'and settle on a price for Helvetia.'

Humphries immediately jumped in, 'My original offer was based on your total assets, which have gone down almost to nothing since the fire in your warehouse.'

'Which was deliberately set,' Fuchs said.

'Deliberately set?'

'It was no accident. It was arson.'

'You have proof of that?'

'We have no forensics experts on Ceres. No criminal investigators.'

'So you have no proof.'

'Mr Fuchs,' Verwoerd said, 'we are prepared to offer you three million international dollars for the remaining assets of Helvetia Ltd, which – frankly – amounts to the goodwill you've generated among the miners and prospectors, and not much more.'

Fuchs stared at her for a long, silent moment. So sure of herself, he thought. So cool and unruffled and, yes, even beautiful, in a cold, distant way. She's like a sculpture made of ice.

'Well?' Humphries asked. 'Frankly, three million is pretty much of a gift. Your company's not worth half that much, in real terms.'

'Three hundred million,' Fuchs murmured.

'What? What did you say?'

'You could make your offer three hundred million. Or three billion. It doesn't matter. I'm not going to sell to you.'

'That's stupid!' Humphries blurted.

'I won't sell to you at any price. Never! I'm going back to Ceres and starting all over again.'

'You're crazy!'

'Am I? Perhaps so. But I would rather be crazy than give in to you.'

'You're just going to get yourself killed,' Humphries said.

'Is that a threat?'

Again Humphries looked at Verwoerd, then turned back to Fuchs. He smiled thinly. 'I don't make threats, Fuchs. I make promises.'

Fuchs got to his feet. 'Then let me make a promise in return. If you want to fight, I can fight. If you want a war, I'll give you a war. And you won't like the way I fight, I promise you that. I've studied military history; it was required in school. I know how to fight.'

Humphries leaned back in his desk chair and laughed.

'Go ahead and laugh,' Fuchs said, pointing a stubby finger at him. 'But consider: you have a great deal more to lose than I do.'

'You're a dead man, Fuchs,' Humphries snapped.

Fuchs nodded agreement. 'One of us is.'

With that, he turned and strode out of Humphries' office.

For several moments, Humphries and Verwoerd sat there staring at the doorway Fuchs had gone through.

'At least he didn't slam the door,' Humphries smirked.

'You've made him angry enough to fight,' Verwoerd said, with a troubled frown. 'You've backed him into a corner and now he feels he has nothing to lose by fighting.'

Humphries guffawed. 'Him? That little weasel? It's laughable. He knows how to fight! He's studied military history!'

'Maybe he has,' she said.

'So what?' Humphries replied testily. 'He's from Switzerland, for god's sake! Hardly a martial nation. What's he going to do, smother me in Swiss cheese? Or maybe yodel me to death.'

'I wouldn't take it so lightly,' said Verwoerd, still looking at the empty doorway.

17

'Piracy?' Hector Wilcox's eyebrows rose almost to his silver-grey hairline.

Erek Zar looked uncomfortable, unhappy, as the two men strolled along the lane through the park just outside the IAA office building. Spring was in the air, the trees were beginning to bud, the local St Petersburg populace was thronging the park, glad to see the sun. Women were sunbathing on the grass, their long dark coats thrown open to reveal their thick, lumpy bodies clad only in skimpy bikinis. It's enough to make a man take to celibacy, Wilcox thought, eyeing them with distaste.

Zar was normally a placid, cheerful, good-natured paper shuffler whose most urgent demands were for an extra day off here and there so he could nip off to his family in Poland for a long weekend. But now the man's ruddy, round face was dead serious, flushed with emotion.

'That's what he's charging,' Zar said. 'Piracy.'

Wilcox refused to have his postprandial constitutional destroyed by an underling suddenly gone bonkers.

'Who is this person?'

'His name is Lars Fuchs. Tomasselli brought the matter to me. Fuchs is accusing Humphries Space Systems of piracy, out in the Asteroid Belt.'

'But that's ridiculous!'

'I agree,' Zar said swiftly. 'But Tomasselli's taken it seriously and opened an official file on it.'

'Tomasselli,' said Wilcox, as if the word smelled bad.

'That excitable Italian. He saw a conspiracy when Yama-gata made that takeover offer to Astro Corporation.'

'The takeover was never consummated,' Zar pointed out, 'mainly because Tomaselli got the GEC to go on record as opposing it.'

'And now he's taking accusations of *piracy* seriously? Against Humphries Space Systems?'

Nodding unhappily, Zar said, 'He claims there's some evidence to substantiate the accusation, but as far as I can see it's all circumstantial.'

'What on earth does he expect me to do about it?' Wilcox grumbled mildly. He was not the kind of man who lost his self-control. Not ever. You didn't get as far up on the intricate chain of command of the International Astronautical Authority as he had by recklessly blowing off steam.

'It's an open file now,' Zar said, apologetically.

'Yes. Well, I suppose I'll have to look it over.' Wilcox sighed. 'But, really, *piracy*? In the Asteroid Belt? Even if it's true, what can we do about it? We don't even have an administrator on Ceres, for goodness' sake. There isn't an IAA presence anywhere in the Belt.'

'We have two flight controllers at Ceres.'

'Bah!' Wilcox shook his head. 'What do they call them-selves out there? Rock rats? They pride themselves on their independence. They resisted the one attempt we made to establish a fully-fledged office on Ceres. So now they're crying to us about piracy, are they?'

'It's only one person making the accusation: this man Fuchs.'

'A maniac, no doubt,' said Wilcox.

'Or a sore loser,' Zar agreed.

The Waltzing Matilda

Big George's stomach rumbled in complaint.

He straightened up – no easy task in the spacesuit – and looked around. *Waltzing Matilda* hung in the star-strewn sky over his head like a big dumbbell, its habitat and logistics modules on opposite ends of a kilometre-long buckyball tether, slowly rotating around the propulsion module at the hub.

Been too many hours since you've had a feed, eh, he said to his stomach. Well, it's gonna be a few hours more before we get any tucker, and even then it'll be mighty lean.

The asteroid on which George stood was a dirty little chunk of rock, a dark carbonaceous 'roid, rich in hydrates and organic minerals. Worth a bloody fortune back at Selene. But it didn't look like much: just a bleak lump of dirt, pitted all over like it had the pox, with rocks and pebbles and outright boulders scattered across it. Not enough gravity to hold down a feather. Ugly chunk of rock, that's all you are, George said silently to the asteroid. And you're gonna get uglier before we're finished with ya.

Millions of kilometres from anyplace, George realized, alone in this cold and dark except for the Turk sittin' inside *Matilda* monitoring the controls, squattin' on this ugly chunk of rock, sweatin' inside this suit like a teen on his first date and me stomach growlin' 'cause we're low on rations.

And yet he felt happy. Free as a bloomin' bird. He had to make a conscious effort not to sing out loud. That'd startle the Turk, he knew. The kid's not used to any of this.

Shaking his head inside the fishbowl helmet, George returned to his work. He was setting up the cutting laser, connecting its power pack and control module, carefully cleaning its copper mirrors of clinging dust and making certain they were precisely placed in their mounts, no wobbles. It was all hard physical work, even though none of the equipment weighed anything in the asteroid's minuscule gravity. But just raising your arms in the stiff, ungainly suit, bending your body or turning, took a conscious effort of will and more muscular exertion than any flatlander could ever appreciate. Finally George had everything set, the laser's aiming mirrors pointing to the precise spot where he wanted to start cutting, the power pack's superconducting coil charged and ready.

George was going to slice out chunks of the asteroid for *Matilda* to carry back to Selene. The prospector who'd claimed the rock wouldn't make a penny from it until George started shipping the ores, and George was far behind schedule because the wonky laser was malfunctioning time and again. No ores, no money: that was the way the corporations worked. And no food, George knew. It was a race now to see if he could get a decent shipment of ores off toward Selene before *Matilda's* food locker was empty.

As he worked, a memory from his childhood school days back in Adelaide returned unbidden to his mind; a poem by some Yank who'd been in on the Yukon gold rush nearly two centuries ago:

> Were you ever out in the Great Alone,
>   when the Moon was awful clear,
> And the icy mountains hemmed you in with
>   a silence you most could *hear*;
> With only the howl of a timber wolf, and
>   you camped out there in the cold,

> A half-dead thing in a stark, dead world,
>   clean mad for the muck called gold;
> While high overhead, green, yellow and red,
>   the
> Northern Lights swept in bars? –
> Then you've a hunch what the music meant
>   . . . hunger and night and the stars.

George nodded solemnly as he checked out the laser's focus. Hunger and night and the stars, all right. We've got plenty of that. And a stark, dead world, too, aren't you? he said to the impassive asteroid. Come to think of it, you've prob'ly got some gold tucked away inside you, huh? Strange kinda situation when water's worth more'n gold. Price of gold's dropped down to its value as an industrial metal. Jewellers must be going bonkers back Earthside.

'George?' the Turk's voice in his helmet speaker startled him.

'Huh? What'sit?'

The kid's name was Nodon. 'Something is moving out at the edge of our radar's resolution range.'

'Moving?' George immediately thought that maybe this asteroid had a smaller companion, a moonlet. But at the extreme range of their search radar? Not bloody likely.

'It has a considerable velocity. It is approaching very fast.'

That was the longest utterance the kid had made through the whole flight. He sounded worried.

'It can't be on a collision course,' George said.

'No, but it is heading our way. Fast.'

George tried to shrug inside the spacesuit, failed. 'Well, keep an eye on it. Might be another ship.'

'I think it is.'

'Any message from 'im?'

143

'No. Nothing.'

'All right,' said George, puzzled. 'Say hello to him and ask his identification. I'm gonna start workin' the ores here.'

'Yes, sir.' The kid was very respectful.

Wondering what – or who – was out there, George thumbed the activator switch and the laser began to slash deeply into the asteroid's rocky body. In the airless dark there was no sound; George couldn't even feel a vibration from the big ungainly machine. The dead rock began to sizzle noiselessly along a pencil-slim line. The cutting laser emitted in the infrared, but even the guide beam of the auxiliary laser was invisible until the cutting raised enough dust to reflect its thin, red, pointing finger.

Be a lot easier if we could get nanomachines to do this, George thought. I've got to twist Kris Cardenas' arm when we get back to Ceres, make her see how much we need her help. Little buggers could separate the different elements in a rock, atom by atom. All we'd hafta do is scoop up the piles and load 'em on the ship.

Instead, George worked like a common labourer, prying up thick house-sized slabs of asteroidal rock as the laser's hot beam cut them loose, clamping them together with buckyball tethers and ferrying them to Matilda's bulky propulsion module, which was fitted with attachment points for the cargo. By the time he had carried three such loads, using the jetpack of his suit to move the big slabs, feeling a little like Superman manhandling the massive yet weightless tonnages of ore, he was soaked with perspiration.

'Feels like a bloody swamp in this suit,' he complained aloud as he started back toward the asteroid. 'Smells like one, too.'

'It is a ship,' said Nodon.

'You're sure?'

'I can see its image on the display screen.'

'Give 'em another hail, then. See who they are.' George didn't like the idea of another ship in the vicinity. It can't be coincidence, he told himself.

He landed deftly on the asteroid about fifty metres from where the laser was still slicing up the rock. Why would a ship be heading toward us? Who are they?

Dorik Harbin sat at the controls of *Shanidar*, his dark, bearded face impassive, his darker eyes riveted on the CCD display from the ship's optical sensors. He could see the flashes of laser-heated rock spurting up from the asteroid and the glints of light they cast on the *Waltzing Matilda*, parked in orbit around the asteroid. The information from Grigor had been accurate, as usual. There was the ship, precisely where Grigor had said it would be.

Death was no stranger to Dorik Harbin. Orphaned from birth, he was barely as tall as the assault rifle the village elders gave him when Harbin had dutifully marched with the other preteens to the village down the road, where the evil people lived. They had killed his father before Harbin had been born and raped his pregnant mother repeatedly. The other boys sometimes sniggered that Dorik was conceived by one of the rapists, not the father that the rapists had hacked to death.

He and his ragamuffin battalion had marched down to that evil village and shot everyone there: all of them, men, women, children, babies. Harbin even shot the village dogs in a fury of vengeance. Then, under the pitiless eyes of the hard-faced elders, they had set fire to each and every house in that village. Dousing the bodies with petrol where they lay, they burned the dead too. Some of them were only wounded, pretending to be dead to escape the vengeance they had reaped, until the flames ignited their clothing.

Harbin still heard their screams in his sleep.

When the blue-helmeted Peacekeeper troops had come into the region to pacify the ethnic fighting, Harbin had run away from his village and joined the national defence force. After many months of living in the hills and hiding from the Peacekeepers' observation planes and satellites, he came to the bitter conclusion that the so-called national defence force was nothing more than a band of renegades, stealing from their own people, looting villages and raping their women.

He ran away again, this time to a refugee camp, where well-clad strangers distributed food while men from nearby villages sold the refugees hashish and heroin. Eventually Harbin joined those blue-helmeted soldiers; they were looking for recruits and offered steady pay for minimal discomfort. They trained him well, but more importantly they fed him and paid him and tried to instill some sense of discipline and honour in him. Time and again his temper tripped him; he was in the brig so often that his sergeant called him 'jailbird.'

The sergeant tried to tame Harbin's wild ferocity; tried to make a reliable soldier out of him. Harbin took their food and money and tried to understand their strange concepts of when it was proper to kill someone and when it was not. What he learned after a few years of service in the miserable, pathetic, deprived regions of Asia and Africa was that it was the same everywhere: kill or be killed.

He was picked for a hurry-up training course and sent with a handful of other Peacekeeper troops to the Moon, to enforce the law against the renegade colonists of Moonbase. They even allowed the specially-selected troopers dosages of designer drugs which, they claimed, would enhance their adaptation to low gravity. Harbin knew it was nothing more than a bribe, to keep the 'volunteers' satisfied.

Trying to fight the tenacious defenders of Moonbase from inside a spacesuit was a revelation to Harbin. The Peace-keepers failed, even though the lunar colonists took great pains to avoid killing any of them. They returned to Earth, not merely defeated but humiliated. His next engagement, in the food riots in Delhi, finished him as a Peacekeeper. He saved his squad from being overrun by screaming hordes of rioters, but killed so many of the 'unarmed' civilians that the International Peacekeeping Force cashiered him.

Orphaned again, Harbin took up with mercenary organizations that worked under contract to major multinational corporations. Always eager to better himself, he learned to operate spacecraft. And he quickly saw how fragile spacecraft were. A decent laser shot could disable a vessel in an eyeblink; you could kill its crew from a thousand kilometres before they realized they were under attack.

Eventually he was summoned to the offices of Humphries Space Systems, the first time he had returned to the Moon since the Peacekeepers had been driven off. Their chief of security was a Russian named Grigor. He told Harbin he had a difficult but extremely rewarding assignment for a man of courage and determination.

Harbin asked only, 'Who do I have to kill?'

Grigor told him that he was to drive the independent prospectors and miners out of the Belt. Those working under contract to HSS or Astro were to be left untouched. It was the independents who were to be 'discouraged.' Harbin grimaced at the word. Men like Grigor and the others back at Selene could use delicate words, but what they meant was anything but refined. Kill the independents. Kill enough of them so that the rest either quit the Belt or signed up with HSS or Astro Corporation.

So this one had to die, like the others.

'This is *Waltzing Matilda*,' he heard his comm speaker announce. The face on his display screen was a young male Asian, head shaved, eyes big and nervous. His cheeks seemed to be tattooed. 'Please identify yourself.'

Harbin chose not to. There was no need. The less he spoke with those he must kill, the less he knew about them, the better. It was a game, he told himself, like the computer games he had played during his training sessions with the Peacekeepers. Destroy the target and win points. In this game he played now, the points were international dollars. Wealth could buy almost anything: a fine home in a safe city, good wines, willing women, drugs that drove away the memories of the past.

'We are working this asteroid,' the young man said, his shaky voice a little higher-pitched than before. 'The claim has already been registered with the International Astronautical Authority.'

Harbin took in a deep breath. The temptation to reply was powerful. It doesn't matter what you have claimed or what you are doing, he answered silently. The moving finger has written your name in the book of death, nor all thy piety nor wit shall lure it back to cancel half a line; nor all thy tears wash out a word of it.

By the time he'd made his eighth ore-ferrying trip, George felt dead tired. And starving.

He turned off the laser and said into his helmet microphone, 'I'm comin' in.'

The Turk replied only, 'Copy that.'

'I'm sloshin' inside this suit,' George said. 'The power pack needs rechargin', too.'

'Understood,' said Nodon.

George unhooked the power pack and toted it in his arms back to *Matilda*'s airlock. It was twice his size, and even though it weighed virtually nothing he was careful handling it; a mass that big could squash a man no matter what the ambient gravity. The law of inertia had not been repealed.

'What's our visitor doin'?' he asked as he sealed the lock's outer hatch and started pumping air into it.

'Still approaching on the same course.'

'Any word from 'im?'

'Nothing.'

That worried George, though by the time he had wormed his way out of the ripe-smelling suit and plugged the big power pack into the ship's recharging unit, his first priority was food.

He half-floated up the passageway to the galley.

'Spin 'er up a bit, Nodon,' he hollered to the bridge. 'Gimme some weight while I chow down.'

'One-sixth g?' the Turk's voice came back down the passageway.

'Good enough.'

A comfortable feeling of weight returned as George pulled a meagre prepackaged snack from the freezer. Should've loaded more food, he thought. Didn't expect to be out here this long.

Then he heard a scream from the bridge. The air-pressure alarm started hooting and the emergency hatches slammed shut as the ship's lights went out, plunging George into total darkness.

18

Amanda was aghast. 'You refused to sell at any price?'

Fuchs nodded grimly. Some of the blazing fury he had felt during his meeting with Humphries had burned off, but still the smouldering heat of anger burned deep in his guts. Only one thing was certain: he was going to fight. On the way from Humphries' office to their hotel suite Fuchs had made up his mind once and for all. He was going to wipe the smug smile from Humphries' face, no matter what it cost.

Amanda was in the sitting room of their suite when Fuchs barged through the door, angry and impatient. He saw the expectant look on her face and realized she'd been waiting for him all the while; she'd never gone shopping or done anything other than wait for his return.

'I couldn't do it,' Fuchs said, so low that he wasn't sure she'd heard him. He cleared his throat, repeated, 'I couldn't sell to him. Not at any price.'

Amanda sank into one of the small sofas scattered about the room. 'Lars . . . what do you expect to do now?'

'I don't know,' he told her. That wasn't quite true, but he wasn't sure of how much he could tell her. He sat in the chair next to Amanda and took her hands in his. 'I told him I was going back to Ceres and start over.'

'Start over? How?'

He tried to smile for her, to hide his true thoughts. 'We still have *Starpower*. We can go back to prospecting, I suppose.'

'Live aboard the ship again,' she murmured.

'I know it's a step backward.' He hesitated, then found the courage to say, 'You don't have to come with me. You can stay on Ceres. Or . . . or wherever you would prefer to live.'

'You'd go without me?' She looked hurt.

Fuchs knew that if he told her his real plans, his true goal, Amanda would be terrified. She would try to talk him out of it. Or worse, once she realized that he was unshakable, she would insist on staying with him every step of the way.

So he temporized. 'Amanda, dearest . . . it wouldn't be fair for me to ask you to live that way again. I've made a mess of things, it's up to me to—'

'Lars, he'll kill you!'

She was truly frightened, he saw.

'If you go back to the Belt by yourself,' Amanda said urgently, 'he'll have someone track you down and murder you.'

Fuchs remembered Humphries' words: *You're a dead man, Fuchs.*

'I can take care of myself,' he said grimly.

Amanda thought, I've got to go with him. Martin won't strike at Lars if there's a possibility of hurting me.

Aloud, she said to her husband, gently, soothingly, 'I know you can take care of yourself, darling, but who's going to take care of me?' And she reached up to stroke his cheek.

'You'd go with me?'

'Of course.'

'You *want* to go with me?' He was filled with joyful wonder at the idea.

'I want to be with you, Lars,' Amanda said softly, 'wherever you go.'

To herself, though, she said, It's me that Martin wants.

I'm the cause of all this. I'm the reason my husband is in such danger.

And Fuchs was saying to himself, She wants to be away from Humphries. She's afraid of him. She's afraid that if I'm not near enough to protect her, he'll steal her away from me.

And the embers of his anger burst into flaming rage again.

Waltzing Matilda

The emergency lights came on, dim but better than utter darkness. George groped through the shadows along the narrow passageway from the galley to the closed hatch of the bridge. He tapped the code on the bulkhead keypad and the hatch popped open slightly.

At least there's proper air pressure in the bridge, George thought as he pushed the hatch all the way open. Hatch wouldn't have opened otherwise.

Nodon was sitting in the command pilot's chair, eyes wide with shock or fright, hands racing along the console keyboard. The regular lights came back on, but they seemed weaker than usual.

'What th' fook happened, mate?' George asked, sliding into the co-pilot's chair.

'I got an electric shock,' said Nodon. 'A spark jumped from the panel and the lights went out.'

George could see the kid was checking out all the ship's systems. The control panel's displays flickered almost too quickly for the eye to register as Nodon raced through one system diagnostic after another.

The kid's good, George thought. I made the right decision when I hired him.

Nodon was a skinny youngster who'd claimed to be twenty-five, but George figured the kid was barely out of his teens. No real experience, outside of working on computers back on Ceres, but he had an intensity, a bright, eager desire to succeed, that made George pick him as his crewman for this mining job. George called him 'Turk' but Nodon was actually a Mongol, with the decorative spiral tattoos on both his cheeks to prove it. He claimed he'd been born on the Moon, of miners who'd fled Earth when the Gobi Desert engulfed the grasslands of their ancestral homeland. He was all bone and sinew, skin the colour of old parchment, head shaved, big, expressive, deep brown eyes. He'd look damned handsome if it weren't for those bloody scars, George thought. He was trying to grow a moustache; so far it was nothing more than a few wisps that made his upper lip look dirty.

Sitting tensely in the command chair, flicking through diagnostics almost faster than George could follow, Nodon wore only a comfortable sleeveless mesh shirt over a pair of ragged shorts.

'The power generator is off-line,' he said. 'That's why the lights went out.'

'We're on batteries now?' George asked.

'Yes, and—'

The alarms hooted again and George felt his ears pop. The airtight hatch slammed shut once more.

'Jeezus God!' George shouted. 'The bugger's shootin' at us!'

Dorik Harbin scowled at his display screens. His first shot should have taken out the ship's habitat module, but they increased their spin just a split-second before he'd fired. He hit *something*, he was certain of that, but it wasn't a fatal hit.

It had taken a few minutes for the big laser to recharge; this had given Harbin enough time to choose his target carefully. He had the full schematics of *Waltzing Matilda* on one of the screens, courtesy of Humphries Space Systems. Their intelligence data was well nigh perfect. Harbin knew where to find the ships he went after, and what each ship's layout was.

Not much of a challenge to a soldier, he thought. But then, what soldier wants challenges? When you put your life on the line, the easier the job the better. For just the flicker of a moment he thought about the fact that he was shooting at unarmed civilians. Perhaps there was a woman aboard that ship, although the HSS intelligence data didn't indicate that. What of it, he told himself. That's the target and you're being paid to destroy it. It's a lot easier than killing people face to face, the way you had to in Delhi.

That had been a mess, a fiasco. One battalion of mercenary troops trying to protect a food warehouse against a whole city. That idiot commander! Stupid Frenchman. Harbin still saw the maddened faces of the ragged, half-starved Indians, bare hands against automatic rifles and machine guns. Still, they nearly swarmed us down. Only when he was foolish enough to let one of the women get close enough to knife him did his blood-rage surge and save him. He shot her point-blank and led a howling murderous charge that sent the mob running. He stopped firing into their backs only when his automatic rifle finally jammed from overheating.

He pushed the nightmare images out of his mind and concentrated on the job at hand. By the time he was ready to fire again, *Matilda*'s spin had moved the hab module enough so that it was partially shielded by the big slabs of ores the miners had hung on their central propulsion module. But their main comm antenna was in his sights. He squeezed off a shot. The laser's capacitors cracked loudly and he saw a flash of light glance off the rim of the antenna. A hit.

Now to get the auxiliary antennas, he said to himself. I'll have to move in closer.

'Shooting at us?' Nodon's voice went high with sudden fright.

'Fookin' bastard,' George growled. 'Get into your suit. Quick!'

Nodon bolted from his chair and went to the hatch. He tapped out the keyboard code swiftly and the hatch swung open all the way.

'The air pressure is falling,' he called over his shoulder as George followed him down the passageway toward the airlock.

George was thinking, If we had the bloody laser on board we could give the bastard a taste of his own medicine. But the laser was sitting on the asteroid and its power pack was recharging; at least, it had been until the generator had been hit.

As they scrambled into their suits, George said, 'We'd better power down the ship. Save the batteries.'

Nodon was already pulling his bubble helmet over his head. 'I'll go to the bridge and do it,' he said, his voice muffled by the helmet.

'Turn off everything!' George yelled after his retreating back. 'Let 'em think we're dead!'

He added silently, It won't be far from wrong, either.

Nodon returned from the bridge as George was closing the neck seal of his helmet. Leaning toward the kid so their helmets touched, he said, 'Don't even use the suit radio. Play dead.'

The kid looked worried, but he forced a sickly grin as he nodded back to George.

They got to the airlock and went out together. George grasped Nodon's suited arm and, without using his jetpack, pushed off toward the big slabs of ores attached to *Matilda*'s fusion engine. Get into the shadow of those chunks, he thought. Huddle up close to 'em and maybe this fookin' killer won't see us.

Perspective was tricky in microgravity. Once George and

his young crewman got to the nearest of the slabs, it seemed as if they were lying on a huge, hard bed, side by side, looking up at the slowly revolving shape of their habitation module as it swung on its long tether.

The other ship glided into George's view. It was small, little more than a hab unit set atop a fusion engine and a set of bulbous propellant tanks. It looked almost like a cluster of mismatched grapes. Then he recognized the bulky shape of a high-power laser hanging just below the hab module. This ship was meant to be a destroyer, nothing else.

The guide beam from the ship's auxiliary laser played over *Matilda*'s habitation module. George watched as the smaller ship manoeuvred leisurely, the evil red spot of the guide beam sliding away from the hab unit. For a moment it was lost in the depth of space, but then George's heart clutched in his chest. The red spot was moving across the slab on which he and Nodon were clinging.

He knows we're here! George thought, sweat breaking out on his face. He's gonna slice us!

But the red spot slid across the slab more than ten metres below their boots. It stopped on the bell-shaped nozzle of their fusion engine, then walked slowly up to the throat of the nozzle. A light flashed there. George blinked against the sudden, unexpected glare.

Nodon bumped his helmet against George's. 'The engine!' he whimpered.

Another flash. This time George saw shards of metal fly off the rocket nozzle, glinting briefly in the pale sunlight as they spun out of sight, into the endless darkness.

Again the laser fired. This time it hit the piping that fed cryogenic hydrogen into the nozzle's cooling capillaries. Fookin' bastard knows his business, George thought grimly. He's disabled the engine with three bloody shots.

The attacking ship drifted out of George's sight, beyond

the edge of the slab on which he and Nodon hid. For moments that seemed like hours, the two men lay there unmoving. What are we gonna do? George wondered. How can we get home without the main engine?

In the darkness, George felt Nodon's helmet touch his again. 'Do you think he's gone?' the young man asked.

Before George could answer, he caught another glint in the corner of his eye. Pushing slightly away from the slab, he saw that their attacker was punching holes in their propellant tanks. Thin cold jets of cryogenic hydrogen and helium-three hissed noiselessly into the vacuum, brief whitish wisps of gas that dissipated into the emptiness of space in an eyeblink.

'We're movin',' George muttered, even though Nodon could not hear him. Like a child's balloon when he lets the air out of it, the gases escaping from the punctured tanks were pushing *Matilda* slowly away from the asteroid.

'We're gonna get a fookin' tour of the solar system,' George said aloud. 'Shame we'll be too dead to enjoy the sights.'

19

'I'm surprised he hasn't had us thrown out of this hotel already,' Fuchs said morosely.

Pancho Lane tried to smile encouragingly. Lars and Amanda both looked so down, so – *bewildered* was the word for it, Pancho decided. Overrun by events and their own emotions.

'Hey, don't worry about the hotel,' she said, trying to sound cheerful. 'Astro'll pay for it if Humphries reneges.'

Fuchs was still in the light grey business suit he'd worn for his meeting with Humphries. Amanda was wearing a pale turquoise knee-length frock, modest enough, but she still made Pancho feel gawky and shapeless, as usual. Mandy didn't mean to, but whenever Pancho was near her she felt like a beanpole standing beside a vid star.

'We're going back to Ceres,' Amanda said. 'Back to prospecting.'

The two of them were sitting glumly on the sofa set beneath a hologram of Valles Marineris on Mars: the grandest Grand Canyon in the solar system.

'What about Helvetia Ltd?' Pancho asked. 'You're not gonna let Humphries muscle you out of business, are you?'

Fuchs grunted. 'What business? Our inventory went up in flames.'

'Yeah, but the insurance oughtta cover enough of it to get you started again.'

Fuchs shook his head wearily.

'You got a lot of goodwill out there on Ceres,' Pancho urged. 'Shouldn't oughtta let that go to waste.'

Amanda's brows rose hopefully.

'Don't want to let Humphries get a monopoly, do you, Lars ol' buddy?'

'I'd prefer to strangle him,' Fuchs growled.

Pancho leaned back in her chair, stretched her long lean legs. 'Tell you what: Astro'll advance you the credit to restock your warehouse, up to the limit that the insurance will pay you.'

Fuchs looked at her. 'You can do this?'

'I'm learnin' how to play the board of directors. I got a clutch of 'em on my side. They don't want Humphries to monopolize the Belt any more'n you do.'

Amanda asked, 'Is your group strong enough to let you do what you just offered to do?'

Nodding, Pancho replied, 'Take my word for it.'

Turning to her husband, Amanda said hopefully, 'Lars, we could start Helvetia all over again.'

'With a smaller inventory,' he grumbled. 'The insurance won't cover everything we lost.'

'But it's a start,' Amanda said, smiling genuinely.

Fuchs did not smile back. He looked away from his wife. Pancho thought there was something going on inside his head that he didn't want Mandy to see.

'I'm going back to prospecting,' he said, his eyes focused on the far wall of the sitting room.

'But—'

'I'll take *Starpower* back as soon as the current lease on her is finished.'

'But what about Helvetia?' Amanda asked.

He turned toward her once more. 'You'll have to run Helvetia. You can stay on Ceres while I take the ship out.'

Pancho studied them. There was something going on

between them, some hidden agenda someplace, that she couldn't fathom.

'Lars,' said Amanda, in a very soft voice, 'are you certain that this is what you want to do?'

'It's what I must do, darling.' His voice sounded implacable.

Pancho invited them both to dinner at the Earthview Restaurant, off the hotel's lobby.

'Strictly a social evening,' she told them. 'No talk about Humphries or Ceres or any kind of business at all. Okay?'

They agreed, half-heartedly.

So naturally they talked about business through the entire meal. Pancho's business.

The standing joke about the Earthview was that it was the finest restaurant within four hundred thousand kilometres. Which was perfectly true: the two other eateries in Selene, up in the Grand Plaza, were mere bistros. Two levels beneath the lunar surface, the Earthview featured sweeping windowwalls that displayed holographic views from the Moon's surface. It was almost like looking through real windows at the gaunt, cracked floor of the giant crater Alphonsus and its worn, slumped ringwall mountains. But the Earth was always in that dark sky, hanging like a splendid glowing jewel of sparkling blue and glowing white, ever changing yet always present.

The Earthview prided itself on having a human staff, no robots in sight. Pancho always felt that a truly top-rate restaurant should use tablecloths, but the Earthview used glittering placemats made of lunar honeycomb metal, thin and supple as silk.

None of them had changed clothes for dinner. Fuchs was still wearing his suit, Amanda her turquoise dress. Pancho, who favoured coveralls and softboots, had started the day in a business outfit of chocolate-brown slacks, pale yellow sweater and light tan suede vest. Amanda had loaned her a light auburn Irish lace stole to 'dress up your outfit.'

Once their handsome young waiter had brought their drinks and taken their dinner order, an awkward silence fell over their table. They had agreed not to talk business. What other topic of conversation was there?

Pancho sipped at her margarita and watched the waiter's retreating back. Nice buns, she thought. Wonder if he's married?

'So, what have you been doing lately, Pancho?' Amanda finally said, more to break the silence than any other reason.

'Me? I'm followin' up on something Dan Randolph talked about years ago: scoopin' fusion fuels from Jupiter.'

Fuchs' ears perked up. 'Fusion fuels?'

'Yeah. You know, helium-three, tritium, other isotopes. Jupiter's atmosphere is full of 'em.'

'That's a steep gravity well,' said Amanda.

'Tell me about it,' Pancho said. 'You know I've been approached by some nuts who want to go skimmin' Jupiter's atmosphere as a *stunt*? They even brought a network producer with 'em.'

'Insanity,' Fuchs muttered.

'Yeah, sure. But then there's a gaggle of scientists who wanta set up a research station in orbit around Jupiter. Study the moons and all.'

'But the radiation,' Amanda said.

'Tight orbit, underneath the Jovian Van Allen belts. Might be doable.'

'Astro would fund this?'

'Hell no!' Pancho blurted. 'Universities gotta come up with the funding. We'll build the sucker.'

'And use it as a platform for mining Jupiter's atmosphere,' Amanda added.

Pancho smiled at her. Sometimes I forget how smart she is, Pancho thought. I let her sweet face and nice boobs fool me.

Then she looked at Fuchs. He sat with his drink untouched before him, his eyes staring off into some private universe. Whatever he's thinking about, Pancho realized, he's a zillion kilometres from here.

Waltzing Matilda

Once they got back inside the ship, it took George and Nodon hours to patch the holes punched through the hull by the attacker's laser and check out all the systems. They were both dead tired by the time they were able to take off their spacesuits and clump wearily, fearfully to the bridge.

George took the command chair, Nodon slipped into the chair at his right.

'You run a diagnostic on the power generator,' said George. 'I'll check the nav computer and see where th' fook we're headin'.'

They worked in silence for another twenty minutes.

At last Nodon said, 'I can repair the generator. He knocked out one set of electrodes. We have spares.'

George nodded. 'Okay, then. If you can get the generator back on line we won't hafta worry about electrical power for the life support systems.'

Nodding, Nodon said, 'That is good news.'

'Right. Now here's the bad news. We're up shit creek without a paddle.'

Nodon said nothing. He held his bony face impassive, but George saw that even his shaved pate was sheened with perspiration. It sure isn't the temperature in here, George told himself. In fact, the bridge felt decidedly chilly.

With a heavy sigh, George said, 'He knocked enough holes in the propellant tanks to send us jettin' deeper into the Belt.'

'And the main engine is beyond repair.'

'Prob'ly.'

'Then we will die.'

'Looks that way, mate. Unless we can get some help.'

'The comm system is down. He must have lasered the antennas.'

George nodded. 'So that's what the soddin' bastard was doing.'

'He was very thorough.'

Sitting there, staring at the control panel with half its tell-tale lights glowering red, George tried to think.

'We're okay on life support,' he mused aloud.

'Once the generator is running again,' Nodon corrected. 'Otherwise the batteries will run out in . . .' He glanced at the display '. . . eleven hours.'

'Better fix the generator, then. That's our first priority.'

Nodon started to get up from his seat. He hesitated, asked, 'And our second priority?'

'Figurin' out if we can nudge ourselves into a trajectory that'll bring us close to Ceres before we starve to death.'

20

Amanda would have preferred to stay in Selene for just a few days more, but Fuchs insisted that they start back for Ceres as soon as possible. He learned from Pancho that an Astro ship was due to depart for Ceres the next day, carrying a load of equipment that Helvetia had ordered before the warehouse fire.

'We'll go back on that ship,' Fuchs told his wife.

'But it's a freighter. It won't have passenger accommodations,' Amanda protested.

'We'll go back on that ship,' he repeated.

Wondering why her husband was so insistent on returning as quickly as possible, Amanda reluctantly packed her travel bag while Fuchs called Pancho to beg a ride.

The next morning they rode the little automated tractor through the tunnel that led out to Armstrong Spaceport and climbed aboard the spindly-legged shuttlecraft that would lift them to the *Harper*. The ship was in lunar orbit, but rotating at one-sixth g. Fuchs felt grateful that he would not have to endure weightlessness for more than the few minutes of the shuttlecraft's flight.

'Newest ship in the solar system,' said her captain as he welcomed them aboard. He was young, trim, good-looking, and stared openly at Amanda's ample figure. Fuchs, standing beside her, grasped his wife's arm possessively.

'I'm afraid, though, that she's not built for passenger service,' the captain said as he led them down the habitat module's central passageway. 'All I can offer you is this cabin.'

He slid back an accordion-pleated door. The cabin was barely large enough for two people to stand in.

'It's kind of small,' the captain said, apologetically. But he was smiling at Amanda.

'It will do,' said Fuchs. 'The trip is only six days.'

He stepped into the compartment, leading Amanda.

The captain, still out in the passageway, said, 'We break orbit in thirty minutes.'

'Good,' said Fuchs. And he slid the door shut.

Amanda giggled at him. 'Lars, you were positively rude to him!'

With a sardonic grin, he said, 'I thought his eyes would fall out of his head, he was staring at you so hard.'

'Oh, Lars, he wasn't. Was he?'

'He most certainly was.'

Amanda's expression became sly. 'What do you think he had on his mind?'

His grin turned wolfish. 'I'll show you.'

Even though they took place in the tropical beauty of La Guaira, on the Caribbean coast of Venezuela, the quarterly meetings of Astro Manufacturing Corporation's board of directors had turned into little short of armed confrontations. Martin Humphries had built a clique around himself and was working hard to take control of the board. Opposing him was Pancho Lane, who had learned in her five years on the board how to bring together a voting bloc of her own.

As chairman of the board, Harriett O'Banian tried her best to steer clear of both groups. Her job, as she saw it, was to make Astro as profitable as possible. Much of what Humphries wanted to do was indeed profitable, even though Pancho opposed virtually anything Humphries or one of his people proposed.

But now Pancho was proposing something that might become an entirely new product line for Astro, and Humphries seemed dead set against it.

'Scoop gases from the atmosphere of Jupiter?' Humphries was scoffing. 'Can you think of anything – any idea at all – that carries more risk?'

'Yeah,' Pancho snapped. 'Lettin' somebody else get a corner on the fusion fuels market.'

Red-haired Hattie O'Banian was no stranger to outbursts of temper. But not while she chaired the board. She rapped on the long conference table with her knuckles. 'We *will* have order here,' she said firmly. 'Mr Humphries has the floor.'

Pancho slumped back in her chair and nodded unhappily. She was seated almost exactly across the table from Humphries. O'Banian had to exert some self-control to keep from smiling at her. Pancho had come a long way since her first awkward days on the board. Underneath her west Texas drawl and awshucks demeanour, she had a sharp intelligence, quick wit, and the ability to focus on an issue with the intensity of a laser beam. With Hattie's help, Pancho had learned how to dress the part of a board member: today she wore a trousered business suit of dusky rose, accented with jewellery. Still, Hattie thought, her lanky, long-legged tomboy image came through. She looked as if she wanted to reach across the table and sock Humphries between the eyes.

For his part, Humphries seemed perfectly at ease in a casual cardigan suit of deep blue and pale lemon turtleneck shirt. He wears clothes well, Hattie thought, and hides his thoughts even better.

'Martin,' said O'Banian. 'Do you have anything else to add?'

'I certainly do,' Humphries said, with a crafty little smile.

He turned his gaze to Pancho for a moment, then looked back at O'Banian. 'I am opposed to fly-by-night schemes that promise a jackpot at the end of the rainbow but are in reality fraught with technical risks. And human dangers. Sending a ship to Jupiter in a crazy attempt to scoop hydrogen and helium isotopes from that planet's atmosphere is utter madness, pure and simple.'

Half a dozen board members nodded agreement. O'Banian noticed that a couple of them were not usually on Humphries' side in these quarrels.

'Ms Lane? Do you have anything more to say in support of your proposal?'

Pancho sat up ramrod straight and looked squarely at Humphries. 'I sure do. I've presented the facts, the engineering analysis, the cost estimates and the profit probabilities. The numbers show that scooping fusion fuels is within the capabilities of existing technology. Nothing new needs to be invented.'

'A ship that dives into Jupiter's atmosphere to collect its gases?' blurted out one of the older men down the table. He was paunchy, bald, red-faced.

Pancho forced-smile at him. 'A ship that's being tele-operated from Jupiter orbit. It's well within existing capabilities.'

'There's no base in the Jupiter system for a remote operating team; we'd have to set it up it ourselves.'

'That's true,' Pancho said evenly. 'I didn't say it was existing state-of-the-art hardware. But it is within existing capabilities. We just have to build it and test it.'

'At what cost?' asked the grey-haired woman sitting two chairs down from Pancho.

'You have all the cost figures in my presentation,' Pancho said. Then, turning to O'Banian, she asked, 'Can I finish my say without bein' interrupted, please?'

O'Banian nodded. Raising her voice slightly, she said, 'Let's give Pancho the same courtesy we gave Martin, everyone.'

Pancho said, 'Thanks, y'all. Earth needs energy sources that won't put greenhouse gases into the atmosphere. Fusion is the answer, and fusion based on helium-three is the most efficient fusion system that's been built so far. There's trillions of dollars *per year* waitin' for the company that can supply fusion fuels for Earth. And don't forget that Selene, the Mars bases, Ceres and lots of other facilities off-Earth will buy fusion fuels, too. Not to mention the market for spacecraft propulsion.'

'Selene sells us deuterium-three,' said the red-faced bald man. 'They scoop it up out of the ground.'

Pancho countered, 'There's not enough deuterium on the Moon to satisfy the potential market demand.'

'But going all the way out to Jupiter . . . that will make the price too damned high, won't it?'

'Not once we get the facilities runnin'. It'll be a long-haul cargo run, a pipeline operation. We won't hafta undercut Selene's price; we'll just offer a million times more fusion fuels than Selene can dig up.'

The man mumbled to himself, unconvinced.

Pancho looked back to O'Banian, but before the chairwoman could say anything, she went on, 'One more thing. If we don't do this, Humphries Space Systems will.'

Humphries shot up from his chair and pointed an accusing finger at Pancho. 'That's a deliberate insult!'

'That's the truth and you know it!' Pancho fired back.

The board room erupted with angry voices.

O'Banian banged on the table, hard. 'Quiet! All of you.'

'Do I still have the floor?' Pancho asked, once the commotion calmed down. Humphries was glaring at her from across the table.

O'Banian threw an irritated look at Pancho. 'As long as you refrain from personal attacks on other board members,' she answered stiffly.

'Okay,' said Pancho. 'But it seems to me like we got a problem here. *Mr* Humphries here is in a position to block new ideas and then take 'em back to his own corporation and run with 'em.'

'You're accusing me of unethical behaviour!' Humphries barked.

'Damn' right,' said Pancho.

'Wait! Quiet!' O'Banian demanded. 'I will not have this meeting break down into a personal quarrel.'

The oldest member of the board, a frail-looking gentleman who hardly ever said a word, spoke up. 'It seems to me,' he said in a whispery voice, 'that we do indeed have a conflict of interest here.'

'That's nonsense,' Humphries snapped.

'I'm afraid that the point has to be considered,' O'Banian said. She tried to make it as mild and noncommittal as possible, but she was not going to let this point pass without a full discussion. She deliberately kept her eyes away from Pancho, afraid that her gratitude would show.

The discussion wrangled on for nearly two hours. Each board member demanded to have his or her say, whether or not the same sentiment had already been expressed by someone else. O'Banian sat patiently through it all, watching their egos on parade, trying to figure out how she could bring this to a vote. Throw Humphries off the board? Gladly. But there weren't enough votes for that. The best she could hope for was to pull his fangs.

Humphries was no fool. He too listened to the board members' repetitious ramblings, clearly impatient, obviously calculating his odds. By the time it was his turn to speak in his own defence, he had come to a decision.

Rising to his feet, he said slowly, calmly, 'I'm not going to dignify the accusation that Ms Lane made by trying to defend myself against it. I think the facts speak for themselves—'

'They sure do,' Pancho muttered, loud enough for everyone to hear.

Humphries kept his temper, barely. 'Therefore,' he continued, 'I will withdraw my opposition to this Jupiter concept.'

O'Banian realized she had been holding her breath. She let it out with a gush, surprised at how displeased she felt. She had hoped that Humphries would do the gentlemanly thing and resign from the board.

'But let me tell you this,' Humphries added, with an upraised finger. 'When the costs mount up and the whole idea collapses around our heads, don't say I didn't warn you.'

O'Banian took another breath, then said, 'Thank you, Martin, on behalf of the entire board.'

But Humphries' clique on the board still opposed the Jupiter project. The best they would agree to was to allow Pancho to seek a partner that would share at least one quarter of the project's costs. Failing that, the board would not allow the programme to be started.

'A partner?' Pancho groused. O'Banian threw her a sharp warning look. If Pancho complained openly that no one would join Astro in such a partnership, it merely proved Humphries' point that the idea was impractically far-fetched.

'I think you might open up a dialogue with some of the major utilities corporations,' O'Banian suggested. 'After all, they have the most to gain from an assured supply of fusion fuels.'

'Yeah,' Pancho mumbled. 'Right.'

As the meeting broke up and the board members made their way out of the conference room, muttering and chattering to one another, Humphries came up to O'Banian.

'Are you satisfied?' he asked, in a low, confidential voice.

'I'm sorry it had to come to this, Martin,' she replied.

'Yes, I can see how sorry you are.' He glanced across the room, to where Pancho was talking to the old red-faced man as they filed out of the room. 'Clever work, using Pancho as your stalking horse.'

O'Banian was genuinely shocked. 'Me? Using . . . ?'

'It's all right,' Humphries said, smiling thinly. 'I expect sneak attacks now and then. It's all part of the game.'

'But, Martin, I had no idea—'

'No, of course you didn't. Well, go ahead with this Jupiter nonsense, if you can find some idiot foolish enough to go along with you. Once it flops I'll be able to use it to get you off the board. And that damned grease-monkey, too.'

Waltzing Matilda

'What spooks me,' George was saying, 'is how the fookin' bastard knew where our antennas were.'

He and Nodon were taking off their spacesuits, dog-tired after a five-hour EVA. They had patched the laser-punched holes in the propellant tanks, but most of the hydrogen and helium had already leaked away. Their communications antennas, even the backups, were slagged and useless.

'He must have had complete specs on this ship,' Nodon said, as he lifted off the torso of his hard-shell suit and placed it carefully on its rack. 'Every detail.'

'Every fookin' detail,' George agreed. He sat on the tiny bench in front of the suit racks, filling it so completely that Nodon sat on the deck to start removing his boots. George felt too weary even to bend over and pull his boots off.

Piece by piece they finished unsuiting at last, then made their way to the galley. George mused aloud, 'Y'know, somebody must've given him the specs for this ship.'

'Yes,' Nodon agreed, trailing along behind him. The passageway was too narrow for them to proceed side by side.

'But who? This is a private piece of property, its specs aren't public knowledge. You can't look 'em up on a fookin' net site.'

Nodon scratched his lean, bristly chin, then suggested, 'Could he have access to the manufacturer's records?'

'Or to the maintenance files at Ceres, maybe,' George muttered.

'Yes, that is possible.'

'Either way,' said George, with growing conviction, 'it has to be somebody in Humphries Space Systems. Their people do the maintenance on it.'

'Not Astro?'

'Naw. HSS offered me a bargain price if I signed up for the maintenance contract.'

'Then it must be someone in HSS,' Nodon agreed.

'But why? Why did the bastard attack us?'

'To invalidate the claim to the asteroid, certainly.'

George shook his head irritatedly. 'There's millions of rocks in the Belt. And Humphries is the richest shrewdie in the fookin' solar system. What's he need a lousy asteroid claim for?'

'Perhaps not him,' Nodon said. 'Perhaps someone in his corporation.'

'Yeah.' George nodded. 'Maybe.'

With a resigned shrug, Nodon said, 'It is all academic, anyway.'

'Whatcha mean, mate?'

Tapping a lean finger against the small wallscreen that displayed the galley's contents, Nodon pointed out, 'We have enough food for only another twenty-two days. Perhaps as much as forty days, if we cut our daily ration to starvation level.'

George grunted at him. 'No sense starvin' ourselves. We're gonna die anyway.'

21

Through the week-long trip on the *Harper*, Amanda sensed a strangeness in her husband, something odd, different, something she couldn't put her finger on. He seemed – not, distant, exactly – certainly not distant: Lars spent almost the entire journey in bed with her, making love with a fierce intensity she had never known before.

And yet, even in the midst of their passion there was something withdrawn about him; something that he was hiding from her. She had always been able to read his thoughts before: one look at the set of his jaw and she knew what he was thinking. He had never held anything back from her. But now his face was impassive, his expression guarded. His deepset blue eyes showed her nothing.

It frightened Amanda to realize that Lars was keeping a secret from her. Perhaps more than one.

Once they arrived back at their quarters on Ceres and began unpacking their travel bags, Amanda decided to confront the issue directly.

'Lars, what's the matter?'

He was stuffing a handful of socks and underwear into his bureau drawer. 'The matter?' he asked, without looking up at her. 'What do you mean?'

'Something's on your mind and you're not sharing it with me.'

Straightening up, he came back toward her at the bed. 'I'm thinking of everything that we have to do. The insurance, restocking the warehouse, getting *Starpower* back.'

Amanda sat on the bed, next to her opened bag. 'Yes, of course. And what else?'

His eyes shifted away from her. 'What else? Isn't that enough?'

'There's something more, Lars. Something that's been bothering you since we left Selene.'

He looked down at her, then turned his attention to his travel bag again, started rummaging through it, muttering about his shaving kit.

Amanda put her hand atop his, stopping him. 'Lars, please tell me.'

He straightened up. 'There are some things you shouldn't know, dear.'

'What?' She felt shocked. 'What things?'

He almost smiled. 'If I told you, then you would know.'

'It's about Martin, isn't it? You've been this way ever since your meeting with him.'

Fuchs took a deep breath. She could see his chest expand and then deflate again. He pushed his bag aside and sat next to her on the bed.

'All through our trip back here,' he said, his voice heavy, low, 'I've been trying to think of a way that we can stop him from gaining complete control of the Belt.'

'So that's it.'

He nodded, but she could see that there was still more. His eyes looked troubled, uncertain.

'He wants that. He wants complete control of everyone and everything out here. He wants absolute power.'

Amanda said, 'What of it? Lars, we don't have to fight against him. We can't! You're only one man. You can't stop him.'

'Someone has to do it.'

'But not you! Not us! We can cash in the insurance money and go back to Earth and forget about all this.'

With a slow shake of his head, Fuchs said, 'Perhaps you can forget about it. I can't.'

'You mean you won't.'

'I can't.'

'Lars, you're obsessed with a foolish macho delusion. This isn't a battle between you and Martin. There's nothing to fight about! I love you. After all these years, don't you know that? Don't you believe it?'

'It's gone beyond that,' Fuchs said grimly.

'Beyond . . . ?'

'He's killed people. Friends of ours. Ripley. The men and women aboard the ships that have disappeared. He's a murderer.'

'But what can you do about it?'

'I can fight.'

'Fight?' Amanda felt truly frightened now. 'How? With what?'

He held up his thick-fingered hands and slowly clenched them into fists. 'With my bare hands, if I have to.'

'Lars, that's crazy! Insane!'

He snapped, 'Don't you think I know it? Don't you think it horrifies me down to the bottom of my soul? I'm a civilized man. I'm not a Neanderthal.'

'Then why . . . ?'

'Because I *must*. Because there's an anger in me, a fury that won't let go of me. I *hate* him! I hate his smug certainty. I hate the idea that he can push a button and men are murdered millions of kilometres away while he sits in his elegant mansion and dines on pheasant. And fantasizes about you!'

Amanda's heart sank. I'm the cause of all this, she realized all over again. I've turned this sweet, loving man into a raging monster.

'I'd like to smash his face in,' Fuchs growled. 'Kill him just as he's killed so many others.'

'The way you killed that man in The Pub,' she heard herself say.

He looked as if she had slapped him in the face.

Shocked at her own words, Amanda said, 'Oh, Lars, I didn't mean—'

'You're right,' he snapped. 'Absolutely right. If I could kill Humphries like that, I'd do it. In a hot second.'

She reached up and stroked his cheek as gently, soothingly as she could. 'Lars, darling, please – all you're going to accomplish is getting yourself killed.'

He pushed her hand away. 'Don't you think I'm already marked for murder? He told me he would have me killed. *You're a dead man, Fuchs.* Those were his exact words.'

Amanda closed her eyes. There was nothing she could do. She knew that her husband was going to fight, and there was nothing she could do to stop him. She knew he would get himself killed. Worse, she saw that he was turning into a killer himself. He was becoming a stranger, a man she didn't know, didn't recognize. That frightened her.

'And to what do I owe the pleasure of your visit?' asked Carlos Vertientes.

He's a handsome devil, Pancho thought. Aristocratic Castilian features. Good cheekbones. Neat little salt-and-pepper beard. He really looks like a professor oughtta, not like the slobs and creeps back in Texas.

She was strolling along the *Ramblas* in Barcelona with the head of the university's plasma dynamics department, the tall, distinguished physicist who had helped Lyall Duncan build the fusion propulsion system that now powered most of the spacecraft operating beyond the Moon's orbit. Vertientes looked truly elegant in a dove-grey three-piece suit. Pancho was wearing the olive green coveralls she had traveled in.

Barcelona was still a vibrant city, despite the rising sea level and greenhouse warming and displacement of so many millions of refugees. The *Ramblas* was still the crowded, bustling, noisy boulevard where everyone went for a stroll, a sampling of *tapas* and good Rioja wine, a chance to see and be seen. Pancho liked it far better than sitting in an office even though the crowd was so thick that at times they had to elbow their way past clusters of people who were walking too slowly. Pancho preferred the chatting, strolling crowd to an office that might be bugged.

'Your university's a shareholder in Astro Corporation,' Pancho said, in answer to his question.

Vertientes' finely-arched brows rose slightly. 'We are part of the global consortium of universities that invests in many major corporations.'

He was slightly taller than Pancho, and slim as a Toledo blade. She felt good walking alongside him. With a nod, she replied, 'Yup. That's what I found out when I started lookin' up Astro's stockholders.'

He smiled dazzlingly. 'Have you come to Barcelona to sell more stock?'

'No, no,' Pancho said, laughing with him. 'But I do have a proposition for you – and your consortium.'

'And what might that be?' he asked, taking her arm to steer her past a knot of Asian tourists posing for a street photographer.

'How'd you like to set up a research station in orbit around Jupiter? Astro would foot three-quarters of the cost, maybe more if we can jiggle the books a little.'

Vertientes' brows rose even higher. 'A research station at Jupiter? You mean a manned station?'

'Crewed,' Pancho corrected.

He stopped and let the crowd flow around them. 'You are suggesting that the consortium could establish a manned – and womanned – station in Jupiter orbit at one-quarter of the actual cost?'

'Maybe less,' Pancho said.

He pursed his lips. Then, 'Let's find a cantina where we can sit down and discuss this.'

'Suits me,' said Pancho, with a happy grin.

Waltzing Matilda

George looked sourly at the screen's display.

'Four hundred and eighty-three days?' he asked. He was sitting in the command pilot's chair, on the bridge; Nodon sat beside him.

Nodon seemed apologetic. 'That is what the navigation program shows. We are on a long elliptical trajectory that will swing back to the vicinity of Ceres in four hundred and eighty-three days.'

'How close to Ceres?'

Nodon tapped at the keyboard. 'Seventy thousand kilometres, plus or minus three thousand.'

George scratched at his beard. 'Close enough to contact 'em with our suit radios, just about.'

'Perhaps,' said Nodon. 'If we were still alive by then.'

'We'd be pretty skinny.'

'We would be dead.'

'So,' George asked, 'what alternatives do we have?'

Nodon said, 'I have gone through all the possibilities. We have enough propellant remaining for only a short burst, nowhere nearly long enough to cut our transit time back to Ceres to anything useful.'

'But the thruster's bunged up, useless.'

'Perhaps we could repair it.'

'Besides, if we use the propellant for thrust we won't have anything left for the power generator. No power for life support. Lights out.'

'No,' Nodon corrected. 'I have reserved enough of the

remaining propellant to keep the power generator running. We are okay there. We won't run short of electrical power.'

'That's something,' George huffed. 'When our corpses arrive back in Ceres space the fookin' ship'll be well lit.'

'Perhaps we can repair the rocket thruster,' Nodon repeated.

George scratched at his beard again. It itched as if some uninvited guests had made their home in it. 'I'm too fookin' tired to go out again and look at the thruster. Gotta get some shuteye first.'

Nodding his agreement, Nodon added, 'And a meal.'

Surveying the depleted list on the galley inventory screen, George muttered, 'Such as it is.'

22

Amanda looked up from her screen and smiled as Fuchs entered their one-room apartment. He did not smile back. He had spent the morning inspecting the ruins of Helvetia's warehouse. The fire had turned the rock-walled chamber into an oven, melting what it did not burn outright. Before it consumed all the oxygen in the cave and died out, it reduced all of Fuchs' stock, all that he had worked for, all that he had planned and hoped for, to nothing but ashes and twisted stumps of melted metal. If the airtight hatches hadn't held, the fire would easily have spread down the tunnels and killed everyone in Ceres.

Fuchs trembled with rage at the thought. The murdering vermin don't worry about that. They don't care. So everyone in Ceres dies, what is that to Humphries? What does it matter to him, so long as he gets his way and removes the thorn in his side?

I am that thorn, Fuchs told himself. I am only a little inconvenience, a minor nuisance in his grandiose plans for conquest.

Thinking of the blackened, ruined warehouse, Fuchs said to himself, This thorn in your side will go deeper into your flesh, Humphries. I will infect you, I will inflame you until you feel the same kind of pain that you've inflicted on so many others. I swear it!

Yet, by the time he trod back to his home, coughing in the dust stirred up by his strides, he felt more weary than angry, wondering how he had come to travel down this path, why this weight of vengeance had fallen onto his shoulders. It's not vengeance, he snarled inwardly. It's justice. Someone has to stand for justice; Humphries can't be allowed to take everything he wants without being accountable to anyone.

Then he slid back the door to his quarters and saw Amanda's beautiful, radiant smile. And the anger surged back in full fury. Humphries wants her, too, Fuchs reminded himself. The only way he'll get Amanda is over my dead body.

Amanda got up from her desk and came to him. He took her in his arms, but instead of kissing him, she rubbed her fingers against his cheek.

'You have a smudge on your face,' she said, still smiling. 'Like a little boy who's been out playing in the streets.'

'Soot from the warehouse,' he said bleakly.

She pecked him on the lips, then said, 'I have some good news.'

'Yes?'

'The insurance money was deposited in Helvetia's account this morning. We can get started again without borrowing from Pancho.'

'How much?'

Amanda's smile faded a fraction. 'Just a tad less than half of what we applied for. About forty-eight per cent of our actual loss.'

'Forty-eight per cent,' he muttered, heading for the lav.

'It's more hard cash than we had when we started Helvetia, darling.'

He knew she was trying to cheer him. 'Yes, that's true, isn't it?' he said as he washed his face. His hands were also grimy with soot, he saw.

He let the dryer blow over his face, noisy and rattling, remembering the luxury of having actual cloth towels at the hotel in Selene. We could do that here, Fuchs told himself.

Vacuum clean them on the surface just as they do at Selene. It would save us electrical power, if we could keep the laundry out of the dust up on the surface.

'Any word from *Starpower*?' he asked as he stepped back into the main room.

'She's on the way in,' Amanda said. 'She'll be here when the lease is up, at the end of the month.'

'Good.'

Amanda's expression turned grave. 'Lars, do you think it's a good idea for you to take *Starpower* out? Can't you hire a crew and stay here?'

'Crews cost money,' he said. 'And we'd have to share whatever we find with the crew. I can handle the ship by myself.'

'But you'll be alone . . .'

He knew what she meant. Ships had disappeared out in the Belt. And he was marked for murder by Humphries.

'I'll be all right,' he said. 'They won't know where I'm going.'

Amanda shook her head. 'Lars, all they have to do is tap into the IAA's net and they'll see your tracking beacon. They'll know exactly where you are.'

He almost smiled. 'Not if the tracking beacon is coming from a drone that I release a day or so after I've left Ceres.'

She looked totally surprised. 'But that would be a violation of IAA regulations!'

'Yes, it would. It would also make my life much safer.'

The work of cleaning up the charred mess of his warehouse took several days. It was hard to find men or women to do the menial labour; they demanded the same level of pay they could get working someone's computer systems or crewing one of the prospecting ships. So Fuchs hired all four of the teenagers on Ceres. They were eager to have something to do outside of their school hours, happy to be away from their lesson screens, happier still to be earning spendable money. Still, Fuchs did most of the labour himself, since the kids could only work a couple of hours each day.

After several days, though, the four youngsters failed to show up for work. Fuchs phoned each of them and got a variety of lame excuses.

'My parents don't want me working.'

'I got too much studying to do.'

Only one of them hinted at the truth. 'My father got an e-message that said he could lose his job if he let me work for you.'

Fuchs didn't have to ask who the father worked for. He knew: Humphries Space Systems.

So he laboured alone in the warehouse cave, finally clearing out the last of the charred debris. Then he started putting together new shelving out of discarded scraps of metal from the maintenance bays.

One evening, as he scuffed wearily along the dusty tunnel after a long day of putting up his new shelving, Fuchs was accosted by two men wearing HSS coveralls.

'You're Lars Fuchs, aren't you?' said the taller of the pair. He was young, not much more than a teenager himself: his dirty-blond hair was cropped close to his skull; his coverall sleeves were rolled up past his elbows. Fuchs saw tattoos on both his forearms.

'I am,' Fuchs answered, without slowing down.

They fell in step with him, one on either side. The shorter of the two was still a couple of centimetres taller than Fuchs, with the chunky build of a weightlifter. His hair was long and dark, his face swarthy.

'I've got a piece of friendly advice for you,' said the taller one. 'Take your insurance money and leave Ceres.'

Still shuffling along the tunnel, Fuchs said, 'You seem to know something about my business.'

'Just get out of here, before there's trouble,' the other one said. His accent sounded Latino.

Fuchs stopped and looked them up and down. 'Trouble?' he asked. 'The only trouble that happens here will be trouble that you start.'

The taller one shrugged. 'Doesn't matter who starts it. What matters is, who's still standing when it's over.'

'Thank you,' said Fuchs. 'Your words will be useful evidence.'

'Evidence?' They both looked startled.

'Do you think I'm a fool?' Fuchs said sharply. 'I know what you're up to. I'm wearing a transmitter that is sending every word you say to IAA headquarters in Geneva. If anything happens to me, you two have already been voiceprinted.'

With that, Fuchs turned on his heel and strode away from the two toughs, leaving them dumbfounded and uncertain. Fuchs walked carefully, deliberately, stirring up as little dust as possible. He didn't want them to think he was running away from them; he also didn't want them to see how his legs were shaking. Above all, he didn't want them to figure out that his transmitter was a total bluff, invented on the spot to allow him to get away from them.

By the time he got home, he was still trembling, but now it was with anger. Amanda flashed a welcoming smile at him from the computer desk. Fuchs could see from the wallscreen that she was ordering inventory to stock the warehouse. Most of the machinery and electronic gear she ordered came from Astro Corporation. Now, he saw, she was dealing with foodstuffs and clothing, which came from other companies. He went to wash up as she stared wistfully at the latest Earthside fashions.

By the time he came back into the room, she was finished with the computer. She slid her arms around his neck and kissed him warmly.

'What would you like for dinner?' she asked. 'I just ordered a shipment of seafood from Selene and I'm famished.'

'Anything will do,' he temporized as he disengaged from her and sat at the computer desk.

Amanda went to the freezer as she asked, 'Will you be ready by the time the supplies start arriving?'

Working the computer, his eyes on the wallscreen display, Fuchs barely nodded. 'I'll be ready,' he muttered.

Amanda saw that he was studying the specifications for handheld lasers.

Frowning slightly, she said, 'That looks like the laser that that Buchanan fellow killed Ripley with.'

'It is,' Fuchs said. 'And he tried to kill me with it, too.'

'I've already ordered six of them, with an option for another half dozen when they're sold.'

'I'm thinking of ordering one for myself,' said Fuchs.

'For *Starpower*?'

He looked up at her. His face was grim. 'For myself,' he said. 'As a sidearm.'

23

Starpower swung lazily in the dark, star-choked sky above Ceres. Strange, Fuchs noted as he climbed aboard the shuttlecraft, that the sky still seems so black despite all those stars. Other suns, he thought, billions of them blazing out their light for eons. Yet here on the rubble-heap surface of Ceres the world seemed dark, shadowy with menace.

Shaking his head inside the fishbowl helmet, Fuchs clambered up the ladder and ducked through the shuttlecraft's hatch. No sense taking off the suit until I'm inside *Starpower*, he told himself. The shuttle flight would take mere minutes to lift him from the asteroid's surface to his waiting ship.

The shuttle's hab module was a bubble of glassteel. Two other prospectors were already aboard, waiting to be transferred to their spacecraft. Fuchs said a perfunctory hello to them through his suit radio.

'Hey, Lars,' one of them asked, 'what are you gonna do about the habitat?'

'Yeah,' chimed in the other one. 'We put up good money to build it. When's it going to be finished so we can move in?'

Fuchs could see their faces through their helmets. They weren't being accusative or even impatient. They looked more curious than anything else.

He forced a weak smile for them. 'I haven't had a chance to recruit a new project engineer, someone to replace Ripley.'

'Oh. Yeah. Too bad about the Ripper.'

'You did a good thing, Lars. That sonofabitch murdered the Ripper in cold blood.'

Fuchs nodded his acknowledgement of their praise. The voice of the IAA controller told them the shuttlecraft would lift off in ten seconds. The computer counted off the time. The three spacesuited men stood in the hab module; there were no seats, nothing except a t-shaped podium that held the ship's controls, which weren't needed for this simple flight, and foot loops in the deck to hold them down in microgravity.

Liftoff was little more than a gentle nudge, but the craft leaped away from Ceres' pitted, rock-strewn surface fast enough to make Fuchs' stomach lurch. Before he could swallow down the bile in his throat they were in zero-g. Fuchs had never enjoyed weightlessness, but he put up with it as the IAA controller remotely steered the shuttle to the orbiting ship of the other two men before swinging almost completely around the asteroid to catch up with *Starpower*.

Fuchs thought about hiring a replacement for Ripley. The funding for the habitat was adequate, barely. He had put the task on Amanda's list of action items. She'll have to do it, Fuchs said to himself. She'll have to use her judgment; I'll be busy doing other things.

Other things. He cringed inwardly when he thought of the angry words he had flung at Humphries: *I've studied military history . . . I know how to fight.* How pathetic! So what are you going to do, go out and shoot up Humphries spacecraft? Kill his employees? What will that accomplish, except getting you arrested eventually or killed? You think too much, Lars Fuchs. You are quick to anger, but then your conscience frustrates you.

He had thought long and hard about searching out HSS

vessels and destroying them. Hurt Humphries the way he's hurt me. But he knew he couldn't do it.

After all his bold words, all his blazing fury, the best he could think of was to find an asteroid, put in a claim for it, and then wait for Humphries' hired killers to come after him. Then he'd have the evidence he needed to make the IAA take official action against Humphries.

If he lived through the ordeal.

Once the shuttle made rendezvous with *Starpower* and docked at the spacecraft's main airlock, Fuchs entered his ship and began squirming out of the spacesuit, grateful for the feeling of gravity that the ship's spin imparted. The bold avenger, he sneered at himself. Going out to offer yourself as a sacrificial victim in an effort to bring Humphries down. A lamb trying to trap a tiger.

As he entered the bridge, still grumbling to himself, the yellow MESSAGE WAITING signal was blinking on the communications screen.

Amanda, he knew. Sure enough, the instant he called up the comm message, her lovely face filled the screen.

But she looked troubled, distraught.

'Lars, it's George Ambrose. His ship's gone missing. All communications abruptly shut off several days ago. The IAA isn't even getting telemetry. They're afraid he's dead.'

'George?' Fuchs gaped at his wife's image. 'They've killed George?'

'It looks that way,' said Amanda.

Amanda stared at her husband's face on the wallscreen in their quarters. Grim as death, he looked.

'They killed George,' he repeated.

She wanted to say, No, it must have been an accident. But the words would not leave her lips.

'*He* had George killed,' Fuchs muttered. 'Murdered.'

'There's nothing we can do about it,' Amanda heard herself say. It sounded more like a plea than a statement, even to her own ears.

'Isn't there?' he growled.

'Lars, please . . . don't do anything . . . dangerous,' she begged.

He slowly shook his head. 'Just being alive is dangerous,' he said.

Dorik Harbin studied the navigation screen as he sat alone on the bridge of *Shanidar*. The blinking orange cursor that showed his ship's position was exactly on the thin blue curve representing his programmed approach to the supply vessel.

Harbin had been cruising through the Belt for more than two months, totally alone except for the narcotics and virtual reality chips that provided his only entertainment. A good combination, he thought. The drugs enhanced the electronic illusion, allowed him to fall asleep without dreaming of the faces of the dead, without hearing their screams.

His ship ran in silence; no tracking beacon or telemetry signals betrayed his presence in space. His orders had been to find certain prospectors and miners and eliminate them. This he had done with considerable efficiency. Now, his supplies low, he was making rendezvous with a Humphries supply vessel. He would get new orders, he knew, while *Shanidar* was being restocked with food and propellant.

I'll have them flush my water tanks, too, and refill them, Harbin thought idly as he approached the vessel. After a couple of months recycled water began to taste suspiciously like piss.

He linked with the supply vessel and stayed only long enough for the replenishment to be completed. He didn't

196

leave his own ship, except for one brief visit to the private cabin of the supply vessel's captain. She handed him a sealed packet which Harbin immediately tucked into the breast pocket of his jumpsuit.

'Must you leave so soon?' the captain asked. She was in her thirties, Harbin judged, not really pretty but attractive in a feline, self-assured way. 'We have all sorts of, um . . . amenities aboard my ship.'

Harbin shook his head. 'No thank you.'

'The newest recreational drugs.'

'I must get back to my ship,' he said curtly.

'Not even a meal? Our cook—'

Harbin turned and reached for the cabin's door latch.

'There's nothing to be afraid of,' the captain said, smiling knowingly.

Harbin looked at her sharply. 'Afraid? Of you?' He barked out a single, dismissive laugh. Then he left her cabin and went immediately back to his own ship.

Only after he had broken away from the supply vessel and was heading deeper into the Belt did he open the packet and remove the chip it contained. As he expected, it contained a list of ships to be attacked, together with their planned courses and complete details of their construction. Another death list, Harbin thought as he studied the images passing across his screen.

Abruptly, the specification charts ended and Grigor's lean, melancholy face appeared on the screen.

'This has been added at the last moment,' Grigor said, his dour image replaced by the blueprints of a ship. 'The ship's name is *Starpower*. We do not have a course for it yet, but that data will be sent to you via tight-beam laser as soon as it becomes available.'

Harbin's eyes narrowed. That means I'll have to get to the preplanned position to receive the laser beam and loiter there until they send the information. He did not like the idea of waiting.

'This is top priority,' Grigor's voice droned over the image of *Starpower*'s construction details. 'This must be done before you go after any other ships.'

Harbin wished he could talk back to Grigor, ask questions, demand more information.

Grigor's face appeared on the screen again. 'Destroy this one ship and you might not need to deal with any of the others. Eliminate *Starpower* and you might be able to return to Earth for good.'

Waltzing Matilda

'I have good news,' Nodon said as George pushed through the hatch into the bridge. 'While you were on EVA I wired the back-up laser into the comm system.'

George squeezed into the right-hand seat. 'The back-up laser?'

'From our supply stocks. Back in the storage section.'

'And it works?'

Nodon beamed happily. 'Yes. The laser can carry our communications signals. We can call for help now.'

Breaking into a guarded smile, George asked, 'We'll hafta point it at Ceres, then.'

'The pointing is the problem,' Nodon said, his happiness diminishing. 'At the distance we are from Ceres, the beam disperses only a dozen kilometres or so.'

'So we hafta point it straight onto the optical receivers, then.'

'If we can.'

'And the fookin' 'roid rotates in about nine hours or so, right?'

'I believe so,' Nodon said. 'I can look it up.'

'So that means we'd hafta hit their optical receivers bung on at just the right time when they're pointin' toward us.'

'Yes,' said Nodon.

'Like playin' a fookin' game o' darts over a distance of thousands of kilometres.'

'Hundreds of thousands.'

'Fat chance.'

Nodon bowed his head. For a moment George thought he might be praying. But then he looked up again and asked, 'What of the engine? Can you repair the thruster?'

George grunted. 'Oh, sure. Yeah.'

'You can?'

'If I had a repair shop available and a half-dozen welders, pipefitters and other crew.'

'Oh.'

Heaving a weary sigh, George said, 'We'll hafta depend on the laser, pal. The fookin' engine's a lost cause.'

24

Lars Fuchs didn't spend more than five minutes deciding what he was going to do. He called up the flight history data on *Waltzing Matilda*. Sure enough, Big George and his crewman had been working a fair-sized carbonaceous asteroid, according to the data they had telemetered back to the IAA. They had started mining it, then all communications from their ship had abruptly cut off. Efforts by the IAA controllers on Ceres to contact them had proved fruitless.

Evidence, Fuchs thought as he studied the flight data on his main comm screen. If I can locate *Waltzing Matilda* and find evidence that the ship was attacked, deliberately destroyed, then I can get the authorities Earthside to step in and do a thorough investigation of all these missing ships.

Sitting alone on the bridge of *Starpower*, he tapped the coordinates of the asteroid George had been working into his navigation computer. But his hand hovered over the key that would engage the program.

Do I want the IAA to know where I'm going? He asked himself. The answer has to be a clear *no*. Whoever is destroying the prospectors' and miners' ships must have exact information about their courses and positions. They can use the telemetry data that each ship sends out automatically to track the ships down.

He knew he must run silently; he had known it all along. Not even Amanda will know where I am. The thought of the risk bothered him; the reason for sending out the telemetry signal was so that the IAA would know where each ship was. But what good is that? Fuchs asked himself. When a ship gets in trouble, no one comes out to help. The Belt is too enormous. If I run into a problem I'm on my own. All the telemetry data will do is tell the IAA where I was when I died.

It took the better part of a day for Fuchs to take out *Starpower*'s telemetry transmitter and install it into the little emergency vehicle. Each ship carried at least one escape pod; six people could live in one for a month or more. An example of so-called safety regulations that looked important to the IAA and were in fact useless, ridiculous. An escape pod made sense for spacecraft working the Earth/Moon region. A rescue ship could reach them in a few days, often in a matter of mere hours. But out here in the Belt, forget about rescue. The distances were too large and the possible rescue ships too few. The prospectors knew they were on their own as soon as they left Ceres.

Fuchs grinned to himself as he thought about all the other uses the emergency vehicles had been put to: extra storage capacity; extra crew quarters; microgravity love nest, when detached from the spinning ship so the pod would be weightless.

But you, he said silently as he installed the telemetry transmitter into *Starpower*'s escape pod, you will be a decoy. They will think you are me, while I head silently for George's asteroid.

Once he returned to the bridge and sat in the command chair, he thought of Amanda. Should I tell her what I'm about to do? He wanted to, but feared that his message would be overheard by Humphries' people. It's obvious that they have infiltrated the IAA, Fuchs thought. Perhaps the flight controllers on Ceres are secretly taking money from him.

If something happens to the escape pod, Amanda will think I've been killed. How can I warn her, let her know what I'm doing?

Then he felt an icy hand grip his heart. What would Amanda do if she thought I was dead? Would she mourn me? Try to avenge me? Or would she run to Humphries? That's what *he* wants. That's why he wants me dead. Will Amanda give in to him if she thinks I'm out of the way?

He hated himself for even thinking such a thought. But he could not escape it. His face twisted into an angry frown, teeth clenched so hard his jaws ached, he banged out the keyboard commands that ejected the pod into a long, parabolic trajectory that would send it across the Belt. It took an effort of will, but he did not send a message back to his wife.

I'm alone now, Fuchs thought as he directed *Starpower* toward the asteroid where Big George had last been heard from.

Diane Verwoerd was reading her favorite Bible passage: the story of the crooked steward who cheated his boss and made himself a nice featherbed for his retirement.

Whenever she had qualms about what she was doing, she called up Luke 16: 1–13. It reassured her. Very few people understood the real message of the story, she thought as she read the ancient words on the wallscreen of her apartment.

The steward was eventually fired, when his boss found out about his cheating. But the key to the tale was that the steward's thefts from his master's accounts were not so huge that the master wanted vengeance. He just fired the guy. And all through the years that the steward had been working for this master, he had put away enough loot so he could live comfortably in retirement. A sort of golden parachute that the boss didn't know about.

Verwoerd leaned back languidly in her recliner chair. It adjusted its shape to the curves of her body and massaged her gently, soothingly. It had originally belonged to Martin Humphries, but she had shown him an advertisement for a newer model, which he had immediately bought and then instructed her to get rid of this one. So she removed it from his office and installed it in her own quarters.

With a voice command she ordered the computer to show her personal investment account. The numbers instantly filled the wallscreen. Not bad for a girl from the slums of Amsterdam, she congratulated herself. Over the years she'd avoided the usual pitfalls of prostitution and drug dependency and even steered clear of becoming some rich fart's mistress. So far, so good.

She spoke to the computer again and the list of asteroids whose claims she personally owned appeared on the screen. Only a half dozen of the little rocks, but they were producing ores nicely and building up profits steeply. Taxes would take a sizeable chunk of the money, but Verwoerd reminded herself that no government can tax money that you don't have. Pay the taxes and be glad you owe them, she told herself.

Of course, Martin thought that HSS owned the claims to those asteroids. But with so many others in his clutches, a mere half-dozen was down below his radar horizon. Besides, whenever he wanted to check on anything, he always asked his trusted assistant to do it. So he'll never find out about this little pilfering until after I've left his employment.

She cleared the list from the screen, and the verses from Luke came up again.

I'll be able to retire very comfortably in a couple of years, Verwoerd told herself. It will all work out fine, as long as I don't get too greedy – and as long as I keep Martin at arm's length. The moment I give in to him, my days as an HSS employee are numbered.

She looked at her reflection in the mirror across the room and smiled to herself. Maybe I'll give him a little fling, once I'm ready to retire. Once he fires me, I'll get severance pay. Or at least a nice little going-away present from Martin. He's like that.

Turning from her own image back to the words from the Bible, she frowned slightly at the final verse:

No man can serve two masters; for either he will hate the one, and love the other, or else he will hold to one, and despise the other. You cannot serve God and Mammon.

Perhaps, thought Diane Verwoerd. But I'm not really serving Martin Humphries. I'm working for him. I'm getting rather wealthy off him. But I'm serving only myself, no one else.

Still, she cleared the wallscreen with a single sharp command to the computer. The Bible passage disappeared, replaced by a reproduction of a Mary Cassatt painting of a mother and child.

Dossier: Joyce Takamine

You had to have an education to be considered for a job at Selene. The lunar nation was hiring engineers and technicians, not fruit pickers. Joyce's passport to the Moon was a battered old palmcomp that her father had given her. Through it she could access virtually any class in any university on the nets. She studied every night, even when she was so tired from picking that she could barely find the strength to open the palmcomp's scuffed plastic lid.

The other pickers complained that the flickering light kept them from sleeping, so Joyce moved outside the barracks and kept doggedly at her studies out in the open, under the stars. When she looked up at the Moon and saw Selene's beacon light, it seemed to her as if that laser's bright beam was calling to her.

Once, a guy she briefly slept with stole her palmcomp; just walked off with it, as if he owned it. In a panicked fury, Joyce tracked him down at the next camp and nearly took his head off with a two-by-four. The owner's guards let her go, once she told them the whole story. They had no use for thieves, especially stupid ones who let a scrawny oriental girl cold-cock them.

In three years, Joyce got her degree in computer systems analysis from California Coast University. She applied for an advertised job at Selene. She didn't get it. Four hundred and twenty-seven other people, most of them just as desperate and needy as Joyce, had applied for the same position.

The same day that she was turned down by Selene she got the message that both her parents had died in a freeway pile-up during the earthquake that destroyed the shanty-towns up in the hills above the drowned ruins of San Francisco.

25

Nothing.

Fuchs scowled at the display screens that curved around his command chair, then looked out through the bridge's windows. No sign of *Waltzing Matilda*. Nothing here but the lumpy, irregular shape of an asteroid tumbling slowly in the barren emptiness, dark and pitted and strewn with small boulders and rocks.

This was the last position that the IAA had for Big George's ship. *Matilda*'s telemetering had cut off here, at this location. But the ship was nowhere in sight.

Almost without consciously thinking about it, he put *Starpower* into a tight orbit around the little asteroid. Was George really here? He wondered. If he was, he probably didn't linger very—

Then he saw an area on the 'roid where neat rectangular slabs had been cut out of the rock. George *had* been here! He had started to mine the asteroid. Turning up the magnification on his telescope to max, Fuchs saw that there was still some equipment standing on the surface. He left in a hurry, Fuchs realized, too much of a hurry to pick up all his gear.

It was a cutting laser, Fuchs saw, still standing silently at the edge of one of the cut-out rectangles. I must retrieve it, he said to himself. It could be evidence.

The easiest way to get it would be to suit up and go EVA. But with no one else in the ship, Fuchs decided against that. Instead, he manoeuvred *Starpower* into an orbit that matched the asteroid's own spin, the tip of his tongue apprehensively between his teeth, then slowly, carefully, brought the big ship to within a dozen metres of the rocky surface.

Using the manipulator arms on *Starpower*'s equipment module, Fuchs snatched the laser up off the asteroid and tucked it inside the cargo bay. He was soaked with perspiration by the time the job was done, but felt proud of his piloting.

Mopping his forehead, Fuchs resisted the temptation to call Ceres and ask if they had any fresh data on George's ship. No! he scolded himself. You must remain silent.

Maybe that's what George is doing, he thought. Gone silent, so no one can find him. Obviously he left in a big hurry. Most likely he was attacked, perhaps killed. But if he got away, now he's staying silent to keep his attacker from finding him again.

But what do I do now? Fuchs wondered.

He left the bridge and went to the galley. The brain needs nourishment, he said to himself. I can't think well on an empty stomach. He realized that his coverall shirt was sticky with perspiration. Honest work, he told himself. But it doesn't smell good.

But by the time he washed up and ate a prepackaged meal, he still had no clear idea of what he should do next.

Find George, he thought. Yes, but how?

Back to the bridge he went and called up the search and rescue program from the computer files. 'Ahah!' he said aloud. Expanding spiral.

Standard operational procedure for a search mission was to fly an expanding spiral out from the last known position of the lost spacecraft. The one thing that worried Fuchs, though, was that George might have gone batting off at a high angle off the ecliptic. While the major planets orbited within a few degrees of the ecliptic path, plenty of asteroids roamed twenty or thirty degrees above or below that plane. Suppose George had gone angling away at high thrust? Fuchs knew he'd never find him then.

As it was, the Belt was so huge that even if George stuck close to the ecliptic plane, he could be halfway to hell by now. A few days at high thrust could push a ship all the way back to Earth. Or out past Jupiter.

Still, there was nothing more that Fuchs could do but fly his expanding spiral, and sweep with his radar at high angles above and below his position while he moved away from the asteroid.

He set the course, then got into his spacesuit to slither down the long buckyball cable that connected *Starpower*'s habitation unit with the equipment module. The hollow cable was big enough for a person to squeeze through, but it was not pressurized. He had to wear a suit, and that made crawling along the kilometre-long cable a long, arduous chore. Still, Fuchs had nothing else to do, and he wanted to see the laser that George had left behind.

Dorik Harbin was searching, too.

He had picked up *Starpower*'s telemetry signals within hours of Fuchs' leaving Ceres and tracked the departing ship from a safe distance.

Before the day was out, however, the telemetry signal had abruptly cut off. Harbin debated moving close enough to the ship to sight it visually, but before he could make up his mind to do that, the telemetry came back on and showed that *Starpower* was moving again, cutting diagonally across the Belt at high thrust.

Where could he be going? Harbin asked himself. He must have a specific destination in mind, going at that velocity.

He matched *Starpower*'s course and speed, staying far

enough behind the departing spacecraft so that he wouldn't be spotted. Even if Fuchs was cautious enough to probe behind him with radar, the beam would be so scattered by his own engine's exhaust that he'd never see me, Harbin thought. He stayed within the shadow of Fuchs' exhaust cloud and trailed *Starpower*.

Again he thought of Grigor's comment: destroy *Starpower* and all this hunting and killing might be finished. I'll get my money and a considerable bonus, Harbin thought. I can go back to Earth and find a safe area and live like an emir for the rest of my life.

Where would the best place be, on Earth? I want a warm climate, safe from the rising sea levels, no earthquakes, stable government. A wealthy country, not one where half the population is starving and the other half plotting revolution. Canada, perhaps. Or Australia. They have very tight restrictions on immigration, but with enough money a man can go wherever he wants. Maybe Spain, he thought. Barcelona is still livable and Madrid hasn't had a food riot in years.

26

Hiring reliable people was Amanda's biggest headache. She worried about her husband sailing all alone out into the Belt, trying like so many others to strike it rich. Or was he? Her greatest fear was that Lars was out seeking revenge on Humphries by attacking HSS ships. Even if he didn't get killed he'd become an outlaw, a pariah.

She tried to force such thoughts out of her mind as she worked at restarting their supply business on the insurance money from the fire.

Labour was at a premium on Ceres. Most of the people who came out to the Belt went prospecting, intent on finding a rich asteroid and becoming wealthy from its ores. Even the experienced hands who had learned from bitter experience that most prospectors barely broke even, while the big corporations raked in the profits from selling ores, still went out time and again, always seeking the 'big one' that would make their fortunes. Or they worked as miners, taking the ores from asteroids, either as corporate employees or under contract to one of the big corporations. Miners didn't get rich, but they didn't starve, either.

Amanda had taken courses in economics at college. She understood that the more asteroids were mined, the more plentiful their metals and minerals, the lower their value. A corporation like Astro or HSS could afford to work on a slim profit margin, because they handled such an enormous volume of ores. A lone prospector had to sell at market prices, and the price was always far below their starry-eyed dreams.

She frowned as she dressed for another day of work. *Then why is Lars out there, prospecting? He knows the odds as well as anyone does. And why hasn't he sent any messages to me? He warned me that he wouldn't, but I thought that after a few days he'd at least tell me he's all right.*

The answer was clear to her, but she didn't want to believe it. *He's not prospecting. He's out there on some insane kind of mission to get even with Martin. He wants to fight back – one man against the most powerful corporation in the solar system. He'll get himself killed, and there's nothing I can do about it.*

That was what hurt her the most, that feeling of utter impotence, the knowledge that there was no way she could protect, or even help, the man she loved. *He's gone away from me,* she realized. *Not merely physically; Lars has moved away from me, away from our marriage, away from our relationship. He's let his anger override our love. He's after vengeance now, no matter what it costs.*

Fighting back the tears, she booted up her computer and took up where she'd left off the previous night, searching for people willing to work in the warehouse. In her desperation she had even sent a call to Pancho, back Earthside. Now, as the wallscreen sprang to life, she saw that Pancho had returned her message.

'Show Pancho Lane's message,' she commanded the computer.

Pancho's angular face grinned at her. She appeared to be in an office somewhere in the tropics. Probably Astro's corporate headquarters in Venezuela.

'Got your sad story, Mandy. I can 'preciate how tough it

is to get reliable people to work in your warehouse. Wish I could ship you a couple of my folks, but nobody with a decent job here is gonna go peacefully out to Ceres unless they got asteroid fever and think they're gonna become zillionaires in six weeks.'

Hunching closer to the camera, Pancho went on, 'Lemme warn you about one thing, though: some of the people who might agree to work for you could be HSS plants. Screen ever'body real careful, kid. There's skunks in the woodwork, I bet.'

Amanda shook her head wearily. As if I didn't have enough to worry about, she thought.

Pancho leaned back again and said, 'I'm off to Lawrence, Kansas. Got a meeting with the international consortium of universities to work out a deal to build a research station in Jupiter orbit. Might be some college kids looking for jobs. Lord knows there's enough unemployment around. I'll see what I can find for you. In the meantime, watch your butt. That ol' Humper still wants to take over Astro, and you'n' Lars are standing in his way.'

With a cheerful wave, Pancho signed off. Amanda felt like crawling back into bed and staying there until Lars returned.

If he returned at all.

How long should I search? Fuchs asked himself. It's been three days now, and no sign of George. No sign of anything.

He had known, intellectually, that the Belt was almost entirely empty space. Even in his freshman astronomy course he remembered it being compared to a big, empty theatre that contained only a few specks of dust floating in its vast volume. Now he felt the reality of it. Staring out the windows in the bridge of *Starpower*, studying the screens that displayed the radar scans and telescopic views, he saw that there was nothing out there, nothing but empty space, darkness and eternal silence.

He thought of how Columbus' crew must have felt, alone out in the middle of the Atlantic without even a bird in sight; nothing but empty sea and emptier sky.

Then the comm unit chirped.

Fuchs was startled by the unexpected noise. He turned in the command chair and saw that the communications display showed an incoming message had been received on the optical comm system.

An optical signal? Puzzled, he asked the comm computer to display the message.

The screen flashed into a harsh jumble of colours while the speakers rasped with hisses and squeaks. Only random noise, Fuchs thought. Probably a solar flare or a gamma burster.

But the other sensors showed no evidence of a solar flare and, once he thought about it, Fuchs realized that a gamma-ray burst would not have registered on the optical receiver.

He ordered the navigation program to move *Starpower* back to the area where the optical signal had been detected. Turning a ship of *Starpower*'s mass was no simple matter. It took time and energy. But at last the nav computer reported it was done.

Nothing. The comm system remained silent.

It was a fluke, Fuchs told himself. An anomaly. Still, *something* must have caused it, and he felt certain that it wasn't a glitch in the communications equipment. Nonsense, snapped the reasoning part of his brain. You're convinced because you want it to be a signal. You're letting your hopes overbalance your good sense.

Yes, that's true, Fuchs admitted to himself. But he

ordered the nav system to move *Starpower* along the vector the spurious signal had come from.

Hoping that his gut feeling was closer to the mark than his rational mind, Fuchs followed that course for an hour, then two, then—

The comm screen lit up with a weak, grainy picture of what looked to Fuchs like a bald, emaciated Asian.

'This is the *Waltzing Matilda*. We are disabled and unable to control our course. We need help urgently.'

Fuchs stared at the streaky image for several slack-jawed moments, then flew into a flurry of activity, trying to pin down *Matilda*'s location and move his own ship to her as quickly as possible while getting off a signal to her on every channel his comm system could transmit on.

Dorik Harbin was furious.

It's a decoy! he raged. A stupid, sneaking decoy! And you fell for it. You followed it like an obedient puppy halfway to hell!

He had manoeuvred *Shanidar* slightly away from the exhaust wake of what he'd thought was *Starpower* more out of boredom than any intelligent reason. He'd been following the ship's telemetry signals for several days, intent on finding where it was heading. His standing orders from Grigor were to wait until a ship took up orbit around a particular asteroid, then destroy it. Harbin knew without Grigor's telling him that HSS then claimed the asteroid for itself.

But after several days his quarry showed no indications of searching for an asteroid. It simply puttered along at low thrust, like a tourist boat showing off the local sights. Except that there were no tourists out here and no sights to show; the Belt was cold and empty.

Now Harbin could see clearly in his screens that what

he'd been following was not *Starpower* at all but a crew emergency vehicle, a miserable escape pod.

This was no accident. Fuchs had deliberately set him up while he went off in some other direction. Where? Grigor would not be happy to learn that he'd failed. Harbin swore to himself that he would find Fuchs and destroy the cunning dog as soon as he did.

If he reversed his course it would cost so much of his propellant that he'd need another topping off within a few days. And the nearest HSS ship was at least three days off. Harbin searched his sensor screens. What he needed was a fair-sized rock close enough . . .

He found one, an asteroid that had enough mass for the manoeuvre he had in mind. Too small for a slingshot move, but Harbin eased close to the rock and put *Shanidar* into a tight orbit around it. He checked his nav computer twice before setting up the program. At precisely the proper instant he fired his thrusters and *Shanidar* shot away from the unnamed asteroid in the direction Harbin wanted, at a fraction of the propellant loss that a powered turnaround would have cost.

Now he sped back toward the region where *Starpower* had fired off its decoy. That was easy to calculate: it had to be where *Starpower*'s telemetry signals went off for a few hours. That was when the clever dog had transferred his transmitter to the escape pod. He had been running silent ever since.

Or maybe not, Harbin reasoned. He might be communicating with Ceres on another channel. Or perhaps signaling some other ship.

So Harbin kept all his communications receivers open as he raced back to the area where Fuchs had fooled him into following the decoy.

Chance favours the prepared mind. After two days of

running at full thrust, Harbin picked up the distant, weak signal of Fuchs answering *Waltzing Matilda*'s distress call.

So that's where he's going. Harbin nodded to himself, satisfied that now he could destroy *Starpower* and finish the job on *Waltzing Matilda*.

Waltzing Matilda

George had drifted to sleep in the co-pilot's chair, leaving Nodon to monitor the control console. There wasn't much to monitor. They were still drifting helplessly, alone, slowly starving.

'I have a signal!' Nodon exulted.

His shout roused George from a dream about dining with a beautiful woman in the Earthview Restaurant back in Selene. Groggy with sleep, George knuckled his eyes, wondering which was more important in his dream, the woman or the tucker.

'What signal?' he mumbled.

Nodon was quivering with excitement. 'Look!' He pointed a bony, shaking finger at the comm screen. 'Look!'

George blinked several times. By crikes, there was Lars Fuchs' dour, dead-serious face on the screen. George had never seen anyone more beautiful.

'I have received your distress call and am proceeding at full thrust to your position. Please home on my beacon and keep repeating your signal so my nav system can maintain an accurate track on you.'

Nodon's fingers were already dancing across the keyboard on the control console.

'Ask 'im how long it'll take him to reach us,' George said.

'I have already fed the data into the computer.' Nodon

tapped a few more keystrokes. 'Ah. Here is the answer. Fifty-two hours.'

'A little more'n two days.' George broke into a shaggy smile. 'We can hold up for two more days, can't we, mate?'

'Yes! Certainly!'

27

Harbin listened intently to the messages that Fuchs was beaming out. Coldly, he thought, if the fool kept himself restricted to laser signals I wouldn't have been able to detect him. Radio signals expand through space like a swelling balloon. Like a flower opening up to the sun. A blossom of death, he realized.

He knew that he had to conserve his propellant supply; it was already low enough to be of concern. Not a danger, not yet, but he couldn't roar out to his prey at full thrust, not if he wanted to have enough propellant to get back to an HSS tanker. But there was no rush. Let Fuchs rescue whoever is left alive on *Matilda*. I'll simply cruise toward them and intercept *Starpower* on its way back to Ceres.

He kept his communications receivers open, and soon heard Fuchs reporting excitedly back to Ceres that he had located *Waltzing Matilda* and its two-man crew were still alive. Not for long, Harbin thought.

Then a new thought struck him. It was not all that unusual for a prospector's ship to disappear out in the lonely vastness of the Belt. He had destroyed several of them; others had failed without his help. A single ship like *Waltzing Matilda* could wink out of contact, never to be heard from again, and no one would know the cause. Of course, there were grumbles about piracy here and there, but no one really took that seriously.

On the other hand, if *Matilda*'s crew was alive, they would be able to tell what actually happened to them. They'd inform the IAA that they were deliberately attacked and left for dead. He couldn't allow them to survive.

But on the *other* other hand, Harbin mused, how would it look if the ship that rescued *Matilda*'s crew also disappeared? That would raise the rumbles of piracy to the level of a major investigation.

He shook his head, trying to clear his thoughts. I'm out here alone; I can't call back to Grigor or anyone else for instructions. I've got to make the decision here and now.

It took him less than a minute to decide. Let *Starpower* rescue *Matilda*'s crew and then destroy the lot of them. Perhaps I can kill them before they can blab their whole story to Ceres or the IAA.

Amanda's heart pounded in her chest when she answered the INCOMING MESSAGE signal on her computer and Lars' image took shape on her wallscreen.

He looked tense, there were dark circles under his eyes, but his normally severe, gloomy face was smiling widely.

'I've found them! George and his crewman. They're alive and I'm going to pick them up.'

'What happened to them?' Amanda asked, forgetting that her husband was too far away for interactive conversation.

'Their ship is disabled,' Fuchs was saying, 'but they are both uninjured. That's all I know at the moment. I'll send more information after I've taken them aboard my ship.'

The screen went blank, leaving Amanda awash in a thousand questions. But none of them mattered to her. Lars was all right and he wasn't doing anything dangerous. He was going to rescue George and his crewman and then he'd come back to Ceres, back to her.

She felt enormously relieved.

The airlock compartment felt cramped, crowded, once George and his crewman came through the hatch in their bulky spacesuits. And as soon as they started pulling off their suits, Fuchs nearly gagged from the stench.

'You both need showers,' he said, as delicately as he could manage.

George grinned sheepishly through his wildly tangled beard. 'Yeah. Guess we don't smell so sweet, eh?'

The Asian said nothing, but looked embarrassed. He was only a youngster, Fuchs saw.

As Fuchs led them along the passageway to the lav, George said cheerfully, 'Hope you've got a full larder.'

Fuchs nodded, resisting the urge to hold his nose. Then he asked, 'What happened to you?'

Shooing the silent Nodon into the shower stall, George answered, 'What happened? We were attacked, that's what happened.'

'Attacked?'

'Deliberately shot to pieces by a bloke with a high-power laser on his ship.'

'I knew it,' Fuchs muttered.

Nodon discreetly stepped into the shower stall before peeling off his coveralls. Then they heard the spray of water, saw tendrils of steamy air rising from the stall.

'I guess we're not the first to be chopped,' said George. '*Lady of the Lake, Aswan* . . . four or five others, at least.'

'At least,' Fuchs agreed. 'We'll have to inform the IAA of this. Maybe now they'll start a real investigation.'

'Dinner first,' George said. 'Me stomach's growlin'.'

'A shower first,' Fuchs corrected. 'Then you can eat.'

George laughed. 'Suits me.' Raising his voice, he added, 'If we can get a certain bloke out of the fookin' shower stall.'

Harbin was glistening with perspiration as he exercised on the ergonomics bike. *Shanidar* was cruising at one-sixth g, the same grav level as the Moon, but Harbin's military upbringing unsparingly forced him to maintain his conditioning to Earth-normal standards. As he pedalled away and pumped at the hand bars, he watched the display screen on the bulkhead in front of him.

It was a martial arts training vid, one that Harbin had seen dozens of times. But each time he picked up something new, some different little wrinkle that he had overlooked before or forgotten. After his mandatory twenty klicks on the bike, he would rerun the vid and go through its rigorous set of exercises.

But his mind kept coming back to the central problem he faced. How can I prevent Fuchs from informing Ceres of what happened to *Waltzing Matilda*? He's already sent one brief message to his wife. Once he beams out their whole story the IAA will launch a full investigation.

Almost, he smiled. If that happens, my career in piracy is finished. Grigor's superiors might even decide that it would be safer to terminate me than to pay me off.

It's imperative, then, that I silence *Starpower* as quickly as possible. But how? I can't jam their transmissions; I don't have the proper equipment aboard.

I could accelerate, get to them at top speed, knock them out before they get a message back to Ceres. But then I'd be too low on fuel to get back to a tanker. I'd have to signal Grigor to send a tanker to me.

And what better way to be rid of me than to let me drift alone out here until I starve to death or the recyclers break down? That way Grigor and his HSS bosses get total silence, for free.

With a grim shake of his head, Harbin decided he would continue on his present course and speed. He'd catch up to *Starpower* and destroy the ship. Fuchs would die. Harbin only hoped that he could finish the job before Fuchs told Ceres what was going on.

That's in the lap of the gods, he thought. It's a matter of chance. A quatrain from the *Rubáiyát* came to him:

> Ah, Love! Could thou and I with fate conspire
> To grasp this sorry Scheme of Things entire,
> Would not we shatter it to bits – and then
> Re-mould it nearer to the Heart's desire!

Yes, Harbin thought. That would be pleasant, to shatter this world to bits and rebuild it into something better. To have a woman to stand beside me, to love me, to be my heart's desire.

But that is fantasy, he told himself sternly. Reality is this godforsaken emptiness, this dreary ship. Reality is studying ways to kill.

With a deep, heartfelt breath, he said silently, reality is this damned bike, going nowhere but taking all my energy to get there.

28

Fuchs sat in the galley, nearly stunned with amazement as he watched George wolf down enough food to feed an ordinary man for a week. The crewman, Nodon, ate more sparingly but still put away a good pile of rations.

'. . . then after he slagged our antennas,' George was saying through a mouthful of veggieburger and reconstituted potato, 'he zapped the fookin' thruster nozzle and for good measure popped our propellant tanks.'

'He was very thorough,' Fuchs said.

George nodded. 'I figure he musta thought we were still inside the hab module. Nodon and me played doggo until he left. By then, old *Matilda* was driftin' in the general direction of Alpha Centauri.'

'He assumed you were dead.'

'Or as good as.'

'You've got to tell all this to the IAA,' said Fuchs.

'If we'd'a had our cutting laser on board I would've shot back at th' bastard. He caught us with the laser sittin' on the 'roid and our power pack bein' recharged.'

'I have your laser,' Fuchs said. 'It's in the cargo bay.'

Nodon looked up from his food. 'I will check it out.'

'You do that,' George agreed. 'I'll call up the IAA people in Selene.'

'No,' said Fuchs. 'We'll call IAA headquarters on Earth. This story must be told to the top people, and quickly.'

'Okay. Soon's I polish off some dessert. Whatcha got in the freezer?'

Turning to Nodon, Fuchs said, 'I'm carrying a cutting laser, too. It's stored in the cargo bay, along with yours.'

The Asian asked softly, 'Do you want me to connect them both to power sources?'

Fuchs saw calm certainty in the young man's hooded brown eyes. 'Yes, I think it might be wise to have them both operational.'

George caught their meaning as he got up and stepped to the freezer. 'How're you gonna fire 'em from inside the cargo bay, mate?'

'Open the hatches, obviously,' said Fuchs.

'Better wear a suit, then.'

Nodon dipped his chin in silent agreement.

'You both think he'll be back, then,' said Fuchs.

'Perhaps,' Nodon answered.

'Better to be ready if and when,' George said, as he scanned the inventory list on the freezer's display screen. 'I don't wanna be caught with me pants down again. Could be fatal.'

Diane Verwoerd could see that her boss was getting cold feet. Martin Humphries looked uncomfortable, almost nervous, as they entered the spacious living room of his mansion.

'How do I look?' he asked her, something he never did ordinarily.

He was dressed in a full-fledged tuxedo, complete with a bow tie and plaid cummerbund. She smiled, suppressing the urge to tell him he looked like a chubby penguin.

'You look very debonair,' she said.

'Damned silly business. You'd think that after a couple of centuries they'd figure out something better to wear for formal occasions.'

'I'm impressed that you knotted the tie so perfectly.'

He frowned at her. 'It's pre-tied and you know it. Don't be cute.'

Verwoerd was wearing a floor-length sheath of glittering silver, its long skirt slit nearly to the hip.

'Stavenger didn't invite me to the damned opera out of the goodness of his heart,' Humphries complained as they headed for the door. 'He wants to pump me about something and he thinks I'll be off my guard in a social setting.'

'Cocktails and dinner, and then *Il trovatore*,' Verwoerd murmered. 'That's enough to relax you to the point of stupefaction.'

'I hate opera,' he grumbled as he opened the door.

Stepping out into the garden behind him, Verwoerd asked, 'Then why did you accept his invitation?'

He glared at her. 'You know why. Pancho's going to be there. Stavenger's got something up his sleeve. He may be officially retired but he still runs Selene, the power behind the throne. He lifts an eyebrow and everybody hops to do what he wants.'

As they walked through the lush shrubbery and trees that filled the grotto, Verwoerd said, 'I wonder what it is that he wants now?'

Humphries threw a sour glance at her. 'That's what I pay you to find out.'

The cocktail reception was out in the open, under the dome of the Grand Plaza next to the amphitheatre that housed all of Selene's theatrical productions. When Humphries and Verwoerd arrived, Pancho Lane was standing near the bar, deep in earnest conversation with Douglas Stavenger.

Nearly twice Humphries' age, Doug Stavenger still looked as young and vigorous as a thirty-year-old. His body teemed with nanomachines that kept him healthy and youthful. Twice they had saved him from death, repairing damage to his body that would ordinarily have been lethal.

Stavenger was not an ordinary man. His family had founded the original Moonbase, built it from a struggling research station into a major manufacturing centre for nanomachine-built spacecraft. Stavenger himself had directed the brief, sharp battle against the old UN that had established the lunar settlement's independence from Earthside government. He had chosen the name Selene.

Towing Verwoerd on his arm, Humphries pushed through the chatting crowd of tuxedoed men and bejewelled, gowned women to join Stavenger and Pancho. He nearly pushed himself between them.

'Hello, Martin,' Stavenger said, with an easy smile. He was handsome, his face somewhere between rugged and pretty, his skin slightly lighter than Pancho's, a deep golden tan. It always surprised Humphries to see that Stavenger was considerably taller than himself; the man's compact, broad-shouldered build disguised his height effectively.

Without bothering to introduce Verwoerd, Humphries said, 'It looks like you got half of Selene to come out tonight.'

Stavenger laughed lightly. 'The other half is performing in the opera.'

Humphries noticed the way the two women eyed each other from crown to toe, sizing up one another like a pair of gladiators entering the arena.

'Who's your friend?' Pancho asked. Her gown was floor-length, too, and as deeply black as the men's tuxes. Her cropped hair was sprinkled with something glittery. The diamond necklace and bracelet that she wore probably came from asteroidal stones, Humphries guessed.

'Diane Verwoerd,' Humphries said, by way of introduction, 'Pancho Lane. You already know Doug, here, don't you?'

'By reputation,' Verwoerd said, smiling her brightest. 'And it's good to meet you, at last, Ms Lane.'

'Pancho.'

Stavenger said, 'Pancho's trying to talk me into investing in a research station to be set up in Jupiter orbit.'

So that's it, Humphries said to himself.

'Selene's made a pocketful of profits out of building spacecraft,' Pancho said. 'You can make even more from bringing fusion fuels back from Jupiter.'

'She makes a good case,' Stavenger said. 'What do you think of the idea, Martin?'

'I'm on record against it,' Humphries snapped. As if he doesn't know that, he growled inwardly.

'So I'd heard,' Stavenger admitted.

Three-note chimes sounded. 'Time for dinner,' Stavenger said, offering Pancho his arm. 'Come on, Martin, let's talk about this while we eat.'

Humphries followed him toward the tables that had been set up on the manicured grass outside the amphitheatre. Verwoerd walked beside him, convinced that the four of them would be talking about this Jupiter business all through the opera, even the Anvil Chorus.

Which was all right with her. She loathed *Il trovotore*.

29

With Nodon working in the cargo bay, Fuchs finally got George out of the galley and into the bridge.

'You must tell everything that happened to the IAA,' Fuchs said, setting himself in the command chair.

George took the co-pilot's seat; overflowed it, actually. He may have been hungry, Fuchs thought, but he hadn't lost much weight.

'Be glad to, mate,' George said amiably. 'Just get 'em on the horn.'

Fuchs instructed the comm computer to call Francesco Tomaselli at IAA headquarters in St Petersburg.

'Oh-oh,' said George.

Fuchs saw that he was pointing at the radar display. A single blip showed in the upper right corner of the screen.

'He's here,' George said.

'It could be a rock,' Fuchs heard himself say, even though he didn't believe it.

'It's a ship.'

Fuchs tapped on his command keyboard. 'A ship,' he agreed, after a few moments. 'And it's on an intercept course.'

'I'd better get into a suit and back to the cargo bay with Nodon. You suit up, too.'

As he followed George down to the airlock compartment where the spacesuits were stored, Fuchs heard the comm unit's synthesized voice say, 'Signor Tomasselli is not available at this time. Do you want to leave a message?'

Fifteen minutes later Fuchs was back in the bridge, feeling like a medieval knight in armour, wearing the cumbersome spacesuit.

The blip was centered in the radar display now. Fuchs peered through the window into the dark emptiness out there, but he could see nothing.

'He still approaching?' George's voice rasped in his helmet earphones.

'Yes.'

'We got your laser connected to the main power supply. Ours is down, something's buggered it up.'

'But the one is working?'

'Yeah. Swing the ship around so we can get a clear view of 'im.'

'George,' Fuchs said, 'suppose it's not the ship that attacked you?'

A half-moment of silence, then, 'You think somebody else just happened to drop by? Not bloody likely.'

'Don't shoot at him unless he fires on us first,' Fuchs said.

George grumbled, 'You sound like some bleedin' Yank. "Don't fire until you see the whites of their eyes." '

'Well, we shouldn't—'

The comm screen suddenly flashed brightly, then went blank. With gloved fingers Fuchs tapped out a diagnostic command.

'I think he's hit our main antenna,' he said to George.

'Turn the bloody ship so I can shoot back!'

The air pressure alarm started shrilling and Fuchs heard the safety hatch at his back slam shut.

'He's punctured the hull!'

'Turn, dammit!'

236

Hoping the controls still worked, Fuchs heard a startled voice in his head say *Mein gott*, we're in a space battle!

This might work out after all, Harbin told himself.

His first shot had disabled *Starpower*'s main communications antenna. And just in time, too. Fuchs had already put in a call to the IAA back Earthside.

His second shot had holed their habitation module, he was certain. They were swinging their ship around, trying to protect the hab module by moving it behind their cargo bay. Harbin studied the schematics of *Starpower* while he waited for his laser to recharge.

No sense wasting time or energy. Hit the propellant tanks, drain them dry and then leave them to drift helplessly deeper into the Belt.

He shook his head, though. No, first I've got to disable their antennas. All of them. They could scream their heads off to the IAA while I'm puncturing their tanks. They could tell the whole story before they drift away and starve to death. If they had any sense, they'd be broadcasting on all frequencies now. They must be panicked, too terrified to think clearly.

You have much to be terrified of, Harbin said silently to the people aboard *Starpower*. The angel of death is breathing upon you.

'What's he doin'?' George asked.

'He's hit us several times,' Fuchs replied into his helmet microphone. 'He seems to be concentrating on the hab module.'

'Goin' for the antennas, just like he did to us.'

'The antennas?'

'So we can't call for help.'

Fuchs knew that was wrong. What good would it do us

to call for help? It would take ten minutes or more for our signal to reach Ceres. How could anyone possibly help us?

'I can see him!' Nodon shouted.

'Now we can shoot back at 'im,' George said excitedly. 'Hold us steady, dammit.'

Working the reaction jets that controlled the ship's attitude, Fuchs' mind was racing. He's not worried about our calling for help, he realized. He doesn't want us to tell anyone that we're under attack. He wants us to simply disappear, another ship mysteriously lost out in the Belt. If we get a distress call off then everyone will know that ships are being deliberately destroyed. Everyone will know that Humphries is killing people.

He called up the comm system diagnostics. Every last antenna was gone, nothing but a string of baleful red lights glowering along the display screen.

What can we do? Fuchs asked himself. What can we do?

George blinked at the sweat that stung his eyes maddeningly.

'Are you ready?' he shouted at Nodon, even though the spacesuited crewman was hardly three metres from him.

They were standing on either side of the bulky cutting laser, a collection of tubes and vanes and piping that looked too complicated to possibly work correctly. Yet George saw Nodon nod, tight-lipped, inside his bubble helmet.

'Ready,' he said.

George glanced at the control board, leaning slightly canted against the curving bulkhead of the cargo bay. All the lights in the green, he saw. Good. Looking up through the open cargo bay hatch he could see the distant speck of the attacking ship, a cluster of gleaming, sunlit crescents against the dark depths of infinity.

'Fire!' George said, leaning on the red button so hard he

forced himself up off the metal deck. He raised a gloved hand to the overhead and pushed gently, felt his boots touch the deck plates again.

The cutting laser was a continuous wave device, designed to slice through rock. Its aiming system was so primitive that George had to sight the thing by eye. Its infrared beam was invisible, and the red beam of the low-power guide laser disappeared in the emptiness of space. In the vacuum of the cargo bay, there was no sound, not even a vibration that George could feel.

'Are we hitting him?' Nodon asked, his voice pitched high.

'How the fook should I know?' George snapped. 'I'm not even sure the fookin' kludge is workin'.'

'It's working! Look at the panel.'

It's working, all right, George saw. But is it doing any good?

The first hint that *Starpower* was firing back at him came when Harbin's control board suddenly sprang a half-dozen amber warning lights. Without hesitation, he hit the manoeuvring jets to jink *Shanidar* sideways. It ruined his own shot, but it moved him out of harm's way. Temporarily.

Frowning at the displays, Harbin saw that one of his propellant tanks had been ruptured. He looked up at *Starpower*, hanging out there and saw the big hatch of the ship's cargo bay was open. They must have a laser in there, probably a cutting laser they use for mining. And they're shooting at me with it.

He manoeuvred *Shanidar* away from the open cargo hatch while checking his ship's systems. Fortunately, the propellant tank they holed was almost empty anyway. Harbin could afford to jettison it. Yet, as he did, he began to worry that they might hit remaining tanks before he had the chance to finish them off.

Staring at the dumbbell shape of *Starpower* rotating slowly against the distant, uncaring stars, Harbin's chiselled features twisted into a cruel smile.

'Kill or be killed,' he whispered to himself.

30

It took only a few days of running Helvetia Ltd by herself for Amanda to come to the conclusion that she didn't need to hire a replacement for Niles Ripley. I can do the systems management job myself, she realized.

With the habitat more than halfway finished, what was needed was a general overseer, a straw boss who understood the various engineering fields that contributed to the ongoing construction programme. Amanda had learned a good deal of the technical skills in her training and experience as an astronaut. The only question in her mind was whether she had the strength, the backbone, to boss a gaggle of construction technicians.

Most of them were men, and most of the men were young and full of testosterone. In general, men outnumbered women in Ceres by six to one. The balance on the construction project was actually better: three men to each woman on the team, Amanda saw as she carefully reviewed the personnel files.

Sitting at her desk, she thought, If Lars were here there would be no problem. But if Lars were here he would take over the task, or hire someone to do it. Shaking her head, Amanda told herself, It's up to you, old girl. You've got to do this for Lars, for all the people living here in Ceres.

Looking into the mirror over the dresser of their one-room quarters, Amanda realized, No. Not merely for them. You've got to do this for yourself.

She got to her feet and surveyed herself in the mirror. It's the same old problem: the men will see me as a sex object and the women will see me as competition. That has some advantages, of course, but in this case the drawbacks outweigh the advantages. Time for baggy sweaters and shapeless slacks. Minimal make-up and keep your hair pinned up.

I can do it, she told herself. I can make Lars proud of what I accomplish.

She set a goal for herself: I'll handle this project so well that when Lars returns he'll want me to stay with it to completion.

Despite her best control, though, she could not avoid hearing a fearful voice in her mind that said, *IF* Lars returns.

'He's coming closer!' Nodon shouted.

Wincing inside his bubble helmet, George hollered, 'I can see that! And I can fookin' hear you, too. No need to yell.'

The two spacesuited men tugged at the big aiming mirrors of the cutting laser, clumsy in their suits as they tried to slew the coupled pair of copper slabs on their mounting. The mirror assembly moved smoothly enough; pointing it precisely was the problem. It had been designed for slicing ore samples out of asteroids, not hitting pinpoint targets that were moving.

'Lars, you've gotta rotate us so we can keep 'im in our sights,' George called to the bridge.

'I'm doing my best,' Fuchs snapped. 'I've got to do it all by hand. The steering program wasn't designed for this.'

George tried to squint along the output mirrors' focusing sight and bumped the curving front of his helmet against the device. Cursing fluently, he sighted the laser as best he could.

'Hold us there,' he said to Fuchs. 'Bastard's coming straight at us now.'

'Tell me when to fire,' Nodon said, hunching over the control board.

'Now,' George said. 'Fire away.'

He strained his eyes to see if the beam was having any effect on the approaching ship. We can't miss him, not at this range, George thought. Yet nothing seemed to be happening. The attacking ship bored in closer. Suddenly it jerked sideways and down.

'He's manoeuvring!' Nodon stated the obvious.

'Shut down the laser,' George commanded. To Fuchs, up on the bridge, he yelled, 'Turn us, dammit! How'm I gonna hit him if we can't keep the fookin' laser pointin' at him?'

A string of red lights sprang up across Harbin's control panel. The propellant tanks. He's sawing away at them.

He was in his spacesuit now. Once he'd realized that *Starpower* was shooting back at him he'd put on the suit before bringing *Shanidar* back into the battle.

His steering program was going crazy. The swine had hit a nearly-full tank, and propellant spurting from the rip in it was acting as a thruster jet, pushing him sideways and down from the direction he wanted to go. He had to override the unwanted thrust manually; no time to reprogram the steering to compensate for it. Besides, by the time he could reprogram the stupid computer, the tank would be empty and there'd be no more thrust to override.

In a way, though, the escaping propellant helped. It had jinked *Shanidar* in an unexpected burst, making it difficult for the enemy to keep their laser trained on him.

But I can't afford to lose propellant! Harbin raged silently. They're killing me.

The amphetamines he sometimes took before going into battle were of no use to him now. He was keyed up enough, stimulated to a knife-edge of excitement. What he needed was something to calm him down a little, stretch out time without dulling his reflexes. He had a store of such medications aboard his ship. But inside his spacesuit, his cache of drugs was out of reach, useless to him.

I don't need drugs, he told himself. I can beat them on my own.

He called up the highest magnification his optical sensors could give and focused on the area where he'd briefly seen the red telltale light of their guide laser. That's where the danger is. If I can see the beam of their aiming laser, they can hit me with the infrared cutter.

Swiftly, he came to a plan of action. Fire the thrusters so that I jet up and across their field of view. As soon as I see the light of their guide laser I fire at them. I can get off a pulse and then be up past their field of view before they can fire back. Once I've disabled their laser I can chop them to pieces at my leisure.

With the semicircle of display screens curving around him, Fuchs saw the attacking spacecraft spurt down and away from them, a ghostly issue of gas glinting wanly in the light of the distant Sun. He could see a long, thin slit slashed across one of the ship's bulbous propellant tanks.

'You've hit him, George!' Fuchs said into his helmet microphone. 'I can see it!'

George's reply sounded testy. 'So swing us around so's I can hit 'im again!'

Fuchs tapped at the control keyboard, wishing he was more adept at manoeuvring a spacecraft. *Starpower* was not built for graceful turns. Pancho was right, he remembered. We turn slow and ugly.

In the cargo bay, George stared out at emptiness.

'Where the fook is he?' he wailed.

'Still below your line of sight,' came Fuchs' answer in his earphones.

'So turn us toward him!'

Nodon said, 'The cooling system needs more time to recover. We have inadequate coolant flow.'

'Just need a few seconds, mate,' said George, 'once we get 'im back in our sights.'

He stepped up to the lip of the cargo hatch and looked down in the direction he had last seen the attacking vessel.

'There he is!' George saw. 'Comin' our way again.'

The attacker was zooming up swiftly. George turned back toward the laser. 'Fire her up!' he yelled to Nodon.

'Firing!' Nodon shouted back.

A blinding flash of light stunned George. He felt himself toppling head over heels and then something slammed into him so hard it spun him like an unbalanced gyroscope. Through blurry, tear-filled eyes he saw a spacesuited arm fly past, geysering blood where it had been severed just above the elbow, rotating over and over as it dwindled out of his view. He heard someone bellowing in pain and rage and realized it was himself.

I'm a dead man, Harbin told himself.

Strangely, the knowledge did not seem to frighten him. He sat back in his spacesuit, relaxed now that the tension of battle had drained out of him.

They've killed me, he thought. I wonder if they know it.

His plan to silence the enemy's laser had worked, after a fashion. He'd popped up into their field of view and fired off a full-energy burst as soon as he saw the red dot of their guide laser. They couldn't have revved up their laser in time to hit him, he was certain of that.

Not unless they already had their laser cooking and he'd

sailed right into their beam. Which is exactly what had happened.

Harbin knew he had knocked out their laser with his one quick shot. But in doing so he had sailed *Shanidar* across the continuous beam of their mining laser. It had carved a long gash through two of the remaining propellant tanks and even sliced deeply into the habitation module itself.

I'll have to stay inside this damned suit, he growled to himself. For how long? Until the air runs out. Hours, perhaps a day or so. No longer than that.

He pulled himself out of the command chair, thinking, Of course, I could tap into the ship's air tanks. If the recycler hasn't been damaged, the air could last for months, even a year or more. I'd starve before I asphyxiated.

But what would be the point? I'm drifting, too low on propellant to reach a tanker or any other help. Leaning forward slightly so he could check the control displays through his suit helmet, he saw that the ship's power generator was unscathed. He would have enough electrical power to keep his systems going. He could even patch the hab module's hull, bring the air pressure back to normal, and get out of the suit.

To what avail? To drift helplessly through the Belt until I starve.

You could call the nearest tanker and ask for a retrieval, he told himself. The computer has their positions in its memory and you could contact them with a tight-beam laser signal.

Would they come to my rescue? Not before they checked with HSS headquarters. Grigor will not be happy to learn that I failed to eliminate *Starpower*. By now, Fuchs and his friends are probably screaming their heads off to the IAA. Would Grigor tell them to rescue me, or would he decide that it's better if I just quietly die?

Quietly. Harbin smiled. That's the key. *Do not go gentle into that good night,* he quoted silently. *Rage, rage against the dying of the light.*

On a clear channel, he put through a call to Grigor.

31

George awoke to see Fuchs and Nodon staring down at him, Fuchs looking grim, irritated. Nodon was wide-eyed with fright. Strange to see him, with those fierce carvings in his face, looking so scared, George thought.

'So I'm not in heaven, then,' he said, trying to grin. His voice sounded strained, terribly weak.

'Not yet,' Fuchs growled.

He realized he was lying in one of *Starpower*'s privacy cubicles, his spacesuit removed. Either they've got me tied down or I'm so fookin' feeble I can't move.

'What happened?' he asked.

Nodon glanced at Fuchs, then licked his lips and said, 'The laser blast shattered our laser. The mirror assembly broke loose and . . . and took off your arm.'

He said the last words all in a rush, as if ashamed of them. George looked down, surprised at how much effort it took to twist his head, and saw his left arm ended just short of the elbow. The stump was swathed in plastic spray-bandage.

He felt more fuddled than shocked. Just the barest tendril of pain, now that he thought about it. Not scared. No worries. They must have me doped up pretty good.

'The rest of your arm is in the freezer,' Fuchs said. 'We're heading back to Ceres at high thrust. I will alert Kris Cardenas.'

George closed his eyes and remembered seeing the space-suited arm spiraling out the cargo hatch.

He looked at Nodon. 'You shut off the bleedin', huh?'

The younger man bobbed his head up and down.

'And closed off the suit arm,' George added.

Fuchs said, 'He also went EVA and recovered your arm. I thought for a few minutes that we would lose him altogether.'

'Did you now?' George said, feeling stupid, muffled. 'Thanks, mate.'

Nodon looked embarrassed. He changed the subject. 'You must have hit the other ship a damaging blow. It left at high speed.'

'That's good.'

'We'll be in Ceres in another fourteen hours,' said Fuchs.

'That's good.' George couldn't think of anything else to say. Somewhere, in a deep recess of his mind, he knew that he should be screaming. Prosthetics be damned, I've lost my fooking arm! But the drugs muted his emotional pain as well as the physical. Nothing really seemed to matter. All George wanted was for them to leave him alone and let him sleep.

Fuchs seemed to understand, thank god. 'You rest now,' he said, his tight slash of a mouth turned down bitterly. 'I have a long report to send to the IAA as soon as we can repair one of the antennas.'

'Not this Fuchs person again,' complained Hector Wilcox.

Erek Zar and Francesco Tomaselli were sitting in front of Wilcox's desk, Zar looking decidedly uncomfortable, Tomaselli almost quivering with righteous indignation.

Wilcox's office was imposing, as befitted the Consul-General of the International Astronautical Authority. Slim, sleek, impeccably clothed in a sombre charcoal business suit and dapper pearl-grey tie that nicely set off his silvery hair and trim moustache, Wilcox looked every centimetre the successful administrator, which he believed himself to be. He had arbitrated many a corporate wrangle, directed teams of bureaucrats to generate safety regulations and import duties on space manufactures, and climbed the slippery slope of the IAA's legal department until he sat at its very top, unchallenged, and hailed by his fellow bureaucrats as an example of patience, intelligence and – above all – endurance.

Now he had a charge of piracy to deal with, and it unsettled him down to his very core.

'He sent in a complete report,' Tomasselli said, lean and eager, his dark eyes flashing.

Zar interrupted. 'Fuchs claims his ship was attacked.'

'He *reports*,' Tomasselli resumed, laying emphasis on the word, 'not only that his own ship was attacked, but another as well, and one of the men seriously injured.'

'By a pirate vessel.'

Zar's ruddy, fleshy face coloured deeper than usual. 'That's what he claims.'

'And the evidence?'

'His ship is damaged,' Tomasselli said before Zar could open his mouth. 'He is bringing the injured man to Ceres.'

'Which ships are we talking about?' Wilcox asked, clear distaste showing on his lean, patrician face.

Zar put out a hand to silence his underling. 'Fuchs' ship is named *Starpower*. The other ship that he claims was attacked is *Waltzing Matilda*.'

'Is that one on its way to Ceres, too?'

'No,' Tomasselli jumped in. 'They had to abandon it. The three of them are coming in on *Starpower*, Fuchs and the two men from *Waltzing Matilda*.'

Wilcox gave the Italian a sour look. 'And Fuchs has charged Humphries Space Systems with piracy?'

'Yes,' said both men simultaneously.

Wilcox drummed his fingers on his desktop. He looked out his window at the St Petersburg waterfront. He wished he were in Geneva, or London, or anywhere except here in this office with these two louts and this ridiculous charge of piracy. Piracy! In the twenty-first century! It was ludicrous, impossible. Those rock rats out in the Asteroid Belt have their private feuds and now they're trying to drag the IAA into it.

'I suppose we'll have to investigate,' he said gloomily.

'Fuchs has registered a formal charge,' said Tomasselli. 'He has requested a hearing.'

Which I will have to preside over, Wilcox said to himself. I'll be a laughing stock, at the very least.

'He should arrive at Ceres in a few hours,' Zar said.

Wilcox looked at the man's unhappy face, then turned his gaze to the eager, impetuous Tomasselli.

'You must go to Ceres,' he said, pointing a long, manicured finger at the Italian.

Tomasselli's eyes brightened. 'I will conduct the hearing there?'

'No,' Wilcox snapped. 'You will interview this man Fuchs and the others with him, and then bring the three of them back here, under IAA custody. Take two or three Peacekeeper troopers with you.'

'Peacekeepers?' Zar asked.

Wilcox gave him a wintry smile. 'I want to show that the IAA is taking this situation quite seriously. If these men believe they have been attacked by pirates, then they should have some visible protection, don't you agree?'

'Oh! Yes, of course.'

Tomasselli said, 'One of the men is seriously injured, and all three of them have been living in low gravity for so long that they could not return to Earth unless they spent several weeks in reconditioning exercises.'

Wilcox let a small hiss escape his lips, his only visible sign of displeasure so far, yet he knew that his control was on the fragile brink of crumbling into towering anger.

'Very well, then,' he said icily. 'Bring them to Selene.'

'I will conduct the hearing there?' Tomasselli asked eagerly.

'No,' Wilcox snapped. 'I will conduct the hearing there.'

Zar looked stunned. 'You'll go to Selene?'

Drawing himself up on his dignity, Wilcox replied, 'I have not risen this far in the service of the International Astronautical Authority by avoiding the difficult tasks.'

It was a bald-faced lie, but Wilcox almost believed it to be true, and Zar was willing to accept whatever his superior told him.

32

George could tell from the look on Dr Cardenas' face that the news was not good.

Fuchs and Nodon had rushed him to Ceres' minuscule infirmary as soon as they had landed, Nodon carrying the insulated plastic box that held George's severed arm. Half the population of the asteroid had also tried to crowd into the infirmary, some out of morbid curiosity, most because they heard that Big George had been injured and they knew and liked the red-haired Aussie. Cardenas had firmly shooed all of the bystanders into the tunnel outside, except for Amanda.

Fuchs embraced his wife and she threw her arms around his neck and kissed him solidly.

'You're all right, Lars?' she asked.

'Yes. Fine. Not a scratch.'

'I was so worried!'

'It's George who was hurt. Not me.'

Cardenas put George through the diagnostic scanners, then took the container from Nodon and disappeared into the lab that adjoined the infirmary, leaving George sitting up on one of the three infirmary beds, surrounded by Amanda, Fuchs and Nodon.

'You really were attacked by another ship?' Amanda asked, still not quite believing it could be possible.

George held up the stump of his left arm. 'Wasn't termites did this,' he said.

'I've sent in a full report of the attack to IAA headquarters,' said Fuchs.

Amanda replied, 'They've sent a confirmation. One of their administrators is coming out here to bring you and George and,' she glanced at Nodon, 'you, Mr Nodon, to Selene for a hearing before the chief of the IAA legal department.'

'A hearing!' Fuchs exulted. 'Good!'

'At Selene.'

'Even better. We'll beard Humphries in his own den.'

'Can George travel?' Amanda asked.

'Why not?' George asked back.

That was when Cardenas came back into the infirmary, her expression dark and grave.

George immediately saw the situation. 'Not good news, eh?'

Cardenas shook her head. 'The arm's deteriorated too far, I'm afraid. Too much damage to the nerves. By the time we get you back to Selene, the deterioration will be even worse.'

'Can't you stitch it back on here?' George asked.

'I'm not that good a surgeon, George. I'm not even a physician, really, I'm just pretending to be one.'

George leaned back on the bed. It was hard to tell what was going on behind his shaggy, matted beard and over-grown head of hair.

'They have regeneration specialists at Selene. With some of your stem cells they'll be able to regrow your arm in a few months.'

'Can you do it with nanomachines?' Amanda asked.

Cardenas shot her a strangely fierce look: part anger, part guilt, part frustration.

'Regeneration could be done with nanotherapy,' she said tightly, 'but I couldn't do it.'

Fuchs said, 'But you are an expert in nanotechnology. A Nobel laureate.'

'That was long ago,' Cardenas said. 'Besides, I swore that I wouldn't engage in any nanotech work again.'

'Swore? To whom?'

'To myself.'

'I don't understand.'

Cardenas was obviously struggling within herself. After a few heartbeats she said, 'This isn't the time to tell you the sad story of my life, Lars.'

'But—'

'Go to Selene. They have regeneration experts there, George. They'll grow your arm back for you.'

George shrugged good-naturedly. 'Long as they don't grow it back before our hearing.' He waved his stump. 'I want those IAA bludgers t' see what the bastards did to me.'

Fuchs patted George's good shoulder. 'And I want Humphries to be there to see it.'

That night Fuchs and Amanda spent making love. No words, no talk about what had happened or discussions about what the future might bring. Nothing but animal heat and passion.

Lying beside her afterward, their room lit only by the dimmed numerals of the digital clock, Fuchs realized he had made love to Amanda as if he would never see her again. He had learned something in that battle out in space. His first brush with imminent death had taught him that he had to live life as if it would end in an instant.

I have no future, he told himself in the silence of their darkened room. As long as I'm in this war against Humphries I cannot hope for anything. I must live moment by moment, expecting nothing, ready to accept whatever comes next and deal with it. Only then can I escape the fear; only by shutting out the future can I cope with the present.

Briefly he thought about the frozen zygotes they had waiting in Selene. If I'm killed, Fuchs reflected, at least Amanda will be able to bear our child – if she wants to.

Amanda, lying beside him, pretended to sleep. But she was thinking too. What can Lars accomplish by this hearing with the IAA? Even if they find Humphries responsible for the attacks on all those ships, what can they do about it? Whatever happens, it will only make Martin even more enraged against Lars.

If only Lars would give this up, forget this war of his. But he won't. He'll keep on fighting until they kill him. He'll keep on fighting until he's as murderous and hateful as they are. He'll never stop, no matter how I beg him. He's moving away from me, becoming a stranger to me. Even in bed, he's not the same person any more.

33

'So he's getting a hearing with the IAA,' Humphries said as he mixed himself a vodka and tonic.

The bar in his palatial home was a sizeable room that also served as a library. Bookshelves ran up to the ceiling along two walls and a third wall had shelves full of videodisks and cyberbook chips stacked around a pair of holowindows that showed slowly changing views of extraterrestrial scenery.

Humphries paid no attention to the starkly beautiful Martian sunset or the windswept cloud deck of Jupiter. His mind was on Lars Fuchs.

'The hearing will be held in the IAA offices here in Selene,' said Diane Verwoerd. Seated on a plush stool at the handsome mahogany bar, she nursed a long slim glass of sickly greenish Pernod and water.

Verwoerd was the only other person in the room with Humphries. She was still in her office clothes: a white sleeveless turtleneck blouse under a maroon blazer, with dark charcoal slacks that accentuated her long legs. Humphries had already changed to a casual open-necked shirt and light tan chinos.

'Is he bringing his wife with him?' Humphries asked as he stepped out from behind the bar.

'Probably.' Verwoerd swiveled on her stool to follow him as he paced idly along the rows of leatherbound books.

'You don't know for certain?'

'I can find out easily enough,' she said.

Humphries muttered, 'He wouldn't leave her alone on that rock.'

'It didn't do you any good the last time he brought her here.'

He shot her a venomous look.

'We have something else to worry about,' Verwoerd said. 'This man Harbin.'

Humphries' expression changed. It didn't soften: it merely went from one object of anger to another.

'That's why you wanted to talk to me alone,' he said.

She raised a brow slightly. 'That's why I agreed to have a drink with you, yes.'

'But not dinner.'

'I have other plans for dinner,' she said. 'Besides, you should be thinking about Harbin. Thinking hard.'

'What's the situation?'

She took a sip of her drink, then placed the glass carefully on the bar. 'Obviously, he failed to eliminate Fuchs.'

'From what I've heard, Fuchs nearly eliminated him.'

'His ship was damaged and he had to break off his attack on *Starpower*. Apparently Fuchs was expecting him; at least, that's what Harbin believes.'

'I don't care a termite fart's worth for what he believes. I'm paying him for results and he's failed. Now I'm going to have the idiotic IAA to deal with.'

Humphries kicked at an ottoman that was in his way and sat heavily on the sofa facing the bar. His face was an image of pure disgust.

'You have Harbin to deal with, too.'

'What?' He looked up sharply at her. 'What do you mean?'

'He knows enough to hurt you. Badly.'

'He's never seen me. He dealt entirely with Grigor.'

With deliberate patience, Verwoerd said, 'If Harbin tells

the IAA what he's been doing, do you think they'll lay the blame in Grigor's lap or yours?'

'They can't—'

'Don't you think they're intelligent enough to realize that Grigor would never authorize attacks on prospectors' ships unless you ordered them?'

Humphries looked as if he wanted to throw his drink at her. It's dangerous being the messenger, Verwoerd told herself, when you bring bad news.

'You'll have to eliminate Harbin, then,' he said. 'Maybe Grigor, too.'

And then me? Verwoerd asked herself. Aloud, she replied, 'Harbin's thought of that possibility. He claims he's sent copies of his ship's log to a few friends on Earth.'

'Nonsense! How could he—'

'Tight-beam laser links. Coded data. It's done every day. It's the way he communicated with our own tankers out there in the Belt.'

'Send messages all the way back to Earth?'

Verwoerd took up her drink again. 'It's done every day,' she repeated.

'He's bluffing,' Humphries mumbled.

She got off the stool and stepped toward the sofa where he was sitting. Nudging the ottoman into position with one foot, she sat on it and leaned toward him, arms on her knees, drink in both hands.

'Even if he's bluffing, it's too big a risk to take. Eliminating him won't be easy. He's a trained fighter and he's tough.'

'He's coming here to Selene on an HSS vessel, isn't he?' Humphries pointed out. 'The crew can get rid of him.'

Verwoerd sighed like a schoolteacher facing a boy who hadn't done his homework. 'Then you'd have half a dozen people who'd have something on you. Besides, I don't think the entire crew could take him. As I said, he's trained and he's tough. Things could get quite messy if we try to take him out.'

'Then what do you recommend?' he asked sullenly.

'Let me deal with him. Personally.'

'You?'

She nodded. 'Keep Grigor out of this. Harbin is most likely worried that we want to take him out, especially since he failed with Fuchs and he knows enough to hang us all. Let me show him that it's not that way. I'll offer him a bonus, send him back to Earth with a fat bank account.'

'So he can blackmail me for the rest of his life.'

'Yes, of course. That's exactly what he'll think. And we'll let him go on thinking that until he's living it up on Earth and his guard is down.'

A crooked smile slowly curled across Humphries' lips.

'Delilah,' he murmured.

Verwoerd saw that he was satisfied with her plan. She took a long swallow of the aniseed-flavoured Pernod, then agreed, 'Delilah.'

Humphries' smile turned sardonic. 'Are you going to fuck him, too?'

She made herself smile back. 'If I have to.'

But she was thinking, You don't know whose hair is going to get trimmed, Martin. And there's more than one way to screw a man, even you.

Fuchs had dreaded this moment. He knew it had to come, though. There was no way around it. The IAA official was due to arrive at Ceres in another few hours.

He started packing his travel bag for the trip to Selene. When Amanda took her bag from the closet and laid it on the bed beside his, he told her that he was going without her.

'What do you mean?' Amanda asked, obviously startled by his decision.

'Precisely what I said. George, Nodon and I are going. I want you to remain here.'

She looked puzzled, hurt. 'But, Lars, I—'

'You are *not* going with me!' Fuchs said sharply.

Shocked at his vehemence, Amanda stared at him open-mouthed as if he had slapped her in the face.

'That's final,' he snapped.

'But, Lars—'

'No buts, and no arguments,' he said. 'You stay here and run what's left of the business while I'm in Selene.'

'Lars, you can't go without me. I won't let you!'

He tried to stare her down. This is the hardest part, he realized. I've got to hurt her, there's no other way to do this.

'Amanda,' he said, trying to sound stern, trying to keep his own doubts and pain out of his voice, out of his face. 'I have made up my mind. I need you to remain here. I'm not a little boy who must bring his mother with him wherever he goes.'

'Your mother!'

'Whatever,' he said. 'I'm going without you.'

'But why?'

'Because that's what I want,' he said, raising his voice. 'I know that you think I'd be safer if you were with me, that Humphries won't attack me if he believes you might be hurt, too. Poppycock! I don't need your protection. I don't want it.'

She burst into tears and fled to the lavatory, leaving him standing by the bed in agony.

If he's going to try to kill me, it won't matter to him whether Amanda's with me or not. The closer I get to hurting him, the more desperate he becomes. She'll be safer here, among friends, among people who know her. He wants to kill me, not her. I'll face him without her. It will be better that way.

He was certain he was right. If only he couldn't hear her sobbing on the other side of the thin door.

Hector Wilcox felt extremely uneasy about going to the Moon. His flight from the spaceport at Munich had been terrifying, despite all the reassurances of the Astro Corporation employees. Their stout little Clippership looked sturdy enough when he boarded it. The flight attendant who showed him to his seat went on at length about the ship's diamond-structure hull and the reliability records that Clipperships had run up. All well and good, Wilcox thought. He strapped himself firmly into his seat and, fortified by several whiskies beforehand and a medicinal patch plastered on the inside of his elbow to ward against spacesickness, he gripped the seat's armrests and listened with growing apprehension to the countdown.

Take-off was like an explosion that jolted every bone in his body. He felt squashed down in his seat, then before he could utter a word of complaint he was weightless, floating against the straps of his safety harness, his stomach rising up into his throat despite he medicine patch. Swallowing bile, he reached for the retch bags tucked into the pouch on the seat back in front of him.

By the time the Clippership had docked with the space station, Wilcox was wishing that he'd insisted on holding the damnable hearing on Earth. There were plenty of smiling, uniformed Astro personnel to help him out of the Clippership and into the transfer vehicle that would go the rest of the way to the Moon. Groaning in zero gravity, Wilcox allowed them to haul him around like a helpless invalid and tuck him into a seat on the transfer ship that was far less comfortable then the Clippership's had been.

At least there was some feeling of gravity when the transfer vehicle started its high-thrust burn Moonward. But that dwindled away all too soon and for the next several hours Wilcox wondered if he was going to survive this journey.

Gradually, though, he began to feel better. His stomach didn't feel so queasy; the pressure behind his eyes eased off. If he didn't turn his head or make any sudden moves, zero gravity was almost pleasurable.

Once they landed at Selene's Armstrong spaceport, the light lunar gravity gave Wilcox a renewed sense of up-and-down. He was able to unstrap and get out of his chair without help. He stumbled at first, but by the time he had been checked through customs and rented a pair of weighted boots, he felt almost normal.

The soothing elegance of the Hotel Luna's lobby helped Wilcox to feel even more at home. Quiet luxury always pleased him, and although the lobby was slightly tatty here and there, the general tone and atmosphere of the place was reassuring. The local IAA flunkies had taken the best suite in Selene's only hotel for him. Spare no expense, Wilcox thought as he looked around the sumptuous sitting room, so long as it's coming out of the taxpayers' pocketbook and not my own. An assistant manager brought him to the suite, unpacked his bags for him, and even politely refused the tip Wilcox proferred. The hotel staff had prepared everything for him, including a well-stocked bar. One good jolt of whisky and Wilcox felt almost normal again.

There was a tap on the door and before Wilcox could say a word, the door slid open and a liveried servant pushed in a rolling table laden with covered dishes and a half-dozen bottles of wine.

Surprised, Wilcox began to protest, 'I didn't order—'

Then Martin Humphries walked into the suite, all smiles.

'I thought you'd appreciate a good meal, Hector,' said Humphries. 'This is from my own kitchen, not the regular hotel fare.' Gesturing toward the bottles, he added, 'From my own cellar, too.'

Wilcox broke into a genuinely pleased smile. 'Why, Martin, for goodness sake. How kind of you.'

As the waiter silently set out their dinner, Humphries explained, 'We shouldn't be seen in a public restaurant together, and I couldn't invite you down to my home without it seeming improper . . .'

'Quite so,' Wilcox agreed. 'Too many damnable snoops willing to believe the worst about anyone.'

'So I decided to bring dinner to you. I hope you don't mind.'

'Not at all! I'm delighted to see you again. How long has it been?'

'I've been living here in Selene for more than six years now.'

'Has it been that long?' Wilcox brushed his moustache with a fingertip. 'But, eh . . . aren't we running the risk of seeming impropriety? After all, with the hearing coming up—'

'No risk at all,' Humphries said smoothly. 'This man is a loyal employee of mine, and the hotel people can be relied on to be discreet.'

'I see.'

'You can't be too careful these days, especially a man in such a high position of trust as you are.'

'Rather,' said Wilcox, smiling as he watched the waiter open the first bottle of wine.

34

Dorik Harbin looked around the spare one-room apartment. Good enough, he thought. He knew that in Selene, the lower the level of your living quarters, the more expensive. It was mostly nonsense: you were just as safe five metres below the Moon's surface as you were at fifty or even five hundred. But people let their emotions rule them, just as on Earth they paid more for an upper floor in a condo tower, even though the view might be nothing more than another condo tower standing next door.

He had been tense during the flight in from the Belt. After leaving the crippled *Shanidar* with an HSS tanker, he had received orders from Grigor to report to Selene. They had provided him with a coffin-sized berth on an HSS freighter that was hauling ores to the Moon. Harbin knew that if they were going to assassinate him, this would be the time and place for it.

Apparently Grigor and his superiors believed his claim that he had sent complete records of *Shanidar*'s campaign of destruction to several friends on Earth. Otherwise they would have gotten rid of him, or tried to. Harbin had no friends on Earth or anywhere else. Acquaintances, yes, several people scattered here and there that he could trust a little. No family; they had all been killed while he was still a child.

Harbin had sent a rough ship's log from *Shanidar* to three persons he had known for many years: one had been the sergeant who had trained him in the Peacekeepers, now retired and living in someplace called Pennsylvania; another, the aged imam from his native village; the third was the widow of a man whose murder he had avenged the last time he had visited his homeland.

The instructions he had sent with the logs – a request, really – were to give the data to the news media if they learned that Harbin had died. He knew that if Grigor received orders to kill him, no one on Earth would likely hear of his death. But the faint possibility that *Shanidar*'s log might be revealed to the public was enough to stay Grigor's hand. At least, Harbin estimated that it was so.

It would have been easier to keep his murder quiet if they'd killed him on the ship coming in, Harbin thought. The fact that he was now quartered in this one-room apartment in Selene told him that they did not plan to kill him. Not yet, at least.

Almost, he relaxed. The room was comfortable enough, nearly spacious compared to the cramped quarters of a spacecraft. The freezer and cupboards were well stocked; Harbin decided to throw everything in the recycler and buy his own provisions in Selene's food market.

He had his head under the sink, checking to see if there were any unwanted attachments to his water supply, when he heard a light tap at his door.

Grigor, he thought. Or one of his people.

He got to his feet, closed the cabinet, and walked six steps to the door, feeling the comfortable solidity of the electrodagger strapped to the inside of his right wrist, beneath the loose cuff of his tunic. He had charged the battery in the dagger's hilt as soon as he had entered the apartment, even before unpacking.

He glanced at the small display plate beside the door. Not Grigor. A woman. Harbin slowly slid back the accordion door balanced on the balls of his feet, ready to spring aside if this woman pointed a weapon at him.

She looked surprised. She was almost Harbin's own height, he saw: slim, with smoky dark skin and darker hair curling over her shoulders. She wore a sleeveless sheer sweater that revealed little but suggested much, form-fitting slacks and soft, supple-looking boots.

'You are Dorik Harbin?' she asked, in a silky contralto voice.

'Who are you?' he countered.

'Diane Verwoerd,' she said, stepping into the room, forcing Harbin to swing back from the doorway so she could enter. 'I'm Martin Humphries' personal assistant.'

Diane looked him up and down and saw a tall, lean, *hard*-looking man with a fierce, dark beard and a world of suspicion in his cold blue eyes. Strange, startling eyes, she thought. Dead man's eyes. Killer's eyes. He was wearing ordinary coveralls that looked faded from long use, but clean and crisp as a military uniform. A strong, muscled body beneath the clothes, she judged. An impressive man, for a hired killer.

'I was expecting Grigor,' Harbin said.

'I hope you're not disappointed,' she said, heading for the couch across the room.

'Not at all. You said you are Mr Humphries' personal assistant?'

She sat and crossed her long legs. 'Yes.'

'Will I meet him?'

'No. You will deal with me.'

He did not reply. Instead, Harbin went to the refrigerator and took out a bottle of wine. She watched him open it, then search in the cabinet above the sink for wine glasses. Is he using this time to think of what he should say? Verwoerd asked herself. Finally he pulled out two simple tumblers and splashed some wine into them.

'I arrived only a few hours ago,' he said, handing her one

269

glass, then pulling up the desk chair to sit facing her. 'I don't know where things are yet.'

'I hope this room is comfortable for you,' she said.

'It will do.'

She waited for him to say more, but he simply studied her with those icepick eyes. Not undressing her. There was nothing sexual in it. He was . . . she tried to find the right word: *controlled*. That's it: he's completely under control. Every gesture, every word he speaks. I wonder what he looks like beneath the beard, Verwoerd thought. Is he the ruggedly handsome type, or does the beard hide a weak chin? Ruggedly handsome, she guessed.

The silence stretched. She took a sip of the wine. Slightly bitter. Perhaps it will improve after it's breathed a while. Harbin did not touch his wine; he simply held the glass in his left hand and kept his eyes riveted on her.

'We have a lot to discuss,' she said at last.

'I suppose that's true.'

'You seem to be afraid that we want to get rid of you.'

'That's what I would do if I were in your position. I'm a liability to you now, isn't that so?'

He's brutally frank, she thought. 'Mr Harbin, please let me assure you that we have no intention of causing you harm.'

He smiled at that, and she saw strong white teeth behind the dense black beard.

'In fact, Mr Humphries has told me to give you a bonus for the work you've done.'

He gave her a long, hard look, then said, 'Why don't we stop this fencing? You wanted me to kill Fuchs and I failed. Now he's here in Selene ready to testify that you're behind the attacks on prospectors' ships. Why should you pay me a bonus for that?'

'We'll pay for your silence, Mr Harbin.'

'Because you know that if you kill me the ship's log will go to the news media.'

'We have no intention of killing you.' Verwoerd nodded toward his untouched glass. 'You can drink all the wine you want.'

He put the tumbler down on the thinly carpeted floor. 'Ms Verwoerd—'

'Diane,' she said, before she had a chance to think about it.

He tilted his head slightly. 'Diane, then. Let me explain how this looks to me.'

'Please do.' She noted that he did not tell her to use his first name.

'Your corporation hired me to scare the independent prospectors out of the Belt. I knocked off several of their ships, but this man Fuchs caused a fuss. Then you instructed me to get rid of Fuchs, and this I failed to do.'

'We are disappointed, Mr Harbin, but that doesn't mean there's any reason for you to fear for your safety.'

'Doesn't it?'

'We'll handle this hearing. In a way, it's an opportunity for us to deal with Fuchs in a different manner. Your part of this operation is finished. All we want to do is pay you off and thank you for your work. I know it wasn't easy.'

'People like you don't come to people like me for easy jobs,' Harbin said.

He's not afraid, Verwoerd saw. He's not frightened or disappointed or angry. He's like a block of ice. No visible emotions. No, she corrected herself. He's more like a panther, a lithe, deadly predator. Every muscle in his body under control, every nerve alert and ready. He could kill me in an instant if he wanted to.

She felt strangely thrilled. I wonder what he would be like if I could break through that control of his. What would it be like to have all that pent-up energy inside me? Not now.

Later, she commanded herself. After the hearing is over. If we come out of the hearing okay, then I can relax with him. If we don't . . . I'd hate to be the one sent to terminate him. If it comes to that, we'll need a team of people for the job. A team of very good people.

Then she thought, Why think about terminating him? Use him!

Can I make him loyal to me? she asked herself. Can I use him for my personal agenda? Smiling inwardly, she thought, It could be fun. It could be very pleasurable.

Aloud, she said, 'There is one more task you could do for us before you . . . eh, retire.'

'What is that?' he asked, his voice flat, his eyes riveted on hers.

'You'll have to go to Ceres. I can arrange a high-thrust flight for you. But it must be very quiet; no one is to know. Not even Grigor.'

He stared at her for long, intense moment. 'Not even Grigor?' he muttered.

'No. You will report directly to me.'

Harbin smiled at that, and she wondered again how he would look without his beard.

'Do you ever shave?' she asked.

'I was going to, when you knocked at my door.'

Hours later, sticky and sweaty in bed beside him, Diane grinned to herself. Being Delilah was thoroughly enjoyable.

Harbin turned to her and slid a hand across her midriff. 'About this business on Ceres,' he said, surprising her.

'Yes?'

'Who do I have to kill?'

35

Much to Hector Wilcox's misgiving, Douglas Stavenger invited himself to the hearing. Two days before the hearing was to begin, Stavenger invited Wilcox to dinner at the Earthview Restaurant. Wilcox knew it was not a purely social invitation. If the youthful founder of Selene wanted to be in on the hearing there was nothing the IAA executive could do about it without raising hackles.

Stavenger was very diplomatic, of course. He offered a conference room in Selene's offices, up in one of the towers that supported the dome of the Grand Plaza. The price of his hospitality was to allow him to sit in on the hearing.

'It'll be pretty dull stuff, mostly,' Wilcox warned, over dinner his second night on the Moon.

'Oh, I don't think so,' said Stavenger, with the bright enthusiasm of a youth. 'Anything involving Martin Humphries is bound to be interesting.'

So that's it, Wilcox said to himself as he picked at his fruit salad. He's following Martin's trail.

'You know, Mr Humphries won't be present at the hearing,' he said.

'Really?' Stavenger looked surprised. 'I thought that Fuchs was accusing him of piracy.'

Wilcox frowned his deepest. 'Piracy,' he sneered. 'Poppy-cock.'

Stavenger smiled brightly. 'That's what the hearing is for, isn't it? To determine the validity of the charge?'

'Oh, yes, of course,' said Wilcox hastily. 'To be sure.'

Fuchs had not slept well his first two nights in Selene, and the night before the hearing began he expected to be too jumpy to sleep at all, but strangely, he slept soundly the whole night through. Pancho had come up to Selene and treated him to a fine dinner at the Earthview Restaurant. Perhaps the wine had something to do with my sleeping, he told himself as he brushed his teeth that morning.

He had dreamed, he knew, but he couldn't remember much of his dreams. Amanda was in them, and George, and some vague, dark, looming danger. He could not recall any of the details.

When his phone chimed he thought it must be Pancho, ready to pick him up and go with him to the hearing room.

Instead, the wallscreen showed Amanda's beautiful face. Fuchs felt a rush of joy that she had called. Then he saw that she looked tired, concerned.

'Lars, darling, I'm just calling to wish you well at the hearing and to tell you that I love you. Everything here is going quite well. The prospectors are giving us more business than we can handle and there hasn't been a bit of trouble from any of the HSS people.'

Of course not, Fuchs thought. They don't want to raise any suspicions while this hearing is going on.

'Good luck in the hearing, darling. I'll be waiting for you to call and tell me how it turned out. I miss you. I love you!'

Her image winked out, the wallscreen went blank. Fuchs glanced at the clock on his bed table, then swiftly ordered the computer to reply to her message.

'The hearing begins in half an hour,' he said, knowing that by the time Amanda heard his words the meeting would almost be starting. 'I'm sorry I didn't bring you with me. I miss you, too. Terribly. I'll call as soon as the hearing ends. And I love you, too, my precious. With all my heart.'

The phone chimed again. This time it was Pancho. 'Rise and shine, Lars, ol' buddy. Time to get this bronco out of the chutes.'

Fuchs was disappointed that Humphries did not show up for the hearing. On thinking about it, though, he was not surprised. The man is a coward who sends others to do his dirty work for him, he thought.

'Hey, look,' Pancho said as they entered the conference room. 'Doug Stavenger's here.'

Stavenger and half a dozen others were sitting in the comfortable chairs arranged along one wall of the room. The conference table had been moved to the rear wall and set out with drinks and finger foods. A smaller table was at the other side of the room, flanked by two chairs already occupied by men in business suits. One of them was overweight, ruddy, red-haired; the other looked as lean and jittery as a racing greyhound. They each held palmcomps in their laps. The wallscreen behind the table showed the black and silver logo of the International Astronautical Authority. Two clusters of chairs had been arranged in front of the table. George and Nodon were already seated there. Fuchs saw that the other set was fully occupied by what he presumed to be HSS personnel.

'Good luck, buddy,' Pancho whispered, gesturing Fuchs toward the chairs up front. She went back to sit beside Stavenger.

Wondering idly who was paying for the food and drink that had been set out, Fuchs took the chair between Big George and Nodon. He had barely sat down when one of the men seated up front announced, 'This hearing will come to order. Mr Hector Wilcox, chief counsel of the International Astronautical Authority, presiding.'

Everyone got to their feet and a grey-haired distinguished-looking gentleman in a Savile Row three-piece suit came in from the side door and took his place behind the table. He put a hand-sized computer on the table and flicked it open. Fuchs noticed that an aluminium carafe beaded with condensation and a cut crystal glass rested on a corner of the table.

'Please be seated,' said Hector Wilcox. 'Let's get this over with as efficiently as we can.'

It begins, Fuchs said to himself, his heart thudding under his ribs, his palms suddenly sweaty.

Wilcox peered in his direction. 'Which of you is Lars Fuchs?'

'I am,' said Fuchs.

'You have charged Humphries Space Systems with piracy, have you not?'

'I have not.'

Wilcox's brows shot toward his scalp. 'You have not?'

Fuchs was amazed at his own cheek. He heard himself say, 'I do not charge a corporation with criminal acts. I charge a person, the man who heads that corporation: Martin Humphries.'

Wilcox's astonishment turned to obvious displeasure.

'Are you implying that the acts you call piracy – which have yet to be established as actually occurring – were deliberately ordered by Mr Martin Humphries?'

'That is precisely what I am saying, sir.'

On the other side of the makeshift aisle, a tall, dark-haired woman rose unhurriedly to her feet.

'Your honour, I am Mr Humphries' personal assistant, and on his behalf I categorically deny this charge. It's ludicrous.'

Big George hopped to his feet and waved the stump of his arm over his head. 'Y'call this ludicrous? I di'n't get this pickin' daisies!'

'Order!' Wilcox slapped the table with the flat of his hand. 'Sit down, both of you. I will not have outbursts in this hearing. We will proceed along calm, reasoned lines.'

Verwoerd and George resumed their seats.

Pointing a bony finger at Fuchs, Wilcox said, 'Very well, then. Before we get to this alleged piracy, there is the matter of your deliberate deception as to the whereabouts of your ship, the . . . eh,' Wilcox glanced at his diminutive computer screen, 'the . . . *Starpower*, is it not?'

'I had to keep my position secret,' Fuchs replied, 'for my own safety. They would have–'

'Safety indeed,' snapped Wilcox. 'Safety regulation *require* that every ship carry a tracking beacon so that our flight controllers can maintain a record of your position at all times.'

'Fat lot o' good that does out in th' Belt,' George stage-whispered.

'Nonetheless, it is a safety regulation,' Wilcox said, his voice rising. 'And you flouted it, Captain Fuchs.'

'For my own safety,' Fuchs shot back stubbornly. 'Against the killers that Martin Humphries has hired.'

Wilcox glared at him for a wordless moment, then said through clenched teeth, 'If you have evidence to sustain a charge of piracy, let us hear it. We'll look into the responsibility for such acts after we ascertain that they have actually happened.'

Fuchs slowly rose, feeling a trembling anger in his gut. 'You have the transcription of the battle between my ship, *Starpower*, and the ship that attacked us. You have seen the damage inflicted on *Starpower*. Mr Ambrose, here, lost his arm in that battle.'

Wilcox glanced over his shoulder at the ruddy-faced IAA flunkey, who nodded once. 'Noted,' he said to Fuchs.

'That same ship earlier attacked Mr Ambrose's ship, *Waltzing Matilda*, and left him and his crewman for dead.'

'Do you have any evidence for this, other than your unsupported word?' Wilcox asked.

'*Waltzing Matilda* is drifting in the Belt. We can provide approximate coordinates for a search, if you wish to undertake it.'

Wilcox shook his head. 'I doubt that such a search will be necessary.'

'Earlier,' Fuchs resumed, 'several others vessels were attacked: *The Lady of the Lake*, *Aswan*, *The Star*—'

Verwoerd called from her chair, 'There is no evidence that any of those ships were attacked.'

'They disappeared without a trace,' Fuchs snapped. 'Their signals cut off abruptly.'

With a smile, Verwoerd said, 'That is not evidence that they were attacked.'

'Quite so,' said Wilcox.

'In most of those cases, the asteroids that those ships claimed were later claimed by Humphries Space Systems,' Fuchs pointed out.

'What of it?' Verwoerd retorted. 'HSS ships have laid claim to many hundreds of asteroids. And if you examine the record carefully, you will see that four of the six asteroids in question have been claimed by entities other than HSS.'

Wilcox turned toward the lean assistant on his left. The man nodded hastily and said, 'Three of them were claimed by a corporation called Bandung Associates and the fourth by the Church of the Written Word. None of these entities are associated with HSS; I checked thoroughly.'

'So what this hearing boils down to,' Wilcox said, turning back to Fuchs, 'is your assertion that you were attacked.'

'For that I have evidence, and you have seen it,' Fuchs said, boiling inside.

'Yes, yes,' said Wilcox. 'There's no doubt that you were attacked. But attacked by whom? That's the real question.'

'By a ship working for HSS,' Fuchs said, feeling he was pointing out the obvious. 'Under the orders of Martin Humphries.'

'Can you prove that?'

'No employee of HSS would take such a step without the personal approval of Humphries himself,' Fuchs insisted. 'He even had one of my people killed, murdered in cold blood!'

'You are referring to the murder of a Niles Ripley, are you not?' asked Wilcox.

'Yes. A deliberate murder to stop our construction of the habitat we're building—'

Verwoerd interrupted. 'We concede that Mr Ripley was killed by an employee of Humphries Space Systems. But it was a private matter; the killing was neither ordered nor condoned by HSS. And Mr Fuchs personally dispatched the killer, in a violent act of vigilantism.'

Wilcox fixed Fuchs with a stern gaze. 'Frontier justice, eh? It's too bad that you executed him. His testimony might have supported your case.'

Feeling exasperated, Fuchs said, 'Who else would benefit from all these criminal acts?'

With a wry smile, Wilcox said, 'I was hoping you could tell me, Mr Fuchs. That's why we've gone to the expense and trouble of holding this hearing. Who is responsible here?'

Fuchs closed his eyes briefly: I don't want to bring Amanda into this. I don't want to make this seem like a personal feud between Humphries and me.

'Do you have anything else to offer, Mr Fuchs?'

Before he could reply, George got to his feet again and said, very calmly, 'Everybody on Ceres knows that Humphries is tryin' to squeeze Fuchs out of the Belt. Ask anybody.'

'Mr . . .' Wilcox glanced down at his computer screen. 'Ambrose, is it? Mr Ambrose, what "everybody knows" is not evidence in a court of law. Nor in this hearing.'

George sat down, mumbling to himself.

'The fact is,' Fuchs said, struggling to keep from screaming, 'that someone is killing people, someone is attacking prospectors' ships, *someone* is committing terrible crimes in the Asteroid Belt. The IAA must take action, must protect us . . .' He stopped. He realized he was begging, almost whining.

Wilcox leaned back in his chair. 'Mr Fuchs, I quite agree that your frontier is a violent, lawless place. But the International Astronautical Authority has neither the power nor the legal authority to serve as a police force across the Asteroid Belt. It is up to the citizens of the Belt themselves to provide their own protection, to police themselves.'

'We are being systematically attacked by Humphries Space Systems personnel!' Fuchs insisted.

'You are being attacked, I grant you,' Wilcox responded, with a sad, condescending smile. 'Most likely by renegades from among your own rough and ready population. I see no evidence linking Humphries Space Systems to your problems in any way, shape or manner.'

'You don't want to see!' Fuchs raged.

Wilcox stared at him coldly. 'This hearing is concluded,' he said.

'But you haven't—'

'It's finished,' Wilcox snapped. He stood up, grabbed his computer, clicked its lid shut and tucked it into his jacket pocket. Then he turned and strode out of the room, leaving Fuchs standing there, frustrated and furious.

36

Straining to keep a satisfied smile off her face, Diane Verwoerd led the squad of Humphries employees out of the hearing, leaving Fuchs and his two friends standing there in helpless, confused frustration.

Out in the corridor she made polite small talk with Douglas Stavenger and Pancho Lane as they left, looking disappointed at the outcome of the hearing. Verwoerd knew that Pancho was Humphries' chief opponent on the board of Astro Corporation, and that Humphries would not be satisfied until he had full control of Astro. Which means, she told herself, that once we've finally gotten rid of Fuchs, Pancho is next.

She hurried to the power stairs that led down to her office. Once there, alone, she put through a tight-beam laser call to Dorik Harbin. He should be arriving at Ceres in another hour or so, she knew.

It took nearly twenty minutes before his face appeared on her wallscreen: smoulderingly handsome without the beard, his chin firm and hard, his eyes icy blue, intent.

'I know you can't reply to this before you land,' she said to Harbin's image. 'But I wanted to wish you good luck and tell you that . . . well, I'm counting the minutes until you get back here to me.'

She took a deliberate breath, then added, 'I've made arrangements with the HSS people at Ceres. The drugs you need will be there, waiting for you.'

Verwoerd cut the connection. The screen went dark.

Only then did she smile. Keep him personally bound to you, she told herself. Use his weaknesses; use his strengths. He's going to be very valuable, especially if you ever have to protect yourself from Martin.

She turned and studied her reflection in the mirror on the far wall of her office. Delilah, she said to herself, and laughed.

'So whattawe do now?' George asked as he, Fuchs and Nodon made their way down the power stairs.

Fuchs shook his head miserably. 'I don't know. This hearing was a farce. The IAA has given Humphries a free hand to do whatever he wants.'

'Looks that way,' George agreed, scratching at his beard.

Nodon said nothing.

'Amanda,' Fuchs said. 'I must tell her what's happened. I must tell her that I've failed.'

Harbin looked over the eight men that had been assigned to his command. A ragtag bunch, at best. Roughnecks, hoodlums, petty thugs. Not one of them had a scrap of combat training or true military discipline. But then, he remembered, this isn't really a military operation. It's a simple theft, nothing more.

He had spent the high-g flight from Selene studying the plan and background information Diane had given him, but he had expected to have reliable men to work under him, not a gaggle of hooligans. Steeling himself to his task, Harbin silently repeated the mantra that the workman does not blame his tools, and the warrior must fight with what he has at hand. The first task was to instill these morons with some purpose other than cracking skulls and making money.

Harbin assumed that none of the louts assigned to him

gave a damn about what had happened to the hotheaded Trace Buchanan, but the doctrine that his old sergeant had drilled into him asserted that it was beneficial to a unit's cohesion and teamwork to build group solidarity in any way possible.

So he said to them, 'You remember what that man Fuchs did to Trace Buchanan?' It was purely a rhetorical question.

They nodded unenthusiastically. Buchanan had been a bully and a fool; he did not have friends, only associates who were afraid to make him angry. None of them mourned the late Mr Buchanan.

But Harbin felt he had to whip up some enthusiasm among his eight underlings. He had brought them together in the cramped little office at the HSS warehouse: eight men who had been flown to Ceres specifically because they could follow orders and weren't strangers to mayhem.

'Okay,' Harbin told them. 'Tonight we even the score. Tonight we hit Fuchs' warehouse and clean it out once and for all.'

'I got a better idea,' said Santorini.

Harbin felt the old anger simmering inside him. Santorini had the intelligence of a baboon. 'What is it?'

'You wanna get even with Fuchs, why don't we do his wife?'

The others all grinned at the thought.

Are these the best that Diane could hire? Harbin asked himself. Or did somebody in her office merely scrape a few barroom floors and send these specimens here to Ceres?

'Our orders are to leave her strictly alone,' he said sharply. 'Those orders come from the top. Don't even go near her. Understand? Anybody who even looks in her direction will be in deep shit. Is that clear?'

'Somebody up there likes her,' one of the lunks said.

'Somebody up there's got the hots for her,' agreed the goon next to him.

Harbin snarled, 'That *somebody* will fry your testicles and then feed them to you in slices if you don't follow orders. Our job is to hit the warehouse. We go in, we do the job, and then we leave. If we do it right you can all go back to Earth with a big fat bonus in your accounts.'

'Plenty of slash back home.'

'Yeah, 'specially if you got money.'

Harbin let them think about how they were going to enjoy their bonuses. Get them away from thinking about Fuchs' wife. Diane had been very specific about that. She is not to be harmed or even threatened. Not in any way, shape or form.

The warehouse was something else.

'Where the hell have you been?' Humphries snapped.

Verwoerd allowed herself a small smile. 'I took a long lunch. A victory celebration.'

'The whole damned afternoon?'

Humphries was sitting in the mansion's dining room, alone at one end of the long rosewood table, the remains of his dinner before him. He did not invite his assistant to sit down.

'I expected you here as soon as the hearing ended.'

'You got the news without me,' she said coolly. 'In fact, you knew how the hearing would turn out before it ever started, didn't you?'

His frown deepened. 'You're pretty damned sassy this evening.'

'Fuchs is on his way back to Ceres,' she said. 'By the time he gets there he won't have a warehouse. His company will be broke, he'll be ruined, and you'll be king of the Asteroid Belt. What more do you want?'

She knew what he wanted. He wanted Amanda Cunningham Fuchs. For that, though, it won't be enough to ruin Fuchs, she thought. We'll have to kill the man.

Humphries' frown dissolved slowly, replaced by a sly smile. 'So,' he asked, 'what are you doing for sex now that you've sent your soldier boy off to Ceres?'

Verwoerd tried to keep the surprise off her face. The sneaking bastard has been keeping me under surveillance!

'You bugged his quarters,' she said coldly.

Grinning, Humphries said, 'Would you like to see a replay?'

It took her a moment to get her emotions under control. Finally she managed to say, 'He's an interesting man. He quotes Persian poetry.'

'In bed.'

Still standing, Verwoerd stared down at him for a long moment, then conceded the point with a curt nod, thinking, he probably has my apartment bugged, too! Does he know about Bandung Associates?

But Humphries seemed more amused than annoyed. 'I have a proposition for you.'

Guardedly, she asked, 'What kind of a proposition?'

'I want you to bear my child.'

She could feel her eyes go round. 'What?'

Laughing, Humphries leaned back in the cushioned dining room chair and said, 'You won't go to bed with me, the least you can do is carry my child for me.'

She pulled out the chair closest to her and sank slowly into it.

'What are you saying?' she asked.

Almost offhandedly, Humphries said, 'I've decided to have a child. A son. My medical experts are picking the best possible egg cells for me to inseminate. We're going to clone me. My son will be as close to me as modern biological science can make him.'

'Human cloning is outlawed,' Verwoerd murmured.

'In most nations on Earth,' Humphries conceded. 'But even on Earth there are places where a man of means can have himself cloned. And here in Selene, well – why not?'

Another little Martin Humphries, Verwoerd thought. But she said nothing.

'The cloning procedure is still a bit dicey,' he went on, as casually as a man discussing the stock market, 'but my people should be able to produce some viable fertilized eggs and get a few women to carry them.'

'Then why do you want me?'

He waved a hand. 'You're a very good physical specimen; you ought to make a good home for my clone. Besides, it's rather poetic, don't you think? You won't have sex with me, but you'll bear my son. That toy boy of yours isn't the only one with a poetic soul.'

'I see,' Verwoerd said, feeling slightly numbed by his cheerful arrogance.

'What I need is several wombs to carry the zygotes to term. I've decided you'd be perfect for the job. Young, healthy, and all that.'

'Me.'

'I've gone through your medical records and your family history,' Humphries said. 'You might say that I know you inside out.'

She was not amused.

'You carry my son to term,' he said, his smile fading, his tone more commanding. 'You'll get a very sizeable bonus. I'll even transfer a couple more of my asteroids to your Bandung Associates.'

The pit of her stomach went hollow.

'Did you think you could embezzle three very profitable asteroids from me without my finding out about it?' Humphries asked, grinning with satisfaction.

Verwoerd knew it was hopeless. She felt glad that she had Dorik on her side.

37

As they pulled up their convoy of four minitractors to the entrance of the Helvetia warehouse, Harbin saw that there were only two people on duty there, and one of them was a woman, grey-haired and grandmotherly, but with a hard, scowling face. She was stocky, stumpy, built like a weight-lifter.

'What do you guys want?' she demanded as Harbin got down from the lead tractor.

'Don't give us a hard time, grandmother,' he said gently. 'Just relax and do what you're told.'

A face-to-face job like this was very different from shooting up spacecraft in the dark emptiness of the Belt. That was like a game; this was blood. Be still, he commanded silently. Don't make me kill you. But he felt the old rage building up inside him: the manic fury that led to death.

'What are you doing here?' the woman repeated truculently. 'Who the hell are you assholes?'

Working hard to keep his inner rage under control, Harbin waved his undisciplined team into the Helvetia warehouse. They all wore breathing masks, nothing unusual in the dusty tunnels of Ceres. They also wore head-hugging caps that had been ferried in all the way from Earth; with the caps on, no one could see a man's hair colour or style. Harbin also made certain none of his crew had any name tags or other identification on themselves. If Trace Buchanan had taken that simple precaution he would undoubtedly still be alive now, Harbin thought.

'What's this goddam parade of tractors for?' the woman demanded.

She was wearing a breathing mask, too. So was the skinny kid standing a few paces down the shadowy aisle of tall shelves.

'We're here to empty out your warehouse,' Santorini said, strutting up to her.

'What the hell do you mean?' the woman asked angrily, reaching for the phone console.

Santorini swatted her to the floor with a backhand smack. The kid back in the stacks threw up his hands in the universal sign of surrender.

'Come on,' Santorini said, waving to the rest of them.

Harbin nodded his approval. They started to move in. The kid stood absolutely still, frozen in terror to judge from the look on his ashen face. Santorini kicked him in the stomach so hard he bounced off the shelving and collapsed groaning to the floor.

'How's that for martial arts?' Santorini shouted over his shoulder as the others revved up the minitractors and trundled into the warehouse, raising billows of black dust.

Swaggering little snot, Harbin thought, looking at the woman Santorini had knocked down. Her lip was bloody, but the look in her eyes proclaimed pure malevolent fury. She struggled to her feet, then lurched toward the phone console.

Harbin grabbed her by one shoulder. 'Be careful, grandmother. You could get hurt.'

The woman growled and swung her free fist into Harbin's temple. The blow surprised more than hurt him, but it triggered his inner anger.

'Stop it,' he snarled, shaking her.

She aimed a kick at his groin. Harbin twisted sideways to catch it on his hip but it still hurt. Without thinking he slid the electrodagger out of its sheath on his wrist and slit her throat.

The old woman gurgled blood and collapsed to the floor like a sack of wet cement.

Fuchs' black mood of frustration and anger deepened into an even darker pit of raging fury as he and Nodon boarded the Astro Corporation ship *Lubbock Lights* bound for Ceres. They had said a lingering goodbye to George at the Pelican Bar the night before.

'I'll be back at the Belt as soon's me arm grows back,' George had promised several times, over many beers.

Pancho had bought all their rounds, drinking with them in gloomy comradeship.

Now, with a thundering headache and a towering hatred boiling inside him, Fuchs faced the four-day journey back to Ceres with the exasperation of a caged jungle beast.

When the message came in from Amanda he nearly went berserk.

He was in his privacy compartment, a cubicle barely large enough to hold a narrow cot, trying to sleep. Each time he closed his eyes, he saw Martin Humphries sneering at him. And why not? Fuchs raged at himself. He has gotten away with murder. And piracy. No one can stop him; no one will even stand up to him except me, and I'm powerless; a pitiful, impotent, useless fool.

For hours he tossed on the cot, clad only in a pair of shorts, sweating, his hair matted, his jaw stubbled with a two day growth of beard. Stop this fruitless nonsense! he raged at himself. It's useless to pound your head against a wall. Think! Prepare! If you want revenge on Humphries you must out-think him, you must make plans that are crystal clear, find a strategy that will crush him once and for all. But each time he tried to think clearly, logically, his anger rose like a tide of red-hot lava, overwhelming him.

The phone buzzed. Fuchs sat up on the cot and told the computer to open the incoming message.

Amanda's face filled the screen on the bulkhead at the foot of the cot. She looked tense, even though she tried to smile.

'Hello, dear,' she said, brushing at a stray lock of hair that had fallen across her forehead. 'I'm fine, but they've looted the warehouse.'

'What? Looted?'

She couldn't hear or see him, of course. She had sent the message a good fifteen minutes earlier.

'They killed Inga. Out of pure bloodthirsty spite, from what Oscar told me. You remember him, Oscar Jiminez. He's the young boy I hired to help handle the stock.'

She's terrified, Fuchs realized, watching the lines of strain on her face, listening to her ramble on.

'They came in during the night shift, when only Inga and Oscar were there, about nine or ten of them, according to Oscar. They beat him and slit Inga's throat. The man who did it laughed about it. Then they emptied the warehouse. Every box, every carton, every bit of stock we had. It's all gone. All of it.'

Fuchs' teeth were grinding together so furiously his jaw began to ache. Amanda was trying hard to keep from crying.

'I'm perfectly fine,' she was saying. 'This all happened late last night. The morning shift found Inga on the floor in a pool of blood and Oscar tied and gagged in the rear of the warehouse. And-and that's the whole story. I'm all right, no one's bothered me at all. In fact, everyone seems to be very protective of me today.' She brushed at her hair again. 'I suppose that's all there is to say, just at this moment. Hurry home, darling. I love you.'

The screen went blank. Fuchs pounded a fist against the unyielding bulkhead and roared a wordless howl of frustration and rage.

He leaped off the cot and ripped open the flimsy sliding door of his cubicle. Still clad in nothing but his shorts he stormed up the ship's passageway to the bridge.

'We must get to Ceres as fast as possible!' he shouted to the lone crew woman sitting in the command chair.

Her eyes popped wide at the sight of him.

'Now! Speed up! I have to get to Ceres before they murder my wife!'

The woman looked at Fuchs as if he were a madman, but she summoned the captain, who came onto the bridge wrapped in a knee-length silk robe, rubbing sleep from his eyes.

'My wife is in danger!' Fuchs bellowed at the captain. 'We must get to Ceres as quickly as possible!'

It was maddening. Fuchs babbled his fears to the captain, who finally understood enough to put in a call to IAA mission control for permission to increase the ship's acceleration. It took nearly half an hour for a reply to come back from IAA headquarters on Earth. Half an hour while Fuchs paced up and down the bridge, muttering, swearing, wondering what was happening at Ceres. The captain suggested that they both put on some clothes, and went back to his quarters. Nodon appeared, then left without a word and returned minutes later carrying a pair of coveralls for Fuchs.

Tugging them on and sealing the velcro closures, Fuchs asked the crew woman to open a communications channel to Ceres. She did so without hesitation.

'Amanda,' he said, 'I'm on the way. We are asking for permission to accelerate faster, so I might be able to reach you before our scheduled arrival time. I'll let you know. Stay in your quarters. Ask some of the people who work for us to act as guards at your door. I'll be there as soon as I can, darling. As soon as I can.'

By the time the captain returned to the bridge, face washed, hair combed, and wearing a crisp jumpsuit with his insignia of rank on the cuffs, the answer arrived from IAA control.

Permission denied. *Lubbock Lights* will remain at its current velocity vector and arrive at Ceres in three and a half more days, as scheduled.

Trembling, Fuchs turned from the robot-like IAA controller's image on the screen to the uniformed captain.

'I'm sorry,' said the captain, with a sympathetic shrug of his shoulders. 'There's nothing I can do.'

Fuchs stared at the man's bland, scrubbed face for half a moment, then smashed a thundering right fist into the captain's jaw. His head snapped back and blood flew from his mouth as he buckled to the deck. Turning on the gape-mouthed crew woman, Fuchs ordered, 'Maximum acceleration. *Now*!'

She glanced at the unconscious captain, then back at Fuchs. 'But I can't—'

He ripped an emergency hand torch from its clips on the bulkhead and brandished it like a club. 'Get away from the controls!'

'But—'

'Get out of that chair!' Fuchs bellowed.

She jumped to her feet and stepped sideways, slipping along the curving control panel, away from him.

'Nodon!' Fuchs called.

The young Asian stepped through the open hatch. He

glanced nervously at the captain lying on the deck, then at the frightened crew woman.

'See that no one enters the bridge,' Fuchs said, tossing the hand torch to him. 'Use that on anyone who tries to get in here.'

Nodon gestured the woman toward the hatch as Fuchs sat in the command chair and studied the control board. Not much different from *Starpower* or the other vessels he'd been on.

'What about the captain?' the crew woman asked. He was groaning softly, his legs starting to move a little.

'Leave him here,' said Fuchs. 'He'll be all right.'

She left and Nodon swung the hatch shut behind her.

'Lock it,' Fuchs ordered.

The captain sat up, rubbed at the back of his neck, then looked up blearily at Fuchs sitting at the controls.

'What the hell do you think you're doing?' the captain growled.

'I'm trying to save my wife's life,' Fuchs answered, pushing the ship's acceleration to its maximum of one-half normal Earth gravity.

'This is piracy!' the captain snapped.

Fuchs swung around in the command chair. 'Yes,' he said tightly. 'Piracy. There's a lot of it going around, these days.'

38

'He's *what*?' Hector Wilcox could not believe his ears.

Zar looked stunned as he repeated, 'He's taken over the *Lubbock Lights*. He's accelerating at top speed to Ceres. Our flight controllers have ordered him to cease and desist, but he's paying no attention to them.'

Wilcox sagged back in his desk chair. 'By god, the man's committed an act of piracy.'

'It would seem so,' Zar agreed cautiously. 'According to our people on Ceres, someone broke into Fuchs' warehouse and cleaned out everything. They murdered one of the people working there. A woman.'

'His wife?'

'No, an employee. But you can understand why Fuchs wants to reach Ceres as quickly as he can.'

'That doesn't justify piracy,' Wilcox said sternly. 'As soon as he arrives at Ceres, I want our people there to arrest him.'

Zar blinked at his boss. 'They're only flight controllers, not policemen.'

'I don't care,' Wilcox said sternly. 'I won't have people flouting IAA regulations. This is a matter of principle!'

Diane Verwoerd had spent most of the morning combing her apartment for bugs. She found none, which worried her. She felt certain that Humphries had bugged her place; how else would he know what she was doing? Yet she could find no hidden microphones, no microcameras tucked in the ventilator grilles or anywhere else.

Could Martin have been guessing about Bandung Associates? She had thought she'd covered her trail quite cleverly, but perhaps naming her dummy corporation after the city in which her mother had been born wasn't so clever after all.

Whatever, she decided. Martin knows that I've winkled him out of several choice asteroids and he's willing to let that pass – if I carry his cloned baby for him.

She shuddered at the thought of having a foreign creature inserted into her womb. It's like the horror vids about alien invaders we watched when we were kids, she thought. And she had heard dark, scary stories about women who carried cloned fetuses. It wasn't like carrying a normal baby. The afterbirth bloated up so hugely that it could kill the woman during childbirth, they said.

But the rational part of her mind saw some possible advantages. Beyond the monetary rewards, this could put me in a position of some power with Martin Humphries, she told herself. The mother of his clone. That puts me in a rather special position. A very special position, actually. I might even gain a seat on his board of directors, if I play my cards well.

If I live through it, she thought, shuddering again.

Then she thought of Harbin. Beneath all that steely self-control was a boiling hot volcano, she had discovered. If I play him correctly, he'll sit up and roll over and do any other tricks I ask him to perform. A good man to have at my side, especially if I have to deal with Martin after the baby is born.

The baby. She frowned at the thought, wondering, Should I tell Dorik about it? Eventually, I'll have to. But not now. Not yet. He's too possessive, too macho to accept the fact that I'll be carrying someone else's baby while I'm letting him make love to me. I'll have to be very careful about the way I handle that little bit of news.

She walked idly through her apartment, thinking, planning, staring at the walls and ceilings as if she could make the electronic bugs appear just by sheer willpower. Martin was snooping on her, she felt certain of it. He certainly got his jollies watching her with Dorik.

With a reluctant sigh she decided she would have to call in some expert help to sweep the apartment. The trouble is, she told herself, all the experts I know are HSS employees. Can I get them to do the job right?

Then she thought of an alternative. Doug Stavenger must know some experts among Selene's permanent population. She'd ask Stavenger to help her.

Both of the IAA flight controllers were waiting at the cave that served as a reception area at Ceres' spaceport when Fuchs returned. He had left *Lubbock Lights* in orbit around the asteroid, turning the ship back to its captain, and ridden a shuttlecraft down to the surface. The two controllers left their posts in the cramped IAA control centre and went to the reception area to meet him.

As Fuchs stepped out of the pressurized tunnel that connected the shuttlecraft to the bare rock cave, the senior controller, a thirtyish woman of red hair and considerable reputation among the men who frequented The Pub, cleared her throat nervously and said:

'Mr Fuchs, the IAA wants you to turn yourself in to the authorities to face a charge of piracy.'

Fuchs ignored her and started for the tunnel that led to the underground living quarters. She glanced at her partner, a portly young man with a round face, high forehead, and a long ponytail hanging halfway down his back. They both started after Fuchs.

He said, 'Mr Fuchs, please don't make this difficult for us.'

Kicking up clouds of dark grey dust as he shuffled into the tunnel, Fuchs said, 'I will make it very easy for you. Go away and leave me alone.'

'But, Mr Fuchs.'

'I have no intention of turning myself in to you or anyone else. Leave me alone before you get hurt.'

They both stopped so short that swirling clouds of dust enveloped them to their knees. Fuchs continued shambling down the tunnel, heading for his quarters and his wife.

He was no longer the raging, bellowing puppet yanked this way and that by strings that Martin Humphries controlled. His fury was still there, but now it was glacially cold, calm, calculating. He had spent the hours in transit to Ceres calculating, planning, preparing. Now he knew exactly what he had to do.

There was no guard at his door. Hands trembling, Fuchs slid it open. And there was Amanda sitting at the work desk, her eyes wide with surprise.

'Lars! No one told me you had arrived!' She jumped out of her chair and threw her arms around his neck.

'You're all right?' he asked, after kissing her. 'No one has tried to harm you?'

'I'm fine, Lars,' she said. 'And you?'

'I've been charged with piracy by the IAA. They probably want me to turn around and return to Selene for a trial.'

She nodded gravely. 'Yes, they sent me a message about it. Lars, you didn't need to take over the ship. I'm quite all right.'

Despite everything, he grinned at her. Feeling her in his arms, most of his fears dissolved. 'Yes,' he breathed, 'you're more than all right.'

Amanda smiled back at him. 'The door's still open,' she pointed out.

He stepped away from her, but instead of closing the door, went to the desk. The wallscreen showed a form letter from their insurance carrier. Fuchs scanned it as far as the line telling them that their policy had been terminated, then blanked the screen.

'I've got to go to the warehouse,' he said. 'Nodon will be waiting there for me.'

'Nodon?' Amanda asked. 'George's crewman?'

'Yes,' said Fuchs as he called up Helvetia's personnel file. 'He was with us at that farce of a hearing in Selene.'

'I know.'

Looking up at her, he asked, 'Which of these people witnessed Inga's murder?'

'Oscar Jiminez,' Amanda said, pulling up the room's other chair to sit beside him.

'Him I must speak to,' Fuchs said. He got up from his chair and went to the door, leaving Amanda sitting there alone.

Nodon was waiting for him at the warehouse. Feeling uneasy, irritable, Fuchs called Jiminez and two other Helvetia employees, both men, both young. When they all arrived at the warehouse's little office area, the place felt crowded and suddenly warm from the press of their bodies. Jiminez, skinny and big-eyed, stood between the two other men.

'In a day or two,' Fuchs told them, 'we're going to the HSS warehouse and take back the material they stole from us.'

The men looked nervously at one another. 'And we're going to administer justice to the men who murdered Inga,' he added.

'They've gone,' Jiminez said, in a voice pitched high with tension.

'Gone?'

'The day after the raid on our warehouse,' said one of the older men. 'Nine HSS employees left on one of their ships.'

'Where is it bound?' Fuchs demanded. 'Selene?'

'We don't know. Maybe it's going to Earth.'

'We'll never get them once they reach Earth,' Fuchs muttered.

'They brought in another bunch on the ship that took them away,' said the other man, a trim-looking welterweight with a military buzz cut and jewellery piercing his nose, both eyebrows and both earlobes.

'I suppose they are guarding the HSS warehouse,' Fuchs said, glancing at Nodon, who remained silent, taking it all in.

The young man nodded.

'Very well, then,' Fuchs said. He took a deep breath. 'This is what we're going to do.'

Dossier: Joyce Takamine

'It's not what you know,' he told her, time and again. 'It's who you know.'

Joyce 'graduated' from picking to helping run one of the big farm management companies. Armed with her degree in computer analysis, she had worked up the courage to ask the young man running the company's local office for a job. He offered to discuss the possibilities over dinner, in his mobile home. They ended the evening in his bed. She got the job and lived for the next two years with the young man, who constantly reminded her about 'the great American know-who.'

When Joyce took his advice and left him for an older man who happened to be an executive with Humphries Space Systems, the young man was shocked and disillusioned.

'But it's what you've been telling me to do all along,' Joyce reminded him.

'Yeah,' he admitted, crestfallen. 'I just didn't think you'd take my advice so literally.'

Joyce stayed with the executive only long enough to win a position at HSS's corporate offices in Selene. She left the tired old Earth at last, and moved to the Moon.

39

Two days passed.

Amanda spent the time trying to find out what her husband was up to. To no avail. It was clear to her that Lars was planning something, that he was putting together some scheme to fight back against Humphries. But he would not tell her a word of it.

Lars is a different man, she realised. I hardly recognize him. He's like a caged animal, pacing, waiting, planning, looking for a way to break free. He's dead set on wreaking vengeance on the people who looted his warehouse and killed Inga, but he won't reveal his thinking to me.

In bed he relaxed a little, but still he kept his own counsel. 'The only law out here is the law we enforce for ourselves,' he said in the darkness as he lay next to her. 'If we don't fight back he'll turn us all into his slaves.'

'Lars, he's hired trained mercenaries. Professional killers,' Amanda pleaded.

'Scum,' her husband answered. 'I know how to deal with scum.'

'They'll kill you!'

He turned to her, and she could feel the heat radiating from his body. 'Amanda, my darling, they are going to kill me anyway. That's what he wants. Humphries wants me dead and he won't be satisfied until I'm killed and you're at his mercy.'

'But if you'd only—'

'Better for me to strike at him when and where he doesn't

expect it,' Fuchs said, reaching for her. 'Otherwise, we just wait here like sheep ready to be slaughtered.'

'But what are you going to do? What do you—'

He silenced her with a finger on her lips. 'Better that you don't know, my darling. You can't be any part of this.'

Then he made love to her ardently, furiously. She revelled in his passion, but she found that not even the wildest sex could divert him from his aim. He was going to attack HSS, attack Humphries, extract vengeance for the killings that had been perpetrated. He was going to get himself killed, she was certain.

His singlemindedness frightened Amanda to the depths of her being. Nothing can move him a centimetre away from this, she realized. He's rushing toward his own death.

The morning of the third day she found an incoming message from IAA headquarters on Earth. A ship had been dispatched to Ceres, carrying a squad of Peacekeeper troops. Their assignment was to arrest Lars Fuchs and return him to Earth for trial on a charge of piracy.

Fuchs smiled grimly when she showed him the message.

'Piracy.' He practically spat the word. '*He* destroys ships and loots and murders and they say I have no proof. Me, they accuse of piracy.'

'Go with them,' Amanda urged. 'I'll go with you. You can tell them that you were in a state of emotional distress. Surely they'll understand—'

'With Humphries pulling the strings?' he snapped. 'They'll hang me.'

It was hopeless, Amanda admitted.

Fuchs sat in the empty Helvetia warehouse, going over his plan with Nodon.

'It all hinges on the people you've recruited,' he said.

Nodon dipped his chin once in acknowledgement.

The two men were sitting at the desk just off the entrance to the warehouse, in a pool of light from a single overhead fluorescent shining in the otherwise darkened cave. The shelves were empty. No one else was there. Beyond the entrance, the tunnel led, in a slight downward slope, toward the living quarters and life support equipment; in the other direction, to the HSS warehouse and the reception area where incoming personnel and freight arrived and outgoing flights departed.

'You're certain these men are reliable?' Fuchs asked for the twelfth time that evening.

'Yes,' Nodon replied patiently. 'Men and women both; most of them are from families I have known for many years. They are honourable persons and will do what you command.'

'Honourable,' Fuchs murmured. Honour meant that a person would take your money and commit mayhem, even murder, to earn that pay. I'm hiring mercenary killers, he told himself. Just as Humphries has. To fight evil you have to do evil things yourself.

'They understand what they must do?'

Nodon allowed himself a rare smile. 'I have explained it all to them many times. They may not speak European languages very well, but they understand what I have told them.'

Fuchs nodded, almost satisfied. Through Nodon he had hired six Asians, four men and two women. Pancho had allowed them to ride to Ceres on an Astro freighter, and now they waited aboard the half-finished habitat orbiting the asteroid. As far as Pancho or anyone else was concerned, they had been recruited to restart construction of the habitat. Only Fuchs and Nodon – and the six themselves – knew better.

'All right,' Fuchs said, struggling against the surge of doubts and worries that churned in his guts. 'At midnight, then.'

'Midnight,' Nodon agreed.

With a sardonic smile, Fuchs added, 'We've got to get this over and done with before the Peacekeeper troops arrive.'

'We will,' Nodon said confidently.

Yes, Fuchs thought, this will be over and done with in a few hours, one way or the other.

The nearest thing to a restaurant on Ceres was The Pub, where mechanical food dispensers standing off in one corner offered packaged snacks and even microwaveable full meals of a sort.

Fuchs made a point of taking Amanda out to dinner that night. The Pub was usually noisy but this particular evening the crowd was hushed; everyone seemed tense with expectation.

That worried Fuchs. Had news of his planned attack leaked out? Humphries' people could be waiting for him; he could be leading his men into a trap. He mulled over all the possibilities as he picked listlessly at his dinner.

Amanda watched him with worried eyes. 'You haven't been eating right ever since you came back from Selene,' she said, her tone more concerned than accusatory.

'No, I suppose I haven't.' He tried to make a careless shrug. 'I sleep well, though. Thanks to you.'

Even in the dim lighting he could see her cheeks flush. 'Don't try to change the subject, Lars.' But she was smiling as she spoke.

'Not at all. I merely—'

'Do you mind if I sit with you?'

They looked up and saw Kris Cardenas holding a dinner tray in both hands.

'No, of course not,' said Amanda. 'Do join us.'

Cardenas put her tray on their table. 'The place is crowded tonight,' she said as she sat on the vacant chair between them.

'But awfully quiet,' Amanda said. 'It's as if everyone here is attending a funeral.'

'The Peacekeepers are due to arrive tomorrow,' Cardenas said, jabbing a fork into her salad. 'Nobody's happy with the thought.'

'Ah, yes,' said Fuchs, feeling relieved. 'That's why everyone is so morose.'

'They're worried it's the first step in a takeover,' Cardenas said.

'Takeover?' Amanda looked startled at the idea. 'Who would take control of Ceres? The IAA?'

'Or the world government.'

'The world government? They don't have any authority beyond geosynchronous Earth orbit.'

Cardenas shrugged elaborately. 'It's their Peacekeepers that arrive tomorrow.'

'Looking for me,' Fuchs said unhappily.

'What do you intend to do?' Cardenas asked.

Looking squarely at Amanda, Fuchs said, 'I'm certainly not going to fight the Peacekeepers.'

Cardenas chewed thoughtfully for a few moments, swallowed, then said, 'We did at Selene.'

Shocked, Amanda asked, 'What are you suggesting, Kris?'

'Nothing. Nothing at all. I'm just saying that six Peacekeeper troops in their nice little blue uniforms aren't enough to force you to go back Earthside with them, Lars. Not if you don't want to go.'

'You mean we should fight them?' Amanda said, her voice hollow with fright.

Cardenas leaned closer and replied, 'I mean that I could name a hundred, a hundred and fifty rock rats here who'd protect you against the Peacekeepers, Lars. You don't have to go with them if you don't want to.'

'But they're armed! They're trained soldiers!'

'Six soldiers against half the population of Ceres? More than half? Do you think they'd fire on us?'

Amanda looked at Fuchs, then back to Cardenas. 'Wouldn't they just send more troops, if these six were turned away?'

'If they tried that, I'm willing to bet that Selene would step in on our side.'

'Why would Selene—?'

'Because,' Cardenas explained, 'if the world government takes over Ceres, Selene figures they'll be next. They tried it once, remember.'

'And failed,' Fuchs said.

'There are still nutcases Earthside who think their government should control Selene. And every human being in the whole solar system.'

Fuchs closed his eyes, his thoughts spinning. He had never had the faintest inkling that Selene could become involved in his fight. This could lead to war, he realized. An actual war, bloodshed and destruction.

'No,' he said aloud.

Both women turned toward him.

'I will not be the cause of a war,' Fuchs told them.

'You'll surrender to the Peacekeepers tomorrow, then?' Cardenas asked.

'I will not be the cause of a war,' he repeated.

After dinner, Fuchs led Amanda back to their quarters. She leaned heavily on his arm, yawning drowsily.

'Lord, I don't know why I feel so sleepy,' she mumbled.

Fuchs knew. He had worried, when Cardenas sat at their table, that he wouldn't be able to slip the barbiturate into his wife's wine. But he had gotten away with it, Kris hadn't noticed, and now Amanda was practically falling asleep in his arms.

She was too far gone to make love. He helped her to undress; by the time she lay her head on the pillow she was peacefully unconsciousness.

For a long time Fuchs gazed down at his beautiful wife, tears misting his eyes.

'Goodbye, my darling,' he whispered. 'I don't know if I will ever see you again. I love you too much to let you risk your life for my sake. Sleep, my dearest.'

Abruptly he turned and left their apartment, carefully locking the door as he stepped out into the tunnel. Then he headed for the warehouse and his waiting men.

40

Oscar Jiminez was clearly worried as Fuchs led Nodon and four others of his employees up the tunnel toward the HSS warehouse.

'There's only six of us,' he said, his voice low and shaky as he shuffled along the dusty tunnel beside Fuchs. 'I know it's after midnight, but they've probably got at least ten guys in the warehouse.'

Fuchs and Nodon carried hand lasers, fully charged. The others held clubs of asteroidal steel, made from the Helvetia warehouse shelving. All of them wore breathing masks to filter out the dust they were raising as they marched purposefully up the tunnel.

'Don't worry,' Fuchs assured him calmly. 'You won't have to fight. If all goes as I've planned, there won't be a fight.'

'But then why—'

'I want you to identify the man who murdered Inga.'

'He won't be there,' the teenager said. 'They took off. I told you.'

'Perhaps. We'll see.'

'Anyway, they were wearing breathing masks and some kind of hats. I couldn't identify the guy if I saw him.'

'We'll see,' Fuchs repeated.

Fuchs stopped them at one of the safety hatches that stood every hundred metres or so along the tunnel. He nodded to one of the men, a life support technician, who pried open the cover of the hatch's set of sensors.

Fuchs motioned his men through the open hatch as the technician fiddled with the sensors.

'Got it,' he said at last.

An alarm suddenly hooted along the tunnel. Fuchs twitched involuntarily even though he had expected the blaring noise. The technician scurried through the hatch just before it slammed shut automatically.

'Hurry!' Fuchs shouted, and he started racing up the tunnel.

Half a dozen bewildered HSS men were out in the tunnel in front of the entrance to their warehouse, looking up and down as if searching for the source of the alarm. They were clad in light tan coveralls bearing the HSS logo; none of them wore breathing masks.

'Hey, what's going on?' one of them yelled as he saw Fuchs and the others rushing toward them, raising billows of dust.

Fuchs pointed his laser at them. It felt clumsy in his hand, yet reassuring at the same time.

'Don't move!' he commanded.

Five of the six froze in place. Two of them even raised their hands above their heads.

But the sixth one snarled, 'What the fuck do you think you're doing?' and started to duck back inside the warehouse entrance.

Quite deliberately, Fuchs shot him in the leg. The laser cracked once, and the man yowled and went down, face first, into the dust, a smoking charred spot on the thigh of his coveralls. A part of Fuchs' mind marveled that there was no recoil from the laser, no smoke or smell of gunpowder.

They herded the six men inside the warehouse, two of them dragging their wounded companion. Two more HSS men were at the desktop computer, trying to determine what was causing the alarm signal when all the life support systems were solidly in the green. Completely surprised, they raised their hands above their heads when Fuchs trained his laser on them.

They looked disgruntled once they realized that they were prisoners. Fuchs made them sit on the floor, hands on their knees.

Four minitractors were sitting just inside the warehouse entrance. Fuchs detailed four of his men to rev them up; then they went through the aisles, pulling down anything that looked as if it had come from the Helvetia warehouse and loading it on to the tractors.

'There'll be a couple dozen more of our people on their way up here,' said the man Fuchs had shot. He sat with his companions, both hands clutching his thigh. Fuchs could not see any blood seeping from his wound. The laser pulse cauterizes as it burns through the flesh, he remembered.

'No one will come here,' he said to the wounded man. 'The alarm sounded only in this section of the tunnel. Your friends are sleeping peacefully in their quarters.'

Finally the laden tractors were parked out in the tunnel, heaped high with crates and cartons that bore the Helvetia imprint.

'I think that's everything,' said one of Fuchs' men.

'Not quite,' Fuchs said. Turning to Jiminez, he asked, 'Do you recognize any of these men?'

The youngster looked frightened. He shook his head. 'They were wearing breathing masks, like I told you. And funny kind of hats.'

'This one, maybe?' Fuchs prodded the shoulder of the man he had shot.

'I don't know!' Jiminez whined.

Fuchs took a deep breath. 'All right. Take the tractors back to our warehouse.'

Jiminez dashed out into the tunnel, plainly glad to get away.

'You think you're going to get away with this?' the wounded man growled. 'We're gonna break you into little pieces for this. We'll make you watch while we bang your wife. We're gonna make her—'

Fuchs wheeled on him and kicked him in the face, knocking him onto his back. The others scuttled away. Nodon shouted, 'Don't move!' and levelled his laser at them.

Frenzied with rage, Fuchs rushed to one of the storage bins lining the wall and yanked out a length of copper wire. Tucking his laser back into its belt pouch, he wrapped one end of the wire several times around the groaning, half-conscious man's neck, then dragged him toward the high stacks of shelving, coughing and sputtering blood from his broken teeth.

The others watched, wide-eyed, while Fuchs knotted the wire at the man's throat, then tossed the other end of it around one of the slim steel beams supporting the shelving. He yanked hard on the wire and the wounded man shot up into the air, eyes bulging, both hands struggling to untie the wire cutting into his neck. He weighed only a few kilos in Ceres' light gravity, but that was enough to slowly squeeze his larynx and cut off his air.

Blazing with ferocity, Fuchs whirled on the other HSS men, who sat in the dust staring at their leader thrashing, choking, his legs kicking, a strangled, gargling inhuman sound coming from his bleeding mouth.

'Watch!' Fuchs roared at them. 'Watch! This is what happens to any man who threatens my wife. If any of you even *looks* at my wife I'll tear your guts out with my bare hands!'

The hanging man's struggles weakened. He lost control

of his bladder and bowels in a single burst of stench. Then his arms fell to his sides and he became still. The men on the floor stared, unmoving, open-mouthed. Even Nodon watched in terrible fascination.

'Come,' Fuchs said at last. 'We're finished here.'

41

Diane Verwoerd was in bed with Dorik Harbin when her phone buzzed and the wallscreen began blinking with PRIORITY MESSAGE in bright yellow letters.

She disentangled herself from him and sat up.

'It's almost two,' he grumbled. 'Aren't you ever off duty?'

But Diane was already staring at the frightened face of her caller and listening to his breathless, almost incoherent words. Then the screen showed a man hanging by the neck, eyes bulging, tongue protruding from his mouth like an obscene wad of flesh.

'Great god,' said Harbin.

Verwoerd slipped out of bed and began to get dressed. 'I'll have to tell Martin about this personally. This isn't the kind of news you relay by phone.'

She found Humphries still awake and alone in the big mansion's game room.

'We have troubles,' she said as she entered the room.

He was bent over the pool table, cue in hand. Humphries had spent many long hours learning how to shoot pool on the Moon. The one-sixth gravity did not affect the way the balls rolled or caromed, except in subtle ways. A visitor could play a few rounds and think nothing was different from Earth. That's when Humphries would offer a friendly wager on the next game.

'Troubles?' he said, intent on his shot. He made it, the balls clicked and one of the coloured ones rolled to a corner pocket and dropped neatly in. Only then did Humphries straighten up and ask, 'What troubles?'

'Fuchs raided the warehouse and killed one of the men there. Hanged him.'

Humphries' eyes widened. 'Hanged him? By the neck?'

'The others have quit,' Verwoerd went on. 'They want no part of this fight.'

He snorted disdainfully. 'Cowardly little shits.'

'They were hired to bully people. They never thought that Fuchs would fight back. Not like this.'

'I suppose they expect me to pay for their transport back to Earth,' Humphries groused.

'There's more.'

He turned and stacked his cue in its rack. 'Well? What else?'

'Fuchs has stolen an Astro ship, the *Lubbock Lights*. He's left—'

'How the hell could he steal a ship?' Humphries demanded angrily.

Verwoerd kept the pool table between them. 'According to the captain—'

'The same limp spaghetti that allowed Fuchs to commandeer his ship on the way in to Ceres?'

'The same man,' Verwoerd replied. 'He reported to the IAA that a half-dozen Asians boarded the ship under the pretence of loading ores. They were armed and took control of the ship. Then Fuchs came up from Ceres with another oriental, apparently the man who was with him when he was here for the hearing. They packed the captain and regular crew into the shuttlecraft and sent them back down to Ceres.'

'Son of a bitch,' Humphries said fervently.

'By the time the Peacekeepers arrived, Fuchs was gone.'

320

'In one of Pancho's ships.' He grinned. 'Serves her right.'

Verwoerd pursed her lips, weighing the dangers of antagonizing him further against the pleasures of yanking his chain a little bit. 'If possession is nine-tenths of the law,' she said slowly, 'then it's mostly his ship now, not Astro's.'

He glared at her, fuming. She kept her expression noncommittal. A smile now could set off a tantrum, she knew.

He stood in angry silence for several long moments, face flushed, grey eyes blazing. Then, 'So those pansies you hired to clean out Fuchs want to quit, do they?'

'Actually, Grigor hired them,' Verwoerd said. 'And, yes, they want out. Fuchs made them watch while he hanged their leader.'

'And Amanda? She went with him?'

With a shake of her head, Verwoerd answered, 'No, she's still on Ceres. Apparently Fuchs' people took back most of the items that were looted from their warehouse.'

'He left her on Ceres? Alone?'

'He hanged the man because he made some crack about her. Nobody's going to go near her, believe me.'

'I don't want anybody to go near her,' Humphries snapped. 'I want her left strictly alone. I've given orders about that!'

'No one's harmed her. No one's threatened her.'

'Until this asshole opened his big mouth in front of Fuchs.'

'And he strung him up like a common criminal.'

Humphries leaned both hands on the rim of the pool table and hung his head. Whether he was overwhelmed with sorrow or anger or the burden of bad news, Verwoerd could not tell.

At last he lifted his head and said crisply, 'We need

someone to go after Fuchs. Someone who isn't afraid of a fight.'

'But nobody knows where he's gone,' Verwoerd said. 'It's an awfully big area, out there in the Belt. He's not sending out a tracking beacon. He's not even sending telemetry data. The IAA can't find him.'

'He'll run out of fuel sooner or later,' Humphries said. 'He'll have to come back to Ceres.'

'Maybe,' she said, uncertainly.

Pointing a finger at her as if he were pointing a pistol, Humphries said, 'I want somebody out there who can find him. And kill him. I want somebody who knows how to fight and isn't afraid of being shot at.'

'A professional soldier,' Verwoerd said.

Humphries smiled thinly. 'Yes. Like your toy boy.'

She had known from the moment she'd heard about Fuchs' actions that it would come down to this. 'I agree,' she said, keeping her voice even, emotionless. 'Harbin would be perfect for this task. But . . .' She let the word dangle in the air between them.

'But?' Humphries snapped. 'But what?'

'He'll want to be paid a lot more than he's been getting.'

He stared at her for a moment. 'Are you representing him now? Are you his goddamned agent?'

She made herself smile at him. 'Let's just say that I know him a lot better than I did a couple of weeks ago.'

Despite his irritation, Humphries grinned back at her. 'You know him more intimately, eh?'

She stopped smiling and refused to rise to his bait.

'All right, pack him off to track down Fuchs. And get Amanda on the phone for me.'

'The distance is too great for real-time conversation,' she pointed out.

His eyes flashed angrily, but then the tension drained out

of his shoulders. Verwoerd thought: not even you can beat the laws of physics, Martin. With all your money, you still have to accept the facts of time and distance.

'I'll send her a message, then.'

She knew he had sent other messages to Fuchs' wife. She had never answered any of them.

42

As they sped away from Ceres on *Lubbock Lights*, Fuchs familiarized himself with the crew that Nodon had recruited. Silent, blank-faced Asians, Mongols, descendents of Genghis Khan. They didn't look particularly ferocious; they looked more like kids, students, fugitives from some high-tech training school. But they apparently knew their way around a fusion-powered spacecraft.

All the fusion ships were built along two or three basic designs, Fuchs knew. *Lubbock Lights* was a freighter, but now he had armed the vessel with three mining lasers taken from his own warehouse.

Once they were well under way, accelerating through the Belt at a lunar one-sixth g, Fuchs called his crew into the galley. The seven of them crowded the little space, but they stood respectfully before him, their dark eyes showing no trace of emotion.

'You realize that we are outlaws now,' he began, without preamble. 'Pirates. There is no turning back.'

Nodon spoke up. 'We will follow you, sir. For us there is no other choice.'

Fuchs looked from one face to another. Young, all of them. Some with facial tattoos, all of them pierced here and there with plain metal adornments. Already embittered by the way the world had treated them. Nodon had given him their backgrounds. They had all come from poor families who struggled to send their children to university where they could learn how to become rich. All six of them had studied technical subjects, from computer design to electrical engineering to environmental sciences. All six of them had been told, upon graduation, that there were no jobs for them. The world was crumbling, their home cities were being abandoned because of drought and terrible, disastrous storms that flooded the parched valleys and washed away the farmlands instead of nourishing them. All six of their families became part of the huge, miserable, starving army of the homeless, wandering the stark, bitter land, reduced to begging or stealing or giving up to die on the roadside.

These are the statistics that I've read about, Fuchs realized. Ragged scarecrows who have lost their place in society, who have lost their families and their futures. The desperate ones.

He cleared his throat and resumed, 'One day, I hope, we will be able to return to Earth as wealthy men and women. But that day may never come. We must live as best as we can, and accept whatever comes our way.'

Nodon said gravely, 'That is what each of us has been doing, sir, for more than a year. Better to be here and fight for our lives than to be miserable beggars or prostitutes, kicked and beaten, dying slowly.'

Fuchs nodded. 'Very well, then. We will take what we need, what we want. We will not allow others to enslave us.'

Brave words, he knew. As Nodon translated them to the crew, Fuchs wondered if he himself truly believed them. He wondered which of these blank-faced strangers would turn him in for a reward. He decided that he would have to protect his back at all times.

The Asians spoke among themselves in harsh whispers. Then Nodon said, 'There is one problem, sir.'

'A problem?' Fuchs snapped. 'What?'

'The name of this ship. It is not appropriate. It is not a fortunate name.'

Fuchs thought, It's a downright silly name. *Lubbock Lights.* He had no idea who had named the ship or why.

'What do you propose?' he asked.

Nodon glanced at the others, then said, 'That is not for us to say, sir. You are the captain; you must make the decision.'

Again, Fuchs looked from face to impassive face. Young as they were, they had learned to hide their feelings well. What's going on behind their masks, he wondered. Is this a test? What do they expect from me? More than a name for this ship. They're watching, judging, evaluating me. I'm supposed to be their leader; they want to see the quality of my leadership.

A name for the ship. An appropriate, fortunate name.

A single word escaped his lips. '*Nautilus.*'

They looked puzzled. At least I've cracked their shell a little, Fuchs thought.

He explained, 'The *Nautilus* was a submarine used by its captain and crew to destroy evil ships and wreak vengeance on wrong-doers.'

Nodon frowned a little, then translated to the others. There was a little jabbering back and forth, but after a few moments they were all bobbing their heads in agreement. A couple of them even smiled.

'*Nautilus* is a good name,' said Nodon.

Fuchs nodded. '*Nautilus* it will be, then.' He had no intention of telling them that the vessel was fictional, or how it – and its captain – came to their end.

Amanda woke up with a headache throbbing behind her eyes. She turned and saw that Lars was not in bed with her. And the wallscreen showed seven messages waiting.

Strange that there was no sound from the phone. Lars must have muted it, she thought.

Sitting up in the bed, she saw that he was not in the apartment. Her heart sank.

'Lars,' she called softly. There was no answer. He's gone, she knew. He's gone from me. For good, this time.

The first message on the list was from him. Barely able to speak the command, her voice trembled so badly, she told the computer to put it on the screen.

Lars was sitting at the desk in the warehouse, looking as grim as death. He wore an old turtleneck shirt, dead black, and shapeless baggy slacks. His eyes were unfathomable.

'Amanda, my dearest,' he said, 'I must leave you. By the time you get this message I will be gone. There is no other way, none that I can see. Go to Selene, where Pancho can protect you. And no matter what you hear about me, remember that I love you. No matter what I have done or will do, I do it because I love you and I know that as long as you are near me your life is in danger. Goodbye, darling. I don't know if I'll ever see you again. Goodbye.'

Without realizing it, she told the computer to rerun his message. Then again. But by then she couldn't see the screen for the tears that filled her eyes.

Fourteen Months Later

43

She used her maiden name now: Amanda Cunningham. It wasn't that she wanted to hide her marriage to Lars Fuchs; everybody on Ceres, every rock rat in the Belt knew she was his wife. But ever since Fuchs had taken off into the depths of space, she had worked on her own to establish herself and to achieve her goals.

She sold off Helvetia Ltd, to Astro Corporation for a pittance. Pancho, for once, outmanoeuvred Humphries and convinced the Astro board of directors that this was a bargain they could not refuse.

'Besides,' Pancho pointed out to the board, staring straight at Humphries, across the table from her, 'we should be competing out there in the Belt. It's where the natural resources are, and that's where the real wealth comes from.'

Glad to be rid of Helvetia, Amanda watched Pancho begin to develop the warehouse into a profitable facility for supplying, repairing and maintaining the ships that plied the Belt. She lived off the income from the Astro stock that she had acquired from the sale, and concentrated her efforts on another objective, one that had originally been Lars' goal: his idea of getting the rock rats to form some kind of government for themselves so they could begin to establish a modicum of law and order on Ceres. The independent-minded prospectors and miners had been dead set against any form of government, at first. They saw laws as restrictions on their freedom;

order as strangling their wild times when they put in at Ceres for R&R.

But as more and more ships were attacked they began to understand how vulnerable they were. A war was blazing across the Belt, with HSS attacking the independents, trying to drive them out of the Belt, while Fuchs singlehandedly fought back against HSS ships, swooping out of nowhere to cripple or destroy them.

In Selene, Martin Humphries howled with frustrated anger as his costs for operating in the Belt escalated over and again. It became constantly more expensive to hire crews to work HSS ships, and neither the IAA nor Harbin nor any of the other mercenaries that Humphries hired could find Fuchs and kill him.

'They're helping him!' Humphries roared time and again. 'Those goddamned rock rats are harbouring him, supplying him, helping him to knock off my ships.'

'It's worse than that,' Diane Verwoerd retorted. 'The rock rats are arming their ships now. They're shooting back – ineptly, for the most part. But it's getting more dangerous out there.'

Humphries hired still more mercenaries to protect his ships and seek out Lars Fuchs. To no avail.

The people who, like Amanda, actually lived on Ceres – the maintenance technicians and warehouse operators and shop-keepers, bartenders, even the prostitutes – they gradually began to see that they badly needed some kind of law and order. Ceres was becoming a dangerous place. Mercenary soldiers and outright thugs swaggered through the dusty tunnels, making life dangerous for anyone who got in their way. Both HSS and Astro hired 'security' people to protect their growing assets of facilities and ships. Often enough the security people fought each other in the tunnels, The Pub, or the warehouses and repair shops.

Big George Ambrose returned to Ceres, his arm regrown, with a contract to work as a technical supervisor for Astro.

'No more mining for me,' he told his friends at The Pub. 'I'm a fookin' executive now.'

But he brawled with the roughest of them. Men and women began to carry hand lasers as sidearms.

At last, Amanda got most of Ceres' population to agree to a 'town meeting' of every adult who lived on the asteroid. Not even The Pub was big enough to hold all of them, so the meeting was held electronically, each individual in their own quarters, all linked through the interactive phone system.

Amanda wore the turquoise dress she had bought at Selene as she sat at the desk in her quarters and looked up at the wallscreen. Down in the comm centre, Big George was serving as the meeting's moderator, deciding who would talk to the group, and in which order. He had promised, at Amanda's insistence, that everyone who wanted to speak would get his or her turn. 'But it's goin' t'be a bloody long night,' he predicted.

It was. *Everyone* had something to say, even though many of them repeated ideas and positions already discussed several times over. Through the long, long meeting – sometimes strident, often boring – Amanda sat and carefully listened to each and every one of them.

Her theme was simple. 'We need some form of government here on Ceres, a set of laws that we can all live by. Otherwise we'll simply have more and more violence until the IAA or the Peacekeepers or some other outside group come in and take us over.'

'More likely it'd be HSS,' said a disgruntled-looking prospector, stuck on Ceres temporarily while his damaged ship was being repaired. 'They've been trying to take us over for years, now.'

'Or Astro,' an HSS technician fired back.

George cut them both off before an argument swallowed up the meeting. 'Private debates can be held on another channel,' he announced cheerfully, turning the screen over to the lean-faced, sharp-eyed Joyce Takamine, who demanded to know when the habitat was going to be finished so they could move up to it and get out of this dust-filled rathole.

Amanda nodded sympathetically. 'The habitat is in what was once called a catch-22 situation,' she replied. 'Those of us who want it finished so we can occupy it, haven't the funds to get the work done. Those who have the funds – such as Astro and HSS – have no interest in spending them on completing the habitat.'

'Well, somebody ought to do something,' Takamine said firmly.

'I agree,' said Amanda. 'That's something that we could do if we had some form of government to organize things.'

Nearly an hour later, the owner of The Pub brought up the key question. 'But how're we gonna pay for a government and a police force? Not to mention finishing the habitat. That'll mean we all hafta pay taxes, won't it?'

Amanda was ready for that one. In fact, she was glad the man had brought it up.

Noting that the message board strung across the bottom of her wallscreen immediately lit up from one end to the other, she said sweetly, 'We will not have to pay taxes. The corporations can pay, instead.'

George himself interjected the question everybody wanted to ask. 'Huh?'

Amanda explained, 'If we had a government in place, we could finance it with a very small tax on the sales that HSS and Astro and any other corporation make here on Ceres.'

It took a few seconds for George to sort out all the

incoming calls and flash the image of a scowling prospector onto her wallscreen.

'You put an excise tax on the corporations and they'll just pass it on to us by raising their prices.'

Nodding, Amanda admitted, 'Yes, that's true. But it will be a very small rise. A tax of one-tenth of a per cent would bring in ten thousand international dollars for every million dollars in sales.'

Without waiting for the next questioner, Amanda continued, 'HSS alone cleared forty-seven million dollars in sales last week. That's nearly two and a half a billion dollars per year, which means a tax of one-tenth of one per cent would bring us more than twenty-four million in tax revenue from HSS sales alone.'

'Could we finish the habitat on that kind of income?' asked the next caller.

Amanda replied, 'Yes. With that kind of assured income, we could get loans from the banks back on Earth to finish the habitat, just the same as any government secures loans to finance its programmes.'

The meeting dragged on until well past one a.m., but when it was finished, Amanda thought tiredly that she had accomplished her objective. The people of Ceres were ready to vote to form some kind of a government.

As long as Martin Humphries doesn't move to stop us, she reminded herself.

44

Lars Fuchs stood straddle-legged behind the pilot's chair on the bridge of *Nautilus*, carefully studying the screen's display, which showed what looked like an HSS freighter.

According to the communications messages to and from the ship, she was the *W. Wilson Humphries*, the pride of Humphries Space Systems' growing fleet of ore carriers, named after Martin Humphries' late father. She was apparently loaded with ores from several asteroids, heading out of the Belt toward the Earth/Moon system.

Yet Fuchs felt uneasy about approaching her. Fourteen months of hiding in the Belt, of taking his supplies and fuel from ships he captured, of sneaking quick visits aboard friendly independent ships now and then, had taught him wariness and cunning. He was leaner now, still built like a miniature bull but without a trace of fat on him. Even his face was harder, his square jaw more solid, his thin slash of a mouth set into a downturned scowl that seemed permanent.

He turned to Nodon, who was handling the communications console on the bridge.

'What's the traffic to and from her?' he asked, jabbing a thumb toward the visual display.

'Normal telemetry,' Nodon replied. 'Nothing more at present.'

To the burly young woman in the pilot's chair Fuchs said, 'Show me the plot of her course over the past six weeks.' He spoke in her own Mongol dialect now; haltingly, but he was learning his crew's language. He did not want them to be able to keep secrets from him.

One of the auxiliary screens lit up with thin looping curves of yellow set against a sprinkling of green dots.

Fuchs studied the display. If it was to be believed, that yellow line represented the course that the Humphries ship had followed over the past six weeks, picking up loads of ore at five separate asteroids. Fuchs did not believe it.

'It's a fake,' he said aloud. 'If she'd really followed that plot she'd be out of propellant by now and heading for a rendezvous with a tanker.'

Nodon said, 'According to their flight plan, they will increase acceleration in two hours and head inward to the Earth/Moon system.'

'Not unless they've refuelled in the past few days,' Fuchs said.

'There is no record of that. No tankers in the vicinity. No other ships at all.'

Fuchs received brief snippets of intelligence information from the friendly ships he occasionally visited. Through those independent prospectors he had arranged a precarious line of communications back to Ceres by asking them to tell Amanda what frequency he would use to make his next call to her. His calls were months apart, quick spurts of ultra-compressed data that told her little more than the fact that he was alive and missed her. She sent similar messages back by tight laser beam to predesignated asteroids. Fuchs was never there to receive them; he left a receiving set on each asteroid ahead of time that relayed the message to him later. He had no intention of letting Humphries' people trap him.

But now he felt uneasy about this supposed fat, dumb freighter. It's a trap, he heard a voice in his mind warning him. And he remembered that Amanda's latest abbreviated message had included a piece of information from Big George to the effect that Humphries' people were setting up decoy ships, 'Trojan horses,' George called them, armed with laser weapons and carrying trained mercenary troops whose mission was to lure Fuchs into a fatal trap.

'George says it's only a rumour,' Amanda had said hastily, 'but it's a rumour that you should pay attention to.'

Fuchs nodded to himself as he stared at the image of the ship on the display screen. *Some rumours can save your life,* he thought.

To the woman piloting the ship he commanded, 'Change course. Head back deeper into the Belt.'

She wordlessly followed his order.

'We leave the ship alone?' Nodon asked.

Fuchs allowed the corners of his mouth to inch upward slightly into a sour smile, almost a sneer. 'For the time being. Let's see if the ship leaves us alone once we've turned away from it.'

Sitting in the command chair on the bridge of *W. Wilson Humphries* Dorik Harbin was also watching the display screens. He clenched his teeth in exasperation as he saw the ship that had been following them for several hours suddenly veer away and head back into the depths of the Belt.

'He suspects something,' said his second-in-command, a whipcord-lean Scandanavian with hair so light she seemed almost to have no eyebrows. She had a knack for stating the obvious.

Wishing he were alone, instead of saddled with this useless crew of mercenaries, Harbin muttered, 'Apparently.'

The crew wasn't useless, exactly. Merely superfluous. Harbin preferred to work alone. With automated systems he had run his old ship, *Shanidar*, by himself perfectly well. He could go for months alone, deep in solitude, killing when the time came, finding solace in his drugged dreaming.

But now he had a dozen men and women under his

command, his responsibility, night and day. Diane had told him that Humphries insisted on placing troops in his decoy ships; he wanted trained mercenaries who would be able to board Fuchs' ship and carry back his dead body.

'I tried to talk him out of it,' Diane whispered during their last night together, 'but he won't have it any other way. He wants to see Fuchs' dead body. I think he might have it stuffed and mounted as a trophy.'

Harbin shook his head in wonder that a man with such obsessions could direct a deadly, silent war out here among the asteroids. Well, he thought, perhaps only a man who is obsessed can direct a war. Yes, he answered himself, but what about the men and women who do the fighting? Are we obsessed, too?

What difference? What difference does any of it make? How did Khayyám put it?

> The Worldly Hope men set their Hearts upon
> Turns Ashes – or it prospers; and anon,
>   Like snow upon the desert's dusty face
> Lighting a little Hour or two – is gone.

What difference do our own obsessions make? They turn to ashes or prosper. Then they melt like snow upon the desert. What difference? What difference?

He heard his second-in-command asking, 'So what are we going to do? He's getting away.'

He said calmly, 'Obviously, he doesn't believe that we're carrying ores back to Earth. If we turn around and chase him we'll simply be proving the point.'

'Then what do we do?' the Scandanavian asked. The expression on her pale bony face plainly showed that she wanted to go after the other ship.

'We continue to behave as if we are an ore-carrier. No change in course.'

340

'But he'll get away!'

'Or come after us, once we've convinced him that we're what we pretend to be.'

She was clearly suspicious of his logic, but murmured, 'We play cat and mouse, then?'

'Yes,' said Harbin, glad to have satisfied her. It didn't seem to matter to her which one of the two ships was the cat and which the mouse.

In Selene, Douglas Stavenger stood by his office window, watching the kids out in the Grand Plaza soaring past on their plastic wings. It was one of the thrills that could be had only on the Moon, and only in an enclosed space as large as the Grand Plaza that was filled with breathable air at normal Earth pressure. Thanks to the light gravity, a person could strap wings onto her arms and take off to fly like a bird on nothing more than her own muscle power. How long has it been since I've done that, Stavenger asked himself. The answer came to him immediately: too blasted long. He chided himself: for a retired man, you don't seem to have much fun.

Someone was prodding the council to allow him to build a golf course out on the floor of Alphonsus. Stavenger laughed at the idea of playing golf in space suits, but several council members seemed to be considering it quite seriously.

His desk phone chimed, and the synthesized voice announced, 'Ms Pahang is here.'

Stavenger turned to his desk and touched the button that opened his door. Jatar Pahang stepped through, smiling radiantly.

She was the world's most popular video star, 'The Flower of Malaya,' a tiny, delicate, exotic woman with lustrous dark eyes and long, flowing, midnight-black hair that cascaded over her bare shoulders. Her dress shimmered in the glareless overhead lights of Stavenger's office as she walked delicately toward him.

Stavenger came around his desk and extended his hand to her. 'Ms Pahang, welcome to Selene.'

'Thank you,' she said in a voice that sounded like tiny silver bells.

'You're even more beautiful than your images on screen,' Stavenger said as he led her to one of the armchairs grouped around a small circular table in the corner of his office.

'You are very gracious, Mr Stavenger,' she said as she sat in the chair. Her graceful frame made the chair seem far too large for her.

'My friends call me Doug.'

'Very well. And you must call me Jatar.'

'Thank you,' he said, sitting beside her. 'All of Selene is at your feet. Our people are very excited to have you visit us.'

'This is my first time off Earth,' she said. 'Except for two vids we made in the *New China* space station.'

'I've seen those videos,' Stavenger said, grinning.

'Ah. I hope you enjoyed them.'

'Very much,' he said. Then, pulling his chair a bit closer to hers, he asked, 'What can I do, personally, to make your visit more . . . productive?'

She glanced at the ceiling. 'We are alone?'

'Yes,' Stavenger assured her. 'No listening devices here. No bugs of any kind.'

She nodded, her smile gone. 'Good. The message I carry is for your ears alone.'

'I understand,' said Stavenger, also fully serious.

Jatar Pahang was not only the world's most popular video star, she was also the mistress of Xu Xianqing, chairman of the world government's inner council, and his secret envoy to Stavenger and the government of Selene.

45

The art of governing, thought Xu Xianqing, was much like the art of playing the piano: never let your left hand know what your right hand is doing.

It had been a long, treacherous road to the leadership of the world government. Xianqing had left many friends, even members of his own family, by the wayside as he climbed to the shaky pinnacle of political power. The precepts of K'ung Fu-Tzu had been his nominal moral guide, the writings of Machiavelli his actual handbook. During his years of struggle and upward striving, more than once he marvelled inwardly that he – or anyone – had bothered even to try. Why am I driven to climb higher and higher? he asked himself. Why do I take on such pains, such risks, such unending toil?

He never found a satisfactory answer. A religious man might have concluded that he had been chosen for this service, but Xianqing was not a man of faith. Instead, he considered himself a fatalist, and reasoned that the blind forces of history had somehow pushed him to his present pinnacle of authority and power.

And responsibility. Perhaps that was the true, ultimate answer. Xianqing understood that with the power and authority came responsibility. Planet Earth was suffering a cataclysm unmatched in all of human history. The climate was changing so severely that no one could cope with the sudden disastrous floods and droughts. Earthquakes raged. Cities were drowned by rising waters. Farmlands were parched by shifting rainfall patterns, then washed away by savage storms. Millions had already died and hundreds of millions more were starving and homeless.

In many lands the bewildered, desperate people turned to fundamentalist faiths for help and strength. They traded their individual liberties for order and safety. And food.

Yet, Xianqing knew, the human communities on the Moon and in the Asteroid Belt lived as if the travails of their brethren on Earth meant nothing to them. They controlled untold wealth: energy that Earth's peoples desperately needed; natural resources beyond all that Mother Earth could provide for its wretched and despairing children.

The giant corporations sold fusion fuels and solar energy to the wealthy of Earth. They sold metals and minerals from the asteroids to those who could afford it. How can I convince them to be more generous, to be more helpful, Xianqing asked himself every day, every hour.

There was only one way that he could see: seize control of the riches of the Asteroid Belt. The fools who plied that dark and distant region, the prospectors and miners and their corporate masters, were fighting among themselves. The ancient crime of piracy had reappeared out there among the asteroids. Murder and violence were becoming commonplace.

The world government could send an expedition of Peacekeepers to Ceres to restore order, Xianqing thought. They could stop the mayhem and bring peace to the region. And thereby, they could gain control of those precious resources. The prospectors and miners would grumble, of course. The corporations would howl. But what could do they do in the face of a *fait accompli*? How could they protest against the establishment of law and peace along that murderous frontier?

One thing barred such a prospect: Selene.

The people of the lunar community had fought for their independence and won it. They would not sit back and allow the world government to seize the Asteroid Belt. Would they fight? Xianqing feared that they would. It would not be difficult for them to attack spacecraft that were launched from Earth. We live in the bottom of a gravity well, Xianqing knew. While our vessels fight their way into space, Selene could destroy them, one by one. Or worse yet, cut off all supplies of energy and raw materials from space. Earth would be reduced to darkness and impotence.

No, direct military intervention in the Belt would be counterproductive – unless Selene could be neutralized.

So, Xianqing decided, if I cannot be a conqueror, I will become a peacemaker. I will lead the effort to resolve the fighting in the Asteroid Belt and gain the gratitude of future generations.

His first step was to contact Douglas Stavenger, in secret, through Xu Xianqing's beautiful mistress.

46

'This isn't going to work, Lars,' said Boyd Nielson.

Fuchs muttered, 'That's my worry, not yours.'

'But some of those people down there are just construction workers,' Nielson pleaded. 'Some of them are friends of ours, for god's sake!'

Fuchs turned away. 'That can't be helped,' he growled. 'They shouldn't be working for Humphries.'

Nielson was an employee of Humphries Space Systems, commander of the ore freighter *William C. Durant*, yet he had been a friend of Fuchs' in the early days on Ceres, before all the troubles began. Fuchs had tracked the *Durant* as the ship picked its way from one asteroid to another, loading ores bound back to the Earth/Moon system. With a handful of his crew, Fuchs had boarded Nielson's ship and taken it over. Faced with a half-dozen fierce-looking armed men and women, there was no fight, no resistance from Nielson or his crew. With its tracking beacon and all other communications silenced, Fuchs abruptly changed *Durant*'s course toward the major asteroid Vesta.

'Vesta?' Nielson had asked, puzzled. 'Why there?'

'Because your employer, the high-and-mighty Mr Martin Humphries, is building a military base there,' Fuchs told him.

Fuchs had heard the rumours in the brief flurries of communications he received from Amanda, back at Ceres. HSS people were building a new base on Vesta. More armed ships and mercenaries were going to use the asteroid as the base from which they would hunt down Lars Fuchs and kill him.

Fuchs decided to strike first. He ordered the compliant Nielson to contact Vesta and tell them that *Durant* had been damaged in a fight with Fuchs' ship and needed to put in for repairs.

But now, as the two men stood at the command console on *Durant*'s bridge and Nielson finally understood what Fuchs was going to do, he began to feel frightened. He was a lean, wiry redhead with a pointed chin and teeth that seemed a size too big for his jaw. Nielson's crew were all locked in their privacy cubicles. Nodon and the other Asians were at the ship's controls. Nielson was not the nervous type, Fuchs knew, but as they approached Vesta he started to perspire visibly.

'For the love of mercy, Lars,' he protested.

'Mercy?' Fuchs snapped. 'Did they show mercy to Niles Ripley? Did they show mercy to any of the people in the ships they destroyed? This is a war, Boyd, and in a war there is no mercy.'

The asteroid looked immense in the bridge's main display screen, a massive dark sphere, pitted with numberless craters. Spreading across one of the biggest of the craters, Fuchs saw, was a tangle of buildings and construction equipment. Scorch marks showed where shuttlecraft had landed and taken off again.

'Three ships in orbit,' Fuchs noted, eyes narrowing.

'Might be more on the other side, too,' said Nielson.

'They'll all be armed.'

'I imagine so.' Nielson looked distinctly uncomfortable. 'We could all get killed.'

Fuchs nodded, as if he had made a final calculation and was satisfied with the result.

To Nodon, sitting in the pilot's chair, Fuchs said, 'Proceed as planned.'

Turning to Nielson, 'You should ask them for orbital parameters.'

Nielson's left cheek ticked once. 'Lars, you don't have to do this. You can get away, go back to your own ship, and no harm done.'

Fuchs glowered at him. 'You don't understand, do you? I *want* to do harm.'

Standing on the rim of the unnamed crater in his dust-caked spacesuit, Nguyan Ngai Giap surveyed the construction work with some satisfaction. Half a dozen long, arched habitat modules were in place. Front-loaders were covering them with dirt to protect them against radiation and micrometeor hits. They would be ready for occupation on time, and he had already reported back to HSS headquarters at Selene that the troops could be sent on their way. The repair facilities were almost finished, as well. All was proceeding as planned.

'Sir, we have an emergency,' said a woman's voice in his helmet earphones.

'An emergency?'

'An ore freighter, the *Durant*, is asking permission to take up orbit. It needs repairs.'

'*Durant*? Is this an HSS vessel?' Giap demanded.

'Yes, sir. An ore freighter. They say they were attacked by Fuchs' ship.'

'Give them permission to establish orbit. Alert the other ships up there.'

'Yes, sir.'

Only after he had turned his attention back to the construction work did Giap wonder how *Durant* knew of this facility. HSS vessel or not, this base on Vesta was supposed to be a secret.

'Freighter approaching,' called the crewman on watch in *Shanidar*'s bridge.

Dorik Harbin hardly paid any attention. After the fruitless attempt to decoy Fuchs with the fake ore freighter, he had returned to the repaired and refurbished *Shanidar*, waiting for him in a parking orbit around Vesta. As soon as refuelling was completed, Harbin could resume his hunt for Lars Fuchs. *Shanidar*'s crew had been disappointed that they had put in at Vesta instead of Ceres, where they could have spent their waiting time at the asteroid's pub or brothel. Let them grumble, Harbin said to himself. The sooner we get Fuchs the sooner all of us can leave the Belt for good.

He thought of Diane Verwoerd. No woman had ever gained a hold on his emotions, but Diane was unlike anyone he had ever known before. He had had sex with many women, but Diane was far more than a bedmate. Intelligent, understanding, and as sharply driven to get ahead in this world as Harbin was himself, she knew more about the intrigues and intricacies of the corporate world than Harbin had ever guessed at. She would be a fine partner in life, a woman who could stand beside him, take her share of the burden and then some. And the sex was good, fantastic, better than any drug.

Do I love her? Harbin asked himself. He did not understand what love truly was. Yet he knew that he wanted Diane for himself; she was his key to a better world, she could raise him above this endless circle of mercenary killing that was his life.

He also knew that he would never have her until he found this elusive madman Fuchs and killed him.

'She's carrying a heavy load of ores,' the crewman noticed.

Harbin turned his attention to the approaching ore freighter in the display screen on his bridge. Damaged in a fight with Fuchs, her captain had said. But he could see no signs of damage. Maybe they're hidden by that pile of rocks she's carrying, he thought. More likely the frightened rabbit raced away from the first sign of trouble and scurried here for protection.

Harbin's beard had grown thick again over the months he had been chasing Fuchs across the Belt. He scratched at it idly as a new thought crossed his mind. How did this ore freighter know that we are building a base here? It's supposed to be a secret. If every passing tugboat knows about it, Fuchs will hear of it sooner or later.

What difference? Harbin asked himself. Even if he knows about it, what can he do? One man in one ship, against a growing army. Sooner or later we'll find him and destroy him. It's only a matter of time. And then I can return to Diane.

As he watched the display screen, he noticed that the approaching freighter didn't seem to be braking into an orbit. Instead, it was accelerating. Rushing toward the asteroid.

'It's going to crash!' Harbin shouted.

Manoeuvring a spinning spacecraft with pinpoint accuracy was beyond the competence of any of Fuchs' people. Or of Nielson's crew. But to the ship's computer it was child's play: simple Newtonian mechanics, premised on the first law of motion.

Fuchs felt the ship's slight acceleration as *Durant* followed the programmed course. Standing spread-legged on the bridge, he saw the rugged, pitted surface of the asteroid rushing closer and closer. He knew they were accelerating at a mere fraction of a g, but as he stared at the screen it seemed as if the asteroid was leaping up toward them. Will we crash? He asked himself. What of it? came his own mind's answer. If we die, that's the end of it.

But as *Durant* accelerated silently toward the asteroid its manoeuvring jets fired briefly and the clamps holding nearly fifteen hundred thousand tons of asteroidal ores let go of their burden. The ship jinked slightly and slipped over the curve of the asteroid's massive dark rim, accelerating toward escape velocity. The jettisoned ores spread into the vacuum of space like a ponderous rock slide, pouring down slowly toward the crater where the HSS base was being built.

In that vacuum, a body in motion stays in motion unless some outside force deflects it. In Vesta's minuscule gravity, the rocks actually weighed next to nothing. But their mass was still nearly fifteen hundred thousand tons. They fell gently, slowly toward the asteroid's surface, a torrent of death moving with the languid tumbling motion of a nightmare.

'Sir? Incoming call from *Shanidar*.' The woman's voice in Giap's earphones sounded strained, almost frightened.

Without waiting for him to tell her, she connected Harbin. 'That ship is on a collision course with – no, wait. It's released its cargo!'

It was difficult to look up from inside the spacesuit helmet, but when Giap twisted his head back and slightly sideways all he could see was a sky full of immense dark blobs blotting out the stars.

He heard Harbin's tense, strained voice, 'Break us out of orbit!'

Then the ground jumped so hard he was blasted completely off his feet and went reeling, tumbling into an all-engulfing billow of black dust.

Aboard *Shanidar*, Harbin watched in horror as the rocks dropped ever-so-softly toward the construction site in the crater. The ore freighter was masked by them and heading over the curve of the asteroid's bulk. The men and women down in that crater were doomed, condemned to inexorable death.

'Break us out of orbit!' he shouted to the woman in the pilot's chair.

'Refuelling isn't completed!'

'Forget the motherhumping refuelling!' he yelled. Pounding the intercom key on the console before him, he called to the crew, 'Action stations! Arm the lasers! *Move!*'

But he knew it was already too late.

With nothing to impede their motion the landslide of rocks glided silently through empty space until they smashed into the surface of Vesta. The first one missed the buildings, but blasted into the rim of the crater, throwing up a shower of rocky debris that spread leisurely across the barren landscape. The next one obliterated several of the metal huts dug halfway into the crater floor. Then more and more of the rocks pounded in, raising so much dust and debris that Harbin could no longer see the crater at all. The dust cloud rose and drifted, a lingering shroud of destruction and death, slowly enveloping the entire asteroid, even reaching out toward his ship. Harbin unconsciously expected it to form a mushroom shape, as nuclear bombs did on Earth. Instead the cloud simply grew wider and darker, growing as if it fed on the asteroid's inner core. Harbin realized it would hang over the asteroid for days, perhaps weeks, a dark pall of death.

By the time *Shanidar* had broken out of orbit, the ore freighter was long gone. The damnable dust cloud even interfered with Harbin's attempts to pick it up on a long-range radar sweep.

47

'He *what?*' Martin Humphries screamed.

'He wiped out the base on Vesta,' Diane Verwoerd repeated. 'All fifty-two people on the surface were killed.'

Humphries sank back in his chair. He had been on the phone negotiating a deal to sell high-grade asteroidal nickel-iron to the government of China when Diane had burst into his office, tight-lipped and pale with shock. Seeing the expression on her face, Humphries had fobbed the Chinese negotiator off onto one of his underlings in Beijing as politely as possible, then cut the phone link and asked her what was the matter.

'Wiped out the entire base?' he asked, his voice gone hollow.

'One of our ships in orbit around Vesta got caught in the dust cloud and—'

'What dust cloud?' Humphries demanded irritably.

Verwoerd sank into one of the chairs in front of his desk and explained as much as she knew of Fuchs' attack. Humphries had never seen her look so stunned, so upset. It intrigued him.

'Fifty-two people killed,' she murmured, almost as if talking to herself. 'And the crew of the ship that was damaged by the dust cloud . . . four of them died when their life support system broke down.'

Humphries calmed himself, then asked, 'And Fuchs got away?'

'Yes,' she said. 'Harbin tried to give chase, but he was too low on fuel. He had to turn back.'

'So he's still out there, hatching more mischief.'

'Mischief?' She looked squarely at him. 'This is more than mischief, Martin. This is a massacre.'

He nodded, almost smiled. 'That's right. That's exactly what it was. A deliberate massacre.'

'You look as if you're pleased about it.'

'We can make it work in our favour,' Humphries said.

'I don't see—'

'Those rock rats have been helping Fuchs, giving him fuel and food, giving him information about our ships' schedules and destinations.'

'Yes,' she said. 'Obviously.'

'*Somebody* told him about the base on Vesta.'

'Obviously,' Verwoerd repeated.

'And now he's killed a couple of dozen of his own people. Rock rats. Construction workers. Right?'

She took a deep breath, straightened up in the chair. 'I see. You think they'll turn against him.'

'Damned right.'

'What if they turn against *you*?' Verwoerd asked. 'What if they decide that working for HSS is too dangerous, no matter how good the pay?'

'That's where we play our trump card,' Humphries said. 'Stavenger's been putting out feelers about arranging a peace conference. Apparently the world government's sticking its nose into the situation and Stavenger wants to head them off.'

'A peace conference?'

'Humphries Space Systems, Astro, Selene . . . even the world government will send a representative. Slice up the Asteroid Belt neat and clean, so there's no more fighting.'

'Who'll represent the rock rats?'

He laughed. 'What do we need them for? This is strictly among the major players. The big boys.'

'But it's about them,' Verwoerd countered. 'You can't divide up the Asteroid Belt between HSS and Astro without including them.'

With a shake of his head, Humphries said, 'You don't understand history, Diane. Back in the twentieth century there was a big flap in Europe over some country called Czechoslovakia. It doesn't even exist any more. But at that time, Germany wanted to take it over. England and France met with the Germans in Munich. They decided what to do with Czechoslovakia. The Czechs weren't included in the conference. No need for them; the big boys parcelled it all out.'

Verwoerd shot back, 'And a year later all Europe was at war. I know more history than you think. You can't have a conference about parcelling out the Belt without having the rock rats in on it.'

'Can't we?'

'You'll be throwing them into Fuchs' arms!'

Humphries frowned at that. 'You think so?' he asked.

'Of course.'

'H'mm. I hadn't thought of that. Maybe you're right.'

Verwored leaned toward him slightly. 'But if you included the rock rats, got them to send a representative to the conference—'

'We'd be making them a party to the crime,' Humphries finished for her.

'And the only outsider, the only one who doesn't agree to the settlement, would be Fuchs.'

'Right!'

'He'd be isolated,' Verwoerd said. 'Really alone. He'd

have to give up. Nobody would help him and he'd be forced to quit.'

Humphries clasped his hands behind his head and leaned far back in his big, comfortable chair. 'And he'd also have to face trial for killing all those people on Vesta. I love it!'

48

Much to his surprise, George Ambrose was elected 'mayor' of Ceres.

His official title was Chief Administrator. The election came about once the inhabitants of Ceres reluctantly admitted that they needed some form of government, if only to represent them against the growing mayhem that was turning the Belt into a war zone. Fuchs' destruction of the Vesta base was the last straw; more than two dozen residents of Ceres had been killed in the attack.

Amanda tried to distance herself from her estranged husband's offense by throwing herself into the drive to bring some form of law and order to Ceres. She worked tirelessly to craft a government, searching databases for months to find governmental organizations that might fit the needs of the rock rats. Once she had put together a proposed constitution, the rock rats grumbled and fussed and ripped it to shreds. But she picked up the pieces and presented a new document that addressed most of their complaints. With great reluctance, they voted to accept the new government – as long as it imposed no direct taxes on them.

Staffing the government was simple enough: there were enough clerks and technical supervisors on Ceres to handle the jobs. Many of them were delighted with the prospect of getting an assured salary, although Amanda made certain that each bureaucrat had to satisfy a strict performance review annually to hold onto the job.

Then came the selection of a governing board. Seven

people were chosen at random by computer from the permanent residents of Ceres. No one was allowed to refuse the 'honour.' Or the responsibility. Amanda was not selected by the computerized lottery, which disappointed her. George was, which disappointed him even more.

At their first meeting, the board elected George their chief, over his grudging protests.

'I won't fookin' shave,' he warned them.

'That's all right, George,' said one of the young women on the board. 'But could you just tone down your language a little?'

Thus it was that Big George Ambrose, now the reluctant 'mayor' of the rock rats, became their representative in the conference that took place at Selene, where he had once lived as a fugitive and petty thief.

'I'm not goin' by myself,' George insisted. 'I'll need some back-up.'

The governing board decided they could afford to send two assistants with George. His first real decision as the newly elected Chief Administrator of Ceres was to pick the two people who would go with him. His first choice was easy: Dr Kris Cardenas.

As he tussled in his mind over who the other appointee should be, Amanda surprised him by volunteering for the post.

She popped into his 'office' – actually nothing more than his everyday living quarters – and told him that she wanted to be part of the delegation to Selene.

'You?' George blurted. 'How come?'

Amanda looked away from his eyes. 'I've done as much work to create this government as anyone. More, in fact. I deserve to go.'

George said warily, 'This won't be a fookin' vacation, y'know.'

'I understand that.'

He offered her his best chair, but she shook her head and remained standing in the middle of his one-room residence. She seemed calm, and very determined. The place was pretty messy, George thought: bed's not made, plates in the sink. But Amanda simply stood there staring off into infinity, seeing – what? George wondered.

'Humphries is there, in Selene,' he said.

Amanda nodded, her face expressionless, frozen, as if she were afraid to show any emotion at all.

'Lars won't like you goin'.'

'I know,' she said, her voice almost a whisper. 'I've thought it all out, George. I must go with you. But I don't want Lars to know. Please don't tell him.'

Scratching his beard, trying to sort out what she was saying, George asked, 'How can I tell 'im? The only way I get any word to him is through you.'

'I've got to go with you, George,' Amanda said, almost pleading now. 'Don't you see? I've got to do whatever I can to put an end to this fighting. To save Lars before they find him and kill him!'

George nodded, finally understanding. At least, he thought he did.

'All right, Amanda. You can come with us. I'll be glad to have you.'

'Thank you, George,' she said, smiling for the first time. But there was no happiness in it.

Amanda had wrestled with her conscience for two days before asking George to let her go with him to Selene. She knew that Lars would not want her to be so near to Humphries, especially without him there to protect her. She herself did not fear Humphries any longer; she felt that she could handle him. Martin wouldn't hurt me, she told herself. Besides, George and Kris will be there to chaperone me.

What worried her was Lars' reaction. He would be dead-set against her going to Selene, to Humphries' home territory. Yet Amanda decided to go, after two days of inner turmoil.

Without telling Lars.

A total of twenty-two ships made the rendezvous above the ruined base on Vesta. The dust cloud from Fuchs' attack had finally settled, but Harbin could see nothing of the base; not even the crater in which it had been situated was visible anymore. It was all obliterated by a new set of overlapping craters, fresh, sharp, raw-looking circular scars on the asteroid's dark surface. They reminded Harbin of the scars left on sperm whales by the suckers of giant squids' tentacles.

With no little bit of irony, Dorik Harbin considered his position as he stood on the bridge of *Shanidar*. A man who treasured his solitude, who had never wanted to be dependent on anyone else, he was now the commander of an entire fleet of spacecraft: attack ships, tankers, even surveillance drones that were spreading across the Belt seeking one infinitesimal speck in all that dark emptiness – Lars Fuchs.

Although he far preferred to work alone, Harbin had been forced to admit that he could not find Fuchs by himself. The Belt was too big, the quarry too elusive. And, of course, Fuchs was aided covertly by other rock rats who gave him fuel and food and information while they secretly applauded his one-man war against Humphries Space Systems. Probably Astro Corporation was also helping Fuchs. There was no evidence of it, Harbin knew; no outright proof that Astro was supplying the renegade with anything more than gleeful congratulations on his continuing attacks.

But Humphries himself was certain that Astro was behind Fuchs' success. Diane had told Harbin that Humphries was wild with rage, willing now to spend every penny he had to track down Fuchs and eliminate him, once and for all. This armada was the result: its costs to Humphries were out of all proportion to the damage that Fuchs had done, but Humphries wanted Fuchs destroyed, no matter what the cost, Diane said.

Diane. Harbin reflected soberly that she had become a part of his life. I've become dependent on her, he realized. Even with the distance between them, she protected him against Humphries' frustrated anger. She was the one who had convinced Humphries to give Harbin command of this all-out campaign against Fuchs. She was the one who would be waiting for him when he returned with Fuchs' dead body.

Well, he thought as he surveyed the display screens showing a scattering of his other ships, now I have the tools I need to finish the job. It's only a matter of time.

The surveillance probes were already on their way to quarter the Belt with their sensors. Harbin gave the orders to his fleet to move out and start the hunt.

Self-satisfaction showed clearly on Martin Humphries' face as he sat down at the head of the long dining table in his mansion. Diane Verwoerd was the only other person at the table, already seated at his right.

'Sorry I'm late for lunch,' Humphries said, nodding to the servant waiting to pour the wine. 'I was on the phone with Doug Stavenger.'

Verwoerd knew her boss expected her to ask what the call was about, but she said nothing.

'Well, he's done it,' Humphries said at last, just a little bit nettled. 'Stavenger's pulled it off. We're going to have a peace conference right here at Selene. The world government's agreed to send their number-two man, Willi Dieterling.'

Diane Verwoerd made herself look impressed, 'The man who negotiated the Middle East settlement?'

'The very same,' said Humphries.

'And the rock rats are sending a representative?' she prompted.

'Three people. That big Australian oaf and two assistants.'

'Who'll represent Astro?'

'Probably Pancho,' he said lightly. 'She's the real power on the board, these days.'

'It should be interesting,' said Verwoerd.

'It should be,' Humphries agreed. 'It certainly should be.'

Lars Fuchs scowled at his visitor. Yves St Clair was one of his oldest and most trusted friends; Fuchs had known the Quebecois since their university days together in Switzerland. Yet now St Clair was stubbornly refusing to help him.

'I need the fuel,' Fuchs said. 'Without it, I'm dead.'

The two men stood in *Nautilus*' cramped galley, away from the crew. Fuchs had given them orders to leave him alone with his old friend. St Claire stood in front of the big freezer, his arms folded obstinately across his chest. When they had been students together he had been slim and handsome, with a trim little pencil moustache and a smooth line of patter for the women, despite his uncouth accent. In those days his clothes had always been in the latest fashion; his friends joked that he bankrupted his family with his wardrobe. During his years of prospecting in the Belt, however, he had allowed himself to get fat. Now he looked like a prosperous middle-aged bourgeois shopkeeper, yet his carefully draped tunic of sky blue was designed to minimize his expanding waistline.

'Lars,' said St Clair, 'it is impossible. Even for you, old friend, I can't spare the fuel. I wouldn't have enough left to get back to Ceres.'

Fuchs, dressed as usual in a black pullover and baggy slacks, took a long breath before answering.

'The difference is,' he said, 'that you can send out a distress call and a tanker will come out for you. I can't.'

'Yes, a tanker will come out for me. And do you know how much that will cost?'

'You're talking about money. I'm talking about my life.'

St Clair made a Gallic shrug.

Since the attack on Vesta, Fuchs had survived by scrounging fuel and other supplies from friendly prospectors and other ships plying the Belt. A few of them gave freely; most were reluctant and had to be convinced. Amanda regularly sent out schedules for the prospectors, miners, tankers and supply vessels that left Ceres. Fuchs planted remote transceivers on minor asteroids, squirted the asteroids' identification numbers to Amanda in bursts of supercompressed messages, then picked up her information from the miniaturized transceivers the next time he swung past those rocks. It was an intricate chess game, moving the transceivers before Humphries' snoops could locate them and use them to bait a trap for him.

Humphries' ships went armed now, and seldom alone. It was becoming almost impossibly dangerous to try to hit them. Now and again Fuchs commandeered supplies from Astro tankers and freighters. Their captains always complained and always submitted to Fuchs' demands under protest, but they were under orders from Pancho not to resist. The cost of these 'thefts' was submicroscopic in Astro's ledgers.

Despite everything, Fuchs was badly surprised that even his old friend was being stubborn.

Trying to hold on to his temper, he said placatingly, 'Yves, this is literally a matter of life and death to me.'

'But it is not necessary,' St Clair said, waving both hands in the air. 'You don't need to—'

'I'm fighting your fight,' Fuchs said. 'I'm trying to keep Humphries from turning you into his vassals.'

St Clair cocked an eyebrow. 'Ah, Lars, *mon vieux*. In all this fighting you've killed friends of mine. Friends of ours, Lars.'

'That couldn't be helped.'

'They were construction workers. They never did you any harm.'

'They were working for Humphries.'

'You didn't give them a chance. You slaughtered them without mercy.'

'We're in a war,' Fuchs snapped. 'In war there are casualties. It can't be helped.'

'*They* weren't in a war!' said St Clair, with some heat. 'I'm not in a war! You're the only one who is fighting this war of yours.'

Fuchs stared at him. 'Don't you understand that what I'm doing, I'm doing for you? For all the rock rats?'

'Pah! Soon it will be all over, anyway. There is no need to continue this . . . this vendetta between you and Humphries.'

'Vendetta? Is that what you think I'm doing?'

Drawing in a deep, deliberate breath, St Clair said more reasonably, 'Lars, it is finished. The conference at Selene will put an end to this fighting.'

'Conference?' Fuchs blinked with surprise. 'What conference?'

St Clair's brows rose. 'You don't know? At Selene.

Humphries and Astro are meeting to discuss a settlement of their differences. A peace conference.'

'At Selene?'

'Of course. Stavenger himself arranged it. The world government has sent Willi Dieterling. Your own wife will be there, one of the representatives from Ceres.'

Fuchs felt an electric shock stagger him. 'Amanda's going to Selene?'

'She is on her way, with Big George and Dr Cardenas. Didn't you know?'

Amanda's going to Selene, thundered in Fuchs' mind. To Selene. To Humphries.

It took him several moments to focus his attention again on St Clair, still standing in the galley with him, a bemused little smile on his lips.

'You didn't know?' St Clair asked again. 'She didn't tell you?'

His voice venomously low, Fuchs said, 'I'm going to take the fuel I need. You can call for a tanker after I've left the area.'

'You will steal it from me?'

'Yes,' said Fuchs. 'That way you can make a claim to your insurance carrier. You're insured for theft, aren't you?'

Dossier: Joyce Takamine

Joyce was quite content living on the Moon. She lived alone, not celibate, certainly, but not attached to anyone, either. She had achieved most of what she had dreamed of, all those long hard years of her youth.

She was a mature woman now, lean and stringy, hardened by years of physical labour and cold calculation, inured to clambering up the ladder of life by grabbing for any rung she could reach. Now that she was at Selene, with a well-paying job and a secure career path, she felt that she could relax and enjoy life for the first time.

Except – she soon felt bored.

Life became too predictable, too routine. Too safe, she finally realized. There's no challenge to this. I can run my office blindfolded. I see the same people socially every time I go out. Selene's just a small town. Safe. Comfortable. Boring.

So she transferred to the Humphries operation on Ceres, much to her supervisor's shock, and rode out to the Belt.

Ceres was even smaller than Selene, dirty, crowded, sometimes dangerous. Joyce loved it. New people were arriving and departing all the time. The Pub was rowdy, raucous. She saw Lars Fuchs kill a man there, just jam a power drill into the guy's chest like an old-fashioned knight's spear. The guy had admitted to killing Niles Ripley, and he tried to shoot Fuchs right there at the bar.

She served on the jury that acquitted Fuchs and, when the people of Ceres finally started to pull together a ragtag kind of government, Joyce Takamine was one of those selected by lottery to serve on the community's first governing council. It was the first time she had won anything.

49

Humphries gave a party in his mansion for the delegates to the peace conference. Not a large, sumptuous party; just an intimate gathering of the handful of men and women who would meet the next morning in a discreet conference room in Selene's office tower, up in the Grand Plaza.

Pancho Lane was the first guest to arrive. Humphries greeted her in the sprawling living room of his home, with Diane Verwoerd at his side. Diane wore a glittering floor-length sheath of silver, its neckline plunging almost to her waist. Pancho was in a lavender cocktail dress accented with big copper bangle earrings and hoops of copper at her wrists and throat.

Humphries, wearing a collarless burgundy jacket over a space-black turtleneck shirt and charcoal slacks, smirked to himself. Pancho had learned a lot in her years on the Astro board, but she was still gawky enough to show up at the party precisely on time, rather than fashionably late.

Soon enough the other guests began to arrive, and Humphries' servants showed them into the lavishly furnished living room. Willi Dieterling came in with two younger men flanking him; his nephews, he told Humphries as they exchanged introductions.

'May I congratulate you, sir,' Humphries said, 'on your successful resolution of the Mideast crisis.'

Dieterling smiled in a self-deprecating manner and touched his trim grey beard with a single finger. 'I cannot take all the credit,' he said softly. 'Both sides had run out of ammunition. My major accomplishment was to get the arms dealers to stop selling to them.'

Everyone laughed politely.

Dieterling went on, 'With the Mediterranean threatening to flood Israel and the Tigris-Euphrates rivers washing away half of Iraq, both sides were ready to cooperate.'

'Still,' Humphries said as a waiter brought a tray of champagne flutes, 'your accomplishment is something that—'

He stopped and stared past Dieterling. Everyone turned toward the doorway. There stood Big George Ambrose with his shaggy red hair and beard, looking painfully ill-at-ease in a tight-fitting dinner jacket. On one side of him was Kris Cardenas, in Selene for the first time in more than six years. On George's other side was Amanda, in a plain white sleeveless gown, accented with a simple necklace and bracelet of gold links.

Humphries left Dieterling and the others standing there and rushed to Amanda.

His mouth went dry. He had to swallow hard before he could croak out 'Hello.'

'Hello, Martin,' said Amanda, unsmiling.

He felt like a tonguetied schoolboy. He didn't know what to say.

Pancho, of all people, rescued him. 'Hi, Mandy!' she called cheerfully, walking toward them. 'Good to see ya.'

Humphries felt almost grateful as Pancho introduced Amanda, Cardenas and Big George to Dieterling and his nephews. Then Doug Stavenger came in, with his wife, and the party was complete.

While his guests sipped champagne and chatted, Humphries called one of the waiters over and instructed him to change the seating in the dining room. He wanted Amanda at his right hand.

Two minutes later his butler came up to him and whispered in his ear, 'Sir, Dr Dieterling is supposed to be sitting at your right. Diplomatic protocol—'

'Protocol be damned!' Humphries hissed. 'Rearrange the seating. Now!'

The butler looked alarmed. Verwoerd stepped in and said, 'Let me take care of it.'

Humphries nodded to her. She and the butler headed off to the dining room. Humphries turned back to Amanda. She seemed to glow like a goddess among the chattering mortals arrayed around her.

Dinner was long and leisurely. Humphries was certain that the conversation was sophisticated, deeply significant, a fine way for the delegates to tomorrow's meeting to get to know each other. Bursts of laughter showed that considerable wit sparkled around the table. Humphries heard not a word. All he could see was Amanda. She smiled now and then, but not at him. She chatted with Dieterling, seated on her other side, and with Stavenger, who was across the table from her. She said hardly a word to Humphries and he found it difficult to talk to her, especially with all these others surrounding him.

After-dinner drinks were served in the library-cum-bar. As midnight tolled on the antique grandfather clock in the corner, the guests began to make their farewells. Amanda left with Cardenas and Big George. Pancho stayed until everyone else had gone.

'First in, last out,' she said once she finally put her glass down on the bar. 'I never want to miss anything.'

Humphries let Verwoerd escort Pancho to the door. He stepped behind the bar and poured himself a stiff single malt, neat.

Verwoerd returned, a subtle smile creasing her sultry lips.

'She's even more beautiful in person than her on-screen image.'

'I'm going to marry her,' Humphries said.

Verwoerd actually laughed. 'Not until you get up the nerve to speak to her, I should think.'

Anger flared in his gut. 'Too many people around. I can't say anything meaningful to her in a crowd like that.'

Still smirking, Verwoerd said, 'She didn't have much to say to you, either.'

'She will. I'll see to that.'

Picking up her half-finished drink from the bar, Verwoerd said, 'I noticed that the other woman didn't have much to say to you, either.'

'Dr Cardenas?'

'Yes.'

'We've had our . . . differences, in the past. When she lived here at Selene.'

'She used to run the nanotech lab, didn't she?'

'Yes.' Kris Cardenas had been shut out of her lab because of Humphries. He was certain that Verwoerd knew it; the feline smile on her face told him that she knew and was enjoying his discomfort over it. And his inability to say more than a few words to Amanda. She's *enjoying* watching me turn myself into knots over the woman I love, he fumed silently.

'It'll be interesting to see what they have to say tomorrow, if anything,' Verwoerd mused.

'Tomorrow?'

'At the conference.'

'Oh, yes. The conference.'

'I'm looking forward to it,' said Verwoerd.

'You won't be there.'

Her eyes went wide for just a flash of a second, then she regained control of herself.

'I won't be at the conference? Why not?'

'Because you'll be in the medical lab. It's time for you to be implanted with my clone.'

Verwoerd's self-control crumpled. 'Now? You're going to do that now, with the conference and—'

He had just made up his mind. Seeing the smug superiority on her face had decided him. It's time to show her who's in charge here; time to make her realize she's here to do my bidding.

'Now,' Humphries said, enjoying her shock and confusion. 'I'm going to marry Amanda and you're going to carry my baby.'

50

So it boils down to this, Dorik Harbin said to himself as he read the message on his screen. All this effort and manoeuvring, all these ships, all the killing, and it comes down to a simple little piece of treachery.

He sat in his privacy cubicle and stared at the screen. Some fluncky who had once worked for Fuchs had sold out. For a despicably small bribe he had hacked into Fuchs' wife's computer files and found out where Fuchs had planted communications transceivers. Those little electro-optics boxes were Fuchs' lifeline, his link to information on where and when he could find the ships he preyed upon.

Harbin smiled tightly, but there was no joy in it. He opened a comm channel to his ships and began ordering them to the asteroids where Fuchs' transceivers lay. Sooner or later he would show up at one of those rocks to pick up the latest intelligence information from his wife. When he did, there would be three or four of Harbin's ships waiting for him.

Harbin hoped that Fuchs would come to the asteroid where he himself planned to lie in wait.

It will be good to finish this fight personally, he told himself. Once it's over, I'll be wealthy enough to retire. With Diane.

Diane Verwoerd spent a sleepless night worrying about the ordeal she faced. I'll bear Martin's child without really being impregnated by him. I'll be a virgin mother, almost.

The humour of the situation failed to ease her fears.

Unable to sleep, she went to her computer and searched for every scrap of information she could locate about cloning: mammals, sheep, pigs, monkeys, apes – humans. Most nations on Earth forbade human cloning. The ultraconservative religions organizations such as the New Morality and the Sword of Islam jailed and even executed scientists for merely doing research in cloning. Yet there were laboratories, private facilities protected by the very wealthy, where such experiments were done. Most attempts at cloning failed. The lucky ones suffered spontaneous abortions early. Less fortunate women died in childbirth or gave birth to stillborns.

My chances for presenting Martin with a healthy son are about one in a hundred, Verwoerd saw. My chances for dying are better than that.

She shuddered, but she knew she would go through with it. Because being the mother of Martin Humphries' son was worth all the risk to her. I'll get a seat on the board of directors for this. With Dorik to protect me, there's no telling how far I can go.

Humphries awoke that morning and smiled. It's all coming together nicely, he told himself as he got out of bed and padded into his tiled lavatory. Amanda's here without Fuchs. By the time the conference is over he'll be totally cut off from her and everybody else. I'll have the chance to show her what kind of life she can have with me.

The mirror above the sink showed him a puffy-faced, bleary-eyed unshaven image. Will she want me? he asked himself. I can give her everything, everything a woman could possibly desire. But will she turn me down again? Will she stick with Fuchs?

Not if the man is dead, he thought. Then she'd have no choice. The competition will be over.

His hands trembled as he reached for his electric tooth-brush. Frowning at this weakness, Humphries opened his medicine cabinet and rummaged through the vials lined up there in alphabetical order. A cure for every malady, he said to himself. Most of them were recreational drugs, cooked up by some of the bright researchers he kept on his payroll. I need something to calm me down, Humphries realized. Something to get me through this conference without losing my temper, without making Amanda afraid of me.

As he pawed through the medicine cabinet, the image of Diane Verwoerd's troubled, frightened face flashed in his mind. I wiped her superior smile away, he thought, relishing the memory of her surprise and fear. He tried to remember how many women had carried clones of his, all to no avail. Several had died; one had produced a monstrosity that lived less than a day. Diane's strong, he told himself. She'll come through for me. And if she doesn't – he shrugged. There were always other women for the job.

He found the little blue bottle that he was looking for. Just one, he said silently; just enough to get me through the meeting on an even keel. Later on, I'll need something else, something stimulating. But not yet. Not this morning. Later, when Amanda's here with me.

Pancho dressed carefully for the conference in a pumpkin-orange silk blouse and slacks, with a neat patchwork jacket embellished with highlights of glitter. This is an important conference and I'm representing Astro Corporation, she told herself. Better look like a major player. She thought she would be the first one to show up for the conference, but when she got there Doug Stavenger was already standing by the big window that swept along one wall of the spacious room, looking relaxed in an informal cardigan jacket of teal blue.

'Hello,' he called cheerfully. Gesturing toward the side table laden with coffee urns and pastries, he asked, 'Have you had your breakfast?'

'I could use some coffee,' Pancho said, heading for the table.

The conference room was part of the suite of offices that Selene maintained in one of the twin towers that supported the expansive dome of the Grand Plaza. Gazing through the window down into the Plaza itself, Pancho saw the lovingly maintained lawn and flowering shrubbery, the fully-leafed trees dotting the landscape. There was the big swimming pool, built to attract tourists, and the outdoor theatre with its gracefully curved shell of lunar concrete. Not many people on the walks this early in the morning, she noticed. Nobody in the pool.

Stavenger smiled at her. 'Pancho, are you seriously going to try to hammer out your differences with Humphries, or is this conference going to be a waste of time?'

Pancho grinned back at him as she picked up a coffee cup and started to fill it with steaming black brew. 'Astro is willing to agree to a reasonable division of the Belt. We never wanted a fight; it was Humphries who started the rough stuff.'

Stavenger pursed his lips. 'I guess it all depends, then, on how you define the word "reasonable." '

'Hey, look,' Pancho said. 'There's enough raw materials in the Belt to satisfy ever'body. Plenty for all of us. It's Humphries who wants to take it all.'

'Are you talking about me, Pancho?'

They turned and saw Humphries striding through the door, looking relaxed and confident in a dark blue business suit.

'Nothing I haven't said to your face, Humpy, old buddy,' Pancho replied.

Humphries raised an eyebrow. 'I'd appreciate it if you referred to me as Mr Humphries when the other delegates get here.'

'Sensitive?'

'Yes. In return for your consideration I'll try to refrain from using phrases such as "guttersnipe" or "grease-monkey." '

Stavenger put a hand to his forehead. 'This is going to be a lovely morning,' he groaned.

Actually, the conference went along much more smoothly than Stavenger had feared. The other delegates arrived, and Humphries turned his attention to Amanda, who smiled politely at him but said very little. He seemed almost to be a different person when Fuchs' wife was near: polite, considerate, earnestly trying to win her admiration, or at least her respect.

Stavenger called the meeting to order and everyone took seats along the polished oblong conference table. Pancho behaved like a proper corporate executive and Humphries was affable and cooperative. Each of them made an opening statement about how they wanted nothing more than peace and harmony in the Asteroid Belt. Willi Dieterling then said a few brief words about how important the resources of the Belt were to the people of Earth.

'With so many millions homeless and hungry, with so much of our global industrial capacity wiped out, we desperately need the resources from the Belt,' he pleaded. 'This fighting is disrupting the supply of raw materials that we need to recover from the climate catastrophe that has brought civilization to its knees.'

Stavenger pointed out, 'The people of Selene are ready to help as much as we can. We have industrial capacity here on the Moon, and we can help you to build factories and power generation stations in Earth orbit.'

It was Big George who ended the platitudes.

'We all want peace and brotherhood,' he began, 'but the painful truth is that people are killin' each other out in the Belt.'

Dieterling immediately replied, 'The world government is prepared to offer Peacekeeping troops to you to help you maintain order in the Belt.'

'No thanks!' George snapped. 'We can maintain order for ourselves—' he turned to look squarely at Humphries '—if the corporations'll stop sending killers to us.'

'Corporations, plural?' Pancho asked. 'Astro hasn't sent any killers to the Belt.'

'You've sent your share of goons, Pancho,' said George.

'To protect our property!'

Humphries made a hushing motion with both hands. 'I presume you're both referring to certain actions taken by employees of Humphries Space Systems.'

'Fookin' right,' George said.

With all eyes on him, Humphries said calmly, 'It's perfectly true that some of the people my corporation sent to Ceres have been . . . well, roughnecks.'

'Murderers,' George muttered.

'One man committed a murder, true enough,' Humphries conceded. 'But he acted on his own. And he was punished for it swiftly enough.'

'By Lars Fuchs, I understand,' said Dieterling.

Humphries nodded. 'Now we're getting down to the crux of the problem.'

'Wait a minute,' George interjected. 'Let's not start dumpin' on Lars. Plenty of ships have been knocked off out in the Belt, and it was HSS that started it.'

'That's not true,' Humphries said.

'Isn't it? I was fookin' attacked by one of your butcher boys. Took me arm off. Remember?'

'We went through an IAA hearing over that. No one was able to prove it was one of my ships that attacked you.'

'That doesn't mean it wasn't one of 'em, does it now?'

Stavenger broke into the growing argument. 'Unless we have concrete evidence, there's no use throwing accusations around.'

George glowered at him, but said nothing.

'We do have concrete evidence,' Humphries resumed, with a swift glance at Amanda, 'that Lars Fuchs has attacked ships, killed men, stolen supplies, and now he's wiped out a base we were building on Vesta, in a totally unwarranted and premeditated attack. He's killed several dozen people. He's the reason for all this violence out in the Belt and until he's caught and put away, the violence will continue.'

Absolute silence. Not one of the men or women seated around the conference table said a word in Fuchs' defence. Not even Amanda, Humphries noted with unalloyed delight.

The asteroid had no name. In the catalogue files it was merely 38–4002. Barely a kilometre long, and half that at its widest, it was a dark, carbonaceous body, a loose aggregation of pebble-sized chondrules, more like a bean-bag than a solid rock. Fuchs had left one of his transceivers there weeks earlier; now he was returning to the asteroid to retrieve it and see what information Amanda had been able to beam to him.

She's gone to Selene, he kept repeating in his mind. To a conference. To Humphries. Without telling me. Without mentioning a word of it. He saw St Clair's face again as the man told him the news, almost smirking. *Your wife didn't tell you?* he heard St Clair ask, again and again. *She never even mentioned it to you?*

It's probably in the messages waiting for me, Fuchs told himself. Amanda must have put it into the latest batch of messages just before she left for Selene. For Humphries' home. His guts knotted like fists every time he thought of it.

Why didn't she tell me beforehand? he raged silently. Why didn't she discuss this with me before she decided to go? The answer seemed terribly clear: because she didn't want me to know she was going, didn't want me to know she would be seeing Humphries.

He wanted to bellow his rage and frustration, wanted to order his crew to race to Selene, wanted to take Amanda off the ship that was carrying her to the Moon and keep her safely with him. Too late, he knew. Far too late. She's gone. She's there by now. She's left me.

Nautilus' propellant tanks were full. Fuchs felt a slight pang of conscience about taking the hydrogen and helium fuels from his one-time friend, but he had had no choice. He had parted with St Clair on less than friendly terms, but nevertheless the Quebecois had waited six full hours before putting in an emergency call for a tanker, as Fuchs had ordered him to do.

Shaking his head as he sat in the command chair on *Nautilus*' bridge, Fuchs wondered at how the human mind works. *St Clair knew I wouldn't harm him. He waited the full six hours before calling for help, giving me plenty of time to get safely away. Is he still my friend, despite everything? Or was he afraid I'd come back and fire on him?* Pondering the question Fuchs decided, most likely St Clair was simply playing it safe. *Our friendship is dead, a casualty of this war. I have no friends.*

I have no wife, either. I've driven her away. Driven her into Humphries' territory, perhaps into his arms.

The Asian navigator seated to one side of the bridge said to the woman who was piloting the ship, 'The rock is in visual range.' He spoke in their native Mongol dialect, but Fuchs understood them. *It's not a rock,* he corrected silently. *It's an aggregate.*

Glad to have something else to occupy his mind, Fuchs commanded his computer to put the telescopic view of the asteroid on his console screen. It was tumbling slowly along its long axis, end over end. As they approached the 'roid, Fuchs called up the computer image that showed where they had planted the transceiver.

He hunched forward in his chair, studying the screen, trying to drive thoughts of Amanda out of his mind. It showed the telescope's real-time image of the asteroid with the computer's grid map superimposed over it. Strange, he thought. The contour map doesn't match the visual image any more. There's a new lump on the asteroid, not more than fifty meters from where the transceiver should be sitting.

Fuchs froze the image and peered at it. The asteroids are dynamic, he knew. They're constantly being dinged by smaller chunks of rock. An aggregate like this 'roid wouldn't show a crater, necessarily. It's like punching your fist into a beanbag chair: it just gives and reforms itself.

But a lump? What would cause a lump?

He felt an old, old fervour stirring inside him. Once he had been a planetary geochemist; he had first come out to the Belt to study the asteroids, not to mine them. A curiosity that he hadn't felt in many years filled his mind. What could raise a blister on a carbonaceous chondritic asteroid?

Dorik Harbin was half a day's journey distant from the carbonaceous asteroid, even at the 0.5 g acceleration that was *Shanidar*'s best speed. He had dropped his ship into a grazing orbit around the jagged, striated body of nickel-iron where Fuchs had left one of his transceivers. His navigator was still sweating and wide-eyed with apprehension. His pale blond Scandanavian second-in-command had warned him several times that they were dangerously close to crashing into the rock.

But Harbin wanted to be so close that an approaching ship would not spot him. He wished this chunk of metal was porous, like the carbonaceous rock where one of Fuchs' other transceivers had been found. The crew there had simply detached their habitation module from the rest of their ship and buried it under a loose layer of rubble. Then the remainder of the ship, crewed only by a pilot and navigator, had flown out of range. If Fuchs showed up there, all he would see would be an innocent pile of dirt. A Trojan horse, Harbin thought grimly, that would disgorge half a dozen armed troops while calling on all of Harbin's armada to close the trap.

The Scandanavian was clearly unhappy orbiting mere metres from the scratched and pitted surface of the asteroid. 'We are running the danger of having the hull abraded by the dust that hovers over the rock,' she warned Harbin.

He looked into her wintry blue eyes. So like my own, he thought. Her Viking ancestors must have invaded my village some time in the past.

'It's dangerous!' she said sharply.

Harbin made himself smile at her. 'Match our orbit to the rock's intrinsic spin. If Fuchs comes poking around here, I don't want him to see us until it's too late for him to get away.'

She started to protest, but Harbin cut her off with an upraised hand. 'Do it,' he said.

Clearly unhappy, she turned and relayed his order to the navigator.

'Let's break for lunch,' said Doug Stavenger.

The others around the conference table nodded and pushed their chairs back. The tension in the room cracked. One by one, they got to their feet, stretched, took deep breaths. Stavenger heard vertebrae pop.

Lunch had been laid on in another conference room, down the hall. As the delegates filed out into the corridor, Stavenger touched Dieterling's arm, detaining him.

'Have we accomplished anything?' he asked the diplomat.

Dieterling glanced at the doorway, where his two nephews stood waiting for him. Then he turned back to Stavenger. 'A little, I think.'

'At least Humphries and Pancho are talking civilly to each other,' Stavenger said, with a rueful smile.

'Don't underestimate the benefits of civility,' said Dieterling. 'Without it, nothing can be done.'

'So?'

With a heavy shrug, Dieterling answered, 'It's clear that the crux of the problem is this man Fuchs.'

'Humphries certainly wants him out of the way.'

'As long as he is rampaging out there in the Belt there can be no peace.'

Stavenger shook his head. 'But Fuchs started his . . . rampage, as you call it, in reaction to the violence that Humphries' people began.'

'That makes no difference now,' Dieterling said, dropping his voice almost to a whisper. 'We can get Humphries and Ms Lane to let bygones be bygones and forget the past. No recriminations, no acts of vengeance. They are willing to make a peaceful settlement.'

'And stick to it, do you think?'

'Yes. I'm certain of it. This war is becoming too expensive for them. They want it ended.'

'They can end it this afternoon, if they want to.'

'Only if Fuchs is stopped,' Dieterling said. 'He is the wild card, the terrorist who is beyond ordinary political control.'

Stavenger nodded glumly. 'He's got to be stopped, then. Dammit.'

Humphries stepped into the washroom, relieved himself of a morning's worth of coffee, then washed up and popped another tranquillizing pill. He thought of them as tranquillizers, even though he knew they were much more than that.

As he stepped out into the corridor, Amanda came out of the ladies' room. His breath caught in his throat, despite the pill. She was dressed in a yellow pantsuit that seemed faded from long use, yet in Humphries' eyes she glowed like the sun. No one else was in sight; the others must have all gone into the room where lunch was laid out.

'Hello, Amanda,' he heard himself say.

Only then did he see the cold anger in her eyes.

'You're determined to kill Lars, aren't you?' she said flatly.

Humphries licked his lips before replying, 'Kill him? No. Stop him. That's all I want, Amanda. I want him to stop the killing.'

'Which you started.'

'That doesn't matter any more. He's the problem now.'

'You won't rest until you've killed him.'

'Not—' He had to swallow hard before he could continue. 'Not if you'll marry me.'

He had expected her to be surprised. But her eyes did not flicker, the expression on her utterly beautiful face did not change one iota. She simply turned and headed up the corridor, away from him.

Humphries started after her, but then he heard Stavenger and Dieterling coming up the hall behind him. Don't make an ass of yourself in front of them, he told himself sternly. Let her go. For now. At least, she didn't say no.

52

As Fuchs studied the image of asteroid 38–4002, Nodon ducked through the hatch and stepped into the bridge. Fuchs heard him ask the pilot if the long-range scan showed any other ships in the area.

'None,' said the pilot.

What could raise a lump on a beanbag collection of pebbles? Fuchs asked himself for the dozenth time. *Nautilus* was approaching the asteroid at one-sixth g; they would have to start a braking manoeuvre soon if they were going to establish an orbit around it.

Wishing he had a full panoply of sensors to play across the asteroid's surface, Fuchs noted again that there were several noticeable craters on its surface, but none of them had the raised rims that formed when a boulder crashed into a solid rock. No, this is a collection of nodules, he thought, and the only way to build a blister like that is for something to push the pellets up into a mound.

Something. Then it hit him. Or some*one*.

He turned in his chair and looked up at Nodon. 'Warm up laser number one,' he commanded.

Nodon's big eyes flashed, but he nodded silently and left the bridge.

Turning back to the image of the approaching asteroid, Fuchs reasoned, if something natural pushed up that mound, then there should be a depression around it, from where the pebbles were scooped up. But there isn't. Why not? Because something is buried under that mound. Because someone dug a hole in that porous pile of rubble and buried something in it.

What?

'Cut our approach velocity in half,' he said to the pilot. The Asian complied wordlessly.

Several minutes later, Nodon called from the cargo bay, 'Laser number two is ready.'

'Number two?' Fuchs replied sharply. 'What happened to number one?'

'Its coolant lines are being flushed. Routine maintenance.'

'Get it on line,' Fuchs snapped. 'Get number three on line, too.'

'Yes, sir.' Fuchs could hear Nodon speaking in rapid dialect to someone else down in the cargo bay.

'Slave number two to my console,' Fuchs ordered.

He began to reconfigure his console with fingertip touches on its main display screen. By the time he had finished, the laser was linked. He could run it from the bridge.

He put the asteroid on-screen and focused on that suspicious mound of rubble. He saw the red dot of the aiming laser sparkling on the dark, pebbly ground and walked it to the middle of the mound. Then, with a touch of a finger, he fired the high-power laser. Its infrared beam was invisible to his eyes, but Fuchs saw the ground cascade into a splash of heat, a miniature fountain of red-hot lava erupting, spraying high above the asteroid's surface.

His face set in a harsh scowl, Fuchs held the cutting laser's beam on the spewing geyser of molten rock. Ten seconds. Fifteen. Twenty . . .

The mound erupted. Half a dozen spacesuited figures scurried in all directions like cockroaches startled out of their nest, stumbling across the rough surface of the asteroid.

'I knew it!' Fuchs shouted. The three Asians on the bridge turned toward him.

Nodon called from the cargo bay, 'They were waiting for us to pick up the transceiver!'

Fuchs ignored them all. He swung the laser toward one of the figures. The man had tripped and sprawled clumsily in the minuscule gravity of the little asteroid, then when he tried to get up, he had pushed himself completely off the ground. Now he floated helplessly, arms and legs flailing.

Fuchs walked the laser beam toward him, watched its molten path as it burned across the asteroid's gravelly surface.

'Waiting to trap me, were you?' he muttered. 'You wanted to kill me. Now see what death is like.'

For an instant he wondered who was inside that spacesuit. What kind of a man becomes a mercenary soldier, a hired killer? Is he like my own crew, the cast-offs, the abandoned, so desperate that they'll do anything, follow anyone who can give them hope that they'll live to see another day? Fuchs watched the spacesuited figure struggling, arms and legs pumping frantically as he drifted farther off the asteroid. He certainly had no experience in microgravity, Fuchs saw. And his comrades are doing nothing to help him.

You're going to die alone, he said silently to the spacesuited figure.

Yet he turned off the cutting laser. His hand had touched the screen icon that deactivated its beam before his conscious mind understood what he had done. The red spot of the low-power aiming laser still scintillated on the asteroid's surface. Fuchs moved it to shine squarely on the flailing, contorted body of the mercenary.

Kill or be killed, he told himself. It took an effort, though, to will his hand back to the high-power laser's firing control. He held it there, poised a bare centimetre above it.

'Two ships approaching at high acceleration,' called the pilot. 'No, four ships, coming in from two different directions.'

Fuchs knew he couldn't murder the man. He could not kill him in cold blood. And he knew that their trap had worked.

It all fell in on him like an avalanche. They knew where the transceivers were hidden. Someone had told them. Someone? Only Amanda knew where the transceivers were located. She wouldn't betray him, Fuchs told himself. She wouldn't. Someone must have ferreted out the information somehow. And then sold it to Humphries.

'Six ships,' called the pilot, sounding frightened. 'All approaching at high g.'

Trapped. They were waiting for me to show up. Six ships.

Nodon's voice came over the intercom. 'Lasers one and three ready to fire.'

I'll get them all killed if I try to fight back, Fuchs realized. It's me that Humphries wants, not my crew.

Suddenly he felt tired, bone tired, soul weary. It's over, he realized. All this fighting and killing and what has it gained me? What has it gained anyone? I've walked my crew into a trap, like a fool, like a wolf caught in the hunter's net. It's over. It's finished. And I've lost everything.

With a feeling of resignation that overwhelmed him, Fuchs touched the communications key and spoke, 'This is Lars Fuchs aboard the *Nautilus*. Don't fire. We surrender.'

Harbin heard the defeat in Fuchs' voice. And he cursed Martin Humphries for saddling him with this oversized armada and company of troops. I could have done this by myself, he thought. Given the information about where he planted his transceivers, I could have trapped him by myself, without all these others – all these witnesses.

By himself, Harbin would have sliced Fuchs' ship into bits and killed everyone aboard it. Then he would have carried Fuchs' dead body back to Diane and her boss, so Humphries could glory in his triumph and Harbin could claim the immense bonus that would be rightfully his. Then he would take Diane for himself and leave Humphries to gloat over his victory.

But there were more than a hundred men and women aboard this fleet that Humphries had insisted upon. It was nonsense to believe that each of them would remain quiet if Harbin killed Fuchs after the man had surrendered. It would be too big a story, too much temptation. Someone would cash out to the news media, or to spies from Humphries' competitors in Astro Corporation.

No. Against his instincts, against his judgment, Harbin knew he had to accept Fuchs' surrender and bring the man and his crew back to Ceres. Then he smiled grimly. Perhaps once he's on Ceres something might happen to him. After all, the man's made many enemies there. They might even put him on trial and execute him legally.

53

The implantation procedure was not as exhausting as Diane feared it would be.

She had insisted that all the attending personnel be women, and Selene's medical staff had complied with her demand. They were smiling, soothing, soft-spoken. After an injection of a tranquillizer, they wheeled Diane into the little room where the procedure would take place. The room felt cold. A plastic container sat on the table where the instruments were laid out, steaming icy white vapour. The frozen embryo was in there, Diane realized, her thoughts getting fuzzy from the injection.

It's like being put on the rack by the Spanish Inquisition, she thought. The instruments of torture lay in a neat row beside her. Bright lights glared down at her. The torturers gathered around her, masked and gowned, their hands gloved in skin-thin plastic.

She took a deep breath as they gently placed her feet in the stirrups.

'Just try to relax,' said a soothing woman's voice.

Good advice, Diane thought. Just try.

Humphries was seated up near the head of the table, one chair down from Stavenger. Dieterling was at his left, Pancho Lane across the table from him, and Big George Ambrose at his right. Humphries did not relish being next to the big Aussie; the shaggy redhead was intimidating even when he was doing nothing more than sitting quietly and listening to the others wrangle.

Amanda was on George's other side. Humphries couldn't even glance at her without leaning around the Australian and being obvious about it.

'The essence of agreement is compromise,' Dieterling was saying for the nth time. 'And compromise is impossible without trust.'

Dieterling expects the Nobel Peace Prize for his work in the Middle East, Humphries thought. It won't matter much what he accomplishes or fails to accomplish here. But he's so damned *earnest*. You'd think his own life hinges on what we're doing today.

Pancho, across the table, eyed Humphries for a moment, then said to Dieterling, 'Astro's willing to compromise. I've been sayin' all along that there's so much natural wealth out in the Belt that there's plenty for ever'body. What we need is an agreement about who gets what.'

Stavenger shook his head. 'I don't think you can carve up the Belt the way Spain and Portugal divided up the New World back in the sixteenth century.'

'Yeah,' Big George agreed. 'What about the independents? You can't give the whole fookin' Belt to the corporations.'

'What is required,' Dieterling said, 'is an agreement to forego the use of violence; an agreement to proceed peacefully and respect the rights of others.'

Humphries' phone buzzed in his jacket pocket. Ordinarily he would have been annoyed at the interruption, but at this point he welcomed it.

'Please excuse me,' he said, plucking the phone from his pocket. 'This must be extremely important. I gave orders that I wasn't to be disturbed.'

Stavenger spread his hands. 'This is a good time for a short break, I think.'

Humphries strode off to a corner of the conference room as the others all got up from their chairs.

Tucking the phone's little speaker into his earlobe, Humphries flicked the device open and saw URGENT – PRIORITY 1 printed across its tiny screen.

'Proceed,' he said softly.

Dorik Harbin's dark bearded face formed on the screen. 'Sir, we have captured the man Fuchs and his entire crew. We are on the way back to Ceres with them in custody.'

Kill him! Humphries wanted to cry. Instead, his eyes scanned the conference room. The others were standing at the refreshments table. Amanda was nowhere in sight; probably gone to the rest room, he thought.

Knowing that his response would not reach Harbin for nearly half an hour, Humphries said tightly, 'Good work. Make certain you don't lose him. If he tries to get away, or if anyone tries to free him, take appropriate action.'

Appropriate action, Grigor had assured him, was the euphemistic code phrase that meant *kill the sonofabitch if he twitches an eyebrow*.

Humphries closed the phone and slipped it back into his jacket. His pulse was thudding in his ears; he tasted salty perspiration on his upper lip. It's over, he thought, trying to calm himself. It's finished. I've got him, and now I'm going to get Amanda!

He stayed in the far corner of the room as the others slowly came back to their seats. Amanda returned, looking calm, even dignified. She's grown over the years, Humphries realized. She's become much more sure of herself, much more mature. Stavenger glanced his way, and Humphries – working hard to suppress a grin and look serious – slowly walked to his own chair.

Instead of sitting, though, he gripped the back of the chair and said, 'I have an announcement to make.'

They all looked up at him. Even Amanda.

'The one sticking point in our discussion today has been the one-man guerrilla war of Lars Fuchs.'

Dieterling and several others nodded.

'That problem has been resolved,' Humphries said, looking squarely at Amanda. For an instant she looked startled, frightened, but she recovered quickly and looked squarely into his eyes.

'Lars Fuchs is in custody. He's aboard one of my ships and heading back to Ceres. I presume he'll stand trial there for piracy and murder.'

Absolute silence fell across the conference table. Then Amanda slowly got up from her chair.

'Excuse me, please,' she said. 'I must try to contact my husband.' She turned and headed for the door.

Pancho started to get out of her chair, but thought better of it and sat down again. 'Okay, then,' she said, as Amanda left the conference room. 'We got nothin' in the way of making an agreement we can all live with.'

Humphries nodded, but he was thinking, There's nothing in our way except Fuchs. But he's not going to interfere with my plans any more. He's not going to live much longer.

54

'Will you release my crew once we reach Ceres?' Fuchs asked dully, mechanically.

Harbin replied, 'That's not up to me. That decision will be made—'

'By Martin Humphries, I know,' said Fuchs.

Harbin studied the man. They were sitting at the small table in *Shanidar*'s galley, the only space in the ship where two people could converse in privacy. The hatch to the bridge was shut, by Harbin's orders. Fuchs had looked utterly weary, dispirited, when he had first been brought aboard *Shanidar*. The look of defeat: Harbin had seen it before. A man stops fighting when he becomes convinced that no hope is left; victory begins when the enemy's will to resist crumbles. But now, after a decent meal and a few hours to adjust his thinking to his new situation, Fuchs seemed to be regaining some spark of resistance.

He was a powerfully-built man, Harbin saw, despite his smallish stature. Like a badger, or – what was that American creature? A wolverine, he remembered. Small but deadly. Sharp teeth and utter fearlessness.

For a few moments Harbin contemplated what would happen if Fuchs tried to attack him. He had no doubt that he could handle the man, despite Fuchs' apparent strength and potential ferocity. It would simplify everything if I had to kill him in self-defence, Harbin thought. Perhaps I can goad him into attacking me. His wife is apparently a sore point with him.

But then Harbin thought, To be convincing, I'd need at least one witness. That would be self-defeating. With another person in the room Fuchs probably would be smart enough to keep his hands to himself. If I tried to goad him, the witness would witness that, too.

Fuchs broke into his thoughts with, 'Where is my crew? What have you done with them?'

'They've been placed aboard my other ships,' Harbin said. 'No more than two to a ship. It's safer that way; they won't be tempted to try anything foolish.'

'I expect them to be treated properly.'

Harbin bobbed his head once. 'As long as they behave themselves they will be fine.'

'And I want them released when we get to Ceres.'

Barely suppressing a smile at Fuchs' growing impudence, Harbin said, 'As I told you, that decision will be made by higher authority.'

'I take full responsibility for everything that's happened.'

'Naturally.'

Fuchs lapsed into silence for a few moments. Then he said, 'I suppose I'll have to speak to Humphries directly, sooner or later.'

Harbin answered, 'I doubt that he'll want to speak to you.'

'About my crew—'

'Mr Fuchs,' Harbin said, getting to his feet, 'the fate of your crew is something that neither you nor I has the power to decide.'

Fuchs rose also, barely reaching Harbin's shoulder.

'I think it would be best,' Harbin said, 'if you remained in your privacy cubicle for the rest of the flight. We'll be at Ceres in less than thirty-six hours. I'll have your meals brought to you.'

Fuchs said nothing, but let Harbin lead him down the

passageway to the cubicle they had assigned him. There was no lock on the sliding door, which was so flimsy that a lock would have been useless anyway. Fuchs realized that Harbin had been clever to break up his crew and parcel them out among the other ships in his fleet.

I'm alone here, he thought as Harbin gestured him into the cubicle. The door slid closed. Fuchs sat heavily on the hard springless cot. Like Samson captured and blinded by the Philistines, he told himself. Eyeless in Gaza.

At least I wasn't sold out by Amanda. She'd never be a Delilah, never betray me. Never.

He desperately wanted to believe that.

'The essence of our agreement, then,' said Stavenger, 'is that both Astro and Humphries Space Systems disband their mercenary forces and allow the independent prospectors to operate without harassment.'

'And without placing any controls on the prices for ores,' Humphries added, with a satisfied nod.

'No price controls,' Pancho agreed.

Dieterling said, 'Pardon my bluntness, but don't you feel that your refusal to accept price controls is blatantly selfish?'

'Not at all,' snapped Humphries.

'Works the other way around, Willi,' Pancho said, quite seriously. 'Supply and demand works in favour of the buyer, not the seller.'

'But you buy the ores from the prospectors—'

'And sell the refined metals to you,' Humphries pointed out.

Frowning slightly, Dieterling muttered, 'I'm not an economist . . .'

'I think a free market works in Selene's favour,' Stavenger said. 'And Earth's.'

403

Pancho hunched forward in her chair. 'See, if you leave the market open, then the more ores the prospectors locate the lower the price'll go. Supply and demand.'

'But Earth needs vast amounts of those raw materials,' Dieterling said.

Stavenger put a hand on the diplomat's sleeve, gently. 'Dr Dieterling, I don't think you have any idea of how enormous the resources in the Asteroid Belt are. There are trillions of tons of high-grade ores out there. Hundreds of trillions of tons. We've only begun to scratch the surface, so far.'

'Price controls would work in favour of the prospectors, not the ultimate consumers on Earth,' Humphries said firmly.

'Or Selene,' added Stavenger.

Still worrying that uncontrolled prices for asteroidal ores would somehow work against Earth's best interests, Dieterling reluctantly agreed to drop the issue and allow Astro and HSS to draft an agreement. The International Astronautical Authority would be empowered to adjudicate claims against one corporation or the other.

'There's one remaining problem,' Stavenger pointed out, just as everyone was getting ready to call the conference a success.

Humphries, halfway out of his chair, grumbled, 'What now?'

'Enforcement,' Stavenger said. 'There's nothing in the draft agreement about enforcing the peace.'

Sitting down again, Humphries asked, 'You don't trust us to live up to the terms we agree to?'

Pancho grinned. 'I know you can trust Astro.'

'Sure we can,' Stavenger replied, grinning back at her. 'But I'd prefer to see something on paper.'

George spoke up. 'We'll enforce the peace,' he said.

Everyone turned to him.

'You?' Humphries scoffed. 'The rock rats?'

'We've got a government now, or the beginnings of one,' George said. 'We'll police Ceres. Any complaints from the prospectors, we'll handle 'em.'

'How could you—'

'Everything goes through Ceres,' George explained. 'That's where the ships get fitted out and supplied. We hold the water taps, mate. And the food cupboards and fuel tanks and even the foo – the bleedin' oxygen for breathin'. We'll keep law and order for ya. It's in our own best interests.'

Dieterling turned back to Stavenger. 'Could that work?'

'We can make it work,' said Kris Cardenas, sitting across the table from George.

Stavenger had a strange expression on his face. 'This means that the rock rats will have political control of the Belt.'

'Which is the way it should be,' Cardenas said firmly. 'We're the people who live there, we ought to be able to control our own destiny.'

Looking from her to Stavenger and back again, Dieterling said, 'That is a great deal of power. The entire Asteroid Belt . . .'

'We can handle it,' George said, totally serious. 'Like Kris here said, it's the way things oughtta be.'

55

The conference ended, at last. As the delegates got up from the table and made their way to the door, Humphries remained seated, hands clasped on the tabletop, deep in thought.

'Ain't you goin' home?' Pancho asked as she came around the table.

'In a while,' Humphries said. 'Not right this moment.'

Stavenger was going through the doorway with Dieterling and his two nephews. Big George and Dr Cardenas were already gone; George had been the first out the door, like a schoolboy racing away from the classroom once the bell has rung.

'I don't think Mandy'll be comin' back here,' Pancho said.

Humphries made himself smile up at her. 'We'll see.'

'Suit yourself,' Pancho said.

Humphries watched her saunter out the door, leaving him alone in the conference room. So we'll have peace in the Belt, he said to himself. And the rock rats will enforce it. Sure they will.

He got to his feet and went to the slim podium that had been wheeled into a corner of the room. The audiovisual controls on its surface were simple enough. With a touch of his finger, Humphries lit up the wallscreen at the other end of the conference room. It showed Selene's logo: the androgynous outline of a human being against the full Moon. Scrolling idly through the computer's stored images, he stopped when a map of the Belt came up: the wild tangle of orbits looked like a long-exposure view of a mad raceway.

So we won't bother the independents anymore, Humphries said to himself. We won't call down the wrath of the rock rats and their fledgling government. We won't have to. All the independents will be selling to me or to Astro; there's no third choice. They'll all fall into line now.

He drew in a breath, thinking, Now the fight's between Astro and HSS. Now the *real* war begins. And when it's over, I'll have Astro in my pocket and total control of the Belt. Total control of the whole fricking solar system and everyone in it!

As if on cue, Amanda entered the conference room.

Humphries stared at her. Somehow she looked different: still the most beautiful woman he had ever seen, the most desirable. Yet there was something else about her now, something that almost unnerved him. She looked back at him, her eyes steady, dry. She's not shedding any tears for her husband, Humphries told himself.

'They won't let me speak to him,' Amanda said, her voice so soft he could barely make out the words. She walked along the length of the conference table toward Humphries.

'He's too far out for a two-way conversation,' he said.

'I put through a call to him and they wouldn't even accept it. They told me he's not allowed to receive any messages from anyone.'

'He's being held incommunicado.'

'On your orders.'

'Yes.'

'You intend to kill him, don't you?'

Humphries evaded her unwavering blue eyes. 'I imagine they'll put him on trial at Ceres. He's killed a lot of people.'

'Will he live long enough to face a trial?' Amanda asked, her voice flat, calm, not accusative so much as resigned.

Uncomfortably nervous, Humphries shifted his weight from one foot to another. 'He's a violent man, you know. He might try to escape custody.'

'That would be convenient, wouldn't it? Then he could be killed while trying to escape.'

Humphries came around the podium and stepped toward her, reaching his arms out to her.

'Amanda,' he said, 'it's all over. Fuchs has dug his own grave and—'

'And you're going to see that he goes into it.'

'It's not my doing!' At that moment he almost felt that it was true.

Amanda simply stood there, unmoving, unmoved, her arms at her sides, her eyes focused on him, searching for something, something. He wished he knew what it was.

'What do you want from me?' he asked her.

For a moment she said nothing. Then, 'I want your promise that you won't allow him to be harmed in any way.'

'The rock rats are going to put him on trial for murder.'

'I understand that,' Amanda said. 'I still want your promise that *you* won't do anything to harm him.'

He hesitated, then asked coldly, 'And what will you do in exchange for my promise?'

'I'll go to bed with you,' Amanda said. 'That's what you want, isn't it?'

'No!' he blurted. Almost pleading, he said, 'I want to marry you, Amanda. I love you! I want to give you . . . everything you've ever wanted.'

She waited a heartbeat, then said, 'All I want is Lars' safety.'

'And not me?'

'I owe it to Lars. All this has happened because of me, hasn't it?'

He wanted to lie, wanted to tell her that everything he

had done he had done for her and for her alone. But he couldn't. Facing her, so close to her, he could not lie.

'You were a part of it, Amanda. But only a part. Something like this would have happened anyway.'

'But Lars wouldn't have been caught in the middle of it, would he?'

'Probably not,' Humphries agreed.

'Then I'll marry you, if that's what you want. In exchange for your promise to leave Lars alone.'

Humphries' throat felt dry, parched. He nodded mutely.

'Now you have everything *you* want, don't you?' Amanda said. There was no rancour in it. No trace of anger or bitterness. At last Humphries understood what was different about her, what had changed. She was not the innocent, naïve girl she had once been. Those blue eyes are unsmiling now, calculating.

He couldn't find words. He wanted to make her feel better about this, wanted to make her smile. But he couldn't find any words.

'That is what you want, isn't it?' Amanda insisted.

'Not like this,' he said, finding his voice. And it was the truth. 'Not as part of a – an arrangement.'

Amanda shrugged slightly. 'This is the way it is, Martin. There's nothing either one of us can do to change it. I'll marry you if you swear that you won't harm Lars.'

He licked his lips. 'He'll still have to face trial on Ceres. I can't stop that.'

'I know,' she said. 'I accept that.'

'All right, then.'

'I want to hear you say it, Martin. I want your promise, here and now.'

Drawing himself up to his full height, Humphries said, 'Very well. I promise you, Amanda, that I will do nothing to harm Lars Fuchs in any way.'

'You won't give anyone orders to hurt him.'

'I swear to you, Amanda.'

The breath seemed to sag out of her. 'All right, then. I'll marry you as soon as a divorce can be arranged.'

Or as soon as you become a widow, Humphries thought. Aloud, he said, 'Now it's your turn to make a promise, Amanda.'

Alarm flashed in her eyes momentarily. Then she understood. 'I see. Yes, I promise that I will be your loving wife, Martin. This won't be merely a marriage of appearances.'

Before he could take her hands in his, she turned and walked out of the conference room, leaving him standing alone. For a few moments he felt rejected, wronged, almost angry. But slowly it dawned on him that Amanda had agreed to marry him, to love him. It wasn't the romantic perfection he had fantasized about over all the years, but she had promised to marry him! All right, he thought, she's upset about it now. I've forced her into it and she doesn't like that. She feels an obligation to Fuchs. But that will change. In time, she'll accept it. She'll accept me. She'll love me. I know she will.

Suddenly Humphries was laughing out loud, dancing around the conference table like a manic teenager. 'I've got her!' he shouted to the ceiling. 'I've got everything I've ever wanted! The whole miserable solar system is in my grasp!'

Big George thought they were lucky to snag a ride aboard an HSS ship heading for Ceres on a high-energy trajectory.

'We'll be there in four days,' he said to Kris Cardenas as they picked meal packages from the galley's freezer.

Cardenas was more sceptical about their luck. 'Why is Humphries sending this ship to Ceres on a high-g burn? It's practically empty. We're the only passengers and there isn't any cargo, far as I can tell.'

Sliding his dinner into the microwave, George said, 'From what the crew's buzzin', they're goin' out to pick up the bloke who captured Lars.'

Comprehension lit Cardenas' cornflower-blue eyes. 'So that's it! A triumphal return for the conquering hero.'

'It isn't funny, Kris. We've gotta put Lars on trial, y'know. He's killed people.'

'I know,' she said despondently.

The microwave bell chimed.

'George,' she asked, 'isn't there some way we can save Lars' neck?'

'Sure,' he said, pulling out the tray. 'Sentence 'im to life at hard labour. Or maybe pop 'im into a cryonic freezer for a hundred years or so.'

'Be serious,' Cardenas said.

George sat at the galley's little table and unwrapped his steaming tray. 'Dunno what we can do except give him as fair a trial as we can. He's made a lot of enemies, y'know.'

She slammed her tray back into the freezer and sat glumly beside him. 'I wish there were some way we could save him.'

Already digging into his dinner, George tried to change the subject. 'We'll do what we can for Lars. But, y'know, I been thinkin' . . . why can't you develop nanomachines to take the ores outta the asteroids right there on the spot and refine 'em? That'd make it a snap to mine 'em.'

'It would throw almost all the miners out of work.'

'Maybe so,' George admitted. 'But what if we let 'em buy shares of the nanotech operation? That way they could become fookin' capitalists instead o' grubbin' away at the rocks.'

Harbin personally escorted Fuchs from *Shanidar* to the underground settlement on Ceres. Fuchs was not handcuffed or fettered, but he knew he was a prisoner. Harbin brought two of his biggest men with him; he was taking no chances.

As they rode the ungainly shuttlecraft down to the asteroid's surface, Fuchs spotted the still-unfinished habitat rotating lazily across the star-flecked sky. Will they ever finish it, he asked himself. Will they ever be able to live the way I wanted Amanda and me to live?

Amanda. The thought of her sapped all the strength from him. At least she will be safe, Fuchs thought. Yes, came a mocking voice from within his mind. She'll be quite safe once she's in Humphries' hands. The old anger surged for a moment, but it faded away, replaced with the hopelessness of his situation. He's won her and I've lost, he knew.

As they stepped through the airlock and into the reception area, Fuchs saw a group of four women and three men waiting for him. He recognized them all: former neighbours, former friends.

'We'll take him from here,' said Joyce Takamine, her gaunt, pinched face blankly expressionless. She would not look Fuchs in the eyes.

'Take him where?' Harbin demanded.

'He's under house arrest,' Takamine replied stiffly, 'pending the return of our Chief Administrator. He's going to stand trial for piracy and murder.'

Harbin nodded his agreement and allowed them to lead Fuchs away. It's finished, he told himself. I've done my job. Now for the rewards.

He led his two men to the Humphries office, only a short walk through the dusty tunnel. There a smiling young woman got up from her metal desk and personally escorted the trio to quarters deeper inside the warren of tunnels and cubicles. The two men had to share one room; Harbin got a private apartment. It was still just one room, but it was his alone. Someone had even brought his travel bag and placed it on the bed.

A message from Diane was waiting for him.

She should have looked happy, jubilant, Harbin thought, rejoicing in their victory, his triumph. Instead, her face looked serious, almost grave, in the wallscreen image.

'Dorik, I've set up a high-g flight for you. I want you here at Selene as soon as you can get here. Now that you've taken Fuchs, there's a lot we have to do, a lot of changes in both our lives. I'll tell you all about it when you get here.'

The screen went blank. Harbin stared at it for a few moments, thinking, Not a word of congratulation. Not a syllable of warmth. Well, she's never said she loves me.

He went to the bed and sat on it, suddenly tired. I never expected love, he told himself. Then he realized, not until now. He opened his travel bag and searched through it for the pills that would bring him peace – at least for a little while.

56

Humphries spent the morning making arrangements for his wedding. He had his legal department send a notice of Amanda's divorce suit to Fuchs at Ceres. That ought to put the icing on his cake, he thought delightedly. Maybe he'll commit suicide once he get the news and spare us all the trouble of putting him on trial. Then he decided to buy the Hotel Luna and refurbish it so it would look properly gleaming for his wedding. It won't be a big affair, he thought, just a few dozen friends. And the most important of my business associates, of course. It's got to be first-class all the way. What was that old word the English used, long ago? Posh. That's it. I want this wedding to be small, intimate, and very posh.

Amanda will probably invite Pancho, he realized. So what? I wonder how much family she has back on Earth. I'll bring them all up here. Why not? I'm going to shower her with so much kindness and luxury that she'll fall in love with me whether she wants to or not.

By lunchtime he was still grinning and whistling to himself. He ate at his desk, casually running down the past two days of activities reports. He stopped when he saw that Diane had authorized a high-energy flight to Ceres. The only passengers aboard the vessel were Ambrose and Dr Cardenas.

Why would she do that? he wondered.

And then he remembered, She went through the implantation procedure yesterday. And she still got up and ordered a special flight for those two rock rats?

His mood only slightly dimmed, he called Verwoerd on the phone.

'I'm going to take a stroll through the garden,' he said when her image appeared on the wallscreen. 'Are you up to joining me?'

'I'm trying to catch up on what I missed yesterday,' she said guardedly.

'That can wait. A walk in the fresh air will be good for you.'

She hesitated a fraction of a second, then capitulated. With a nod, she said, 'I'll meet you at your front door.'

He expected that she would show some strain from the procedure she'd been through, but to Humphries' eye Diane Verwoerd looked no different than before the implantation.

'The procedure went well?' he asked as they stepped along the brick path that wound through lushly thick bushes of coral pink oleanders and scarlet azaleas.

She gave him a sidelong glance. 'The report should be on file.'

'I've seen the report,' he replied testily. 'I want to know how you feel.'

'Oh,' said Verwoerd. 'Concerned for the mother of your son?'

'That's right.'

She stayed silent for a few steps, then said at last, 'I'm fine. Mother and fetus in good condition.'

'Good.'

'By the way, let me offer my congratulations.'

He couldn't help breaking into a smile. 'About Amanda? Thank you.'

They passed a little bench of lunar stone. Verwoerd asked, 'Now that you'll be able to make a baby the old-fashioned way, do you still want me to go to term?'

'Of course I do,' he snapped. 'That's my son you're talking about.'

'Your clone.'

'I wouldn't have you abort him. I can have more than one child.'

'But this one,' she patted her stomach lightly, 'carries your genes and nobody else's.'

'Damned right.'

'He won't be exactly like you, you know,' Verwoerd said, a teasing smile playing across her lips. 'Genetically, he'll be identical, but he'll be affected by the enzymes of my body and—'

'I know all that,' Humphries interrupted.

'I'm sure you do.'

He glared at her. 'You're downright sassy today, aren't you?'

'And why shouldn't I be, Martin? I'm carrying your child. You're going to reward me very handsomely for that, aren't you?'

'If the boy is healthy when he's born.'

'No, I don't want to wait until then. I want my payoff now. I want a seat on the board of directors. I've earned it. And I'll be a lot better at it than most of those fossils.'

Power, Humphries thought. She's after power. Aloud, he asked, 'Is that all?'

'I want money, too. I want a lot of money, Martin. I know you can afford it.'

He stopped walking and planted his fists on his hips. 'Since when do you call me by my given name?'

She smiled saucily. 'I'm taking a very large risk for this fetus of yours. I think that works out to a first-name relationship, don't you?'

'No, I don't.'

'Very well then, we'll keep everything strictly on a business level, *Mr* Humphries. I want ten million a year, for life.'

'Ten mil ...' He barked out a bitter laugh. 'You're dreaming. I could get a hundred women to do what you're doing and it wouldn't cost me a fraction of that.'

Verwoerd began walking along the brick path again, slowly. Humphries had no choice but to follow her.

'Yes, I'm sure you could buy a surrogate mother for your clone on the cheap. But I'm worth ten million. Even more, in fact.'

'Are you?' he asked sullenly, realizing now where she was heading.

'I know a lot about you, about what you've done in the Belt. I've been a faithful employee, *Mr* Humphries, and I've kept my mouth shut. But continued silence will cost you ten million per year. You can set up a trust fund; I'll handle the details for you.'

Strangely, Humphries felt no anger. He almost admired her audacity. 'So it's come to this,' he said.

'Yes, it has.'

With a slow, disappointed shake of his head, Humphries said, 'I was afraid you'd get delusions of grandeur. This isn't the first time an employee of mine had tried to extort money from me.'

'Don't you think I'm worth ten mill per year?' she asked, rank impudence on her smiling lips.

Before he could think of an appropriate reply, Verwoerd added, 'And don't think you can conveniently get rid of me. I'm not going to have an accident, Martin. I have a very good insurance policy against accidents of all kinds.'

Then it dawned on him. 'So that's why you're rushing Harbin back here.'

She nodded. 'Dorik's my insurance policy. If you attempt

any violence against me, he'll kill you. He's good at it. Ask Grigor; Grigor's terrified of him.'

'Is he?'

'Yes. And for good reason. You should be terrified of him, too, if you think you can get rid of me. It's cheaper to pay the ten million, Martin. That covers both of us, Dorik and me together.'

'A real bargain,' Humphries growled.

57

It was maddening. All day long Lars Fuchs paced his one room apartment like a caged tiger, to the door, turn around, to the far wall where the wallscreen stood blank and mute. Again and again: the door, then past the bed where he and Amanda had slept together, made love together . . .

He wanted to scream. He wanted to pound the walls, smash down the flimsy door and run through the dusty tunnels until someone shot him down and put an end to it all.

He recalled the phrase the Americans used: cruel and unusual punishment. To be put under house arrest, to be locked in the room that had for so many years been his home, to know that his wife was millions of kilometres away and preparing to marry the man who had ruined his life – better to be dead, better to be out of this endless torture.

He caught a glimpse of himself in the mirror over the bureau and saw a man he hardly recognized, clothes wrinkled and sweat-stained, hair unkempt, jowly face unshaved. He stopped pacing and stared at the image in the mirror: a man steeped in self-pity, wallowing in defeat.

No, he said to himself. I won't let it end this way. They've taken everything from me, but they won't take my self-respect. No one can do that except I myself.

He tore off his sweaty clothes and stepped into the shower. When the spray turned on automatically, he thought about his water allotment, but then he decided, to hell with it; a condemned man has the right to a decent wash. But as the steamy mist enveloped him he thought of the times when he and Amanda had squeezed into the narrow stall together. It took all his strength to keep from crying.

Freshly dressed and shaved, he asked the phone to call George Ambrose. Less than a quarter-hour later, Big George rapped once on his door and slid it back.

'Hullo, Lars,' the big Aussie said, looking slightly shamefaced. 'You wanted to see me?'

Fuchs saw that an armed guard stood out in the tunnel; even with his breathing mask on he recognized the guard as Oscar Jiminez.

'Step in, by all means,' Fuchs said, trying to sound brave. 'I welcome a break in the monotony.'

George slid the door shut again and stood uneasily by it. 'I di'n't think how the hours must drag for you, havin' to stay in here.'

'The only communication I've had from outside was a notice from Humphries' lawyers that Amanda is suing for a divorce.'

'Aw, cripes, Lars,' George said, crestfallen, 'I'm sorry about that.'

'I didn't contest it,' Fuchs went on, almost enjoying the obvious guilt on George's bearded face. 'What difference does it make? I'm going to be executed soon, am I not?'

George's expression turned even gloomier. 'Well, we're settin' up a trial for you. You're gonna need to have somebody to act as your defence counsel.'

'I don't want a trial.' Fuchs was surprised to hear himself say it.

'Neither do I, mate, but we've gotta have it.'

'You don't understand, George. I waive my right to a trial . . . as long as my crew is exonerated and allowed to go free. I take full responsibility for everything.'

'Let your crew go?' George scratched at his beard thoughtfully.

'I gave the orders. They didn't know that my orders would kill the people on Vesta.'

'You take full responsibility?'

'Absolutely.'

'And you admit you killed the construction team on Vesta? Deliberately?'

'I'd do it again,' Fuchs said fervently, 'if the same situation arose.'

George blew out a huge breath. 'Guess we won't need a trial, then.'

'You'll let my crew go free?'

'I'll hafta run it past the rest of the council, but, yeah, I don't see any point in holdin' them if you're willing to take all the blame.'

'I take all the blame,' Fuchs said.

'Okay, then,' said George. 'I guess the only question left is whether you want a blindfold or not.'

Martin Humphries didn't wait for Dorik Harbin to arrive at Selene. He ordered an HSS spacecraft to fly him to a rendezvous with the vessel Harbin was on. He grimaced when he thought about the expense, but he wanted to see this mercenary soldier, this hired killer, without Verwoerd involved.

Even though he had studied Harbin's personnel file to the last detail, Humphries was still surprised when he finally met the man. He's like some prowling jungle cat, Humphries thought as soon as he entered Harbin's compartment. Even in the stark, cramped shipboard cubicle, Harbin reminded him of a panther, restless energy pent beneath a sleekly muscled hide.

He was definitely handsome, in a rugged, almost cruel way. Harbin had shaved off his beard and put on a long-sleeved shirt and khaki slacks for his meeting with Humphries. The clothes were creased so sharply they might as well have been a military uniform. Humphries felt decided civilian in his casual turtleneck pullover and whipcord trousers.

They shook hands and murmured polite greetings to one another. Harbin invited Humphries to sit on the cubicle's sole chair, a plastic recliner, then sat on the edge of the bunk, rigid as if at attention. Even sitting down he looked as if he's ready to leap at his prey, Humphries thought.

'I brought you a gift,' Humphries said genially, pointing to the compartment's blank wallscreen. 'Authorization for any uh . . . medications you might need.'

'You mean drugs,' Harbin said.

'Yes. Recreational, stimulants – anything you want, my pharmacists at Selene will produce them for you.'

'Thank you.'

'Think nothing of it,' said Humphries.

Then there was silence. Harbin simply sat there, appraising Humphries with his spooky ice-blue eyes. I've got to be very careful with this man, Humphries realized. He's like a vial of nitroglycerine: handle him the wrong way and he'll explode.

At last Humphries cleared his throat and said, 'I wanted to meet you personally, to congratulate you on a job well done.'

Harbin said nothing.

'You've earned a sizeable bonus.'

'Thank you.'

'That business about sending copies of your logs to

424

several friends on Earth,' Humphries went on, 'was very clever. It shows a lot of intelligence on your part.'

Harbin's expression changed minutely. A hint of curiosity flickered in his eyes.

'Very clever,' Humphries continued. 'But really unnecessary. You have nothing to fear from me. I'm grateful to you, and I don't turn on the people who do their jobs well. Ask Grigor. Ask anyone.'

Harbin seemed to think it over for a moment. Then, 'I was being cautious.'

'I understand. In a way, I even agree with you. If I'd been in your position, I probably would have done the same thing, more or less.'

'You mentioned a bonus.'

'One million international dollars, paid to any bank you name.'

Harbin didn't move a millimeter, but he seemed somehow to stiffen, like an animal that suddenly senses danger.

'I had expected more,' he said.

'Really? I think a million is very generous.'

'Diane said there would be more.'

There! Humphries cheered silently. He's brought up her name.

'Diane? Diane Verwoerd?'

'Your personal assistant, yes.'

'She has no authority to make you an offer that I haven't approved,' Humphries said sternly.

'But she told me . . .' Harbin's voice trailed off in confusion.

Humphries made himself smile understandingly. 'Diane sometimes exceeds her authority.' With a sly wink, he went on, 'That's the trouble with a woman. If they share your bed they start behaving as if they own you.'

'Share your bed?'

'Didn't you know? She didn't tell you? For god's sake, the woman's carrying my baby.'

Harbin rose slowly to his feet. 'Carrying . . . your baby?'

Trying to keep from showing fear, Humphries sat where he was and said innocently, 'We just found out about it a few days ago. She's pregnant, all right. We've been sending the happy news to all our friends. I'm surprised she didn't tell you.'

58

The drugs only made it worse. Harbin selected carefully among the narcotics available from Humphries' supplier, but he could not eradicate the thought of Diane betraying him. For two days after his arrival in Selene he lay in the apartment Humphries had provided him, trying to smother the pictures that played in his head. The drugs distorted his visions, twisted them and made them physically painful, but they did not bring the peace and oblivion that he sought. Just the opposite. They sharpened the knives that twisted in his flesh; they drove the daggers deeper inside him.

She's been sleeping with him! She's allowed herself to get pregnant by him! All the time she was with me, she was mocking me, manipulating me to do what she wanted, what *they* wanted me to do. She's played me for a fool and she thought she could get away with it.

At last he could stand it no longer. Close to midnight, he lurched out of his apartment into the corridors that honeycombed Selene, bleary-eyed, unshaven, still in the clothes he had slept in for the past two nights. He shambled along the nearly empty corridors, heading for Diane's quarters.

Sleeping alone in his giant bed, Humphries was awakened by the buzz of his private phone. Grumbling, he sat up and told the computer to put his caller on-screen.

The wallscreen showed Grigor's sombre lean face.

'He's left the apartment,' Grigor said without preamble.

Humphries nodded and cut the connection. Wide awake,

now, he bunched the pillows behind him and sat back comfortably, then commanded the computer to show the display from the picocameras built into Diane Verwoerd's apartment. She had searched her quarters several times, seeking the bugs, Humphries knew. But no one had found the microscopic cameras built into the apartment's wiring.

Four dark pictures quartered Humphries' bedroom wall-screen: one view of each room in Diane's apartment: sitting room, bedroom, kitchen, lavatory. He switched to infrared mode and saw that she was lying asleep in her bed. For two days she had searched Selene for Harbin and not found him. Humphries had secreted the mercenary far from her prying eyes. And fed the man with drugs that heightened his normal sense of betrayal, elevated his anger into homicidal fury. Years earlier chemists had developed hallucinogenic PCPs such as angel dust out of the primitive natural amphetamines. What Humphries' people were feeding Harbin was far more sophisticated, fine-tuned to turn him into a raging maniac.

Now Humphries sat back in his bed and waited for the conclusion of this little drama that Diane Verwoerd had brought upon herself. Try to force me to knuckle under to you, will you? Blackmail me? Threaten me? Well, now you'll get what you deserve, you little slut.

Harbin found her door at last. He hesitated a moment, head swimming, fist poised to rap on the door. And give her a chance to call for help? Give her a chance to hide her latest lover?

He forced the lock on the sliding door easily and stepped inside her shadowy living room. It took a few moments for his eyes to adjust to the darkness, then he padded silently to her bedroom door. Something smelled rank, foul, and he realized it was his own body odour. She's done this to me, he told himself. She's made me into a pig.

Like Circe, he thought, peering into the shadows to make out her sleeping form on the bed. The enchantress who turns men into swine.

She was alone, he saw. He moved to the night table and switched on the lamp.

Diane awoke slowly, blinked up at him, then smiled.

'Dorik, where have you been? I've looked everywhere for you.'

Then she saw the murderous look on his unshaved face. She sat up and let the covers slip to her waist.

'What's the matter? What's wrong? You look *terrible*.'

He stared down at her. How many times had he caressed those breasts? How many other men had shared her body?

'Dorik, what's happened?'

His voice, when he found it, was little more than a croak. 'Are you pregnant?'

The shock on her face was all the answer he needed. 'I was going to tell you—'

'With Humphries' baby?'

'Yes, but—'

She got no farther. He seized her by the throat and pulled her off the bed, squeezing hard with both hands. She flailed her arms pitifully as he throttled her. Her eyes glazed, her tongue bulged out of her gagging mouth. Still crushing her larynx with one hand, Harbin grabbed her protruding tongue with the other, dug his nails into it and pulled it out of her lying mouth. Her shriek of pain drowned in the blood gushing from her mouth. Harbin relaxed his grip on her throat just enough to let her choke on her own blood, gurgling, moaning, her hands sliding down his arms until her arms hung limp and dead.

Watching from his bed, Humphries felt his guts churn and heave. He lurched to his feet and staggered to the lavatory,

Diane's last bubbling moans lost in his own retching agony. By the time he had wiped his face and stumbled back into his bedroom, the wallscreen showed Harbin on his knees, sobbing inconsolably, Diane lying on the floor beside him, her face spattered with blood, her eyes staring sightlessly.

He ripped her tongue out! Humphries said to himself, gagging again. My god, he's a monster!

Crawling back into bed, he switched off the camera view and called Grigor, who was waiting patiently in his office.

'Diane Verwoerd's had a heart attack,' Humphries said to his security chief, struggling to keep his voice even. 'A fatal one. Get a reliable crew to her apartment to clean the place up and take care of the body.'

Grigor nodded once. 'And Harbin?'

'Get him tranquillized and tucked away in a safe place. Better bring a team. He won't trank easily.'

'Wouldn't it be better to silence him?'

Humphries laughed bitterly. 'With this hanging over him? He's silenced, believe it. And he's still available to do whatever I need him to do.'

'Still . . .'

'I'll find plenty of work for him, don't worry,' Humphries said. 'Just keep him away from me. I don't want him in the same room with me, ever again.' He thought a moment, then added, 'I don't want him on the same *planet* as me.'

59

Lars Fuchs looked up in surprise when he heard the knock at his door. He shut down the drama he'd been watching – Sophocles' *Antigone* – and called out, 'Come in.'

It was George again, looking grim.

Fuchs rose from his chair. 'To what do I owe this honour?'

'Time to go,' George said.

Even though he knew this moment was inevitable, Fuchs felt startled. His insides went hollow.

'Now?'

'Now,' said George.

There were two armed men outside his door, both strangers to Fuchs. He walked stolidly beside George up the dusty tunnel, trying to suppress the irritation that rasped in his lungs and throat. He couldn't do it, and broke into a racking cough.

'Shoulda brought masks,' George mumbled.

'What difference does it make?' Fuchs asked, as he tried to bring his coughing under control.

George hacked a bit, too, as they walked along the tunnel. Fuchs realized they were headed upward, toward the airlock that opened onto the surface. Maybe that's how they'll execute me, he thought: toss me outside without a suit.

But they stopped short of the airlock. George ushered Fuchs into a sizeable chamber while the two armed guards stayed out in the dust.

Fuchs saw that his former crew were all there. They all turned toward him.

'Nodon . . . Sanja . . . you're all right, all of you?'

The six of them nodded and even smiled. Nodon said, 'We are quite all right, Captain sir.'

'They're leavin',' George said. 'Your ship's been refitted and fuelled up. They're headin' out into the Belt.'

'Good,' Fuchs said. 'I'm glad.'

'And you're goin' with them,' George added, his shaggy face deeply creased with a worried frown.

'Me? What do you mean?'

George took a heavy breath, then explained, 'We're not goin' to execute you, Lars. You're bein' exiled. For life. Get out and don't come back. Ever.'

'Exiled? I don't understand.'

'We talked it over, me an' the council. We decided to exile you. That's it.'

'Exile,' Fuchs repeated, stunned, unable to believe it.

'That's right. Some people won't like it, but that's what we fookin' decided.'

'You're saving my life, George.'

'If you call flittin' out in the Belt like a bloody Flyin' Dutchman savin' your life, then, yeah, that's what we're doin'. Just don't ever try to come back here, that's all.'

For weeks Fuchs had been preparing himself mentally to be executed. He realized now that his preparations had been nothing short of a pitiful sham. An enormous wave of gratitude engulfed him. His knees felt watery; his eyes misted over.

'George . . . I . . . what can I say?'

'Say goodbye, Lars.'

'Goodbye, then. And thank you!'

George looked decidedly unhappy, like a man who had been forced to make a choice between hideous alternatives.

Fuchs went with his crew to the airlock, suited up, and climbed into the shuttlecraft that was waiting to take them to *Nautilus*, hanging in orbit above Ceres.

Half an hour later, as he sat in the command chair on *Nautilus'* bridge, Fuchs sent a final message to Big George:

'Finish the habitat, George. Build a decent home for yourselves.'

'We will,' George answered, his red-bearded face already small and distant in the ship's display screen. 'You just keep yourself outta trouble, Lars. Be a good rock rat. Stay inside the lines.'

It was only then that Fuchs began to understand what exile meant.

60

It was the biggest social event in the history of Selene. Nearly two hundred wedding guests assembled in the garden outside Humphries' mansion.

Pancho Lane wore a pale lavender mid-calf silk sheath that accented her slim, athletic figure. Sapphires sparkled at her earlobes, wrists and her long, graceful throat. Her tightly curled hair was sprinkled with sapphire dust.

'You look like a fookin' million dollars on the hoof,' said Big George.

Pancho grinned at the Aussie. He looked uncomfortable, almost embarrassed, in a formal suit of dead black and an old-fashioned bow tie.

'The way I figure it,' she said, 'if I've got to play the part of a corporate bigwig, I should at least look like one.'

'Pretty damned good,' said George.

'You don't look too bad yourself,' Pancho said.

'Come on,' George said. 'We'd better find our seats.'

Every aspect of the wedding was meticulously controlled by Humphries' people. Each white folding chair set up on the garden's grass had a specific guest's name stenciled on its back, and each guest had been given a specific number for the reception line after the ceremony.

Almost as soon as they sat down, Kris Cardenas joined Pancho and George, looking radiantly young in a buttercup yellow dress that complemented her golden hair.

'Amanda's really going through with it,' Cardenas said, as if she wished it weren't true.

'Looks that way,' George replied, leaning forward in his chair and keeping his voice low. 'Don't think she'd let things get this far and then back out, do you?'

'Not Mandy,' said Pancho, sitting between George and Cardenas. 'She'll go through with it, all right.'

'I feel bad for Lars,' Cardenas said.

Pancho nodded. 'That's why Mandy's marrying Humphries; to keep Lars alive.'

'Well, he's alive, at least,' said George. 'Him and 'is crew are out in the Belt someplace.'

'Prospecting?'

'What else can they do? If he tries to put in here at Selene or anywhere on Earth they'll arrest 'im.'

Cardenas shook her head. 'It doesn't seem fair, exiling him like that.'

'Better than killin' him,' said George.

'I suppose, but still . . .'

'It's done,' George said, with heavy finality. 'Now we've got to look forward, to the future.'

Pancho nodded agreement.

'I want you,' George said to Cardenas, 'to start figurin' out how we can use nanos for mining.'

Cardenas stiffened slightly. 'I told you that I don't think it's a good idea.'

'Stuff it,' George snapped. 'It's a great idea and you know it. Just because—'

The live orchestra that Humphries had brought to Selene for the occasion began to play the wedding march. Everyone got to their feet and turned to see Amanda, in a white floor-length gown, starting down the aisle several paces ahead of the other women in their matching aqua gowns. Amanda walked alone and unsmiling, clutching a bouquet of white orchids and pale miniature roses in both hands.

*   *   *

It won't be that bad a life, Amanda was telling herself as she walked slowly up the aisle to the tempo of the wedding march. Martin isn't a monster; he can be positively sweet when he wants to. I'll simply have to keep my wits about me and stay in command of the situation.

But then she thought of Lars and her heart melted. She wanted to cry, but knew she shouldn't, mustn't. A bride is supposed to smile, she thought. A bride is supposed to be radiantly happy.

Martin Humphries was standing at the makeshift altar up at the head of the aisle. Two hundred-some guests were watching Amanda as she walked slowly, in measured tread, to him. Martin was beaming, looking resplendent in a tuxedo of deep burgundy velvet, standing there like a triumphant champion, smiling at her dazzlingly.

The minister had been flown to Selene from Martin's family home in Connecticut. All the other members of the bridal party were strangers to Amanda.

As the minister started to speak the words of the ceremony, Amanda thought of the fertilized embryos that she and Lars had left frozen in the clinic in Selene. The zygotes were Lars' children, his offspring. And hers.

She glanced at Martin, who would be her legal husband in a few moments. I'll have sex with him, Amanda thought. Of course. That's what he wants. That's what he expects. And I'll give him everything he expects. Everything.

But when I bear a child, it will be Lars' baby, not Martin's. I'll see to that. Martin will never know, but I will. I'll bring Lars' son into the world. That's what I'll do.

When Amanda had to say, 'I do,' she smiled for the first time.

Martin Humphries stood beside the most splendidly beautiful woman in the solar system and knew that

437

she would be his and his alone for as long as he wanted her.

I've got everything I want, he told himself. Almost. He had seen Pancho among the wedding guests, standing there with that big red-headed oaf and Dr Cardenas. Amanda had invited them, they were her friends. Humphries thought he himself would have invited Pancho, just to let her watch him take possession of Amanda.

Pancho thinks the war's over. We have the rock rats under control and the fight between Astro and me can be channelled into peaceful competition. He almost laughed aloud. Amanda glanced at him. She probably thinks I'm smiling for her, Humphries thought. Well, I am. But there's more to it than that. Much more.

I'll have a son with Amanda. The clones will come to term soon and I'll pick the best of the litter, but I'll have a natural son with Amanda, as well. The old-fashioned way. I'll make her forget about Fuchs. I'll drive him out of her memory completely, one way or the other.

Fuchs is finished. They may have let him loose, but he's a dead man anyway. He can't do anything to hurt me now. He's an exile, alone and without friends to help him. I promised Amanda that I wouldn't harm him and I won't have to. He's out of my way now and the rock rats are under control. Now the real battle against Astro can begin. I'll take control of Astro Corporation, and the Belt, and the whole goddamned solar system.

At that moment the minister asked Humphries if he would take Amanda Cunningham as his lawful wedded wife.

His answer to that question, and to his own ambitions, was, 'I will!'

Epilogue

Dorik Harbin writhed and groaned in his drugged sleep as he rode the fusion ship out to the Belt again. Humphries' psychologists had done their best with him, but his dreams were still tortured by visions of Diane dying at his feet. Their drugs couldn't erase the memory; sometimes they made it worse, distorted, sometimes it was Harbin's mother drowning on her own blood while he stood helplessly watching.

When he awoke the visions of her death still haunted him. He heard her last gurgling moans, saw the utter terror in her eyes. She deserved to die, he told himself as he stared out the spacecraft's thick quartz port at the star-flecked emptiness beyond the ship's hull. She lied to me, she used me, laughed at me. She deserved to die.

Yes, said the voice in his mind that he could never silence. Everyone deserves to die. Including you.

He grimaced, and remembered Khayyám's quatrain:

> One Moment in Annihilation's Waste,
> One Moment, of the Well of Life to Taste –
>   The Stars are setting and the Caravan
> Starts for the Dawn of Nothing – Oh, make haste!

Deep in the Asteroid Belt, Lars Fuchs sat uneasily in the command chair of *Nautilus*, staring into the bleak emptiness outside.

This ship is my whole world now, he told himself. This

one ship and these six strangers who crew it. Amanda is gone; she is dead to me. All my friends, my whole life, the woman I love – all dead and gone.

He felt like Adam, driven out of the garden of Eden, kept from returning by an angel with a flaming sword. I can never return. Never. I'll spend the rest of my days out here in this desert. What kind of a life do I have to look forward to?

The answer came to his mind immediately. Martin Humphries has everything I worked for. He possesses my wife. He's driven me into exile. But I will get back at him. No matter how long it takes; no matter how powerful he is. I will have my revenge.

Not like Adam. Not like that snivelling weakling. No, he told himself. Like Samson. Betrayed, blinded, chained and enslaved. Eyeless in Gaza. Yet he prevailed. Even at the cost of his life he had his vengeance. And I will have mine.